MW01594762

A HARD EARNED REASON

K. L. Dziesinski

Copyright © 2015 K. L. Dziesinski
All rights reserved.

ISBN: 1517630851
ISBN 13: 9781517630850
CreateSpace Independent Publishing Platform
North Charleston, South Carolina

If we were seated next to each other on a plane, at a dinner, a concert, a card game, church or a bar you would inevitably ask about my condition, my state. I would respond, depending on my mood and intentions, with a few chapters of my tale. No one has ever heard the cover to cover account. I will relate the facts, three parts, three piles of rocks marking my past.

BEFORE THE HOSPITAL

It took me sixteen years to realize the world would keep spinning even without my footprints. Egocentrism usually fades with age, I was a behind the curve. As a single child of two hardworking Midwestern parents living in a small northern town it was easy to believe everything revolved around me. It mostly did until high school. It is there that evolution throws curve balls, splitters, and wicked sliders. Raging hormones penned in by academic structure; muscle, hair, boobs, zits, attitude popping out everywhere. No compass, GPS, map, manual, or bread crumbs. Nothing to follow, just navigate. There is a funny hat and diploma waiting. Find it. For me Grover Cleveland High resembled the Bataan death march with slightly better food.

I met Iris Skye at a party a few weeks before graduation. She had been in my class for three years but you do not meet everyone when the school has 2200 students. You also do not meet everyone when your social circle could fit in a Dodge Caravan.

I did have friends, guys with a flaw or two. Beezo had a slight stutter, Alfie coke-bottle glasses, Mango limped, Zinger had industrial acne, and Buzz waddled. They were also guys who knew that Herman Hesse was not a Nazi general, that blues is rock with a PHD, that Ronald Reagan did not play Bonzo in the movie only in Washington, and that golf is not a sport. We had our table in the quad at lunch and met up at dances, pizza parlors, games, bowling alleys, and the movies. Safety in numbers. Adolescence can be brutal on lone gazelles.

Through it all I survived. Great grades paid off. Eventually the top percentile pulls away from the herd. A valley of opportunities opens up. Those left behind would continue to feed in the same pasture. Their grass would not get much greener.

With that diploma we go forth and do something else: a job, marriage, college, the service, crime. Take the leap. Iris and I jumped in tandem, our infatuation ensuring a soft landing. Holding hands generated a bolt up the spine. Beezo and the boys became an afterthought. So did the family. Mr. and Mrs. Lawton were relieved. Their son Paul only needed a closet for clothes. Grandchildren were a possibility.

It all made for one hell of a summer. Steaming up the car windows, taking walks, dancing, parties on the beach, talking all night. Life was good, I even got a job.

John Cash Penny, one of the early monarchs of the mercantile trade, sent forth stores like butterflies in spring. One landed down the road from our subdivision. Of course I did not get employed based on merit, I did it the old fashioned way, I knew somebody.

Zinger had an aunt whose cousin was a manager. She got him in, he got me. Minimum wage was enough. Interaction with the public in a controlled setting is a great way to sprout a dormant personality. I blossomed stocking shelves, selling pants, doing the 100% markup boogie. Eight hours a day, two fifteen minute breaks, plus lunch. You learn the value of a dollar when a hamburger and fries equals an hour putting price tags on two hundred pairs of snow boots.

When the eagle flew on Fridays it usually bypassed the bank and headed to my wallet. Saving and minimum wage were mutually exclusive. Acquisition of the most important thing in a young man's world appeared as likely as one of the mannequins coming to life with a Kama Sutra video in her hand.

I needed wheels, a ride, sleigh, chariot, love mobile, a Motown wonder, not Stevie, more like Chief Pontiac, Ransom Olds, Henry Ford. What a marvelous invention, the cure for perspective paralysis with the turn of a key. I needed a new job.

Serendipity is neither a beckoning beacon nor the star in the east leading wise men. It is a cosmic jiggle, a little bump off the ordinary. Taking the trolley a stop too far and finding a great book store. Being on an elevator in Vegas when the door opens and in walks Mick Jagger. Catching a foul ball. Turning the corner just as a shooting star whistles across the sky. Or, spotting a 3 by 5 card on an out of the way bulletin board advertising a job at Krogers.

Barney Kroger, no initials needed, started with a single grocery store in 1883 which lead to 5500 Krogers in 1000 towns by 1920. I joined the parade at the start of my freshman year in college; double the pay of Mr. Penney and 99 per cent less of a markup, the value of volume.

A grocery store is a strange animal; the food comes in the rear and goes out the front. Massive quantities of meat, dairy, produce, cans, bottles, baked goods, sundries arrive on shrink wrapped pallets crammed aboard the modern day mule, the 18 wheel tractor trailer. Fork lifted, released and rushed to fill rows of shelves. Fresh to the back, the aged product goes into a shopping cart, checked out, bagged, taken home. See you next week.

Pushing carts, as they paw over nature's bounty, humanity passes through the aisles, a nonstop review. In the United States consumption greases the wheels of the progress train. A grocery store is a capitalistic microcosm. Dollars earned elsewhere are exchanged for sustenance. Of course if everyone just bought what they needed the nation would be much healthier and Barney's coffers not nearly so full. There would be a lot less waddling, double chins, and folks who only see their feet when they sit down. Instead potato chips and sodas have their own aisle. Cookies, pies, ice cream and all their relatives in the fat food group attract a steady stream of patrons. Profit passes no judgment. Caloric catastrophes pay the light bill.

At Barneys, as in life, there was a pecking order. I was a bagger. Hustling carts, loading up vans, frantically searching for a sale item, mess clean up, and practicing the Zen like art of grocery bagging.

I enjoyed the work. Aside from bowling cantaloupes at beer bottles, using the frozen food cooler as a hangover cure, whipping strawberries at unsuspecting coworkers, and riding shopping carts like rodeo ponies, the job paid well.

It was time to get the wheels, four with rubber and one to steer.

Buying an automobile is like jerking off, it takes a while to get there but that is half the fun. Of course I was in the resale market, caveat emptorville. Unlike a woman of the night a used car has to look good and perform well. Cruising a car lot is like walking the game arcade at the county fair, only the carneys have better teeth and too much after shave. I relied on the same strategy I used with girls; if a car talked to me I liked it. The trick is not to let the commission commando know how much you want that apple green Pontiac with bucket seats, floor shifter, and moon rims. Wander by it a few times with the disinterested look of a Muslim at a pork roast. Then gradually allow yourself to be directed to the prize like a toddler hunting for Easter eggs. "Slide behind the wheel," Mr. Old Spice beckoned. Before my ass hit the faux leather I had a happy ending.

With a car comes responsibility; taxes, title, insurance, fuel, maintenance, soap and water. I did not mind. Roll the window down, rest your elbow on the frame, crank up the tunes, and hit the gas. Make those white lines look like dots. Problems, ailments, disputes, pressures disappear in the rear view mirror. A horsepower holiday is one of the greatest gifts of the industrial revolution; a place machine, here to there, with speed, comfort, quadraphonic sound, night or day, hot or cold and all with a view.

Your car can become your friend. Some people give them names. Lizzie, Rex, Ringo, Luther, Green Hornet, Batmobile. When a driver gets into a mess, having a personal relationship with all that horsepower may save the day. Many more snow covered roads have been conquered by exhortations and steering wheel hugs than by four wheel drive.

My Pontiac was the perfect host as Iris and I hit all the bases before sliding into home one warm August night parked at a turn out by the river. We spent as much time as possible in the back seat with the music down low watching the windows fog over.

The lull between orgasms was filled with discussions of family, friends, and the future. Hopes etched on the steamed glass. A sounding board for ideas, beliefs, and crazy thoughts we would never mouth to anyone else. The world would soon be ours. We were fresh, toned, and ready. The scent emanating from our pores reeked of confidence, disdain, and pleasure. At eighteen you want it all and see no reason why not. Then it is college.

A wise man once said, "Son, stay in school as long as possible, it beats the hell out of working." Translate that into Latin and cut it into stone

The daze and the nights are yours to do with what you may. No one will seek you out. Tuition is the same for A's as D's. Unlike the rest of America, cash cannot grease these wheels. It is your brain. Carve it.

Competition increases, the herd is culled, because everyone does not go to college.. The curve gets steeper. Your educated lungs strain in the thin air up GPA Mountain. Many go solo; others rope off with fellow climbers, while some wait for a phantom tram.

The stakes have been raised. There are not enough parachutes to go around when this plane runs out of gas.

Doing well in academics, as in athletics, is a combination of talent and hard work. The more of the former the less you need of the later. There are many possible variations, like in genetics, some of Mendel's pea plants grow tall and strong while others barely creep over the rim. The major brain muscle is memory. The ability to recall facts, figures, and fluctuations is the ultimate advantage. Tests do not measure intelligence any more than bathroom scales measure strength.

A muscled memory is not a complete positive. The ability to reach back and pull out the name of an obscure German composer also allows for a slide show of past missteps, mispronunciations, mis-appropriations, and missed opportunities to appear at the cranium theatre. Out of nowhere a double feature winds out the moments you casually reached your arm around that first date only to knock off her hair band, followed by calling the well-endowed mother of your best friend Mrs. Tits instead of Kitts. I can throw out a line into the recollection pond and pull in a snapshot of that tattered sign behind the counter at the Northside Grill informing custom-ers "spittoons available upon request." This is true even though I only stopped in there ten years ago to get change for a pay phone. There were many schools of flashback fish in my neuron waters.

As was to be expected I did as well academically at the college level as high school. Grinding grades between beer and bongs. Term papers, blue books, intramural mayhem, potato chips, Pepsi, dirty laundry, cooking, concerts, and assorted experimentation.

Through it all the conscience compass kept me on track. No jail time. No pregnant one night stands. No debts. No depression. No heartache. Until.

My grandfather said that life doesn't start until you fall in love. "It's like going from black and white to color, mono to ste-reo, moonshine to bourbon." he told me as we walked his farm. Gramps believed it was rare for love to last; interruptions were to be expected. "But," he confided, "the awareness of the miracle never leaves, always jangling, loose change in the heart."

Iris and I managed to maintain a relationship that was separated by many clicks of the odometer to her campus. The Pontiac drove those years handling corners of despair and the speed bumps to happiness. Back alleys, dead end streets, t-intersections, freeways, bridges, tunnels, dirt roads, we knew them all. A weekend here and there, holiday visits home, and the phone, kept the embers warm.

We floated in the same river for over three years before Iris headed to shore. She grew up. A real life beckoned. Work, husband, kids, responsibility. I was not ready. It broke my heart. The raft felt empty, the water deeper, and the sun colder. Adrift.

My last semester went by painfully, like a country song. Torn between foolish attempts at reconciliation and self-pity, life went on. Worse than before the relationship began because of the knowledge of what love does bring. The heart begins to heal but your pride still hurts. The future clouds over; an empty seat, a lost smile, a muted lyric, a hug drought, a life now missing. It wasn't that Iris was gone as much as the end of being in love. Grandpa was right. One cannot dance that waltz alone. I needed the change of direction two step. Put your right foot on the gas pedal. Get a Master's degree somewhere down the road.

I headed west to California with one five year old car, one ATM card, one tank of gas, one cooler of soda, one adventure begun, one quarter of breathes exhaled. A Masters in Computer Science please, hold the fine arts, layer on the algorithms, compiler construction, graph theory, parallel architectures, software engineering, database systems, go easy on the artificial intelligence. Another tassel: the best way to climb the tree for those without a pedigree. If you can make magic when others around you are binary baffled, the computer based cashocracy will pay little attention to birthplace, last name, color, creed, weight, hair, hygiene, fashion, hype. Perfect for a potato eyed Midwest boy with a crammed cranium in need of direction.

Interstate 80 rewards those who persevere through corn fields, salt flats, tumble weeds, and exhaust with a Sierra welcome mat: altitude, clean air, sunshine, a rinse cycle for the mind. Trees thrown up the side of granite peaks like sprinkles on an ice cream. Lake Tahoe winking its blue eye, inviting all to the mile high dance as echoes of Eureka bounce down the canyon walls.

Three and one half hours later the Bay area spreads out like an exotic rug before a tourist in Old Delhi. Snap, roll, a whiff of history, "Perhaps this is the one for you." Well yes, starting every day with this beneath my feet would be good. And it was, two years in a studio apartment bordering the Hayward Fault, living on the edge of a cataclysm. A bicycle, backpack and Bart ticket took me where I needed to be. No cash in my pockets cut off access to some of the finer pleasures and pursuits. Free was my mantra. Music in a park, wine tasting at the deli, beer bash at the homes of strangers, prayer breakfast for this or that, a toke here, a snort there. I got high, by and strange; all the while knocking off those credits.

The basic needs were being covered. I met a few women, of course it was hard to offset an aging car, diminishing bank account, drip dry clothes, and cheap hair cut with wit, charm, and potential. I tried. A few dates and even fewer horizontal mambo sessions. Futon Island was a lonely foam outpost.

And then it was over. Six years after I shuffled across the stage at Grover Cleveland it was time. There was no escaping it, life's conveyor belt churned on, dropping me like a box of Wheaties. Out of the educational warehouse, chock full of knowledge, sure to promote software growth and improve energy consumption.

Another graduation, tassel flip, pomp and circumstance day. An extra beer with that slice of pizza. Suddenly I was a hot commodity. Companies large and small reviewed my resume, set up interviews, offered salaries, and stock options. I had crossed the valley. I could see the mountain top. The train was leaving and many people were trying to give me a ticket. For a guy whose biggest decision had been paper or plastic this was a major change of pace.

In the early part of this century Silicon Valley was a three ring circus riding carousal inside a Ferris wheel gondola. Money rained down like manna. Any plan with the words computer and internet found funding. Up-front cash rented space, paid salaries, bought food and percolated ideas. The land between interstates 101 and 280 sure as shit wasn't Kansas and had more than one wizard behind the curtain. They were buying brains and selling dreams. This yellow brick road lead into the ether and munchkins danced along buzzed on expectation.

I got hired here for six months lured away there for the next six, slightly bigger salary for the same expertise. Bought a new car, rented an apartment, and ate better meals. I was not rich but it was a few steps up the ladder. Once prosperity increases you hang on to that higher rung to the last finger nail. A return to lower wood was not an option. Money does not equate to happiness but it can fix a lot of problems. Sharp edges soften. The higher clover becomes home.

I was sliding along, enjoying the pocket jingle and the excitement of digitizing the world.

Then a couple of guys figured out how to speed up the process. I met them at the gas station; they were trying to get the air compressor to work. I pointed out two quarters were required. Joe Weesler and John Zybtow, destined to become two of the filthy rich, proceeded to bitch, piss, and moan that air was free. Then they asked me for change. After filling the tires on a beat up VW bus they graciously handed me the hose. At which point John noticed my Sponge Bob shirt. After a rousing chorus of "Who lives in a pineapple under the sea ...." Joe and John introduced themselves and invited me over to Joe's parent's house for a basement beer. Serenfuckingdipity.

In between cans of Bud I came to realize they were off the charts gifted, reworking connections, spinning viewpoints, exploding the status and the quo. I had a couple of years on them both which really meant for nothing except logistically. Seed money was still sprouting startups on a daily basis and I knew a few frantic farmers. Promises were made and WEEZY was born. I gave notice again, packed up a card board box, and took a new exit to work.

It came to me within the first week. It wouldn't be long; the tingle was there, only a few more strokes. I loaded up on stock, options, and grants. And I worked, long hours, many days, weeks, and months. The silicon wave rose up and we hung ten on WEEZY, through the green pipe line, safely onto shore. Soon it would be lounge chairs on sugar sand beaches with umbrella shaded drinks watching others trying not to drown in the surf.

The announcement arrived one rainy afternoon. Everyone from Joe and John to the janitors gathered in the cafeteria. We knew something was up because of the presence of not one but two suits with leather briefcases and product in their hair. They spoke of merger, buy outs, blending, the SEC, non-compete clauses, relocation, investment, equity, contracts et al. The bottom line, WEEZY was no more. Gulped down whole, and, unlike Jonah, with no hope of return. In exchange everyone in the room was richer, some to a greater degree than others. No one was bitching. However these words were not for public consumption. Keep your mouth shut at the Sirroco.

To the Scirroco we did go and for once coworkers were stumbling over each other to buy drinks, conspiratorial smiles all around. It was not a fancy establishment, two pool tables, some pinball, a beat up juke box, cheap booze and one hinge on the bathroom door. All within blocks of the Silicon Valley computer assembly lines. More millionaires in waiting graced Sirroco's portals than any Gucci store could ever hope to see. A few years into the bonanza, many blondes, brunettes, and red heads discovered the place. Doctors, lawyers, and MBA's became passé.

As we smiled other code crunchers circulated, oblivious to our fortunes. Life changing money they call it, not having to worry about mortgages, tuitions, health care, payments, retirement, bills, and vacations. Shield your eyes from that lightning strike. Talk turned to taxes, accountants, real estate, annuities, and off-shore hideaways. Then, for a few minutes, silence would encircle us to be broken by bust gut laughter. Things were not the same.

As happy hour wound down four women came through the door. I noticed, everyone noticed, we were hardwired to notice. The closest I had ever come to one of these goddesses was waiting in line for the solitary toilet. Today, though, things were different. Programmer Ray happened to be at the bar in search of quarters for the pool table as the long haired, long legged, short of breath group placed their drink orders. Ray, buzzed on rum and impending remuneration, paid the tab and issued an invitation to our corner congress.

They sauntered over like runway models. Chairs were grabbed, throats cleared and introductions made. Jennifer Hays, Iris Camp, Kirsten Woo and Melody Rohn met Gordy, Ray, Fred, Paul and Jeff. Pleasantries were exchanged before silence ensued. And ensued. Drinks were drunk. And drunk. Finally someone asked where we worked and a few nods of recognition accompanied our Weeziness. Then, like an island shower, they were gone. Their memory hung in the air like plumeria, intoxicating.

A little later I walked outside just as a revved up Porsche sped away leaving Iris standing in its wake. She looked upset before flipping the bird at the dimming tail lights. I laughed. She turned and stared in my direction. Then she laughed too. As I walked toward her a thousand lines streaked across my mind like a mctcor shower. Blinded by the light I blurted out, "You need a ride?" Iris looked into my eyes with a flicker of recognition, "You're Paul from Weezy." I just nodded. She looked around for another life boat. Finding none her hand extended, "Yeah, I could use a lift." I then escorted this dream with legs to my late model Buick. Definitely not a Porsche; however there were nice fabric seats.

I drove Iris home, the long way. She pretended not to notice as my speakers blared, "Fat girls and weed that's all I need. They both make you weak in the knees." After switching to a jazz channel I asked where she worked. Iris was between jobs and taking some classes. Having moved from Bakersfield she was fond of almonds, cows, and Buck Owens. I mentioned I square danced in the seventh grade. I also owned a bb gun at one time. We made it to her place without much dead air. A town house on a cul de sac. I parked on the street and Iris thanked me for the ride. She mentioned a dance club in San Jose where her friends were to meet the next night. Then, as she stood in the dashboard light, I heard the words, "I better see you there." The door shut and I stopped tingling long enough to drive away.

What a day. My ship had come in with a blonde at the helm. Well the ship's arrival was a certainty, being invited to the captain's table was still up in the air. Yet there was something comfortable about Iris. The feeling was coming back, old embers glowed, and the edges twinkled.

I slept well and late. Waking up a millionaire brings laughter and daylight dreams. I had three e-mails from Weezerites with various degrees of assurance that, indeed, we had struck the mother lode. I cranked the stereo up and bounced around like a Hare Krishna at a snowed in airport. Jubilation only lasts so long, however, as I chomped down on a salami sandwich with a side of potato sticks and a Heineken chaser it dawned on me that another page had turned. Hell I was in a different book, maybe a different library.

Who to tell first, when and how? "Hey Joe you know that fifty bucks you owe me, forget it." Parents, siblings, extended family, acquaintances. "Yeah I got a few bucks but I am still the same wise ass you know and love."

Those were issues for the future; my immediate concern was my wardrobe, or rather, lack thereof: one old gray suit, a couple of Christmas gift button down shirts, three pairs of dusty loafers, jeans and assorted t-shirts. Dance club fair, probably not. A trip to the mall was in order. Now if I could just find it.

Malls are antiseptic tiled canyons housing sheets of glass fronting product for sale. Squares, piazzas, promenades, downtown replaced by these climate controlled emporiums selling everything from air compressors to diamonds. Step right in and get your hair cut, eyes examined, car tuned, hearing tested, check cashed, and nails done. Boulevards of consumption with registers rattling at a fever pitch from ten till ten.

We file in like ants following a pheromone trail, antennae bouncing. Colonies of calories dot the landscape. Orange Julius, Panda Express, Pizza, Burgers, Smoothies, Cookies. We march: perfumed by paid spritzers, beseeched by garage door hawkers, commandeered by sunglass salesmen, approached by gadgeteers. Plenty of panhandlers line the paths between the anchor establishments. Macy's, Nordstrom, Target, K-Mart hold a mall steady amid winds of economic instability and waves of changing demographics.

I needed a make me look cool at a dance club store, nothing close to that on the directory. So I wandered. I wanted whatever Jerry Lewis used to go from Professor Kelp to Buddy Love in the classic Nutty Professor. At least in the wardrobe department. And the mannerism department. And in the speech department. Without the cigarette. With the drink. I wandered some more until I saw a well-dressed guy walk into Marvins. It had the look. Subdued lighting with midlevel background jazz. Took a breath and entered. First words I heard, "Max, the pizza guy is here."

I almost did a U-turn when it dawned on me, pizza my ass in a few weeks I could buy this place. So I perused $200 shirts, belts, and ties. Shoes priced like a set of Goodyears next to suits worth a month's pay. No one bothered me even though the help outnumbered customers three to one, understandable in my shorts, sandals, and faded t-shirt.

Finally a clerk took pity. Without shame I explained my predicament. No surprise, he had been to the club and new the vibe. Thirty minutes later, after a major dent to the credit card, I left with attire guaranteed to fit me in. The salesman suggested a hair-cut; he called a stylist friend, and made an appointment. I had an hour to ponder that move.

Hair was a flashpoint in my family. At an early age a trip to the barber ranked just above going to the dentist, church, or Aunt Edna's. Dad decided when, where, and how short. This worked well for a number years until I started to notice not only the Playboys on the shop's back shelf but also my reflection in the mirror.

The cells that make arm hair are programmed to stop growing every couple of months so the fuzzy slope from shoulder to wrist stays short. Head hair has no such restraint, can grow for years at a time, and get very long, except at my house. I hoped it was the iner-tia of routine and not some line in the sand parenting issue. After all I had noticed those pictures of dad in bell bottoms and paisley print shirt with studded white belt. His hair hit the eye brows in front and hovered above the shoulders in back.

So when it came to that time of the month I finally resisted. The contemplative look that greeted my declaration of hirsute inde-pendence gave me hope. The transfer of responsibilities between father and son plays out as the boy becomes a man. I would see versions of it as other milestones presented themselves. Evolution has resulted in more nuanced challenges to the silverback. My dad gave me a twenty to use when I was ready, although there was the implication that attention would be paid to my follicle parade.

Over the years several scissor artists have spun that barber chair and gave me my first look at their handiwork Of course at that point options are limited to further cutting, applying product, a hat, or the passage of time. These were all guys with red and white stripes spinning on a pole outside the door. I had always suspected that a stylist had no need for that bloodletting symbol instead preferring to attach a leach to your wallet. However since I did have a semi date, new clothes, and a few bucks to spare I parked in front of Narcissus.

I was greeted at the door, offered water/tea, escorted to a chair near a sink, laid back, shampooed, rinsed, and passed off to Mark, the stylist. He looked down at my head, up at the mirror, into my eyes, back at my hair. "Well, what do we have here?" A challenge I guessed. Then he mentioned his friend at Marvins, the club in San Jose, and my desperate need for a conditioner. I confessed my ignorance of all things of a GQ nature. Mark nodded and went to work, with me facing the mirror. I could watch, the true difference between barber and stylist, that and fifty bucks. Plus tip. For Mark, and the guy who washed my hair, and the one who suddenly appeared and did my nails.

Hit the sidewalk a new man, had the day by the ass. Took the car for a wash and stopped off at Walgreens to refresh my condom supply. Semper paratus, you never know.

"Lets turn the heat up baby before this lovin turns cold" blared from the speakers as the Bott dots on I-280 popped by like flashbulbs on opening night. What a difference a few days can make. I was in the money, my clothes worked, my hair had a life of its own, and winking from the corner was the possibility of love. I howled a thank you to the heavens.

The club had valet but that word was not in my vocabulary, many blocks passed until parking materialized. I paid the cover and made a bee line to the bar for a spot to lean on, a port in the social swirl. The place was large, the disco balls numerous, and the DJ induced beat loud. Not my preferred entertainment location. Music should be live, chairs should be plentiful, and lighting dim. Nonetheless I fit in, thanks to the magic of Marvins and Narcissus. A few cocktail dresses even gave me a look. Then I saw Iris.

She was with a group at a railing overlooking the floor. Drink in hand, twirling a swizzle stick, blonde hair shimmering, smiling, talking. I watched with the echo of, "I better see you there." bouncing between my ears. I heard an invitation. Had one been conveyed or was it just a friendly way to get out the car door. The demons of doubt circled my heart. Should I stay or should I go. I ordered another beer; it was a green bottle place. Iris wasn't moving and I noticed she turned away a few prospective Travoltas. Maybe my name was the only one on her dance card.

Just walk over and say hello. I took that first step a couple of times only to be stopped by pride paralysis. The fear of rejection seizes the joints, grabs the tendons and makes any forward movement impossible. If I was a rooster there would be no eggs.

I ordered another beer. As I stood and pulled out my wallet the bartender waved me off, "The blonde by the rail put it on her tab." I turned and Iris was gone. A disproportionate number of blondes populated my field of vision. My head swiveled like a hungry cat at a fish fry. Then I felt a tap on my shoulder. "Is this seat taken?" Iris grinned as she slid onto my barstool.

"How long have you been here?" she inquired. "My first beer." I lied. "Glad you could make it." Iris replied. When she spoke her eyes toured my face. "Great spot." I lied again. Iris laughed, "You look more like a blues band type of guy." "I appreciate different musical types, just don't ask me to name this song." I grinned and she smiled. We were hitting it off, making time.

18

The club pulsed, a giant squeeze box of motion, scents, voices, alcohol, rhythm, and ardor. Iris introduced me to a few of her friends. We danced up, down, side to side, around, back and forth. With the last spin of the disco ball I offered a ride home and she agreed.

I parked in front of her place and we talked. A lot. I had to start the car a few times to keep the battery charged for the background music. This wasn't a discussion; it was a dialogue of memories, opinions, regrets, hopes, parents, friends, foes. We both were quick with a laugh, sympathy, and a few hugs, catching each other up from birth to the front seat of my practical car. Iris had been a decent student, Girl Scout, high school cheerleader, popular, and eager to get out of Bakersfield. Her mother still lived there. Her dad had died in an automobile accident a few years ago. A good settlement was reached with the other driver.

I told her my tale of travel through the educational jungle and was fairly frank about my wanderings in the dating desert without mentioning the first Iris by name. She asked how I liked Weezy and it took considerable will power not to disclose that the dollar dam was about to burst. I explained my job and Iris appeared genuinely interested. We explored movies, politics, sports, and religion. Iris tried to leave a few times but another topic would reel her back.

Around four in the morning we finally broke down, our last hiss of steam announcing what a great evening it had been. Iris gave me her phone number and we made plans for a movie. She reached over and kissed me. Sparks flew down upon my closed eyes. Then with a smile, she was gone. I watched as she headed up the walk, wondering if she would look back. I started the car just as she reached the door, turned and waved.

I rode home with a smile as a sidekick. A shade had been lifted, light flooded in, old feelings stretched out, wonder returned. I cruised the streets with a shimmering aura, Amen brother all is right.

Going to bed close to the time I usually got up was different. Over a bowl of cereal I thought how many new pearls were about to be strung in the next few months. The designer clothes hit the floor, the tooth brush skied the enamel, no soap as I left her scent on my face. Sleep came easy.

Iris called me a few hours later. We were both still in bed. More historical footnotes were exchanged. She told me about her only love, a boy named Dennis. They had met in high school but a split occurred when he left for college back East. Iris's voice softened as she described that last phone call. "It was hard because he left me." she whispered, "I thought I was going to die." It was like we had been in parallel emotional emergency rooms. Of course with Iris's looks and personality she should have been discharged long before me. So I told her about Iris the First. We excavated disappointment, denial, anger, frustration, loneliness, and depression. Pay loaders worked overtime hauling away relationship debris.

After we hung up I slept through the noon hour only to be awakened by the door bell's chime. It was Josh, a Weezite who worked on the finance side. I only knew him because he was a red vine freak. Josh would attack our candy stash with a vengeance. We took to calling him Sugar Vulture. He walked in and plopped 240 pounds down on my couch. "Paul old boy" he huffed, "We need to talk. Josh then explained that there were a few conditions on the Weezy sale. We first generation employees had two options.

Number one we could take a lump sum buy out, or, as the buyer preferred, accept a smaller initial payment and then agree to act as an on-call consultant for the next five years for $1.5 million per.

He got up and started to explore the kitchen. Slim pickings until stumbling upon my stash of M&Ms. Josh upended a bag and a rainbow of coated chocolate cascaded into his eager mouth. I was a financial neophyte and had no clue which choice to make. Between bags I asked, "What makes the most sense?" Josh came over and put his arm around my neck and said, "I am not authorized to give advice, however, tax wise and every other wise there can be only one correct decision." He then slowly waved two technicolored fingers in front of my face. I signed on the dotted line, said goodbye and took a shower.

Later, standing naked in front of the mirror I gave myself the once over. There were obvious signs of metabolic retreat. Calories burned off by merely being seventeen now took up residence all over my late twenties body. Lack of exercise and poor eating habits had moved belt holes steadily to the left. A few extra pounds but both my dick and feet were still visible as I looked south. Hair sprouted where it should, muscle tone was present, a few patches of skin were tanned. Overall a B minus if you graded on a curve. I gave myself a wink and a smile then got ready for the movies.

The ability to enter into a celluloid creation is magical; action, drama, music, suspense, horror, porno, comedy parading across the big screen surrounded by walls of sound. Escape with buttered popcorn and a soda. Identify with the hero, the villain, the cause, the tribulation. Laugh, clap, cry, boo, scream, moan. A communal experience enjoyed alone. Two hours later walk out into the light or night a little different than when you entered.

I have eaten enough movie popcorn to soak up Lake Huron, washed down with gallons of diet cola along with the occasional rosary of malted milk balls. Matinees, double features, drive-ins, videos and the television lit up my mind. From Casablanca to the Summer of 42, Catch 22 to Apocalypse Now, Blues Brothers to Vanilla Sky, Godfather to Scarface.

Today I had a date. Picked Iris up and drove to one of the few remaining single theatres around: hundreds of seats, monster screen, banging sound. The way a picture was meant to be seen. A throwback to the day people dressed up for encounters with Bogart and Bacall. A plush lobby the size of a basketball court, a maxed out candy counter, and bathrooms full of marble and chrome.

The movie was Chocolat. Comedy, drama, romance all rolled into one; a date trifecta capable of releasing tension and gently shoving a couple toward the deep end of the sensuality pool. Iris held my hand and we smiled. I remained amazed that she was with me. The credits rolled, she took my arm, and soon the early evening breeze blessed us as Lionel Hampton played a swinging version of "Love is in the Air" along my spine. Then Carly Simon wailed "Anticipation" inside my skull as Iris asked, "Can we go to your place tonight?" I gulped and said, "No problem."

The drive home took us past a few McMansions and gated subdivisions. Iris mentioned how it would be nice to live in such a neighborhood.

I had not given it much thought. Never having had more than a T.V., bed, microwave, and a place to shower, nor the dollars needed for such an upgrade, there was no reason to price real estate. Iris seemed quite knowledgeable when it came to financing, tax deductions, and association dues. She looked over and asked, "Wouldn't you love to have your own house with backyard, pool, bbq, and two car garage. It is the American dream isn't it" I gave a half assed grin while pondering the upcoming Weezie windfall. She smiled across the dashboard as the terra cotta roofs faded in the rear view mirror.

Mine was the third apartment complex in a string of hives in the flatlands. I parked and hustled around to open the door, we made it to the stairway, not to heaven, but apartment 301 at the end of the hall.

As I turned the key in the lock Iris placed her hand on my shoulder and gave a little squeeze. Once the door shut we came together, arms entwined and lips pressed. Breaking for a hug I realized her eyes were sweeping across a wasteland of used furniture, faded paint, and comatose plants. I opted for another kiss. It was returned.

We did not exactly waltz to the bedroom. There were no candles, crackling fireplace, satin sheets, champagne glasses, favorite songs, or scattered rose petals. Iris took the lead, I followed. Her sweater, my shirt, pants for pants, ditto socks, boxers, thong, bra. Naked. First time naked. Arousal naked. First time sex.

Slip sliding to the finish line with lust at the wheel, coming in first, as I often did, brought no medals. With Iris, however, there was no checkered flag, just another lap. She gave more than she took. I ran my senses on overdrive exploring firm curves, mounds, and valleys. Then Iris would roll over me like a warm rain and we were in gear. Grinding from first to third without a clutch. Gasping, grunting, and moaning to the end.

Afterglow. Iris's head resting on my chest. Bliss. The mind quiets, the heart slows, and eyes close. Time expands and contracts with each breath. Amazement again hop scotches across my synapses as I looked down upon this blonde Madonna nestled on me like a new born. I hesitate before stroking her hair.

All is well, good night to you, yours and the ships at sea.

Sometime close to dawn we revved up again. Good morning. I drifted back to sleep, exceedingly satisfied. A few hours later a poke to the ribs brought me to life, "Lazy bones, breakfast is served." Iris stood next to the bed in one of my old Ramones t-shirts. Suddenly a pulled blanket rolled my naked ass onto the floor. She laughed and vanished out the door. I found a clean pair of shorts and shirt and made a bathroom groom stop before entering the kitchen. Iris had warmed up a couple of bagels, put some yogurt in a bowl and tossed the last of my cheerios on top. Considering what she had to work with Julia Child would have been proud. Of course Julia would not have been shaking an ass that could stop a train while belting out, "I want to be sedated."

Over breakfast Iris talked me into giving her the shirt, hell she knew more Ramone songs than me. I did the dishes while she changed. I had promised to get her home by noon; she was driving to Bakersfield to see her mother. "Be gone a few days." she said as I dropped her off, "Don't forget me I'll call when I get back." We kissed with familiarity. An evening of heavy breathing had changed the dynamic.

I grinned into the mirror and cranked up the tunes. Some days are gifts.

Another week began in Weezerville. Of course most everyone was walking around like they were on the receiving end of oral sex for breakfast. An impending infusion of massive quantities of cash will do that. Progress still needed to be made, however, and we were soon toiling in our respective corners. For the most part ours was solitary battle. Only occasionally coming together to see if our respective pieces of the puzzle fit together.

We all smiled, me more than most. Meetings were held, agreements signed, and on Friday the dreams were passed out. Snow white envelopes produced numbers with many zeros dancing invitingly across crisp Bank of America checks. Like kids at Christmas we eagerly tore them open with hooting, hollering, and feigning of heart attacks. My particular slice of paper had an eight followed by six zeros, eight hundred thousand dollars, a lifetime of toil for many people. I stuffed it in my pocket and went back to work. Wrap your mind around something familiar when dealing with the impossible. Hours later I packed a few years' worth of vendor freebies, dusty cds, weathered notes and journals. Two boxes and turn out the lights.

I drove to the bank. This was not an ATM transaction. No attention was paid until the teller smoothed the creases out of my check. She looked twice before busting out the "pleased to meet you" smile. "Perhaps you would like to speak with one of our investment counselors, sir" "Just put it in my checking account," I replied, "I have some shopping to do." She gave me a receipt with another big smile. I stuffed it in a pocket and made for the door.

Shopping, no, more like realestating. The neighborhood Iris and I cruised through the other evening felt like a good place to start. Into the hills where elevation not only increased property values, but sprouted gated driveways and manicured lawns. Fawn Lane, Placid Court, Golden Drive. They all looked like easy street to me. I turned a corner and there it was, 201 Partridge Avenue. A tri-level cradled in the arms of several imposing redwoods, stucco, wood, glass, terra cotta working together in architectural harmony.

I called the number on the sign fronting the gate. "Yes I am parked outside the 201 Partridge house," I informed a rather startled agent, "how much is it?" "Well," she stammered. "Let me see, list price is 1.5 million but it has been on the market a while, 1.2 would probably do it. Of course financing is available if you have the down payment." Lady, I thought, that will not be a problem. "Can I have a look around?" "Sure!" she practically yelled into the phone, "This is Grace Hughes, I will be there in fifteen minutes."

Grace pulled up with a look of relief that someone was actually waiting. She was five foot three, with wavy red hair and a few extra pounds, sporting a gold blazer. I exited and walked over. Her smile curved downward as I got closer. My attire did not convey closing costs, points, mortgage material. Nonetheless she opened the lock and began to sing the praises of this recently remodeled, 3600 square foot beauty on a gated half acre of paradise. Grace hustled along and quickly noted walk in closets, stainless steel appliances, marbled bathrooms, den, play room and four bedrooms. Hardly pausing for breath she slid open a door and pointed out the pool, Jacuzzi, horseshoe pit, fruit trees and lush green grass. "Really a very lovely home, I am sure you would be happy here." Grace turned and stared across the yard. The tour was over, time to get back to the office.

I had been following her like a brown eyed puppy, a couple steps behind, without a sound. She lingered, looking at a trellis of wisteria, pale blue flowers climbing the brick wall. As the silence continued, a gust of tension blew by. Grace was in need of a hug, I gave her the next best thing, "So, when can I move in?" She turned in a blur with a you better not be shitting me look. I stood there with my hands in my pockets, bouncing back and forth in my torn

Converse All-Stars. I felt like I was in third grade getting the evil eye from the cafeteria lady when I couldn't find my milk money. Grace piped up, "If you are serious we should be able to turn over the keys within thirty days." "Great," I replied, "what do you need from me?"

Grace still appeared skeptical but she escorted me back into the house and we sat at the kitchen counter. "About financing," she started. I quickly pulled out the bank receipt and slid it toward her manicured, bejeweled fingers. Her eyes scanned the paper expanding from quizzical to comprehension to astonishment. Eight hundred large will do that. "Well, well," she exhaled, "our finance person has worked with this bank before. I do not envision any issues." Grace reached out her hand and gave me a hearty shake. Her blazer glowed a little brighter as we locked up. "See you at the office." "Be right behind you." I said as she pulled a U-turn and motored away.

I did not waver. Buyer's remorse did not cloud my mind. The Century 21 office was buzzing with Grace as the queen bee showing me termite reports, plumbing inspections, building permits, property tax records. I signed a stack of quickly assembled papers. My suddenly good credit paved the way. I could move in while escrow was closing, keys appeared on the desk. The sellers, Mr. and Mrs. Scott Wyn were happy, Grace was happy and I had a house.

A short while later I stood in my apartment, the whole of which could fit in the 201 master bedroom, contemplating what would make the move. Most of the clothes, all of the music, a few pots and pans, sheets, toiletries, towels, one pillow and the futon. I walked over to the manager's office and explained my change of circumstance. There went my last month's rent, security deposit and cleaning fee. Adios. I managed to cram everything into or on top of the car and bounced out onto El Camino. Moving on up, momma look at me.

Darkness was upon the cul de sac as I pulled into the driveway, the neighborhood unaware of my presence. I quickly pulled the car into the massive garage and shut the door. The Buick may have brought suspicion; I needed a better set of wheels.

It did not take long to move my earthly possessions into their new home. The clothes filled a quarter of one closet, the futon looked lonely in the midst of a sea of tan carpeting, kitchen items rested in one drawer and two shelves, half of a bathroom was plenty of room for my assortment of hygiene products, and the stereo found a central spot in the cavernous living room.

I cranked up some Zeppelin and did my best Cruise impersonation bouncing around like a kid on a cotton candy trampoline. At some point a bell interrupted Mr. Plant as he travelled through time and space. I paid it no mind, but there it was again and again.

"No one knows I am here," I thought wrestling with the front door. No one but Grace the yellow jacket who stood smiling on the landing with flowers in one hand and a bottle of champagne in the other. "Hope I am not interrupting," she buzzed "thought you could use some housewarming."

She stared at and then around me. I took the hint and asked her inside. Grace did a 360 and grinned, "I like what you have done with the place." She walked toward the kitchen. "I should have brought glasses and a vase." It was like a thunderstorm had invaded my picnic. "I have something here we can use." I stammered.

A couple of beer steins for the bubbles and a pitcher full of flowers later we sat on the same kitchen counter chairs as earlier in the day. Only now it was becoming quite clear that Grace had a totally different kind of sale in mind. She gave me a shiny eyed look and an ear to ear attentive smile. As Grace went on with information about the neighborhood, supermarkets, dry cleaners, maids, gardeners I paid more attention.

It became clear that with her great smile, blue eyes, flowing hair, full breasts, ready laugh, and dimples, at her fighting weight, Grace would have had her choice of playmates. She was a few years my senior. Had we met in our primes Grace would have looked right through me on her way to the ring. In this time zone, however, I was single, with money and her junior. It was my call whether to answer the bell.

We finished the champagne about the same time Peter Gabriel crooned out the last bars to Red Rain. "You know you're kind of cute." Grace said. Then she quickly crossed space and planted a kiss on my somewhat surprised lips. She lingered, increasing activity until her tongue slid through and bounced around mine. My hands reached toward her hips, slowly sliding upward, over the small of the back and to the shoulders pulling her heaving chest into me before holding her hand as we climbed the stairs and found the darkening bedroom. Once again we entwined limbs, lips, saliva. I pulled back and suggested, "Let's get our clothes off." Grace smiled and began to work the buttons on her blouse. I tossed a sheet over my worn futon.

Grace was enthusiastic and willing. We rolled over, under, up and down, sweat, grunts, groans, exclamatory moans. It was all good. I was in fine form and we went through a few positions before my orgasm face. Once our breathing stopped echoing down the hall Grace whispered something about a "Mighty fine house." before dozing off. I smiled at the vaulted ceiling, "Couldn't agree more."

Light splashed off the walls, rushed through my pupils, and exploded my champagned brain. Not pleasant, but a competing sensation arose from below, a tingling, hardening, pleasure. Grace's lips were wrapped around my morning hard-on. I watched, after a few seconds she looked up, eyes laughing. "I see your up." she giggled.

Then Grace rose, exposing excess flesh that darkness had camouflaged during the night. Mr. Boner gave a one eyed squint past the flanks before disappearing into the slippery crevice. Rolls bounced, breasts flailed, eyes closed. Grace sought her pleasure with quick intensity, falling down upon me, breathing heavily into my ear. My hips thrust upward with increasing fury, she came. I reached over her back and clasped my hands, firmly keeping Grace pinioned. Only the ceiling saw me grunt. Shortly thereafter we shared a thank you kiss. She mentioned an early appointment and the need to get home. "Don't get up, I know the way out. Call me." "Sure."

Over the next few days I went out for provisions at Frys Electronics, making a few commissioned mule skinners happy by purchasing a big, big television and top of the line stereo equipment with speakers wired into bedroom, game room, and backyard.

A week passed before my phone rang. "I just got back." It was Iris. "How is your mother?" I asked. There was a pause, then "Oh mom is fine. I told her all about you." "Why don't we get together?" Another pause, "Not tonight Paul I am tired from driving. How about lunch tomorrow at Kuletos? I have a surprise for you." "Me too." I replied "See you at noon."

I went to bed like kid on Christmas Eve. The next morning I washed the dishes and optimistically brought out new sheets before putting on khakis and a button down shirt. I left the house a little early, ran the car through a wash, and pulled into the parking lot a few minutes past noon. I opened the door and there she was, standing near the bar, turning heads as usual. More than a few eyes watched incredulously as Iris took a few steps, and gave me a hug and kiss.

"Did you miss me?" "Like a rash." I joked. We laughed as the host escorted us to our table.

As we settled in---napkined, menued, watered--- I felt ready to explode my good fortune around her head like fireworks. "You're looking happy." Iris observed. Her eyes sparkled as she reached over and held my hand. The din of the restaurant faded out. "I have some news. A few things I need to tell you." Iris smiled, "Me too." Our waiter, Steve, interrupted with wine recommendations and specials of the day.

"Me first." she said. "You have the floor." I gallantly replied.

"I just got a new car; well it's an old car but new for me. A Mustang just like my dad had when he was young. I can still see the smile on his face when he talked about it. I finally found one like it; I'll take you for a ride after lunch. I know my dad would be happy and proud." She wiped a tear from her eye. I got that twinge that visits the heart when raw emotion storms through.

We sat in silence for a few moments, "So what's your news?" Iris inquired. Feeling the mood needed a shot of grins, I set my fork down, bent forward, looked intently and blurted out, "Not much, Tweezy has been sold, I am a millionaire, bought a house, and am happy to see you." Iris appeared stunned. Her face went momentarily blank, and then she threw back her head and laughed.

"O.K. you have had your fun, really what is the news." she said as a last bite of pasta passed between her lips. I opened my wallet, took out the tattered bank receipt, and slid it across the table. After studying for a few seconds Iris looked up, "You're not joking. Congratulations, holy shit what a kick in the pants."

I retrieved the receipt and asked Steve for the check. "So you want to see my new digs" I got that you got be kidding look, "Sure only we are taking my car." I stood up, "Fine by me."

The Mustang was a thing of beauty, pale blue, plenty of chrome, a horse from another era. Iris turned the key and the engine came to life, exuding power, sounding rich, vibrating. She put it in gear and rolled on to the street. "I can't believe it, feels so good to have this car." Iris grinned. I was jealous. She accelerated and caught the left turn light as it yellowed. Iris looked over, "Fun hey." I nodded enthusiastically; we drove into the hills leaving a few patches of rubber before reaching my home in the trees.

"Oh my," Iris said as we pulled into the driveway. I took her hand and walked to the door. She turned and looked me in the eye, "I can't believe this happened to you. I heard stories about buyouts and stock options but never knew anyone who actually got rich." I gave an aw shucks shoulder shrug. Iris kept looking at me like I had grown another head. "Let's go in," I replied, "could use some help with furniture and stuff."

We toured the rooms. I mimicked a few of Grace's lines, "And over here are heated towel racks and a wonderful Jacuzzi."

Iris was impressed; she loved the backyard saying it was perfect for barbeques. I retrieved a couple of beers from the fridge and turned on the tunes. We sat in the leather recliners positioned between the speakers in the cavernous living room. Iris had questions about Weezy. I explained the process and the decision to take the million and a half for consulting over the next five years.

"I am still the same guy who couldn't dance in the bar the other night."

Iris hopped on my lap and gave me a kiss, "You better not go all Porsche on me." "Not a chance, I have got some Motown muscle on my shopping list."

We kissed as my hands wandered along the edge of her back, across her firm butt, ending with a gentle squeeze to her thigh. Iris gave me hug before asking, "Any more beer?" I slid off the leather like a crock leaving a muddy bank.

After popping the caps on a couple of Becks the doorbell rang. I knew who it was before I peered out the hall window. Grace, sporting jeans, sweatshirt, and sneakers, stood holding another bottle of champagne and more flowers. I didn't think twice before yelling down to Iris, "It's my real estate agent, could you see what she wants, I don't don't feel like talking."

"I'll run interference." Iris shouted back.

Grace's cheery smile vanished when Iris opened the door. Playing handball with my conscience I contemplated going down. By the time right beat wrong 15 to 12 Iris had reached out and took the bottle and bouquet. Grace turned toward her car. She looked back just as I pulled away from the window.

I made my way downstairs with the beers. "She seemed surprised to see me here," Iris said holding out the gifts, "Good taste, how did you meet her?"

"She was the agent for the house," I replied, "made a few bucks on the deal, probably wanted to say thanks.

Iris smiled, "You are so naïve, she has the hots for you. I could see it in her eyes."
I pulled out the pitcher and arranged the flowers.

Iris laughed, "How about I get you a nice crystal vase as a housewarming gift." She put the champagne in the fridge, "No bubbles with beer."

With a quick turn, her shimmering hair taking flight, Iris said, "Since I obviously have some competition how about we give that futon a few bounces before you buy a real bed." She began to run toward the stairs. I caught her just past the landing with a soft take down tackle. We hugged, kissed and rolled into the bedroom. Iris stood up and removed her clothes, slowly and sensuously. The sunlight bathed her like a Greek statue under a window at the Louvre. Iris glowed and she knew it. I was hard before my boxers came off. Iris knew that too.

Laying down a bombing run of kisses upon her neck, descending to her nipples, licking the few hairs between her belly button and the promised land, I commenced the clitoral conga. Iris moved east to west. "I really don't need that." she said. "What the hell." I thought before retreating up and forward, Iris reached down, grabbed and placed my hard on firmly inside. We found a rhythm. Iris put her arms on my back pulling us together. Suddenly the rocket was on the launch pad. Baseball scores, state capitals, binary equations. Not yet Houston. I jerked my head upward and caught a glimpse of Iris. She appeared to looking into the walk in closet. "What the hell." Blast off in t-minus one second.

We dozed while the sun left the room. Iris got dressed as I slept. She left a note near the door. "I am so glad to have met you. Congratulations again. The Mustang needs to get home. I will call you tomorrow. Iris." It would be a taxi ride to retrieve the Buick.

Over the next several weeks Iris and I acted like newlyweds with a trust fund. We went on one helluva shopping spree. More leather chairs, assorted tables, bedroom sets, patio furniture, drapes, blinds, silverware, and dishes. We were often mistaken for a married couple.

Iris was attentive. She spent most nights. We broke in the new bed, watched old movies, listened to music. She cooked, I did the dishes. Iris didn't want a maid, "I am the only woman you need in this house." Getting in the spirit I bought a John Deere rider for the grass, fertilizer for the flowers, and a weed whacker for the fun of it.

One morning Iris noticed an ad for barbeques in the paper. She pointed and asked, "Are you into grilling?" The closest I had ever come was roasting marshmallows over a campfire. "Not exactly but I'm willing to learn."

An hour later we were cruising the aisles at Grills R Us. Like a lot of things in America there were too many choices. Varying degrees of propane powered sizzling capacity. Matt the salesman discussed btu's, warmers, grates, durability. I feigned attention. Iris, on the other hand was interested. She even asked a few questions before deciding on a silver behemoth from Cain Grills. Eight hundred dollars out the door, some assembly required.

Matt was happy, at least 15% worth, as he went for the paper work, only to return a few minutes later with the news that only black models were available. "That's fine." I said. Iris shot me a look, "Paul, black will not match the new patio furniture." Then she turned to Matt, "Why can't we have this one?" He looked slightly perplexed. "Well it is a floor model, been out here a long time. I don't know, have to ask my manager and he doesn't come in for another hour." Iris gave Matt a smile and a slight heave of her chest. "I guess we will have to go somewhere else." Then she looked into his face, he melted. "O.K., don't see the harm, let me get some help and we will wheel it out."

Iris had driven us in the Mustang. She pulled out a large blanket, the store provided a rope and after separating a few parts everything made it into the back seat or trunk.

Unloading was easy enough, tightened a few bolts and wheeled the Cain around back, placing it at the edge of the patio. Iris seemed pleased. "Why don't you start it up and I'll get some hot dogs." I hooked up the propane tank, opened the valve and hit the ignition switch. With a whoosh a blue flame circled the pipes. Iris was watching from the window. I gave her a wave, nothing to this grilling thing.

A routine came to pass, Iris would spend few days, and we would go to movies, concerts, and restaurants. She would leave to see her mother. I would bounce around with home improvement projects. The electric awning over the patio was a real adventure. After buying a road bike I cranked out miles through the western hills. Communication with my parents was sporadic. I had hinted about an upcoming windfall but had not laid out the specifics. Life was pleasantly unchallenging. Thoughts of the future included Iris and kids. It seemed like a natural progression, the next step. I was ready for a new role on a new path. At this point, however, while my devotion had reached the finish line Iris was still out on the track.

One day I took my new wheels, a Cadillac with a northstar V-8, a comfy couch over a Nascar frame, to Tweezy where fine rides spread out like clover.

The name was gone and plenty of different faces made up the expanded population. My old section had been repainted and sprouted cubicles. I spotted Josh the Sugar Vulture beating the side of a candy machine, his frizzy hair bouncing in rhythm. "Try putting some money in." I said. Josh turned and did a double take before wrapping me in a bear hug. "Paul old buddy, old pal. Looking good, new clothes, new hair." He pointed up and down the hall, "As you can see, we've gone corporate." I nodded agreement. "What the hell do you care, I saw your deal, wish I had been here from the beginning, when is the next check due?" "In about six months." Josh finished the other half of his Almond Joy. "Shit, here comes my boss, got to go."

I roamed the halls for a few more minutes. The connection was fading; they would call if my thoughts were needed. I closed the door and didn't look back.

In the Caddy Jim Morrison belted out When the Music's Over. I needed new outlets for my waking hours. Driving along Farm Hill Road I let the horses loose. The excitement of the past few months was winding down. It felt like three days after Christmas when all the toys had been played out. Money was received and spent, my transition was complete. What was is no more. I needed to get out of the shallow end. A road trip was in order. Las Vegas. Viva.

I had been to the adult Disneyland desert oasis a few times. Anything for everyone all the time. Slip into an altered state at this mirage shimmering above the sand. Imported electricity, water, food, drink, women, neon, and sequins. Powered by gaming, the polite term for taking the social security off gray haired ladies tethered to slot machines, the paychecks of farmers and blue collars bused in with double down coupons stuffed in their pockets, tuition money from college kids with a sure fire system, savings of Midwestern couples celebrating anniversaries, and the pocket change of fat whales looking for a Viagra substitute.

In a place that farts cash it is best to tip early and often. Taxi cab drivers smelling like camels, doormen with Cheshire cat smiles, long legged pushed up half naked drink girls, blackjack dealers with snake eyes, waitresses supporting drug addicted boyfriends, illegal immigrants tasked with changing your stained sheets. Slide the sawbucks, what goes around comes around.

It is a three night town, any longer and you may do irreparable damage to your bank account, relationships, skin, and confidence. However, those three days can seem like three weeks.

Sit down anywhere and commiserate with a cross-section of Americana. A cowboy lamenting to a Chinese matron that he could feed his cows for a week on what she just bet. A chunky insurance salesman from St. Joe wondering how they can afford to keep the joint open after he hits for $100. A hyperventilating farmer's daughter from Nebraska anxiously awaiting the drop of the roulette ball. Two grandmas from Escondido giving each other a high five after a jackpot. A sad eyed mechanic nursing a warm beer trying to figure out how to tell his wife the down payment was gone. An overly medicated middle age blonde from Memphis willing to trade a roll in the sack for a keno stake.

Yes, Vegas it would be. Put the mind in the washer and wait for the spin cycle to kick in. I stopped at Tower Records for some asphalt anthems, a little meditation music for the miles ahead. As I looked over some Richard Thompson I heard a familiar laugh. Two rows over was Grace, thumbing through the discount bin. There was a back door. I took a step then stopped. The asshole sign was frantically blinking.

I walked over and tapped her on the shoulder, "Searching for some 80's music?" Grace looked up quizzically. Recognition replaced confusion. Then she gazed down at a U-2 album without saying a word.

"I'm sorry I missed you." I said. "Thanks for the flowers and champagne."

Grace examined a Pink Floyd boxed set, "Hope your girlfriend enjoyed them."

I walked around to the other side of the bin. "She's not my girlfriend, just a good pal."

"Your pal seemed a little possessive; she did not ask me in."

Her eyes scanned my face. "I think she is just a little protective, me coming into some money." I sensed a thaw. "So how have you been?"

"Well," Grace sputtered, "I have stopped waiting for you to call."

I moved over to her side. "Your right, been busy getting the house set up but that is no excuse, how about I buy you that Carole King disc and lunch."

Grace slapped three cds into my gut and walked toward the door. I quickly paid and joined her on the sidewalk.

I escorted Grace to a Vietnamese hole in the wall place around the corner. Thahn Long lacked ambience. Faded travel posters on the wall, worn linoleum on the floor, and a cigarette smoking cook toiling over an open grill. Grace was not impressed; however, somewhere between the roasted crab with garlic noodles and the fried banana dessert she became a customer for life.

After a couple of cold "33's" the world became a better place. I explained to Grace my recent swim up the money can't buy happiness river. Or maybe it was a dive into the what do I do now pond. She had a look halfway between sympathy and give me a break. So I tried harder. "Maybe happiness comes from the journey and not the destination." Grace chuckled, "You sound like a troubled philosopher."

Well there are many twists to every tale. I recognized that my world had flipped severely in the last few months. The Weezy windfall and Iris. A dazzling duet, twin rainbows arcing over me. Most of the money would probably be in the bank but for meeting Iris at the Scirroco. My checking account was never as lonesome as my heart. I was hungry for affection and Iris was four star dining. The house, furniture, and other upgrades were lures for love. I had her on the line, yet there was a part of me that was empty.

"I think I'll take a ride to Vegas." I said, changing subject.

"I have never been there."

"You should go sometime."

"Maybe you should take me sometime."

"Maybe I should."

We smiled at each other. Grace looked at her watch. "Shit I'm late for a showing." She kissed me on the cheek. "Don't be a stranger."

I drove home in a foggy beer buzz. The edge was off and the Caddy coasted as the smooth voice of Charles Brown lamented, "Living in a fool's paradise." I drifted the minutes until the driveway appeared. The garage was empty; there was a note on the back door. "Out shopping for dinner, see you in a little while. Iris."

A midafternoon doze on the soft leather couch was in order. Soon there was inviting turquoise water lapping onto sugar sand beaches fronting a green hued jungle. In this dreamscape I was hang gliding. The wind enveloped me as I dove, rose, looped and roamed over Gauguin's garden. I floated; surf crashed on the reef and palm trees waved me ashore. Limestone cliffs rose up as I soared further inland. Large white birds played in the strong updrafts. Thermals elevated, moist warm air hugged, colors exploded. Suddenly a volcano erupted throwing glowing lava. I circled high above the belching, looking into nature's raging maw, the intense heat surrounded me. The glider canvas crackled, its frame shook, and panic arrived. The shaking increased.

"Get up you lazy bum." Iris pushed my shoulder with her free hand; the other held a brimming Guerra's Meats shopping bag. "Can a lady get a little help." she pleaded. I looked into her blue eyes as the island interlude faded away.

Iris was in the kitchen tossing a salad by the time I convinced my limbs nap time was over. She was wearing cut off denim shorts with dancing white fringe and a faded Giant's t-shirt. As she diced a carrot her breasts swayed in perfect counter balance to her long hair. Iris pointed to two large steaks marinating nearby, "Get the grill ready chef. I have candles and flowers; we deserve a nice romantic dinner."

I walked behind her, put my hands around her waist and nuzzled the back of her neck. She continued to chop. I pressed into her firm behind. Iris waved the knife, "Dessert comes after dinner." My fingers disengaged from their frolic in the fringe. I picked up the T-bones and headed out the sliding door.

It was a beautiful evening. Shadows and sunlight danced across the lawn. The air smelled pure and clean. After placing the steaks on the sideboard I bent down and turned the valve on the propane tank. A sour odor rose and then dissipated. Suddenly a crash came from the house. I ran to the door and found Iris picking up pieces of crystal, her lower lip trembling. As I moved to help she said, "I wanted to surprise you with the vase that I promised weeks ago." Iris brought out the broom and I held the dust pan. Once I deposited the chards in the trash she gave me a big hug. "I had our names etched into the side." "It's OK we can get another." I said before heading back outside.

As my hand reached the handle Iris yelled out, "No not yet, I have something else for you." She motioned toward the chair then did a pirouette. "Pam's was having a sale so I bought something you might like." Iris had my attention. She unbuttoned her shorts and they hit the tile with a hush. Next the shirt came off revealing a low cut shear pale blue camisole which hugged every curve. Her nipples were fighting their captivity. A matching thong complimented the ensemble.

She swayed seductively, rubbing thumb across fingers, "Got any cash, two for one lap dances." "I left my wallet in the other room." "That's OK; I understand you are good for it." Iris wrapped her long legs on either side of the chair and clasped her fingers behind my head. I grabbed, squeezed, pulled and wished for more hands.

Iris stood up and walked toward the sink. She retrieved a towel from the dish rack, set it next to the chair and unzipped my pants. My erection rose up. Iris had rarely engaged in the oral art. It was a pleasant surprise. Her head bobbed, my gasps keeping time, a crescendo resulting in heart stoppage. Trembling slowed as Iris toweled the residue and retrieved her clothes. I managed to stand and zip up. Iris wrapped me in a hug. She whispered, "You're a great guy Paul." Then she kissed me, not with passion but with tenderness. We slowly retreated. "I like you a lot Iris." She got a faraway look and replied, "I know you do, I know."

Iris went back to her meal preparations. I stood and watched her chop an apple before returning to the barbeque.

The steaks were in marinade heaven as I approached the grill and turned the propane valve. It was already open. I pulled the lid up revealing gleaming grates and hit the ignition button.

Light and heat. Flash and torque. Floating and impact. A spectacle of the first order as a violent discharge of concussive flame engulfed me. I was propelled several feet in the air coming to rest like a piece of cardboard blown out of a trash can fire. Rushing air echoed in my brain. My right arm flopped in front of my closing eyes. It looked a little too well done. Then my world blurred as I bobbed in and out of consciousness, body smoldering while my mind drifted back to that paradise in my dream. Shouts intermingled with tropical bird calls, the odor of burnt flesh competed with the scent of island flowers, warm trade winds vied with the brush fire racing across my lungs, the taste of bloody charcoal sparred with sea salt dancing on my lips.

Propane is a liquefied petroleum gas, aromatic hydrocarbon that will vaporize at any temperature above forty four degrees below zero Fahrenheit. A gallon of liquid propane weighs four and one quarter pounds and contains 91,650 BTU's. When it changes into a gas vapor it expands in volume by 270 times. Concentrations may cause flash fires or explosions. A fireball occurs when vaporized propane moves outward and mixes with the surrounding air. A propane flash flame reaches a temperature of 3614 degrees Fahrenheit.

Thermal is a specific type of burn that is caused by hot gases. At a temperature of 140 degrees Fahrenheit human skin begins to burn. Burns are categorized based on depth, area and location. A first degree burn is superficial with red skin. Second degree burns cause blistering with pain. In third degree burns tissue damage extends below hair follicles and sweat glands to the fat layer. The skin becomes charred and leathery, is waxy, pearly or dark khaki with charred blood vessels visible; there is no pain because all nerve endings are dead. Burns that cover more than 15% of the total body surface cause shock.

My eyes opened and shut for no particular reason projecting images onto my visual cortex. A yellow helmet, clouds, tubes, van ceiling, fluorescent lights, surgical gloves and finally a needle. The venom that hypodermic snake injected shut down the theatre. Lights out.

THE HOSPITAL

Patient transported via Ambulance 151, variable consciousness, severe burns to legs, arms, upper chest, face, and scalp, given 10MG Morphine Sulfate IV enroute.

Oxygen-NRBM at 15 lpm, Lung sounds-Right clear, Left clear. Vascular Access-18 gauge MACRO/STD.

Drip TKO at left AC with 1000ccbag. BP 140/ 80, pulse at radial 92, Respirations: 18, labored.

Patient intubated in emergency room, transferred to Burn Surgery ICU for workup and management.

Burn Exam: Patient has second degree burn on anterior aspect of each leg ankle to knee, posterior aspect of both arms wrist to shoulder, upper chest; third degree burn to each side of head.

Assessment: Patient has an estimated 4% total body surface area burn of third degree, 23% of second degree.

Plan: Fluid resuscitation, ventilatory support, nasal gastric tube for nutritional feedings, pain control, sedation.

Lab Orders: Tests-CBC, ER panel, AMI panel, urinalysis screen, arterial blood gas.

Radiology Orders: Chest 1 view IP.

EKG Orders: EKG Stat RN

Medication Orders: zofran, dilaudid, etomidate, vecuronium bromide, succinylcholine chloride, morphine, propofol.

Respiratory Orders: Lactated ringers.

Hospital charts are precise and detached. Cutting a hole in the neck and jamming a tube down the windpipe is a tracheotomy. Using a knife to remove blisters and dead skin to see how deep the flesh is cooked is debridement. Slowly peeling layers of skin until living tissue is exposed is excision. My chart was soon peppered with numerous such descriptions. I was a naked, tube sprouting, wound oozing, assisted breathing mess. Any other animal would have been put out of its misery.

After forty eight hours of modern medicine's best magic the patient was stable but unable to piss, shit, or feed on his own. The life/death teeter totter was merely balanced, not an optimal state. I could breathe independently and my state of consciousness slowly rose from comatose to a few floors below reality. Antibiotic ointments waged war. Cotton gauze and synthetic bandages covered me like tents at a refugee camp. These dressings absorbed drainage and isolated all that is raw from evil microbes and prying bacteria. Restraints were in place preventing arm or leg movement.

My mind fought through dust storms of disjointed memories, dreams, and nightmares.

What the hell had happened? No teller at the memory bank. Had my account been closed for good or was it a temporary hold? I started with the basics: name, age, social security number, hometown, mother's maiden name, all withdrawn without much effort. Next came address, that query, however, arrived just as the narcotic train pulled into the station; I was soon off the tracks.

Address? Address? At first I was back in Apartment 301 just past the strip mall. Next it was a barber chair where a large breasted woman cut my hair with golden scissors.

Suddenly an office desk. "What's in this stuff?" I asked, while passing a purple bong to a faceless woman in a yellow blazer.

"Equity, financing, insurance, tax deductions." she replied.

I walked away coughing as a limousine pulled up knocking over a garbage can full of champagne bubbles. The door was opened by a black capped driver with flowing blonde hair. I found comfort in the back. "Where to sir?" "Home." I said with relief.

Turning up El Camino my seat suddenly turned yellow, the terrain green, I circled a sign announcing House For Sale on a John Deere X540 deluxe mower. Getting closer the signpost morphed into a fire house pole. "We got a push button explosion!" said the Chief. I slid down just after the alarm went off.

"My turn to drive!" I yelled, slamming the fire engine door. Siren wailing, red lights flashing. Rushing through intersections, passing a light blue mustang, careening around a corner, and finally pulling into a driveway at 201 Partridge Avenue. Grabbed a cooler full of beer from the supply locker and headed to the back yard, "I'm medium rare." I announced. "Yes sir." replied the limousine driver throwing a steak on a grill, having exchanged her black cap for a white chef's toque.

I snapped to, riding the tip of the whip.

Medium fucking rare? No. Maybe in the sense of an event occurring very infrequently but certainly not on the chart in the Sizzler kitchen. At that grease pit a good portion of me would be pretty fucking well done. My eyes fixated on the Stanford Burn Unit sign next to the door directly across from my bed. Burned I am, now how did that happen. Just as I started to scratch the soot off my rear view mirror, a whirl and click signaled the release of the sleep patrol, chemical sheep in my veins.

I awoke in the dark. The same sounds fronting dim green and red LED lights. Probably the same day, whatever day that might be. The windshield defogged a little quicker. I knew where I was and what I was, I did not know the why or how. No one to ask and not even sure if speaking was still in my repertoire. I cruised the hippocampus highway and once again took the flashback off-ramp.

The same blonde was working the crowd at PacBell Park, a steaming metal box strapped around her neck. "That will be $11 for two steak sandwiches." I opened my wallet, it was empty. Back pockets empty. Panic ambled over and gave me a poke in the ribs. "You gonna buy those or what!" Left front pocket, not empty. I pulled out a blazing white check with many zeros doing the can-can across its face. Once exposed it grew doubling and doubling again and again. Love handles sprouted out and fell down. I reached up, grabbed a good hunk and held on, rising skyward. The blonde threw down the dogs and ripped open her jacket, exposing. She yelled, "Come with me." I hover; a bulge grows in my pants. The crowd begins to applaud.

I let go and fall slowly down. The blonde cushions my arrival. An ambulance skids around third base and I am strapped to a gurney, boner side down, where a wild eyed paramedic uncaps a syringe, pops a few droplets out the tip, and sticks it in my ass. "Now you know why they call it a meat wagon." he yells over the siren's wail at someone behind me. "This is one USDA Choice honky roast, fresh off the grill." Blue gloves cast a shadow on my face. A carving knife and fork are handed to this angel of mercy just as he finishes tucking a napkin down the front of his shirt. I feel no pain as a he neatly separates a piece of flesh from my arm. "Tastes like chicken."

I awoke with a start, body battling against the restraints. What the hell did they put in the water?

I tried to pull everything tight. Two turns to the right, one to the left, and my mind's tumblers slowly rolled and fell into place, unlocking the truth. It was the grill. The grill in the landscaped backyard of the big house sold to me by Grace of the yellow blazer. The big house holding my Weezy wealth. My riches included a blonde named Iris. Shapely and seductive. Iris bought the steaks for the grill. Push button explosion.

Relief. I was back, partially charred mind and body, but still back.

There are no mirrors in the room of a burn patient, either an act of kindness or a suicide prevention measure. I quickly realized, based on the fact that my head was glued to the bed, that my mug had been toasted. How badly was the unknown. Through barely opened lids I searched the faces of the nurses who visited me the

morning of my resurrection. Trained professionals tended to ointments, dressings, and plastic elixir bags. Concerned expressions
tinged with tenderness without a hint of revulsion. I hoped it was
more than just days of familiarity with my condition..

"Inhaling the byproducts of a propane explosion is not good
for the vocal cords" A nurse informed a much younger woman, a
Florence Nightingale in training no doubt. "Plus the medications
tend to inhibit speech." she continued as if I wasn't in the room.
"Paul here should be able to vocalize any day now." As they headed
out Florence said, "I did hear some weird noises early this morning." Any retort was lost in the hydraulic moan of the closing door

Weird noises, vocalize, propane byproducts. The words slowly registered as if being translated. I heard the conversation but
there was a several second processing delay. I was in psychic in-
tensive care floating in a womb of narcotic amniotic fluid. Pain
was nonexistent, for that matter so was all sensation. This rubber baby bumper world was to be my home for several weeks.
Pushing me back into life would require some serious medication
contractions.

The door opened again and in came a white coated posse of
assorted doctors and hangers on. The leader, Dr. Gibbs, promptly
took up the position directly to my right. The rest pulled their
horses up around my bed. My chart in hand Gibbs held forth in a
dry and competent manner..

"The challenge with this patient is to determine which burns
will do well with conservative therapy and which will do better with
excision and grafting. As you can see we have removed all dead tissue to aid recovery. Dressings, intravenous fluids, antibiotics, and
pain medication have been introduced. We anticipate healing to

result in thick, scabbed surfaces on the legs and arms with the most severe issues in the facial area. Escharotomy will be necessary. Can anyone tell me what that is?"

The posse hemmed and hawed, finally a short, olive skinned man with a middle eastern accent piped up, "A thick scab makes it difficult for blood to flow to the injured area so it is necessary to cut through the scab to promote healing."

"Correct." Gibbs replied as the others feverishly wrote on their note pads. "Now as I said the face," he continued, "will pose some problems. There will be extensive scarring." The group nodded in unison. Mr. Olive muttered under his breath, "It looks like a mardi gras mask."

Gibbs voice raised a notch, "Grafting will be necessary, fortunately this patient has ample healthy skin to harvest from the buttock area. What are some complications related to grafting?"

My eyes scanned the hombres encircling my domain. This time a large, pinked cheeked man tentatively raised his hand. With a nod from Gibbs he began in a southern drawl, "Infection can cause graft failure or pressure can cause the graft to detach from the skin."

"Good, good." Gibbs exclaimed. "What are the three main types of scarring?" This time no one appeared to know. Gibbs sighed and then lectured, "Keloid, hypertrophic and contracture. I anticipate this patient will have all three." A murmur of sympathy passed through the group. "We will bring in a plastic surgeon. Also a psychologist will be needed to help this man deal with the accident and the serious changes to his physical appearance." More murmuring.

Gibbs turned away and headed for the door, the interns at his heels. "Now our next patient presents a different kind of challenge." His voice trailed off as the lock clicked shut. I laid there like the specimen I had become, a hunk of instructional meat. Gibbs and the boys must not have hit the bedside manner chapter yet. It was disconcerting to be talked about but not to. Did they not know I could hear and see, maybe my processor had booted up a little earlier than expected. I understood enough to realize there was a fucked monkey in the room.

Scabs, scars, grafts, mardi gras masks. Harvest skin from my ass and put it on my face. I will be the butt of so many jokes. Got to laugh because I can't cry. I wanted to cry, I wanted to wake up from a bad dream, I wanted to be me again, I wanted to beat my head against the wall, I wanted to yell at Gibbs, I wanted to jerk off, I wanted to die, I wanted to live, I wanted the sleep patrol to come over the ridge.

OPERATIVE REPORT

PATIENT: Paul Lawton

PROCEDURE: Tangential excision and split-thickness skin graft with 3:1 mesh to both sides of face.

ANESTHESIA: General.

INDICATIONS: Mr. Lawton was involved in a propane gas explosion and sustained burns to his lower legs, arms, and facial area including ears. He has been heavily sedated due to perceived psychic trauma evidenced by involuntary extremity contractions and persistent moans and screams. The decision was made to proceed with grafting due to fear of infection.

FINDINGS AT SURGERY: The patient did indeed have areas of third degree burns on the outer portions of each side of the face. He had areas of burns on the arms and legs which required excision.

PROCEDURE: The Watson knife was used to excise the areas down to viable fat. Bleeding was controlled using epinephrine-soaked gauze and cautery and spray thrombin. The Padgett dermatomc was used to harvest skin approximately 11 thousandths of an inch thick. The donor sites were covered with glucan, Adaptic and the skin was then meshed 3:1 using the Brennen mesher. After obtaining hemostatis the skin grafts were stapled in place totaling 2000cm2. Sulfamylon/nystatin solution, fine mesh gauze, and Red Robinson's were placed. The entire package was covered with spandex which was stapled in place.

Patient was then taken back to the burn ICU in stable but critical condition. He had estimated blood loss of 1000ml. He received 200 ml of crystalloid. Three units of packed red blood cells and had urine output of 250ml.

I kept trying to break the surface only to be drawn back down. I would reach where the light invaded the gloom then, grabbed by a powerful hand, retreat into shadow. Repeatedly up down forth back. Eventually a disjointed face straight out of Picasso's pallet bobbed above. A yin to the yang.

Words plunged through, muffled bullets, beckoning: "O.K." "Safe" "Jane" "You are" "Trust" "Will be." "It is" Brown eyes, small nose, purple patch, ears all spun before coalescing inches away. I went for it, busting through, breeching the fresh air.

I awoke with a start, stars twinkling before my eyes. With clarity came the realization I was not alone. Nurse Jane Meyer bent over me with a cup of ice chips in her hand. "There, there." she said with a smile, "Stay calm, I am here to help you." She placed a piece of ice between my lips. A wet, cold welcome wagon circled my mouth. After a few more frozen salvos Nurse Jane said, "We thought you would come back to us today, you have had quite a jolt to your system." I tried to respond. Something akin to a sick dog barking through wet burlap came out. Jane put a finger to her lips. "Don't try to speak, give it a few more days." She set the cup of ice on a tray, picked up a clipboard, looked at her watch and began to write.

Nurse Meyer appeared to be in her early thirties with coal black hair underneath her starched white nursing cap. The right side of her face was stained shades of purple and red. I had seen birth marks before but this stretched from just below her eye, across her check, and ending and inch from her mouth. Large, caring brown eyes shone below pencil thin eyebrows. She was also blessed with a shape of the finest caliber, a genetic anomaly, the top of the totem pole outdone by the bottom.

As my gaze lingered Nurse Jane set down the clipboard and looked into my eyes. "I will be your main care nurse." she stated in a serious tone. "It will be my responsibility to get you out of here as healthy and as early as possible." She put another ice chip in my mouth.

"It will be your responsibility to do everything I say." Jane smiled, "Sort of like a marriage." Then she laughed a bold, infectious ode to joy. One more ice chip. I was beginning to feel like one of Pavlov's dogs. "You get some rest now. I will be back in a little while." "Rest, rest, what the hell have I been doing for God knows how long!" I wanted to yell at my angel of mercy. "Tell me what you have done to me, what have I missed. What about the world, my friends, family." Jane appeared to sense my consternation. "We can talk later." she said with a raised finger. "Remember, your job is to do what I say." Then Jane winked, "At least for now."

I slept without tension, without dreams, without fear. Nurse Jane was there when I opened my eyes, ice chips at the ready. She sat on a chair, picked up the pieces of my life and put them together.

"You had a terrible accident. A grill in your backyard blew up causing a fireball. The explosion threw you into the air burning exposed skin on your lower legs, arms, and face. I understand a friend of yours quickly called 911 and you arrived here within a half hour of the event. Our first task was to save your life. We stabilized your vitals and then went to work on your burns. A lot of dead skin was removed, that is why you have all the bandages. Usually our patients regain consciousness within a day or two; however, you have been a challenge. It was necessary to use heavy sedation until the demons passed. In the meantime we performed two surgeries on your face. Skin from your backside was used to cover burned areas beside both eyes, down to your jaw line and toward each ear. The procedures were successful."

Jane leaned forward and placed more ice in my mouth with her long, delicate fingers. She was increasing the frequency and the dose, hydrating body and mind. I looked into her eyes trying to catch a glimpse of my face in the pupils; dark pools of mystery, black holes of professionalism, taking in information without reflection.

"You have been here fifteen days. I hope that does not upset you too much. Your parents were present for the first week but they had to return home. I have kept them informed of your progress. We will arrange for a phone in a little while. A couple of other people have made inquiries, a man, Josh, and a woman, Iris. I told them it would be some time before you will be able to see them." Of course it is up to you if and when you want to have visitors."

A disembodied voice came over the intercom, "Attention, Nurse Meyer please report to the emergency room. Nurse Meyer." She stood up and squeezed my hand. "Don't worry, we will get through this."

I wanted to believe her.

Two weeks gone, except of course for my initial awakening. Baptized in the river of reclaimed memories, I recalled Dr. Gibbs and his posse and I remembered putting my own jigsaw puzzle in order: Weezy, big money, Iris, Grace, house, nice car, and thoughts of Vegas. How long ago it all came together was not known, neither was why it all fell apart. Denial and anger were still doing the tango around my sawdust floor with depression cutting in from time to time. Acceptance was not yet in the house.

On the positive side I felt no pain. My head was still pinned to the bed restricting my field of vision to islands of bandages. There was a light sheet over the family jewels. My arms remained strapped down. I was primed for a Lilliputian invasion. The little bastards could have a field day.

Jane did say my parents had stayed for a week. It dawned on me that they did not know about my new wealth. I did tell them Weezy was being sold and I should make a profit on the stock. They sounded happy but not impressed. Neither really understood what I did for a living. I had wanted to bring them for a nice vacation over the winter months. Get out of that blowing snow. It was to be a surprise with the house, car, and cash. Instead they got a surprise of a different kind. Our son Paul, picture boy for a weenie roast gone badly, laying there, unresponsive, charcoal with a pulse.

I knew Iris must have been the friend who quickly called the ambulance. We had a relationship of sorts. Josh, on the other hand, was a work buddy. How did he hear of my propane party? Was it a personal or business visit?

Thinking for an extended period of time was not possible. Clouds quickly formed raining Novocain down upon my neurons. Moments of clarity were as rare as a rainbow. Always a few lines short of a paragraph, I could not answer my own questions. Too many distractions floating through the blood stream courtesy of the chemical cocktail entering my arm. Happy hour on the hour. The Drifters on the juke box, ice chips in a cup, and a waitress named Jane.

I dozed, again, only to be awakened by the murmur of female voices. "Keep up the hydration and check the catheter. Watch the dressings for excessive drainage." "Do I deal with the graft sites?" "No, neither the graft nor harvest areas will require your attention. Just monitor the vitals." "Isn't he nightmare afflicted?" "Hopefully that phase has past but pay attention the first few nights." "He's quite the mess, what a shame." "Please remain positive around the patients Nurse Blitz." "Of course, sorry Nurse Meyer."

Sneakered steps padded out the door. Darkness slowly seeped in over the hum of the machines, around the blinking lights and onto the mess that was me. I closed my eyes and took refuge in a small corner of my medicated mind.

Routine blossoms everywhere, even on the Burn Ward. Over the next few days I slept most of the time. "Mother Nature's healing mechanism." according to Nurse Jane. In my waking hours I bore witness to my own red, raw skin as the dressings were changed. The second day brought two developments, my initial conscious experience with a wound care bath and the return of my voice.

Jane informed me in the early afternoon that I would be moved from my bed to a room down the hall for a bath. "We will do this every few days to prevent infection." she explained. "I will increase your pain medication." The she looked me in the eye, "It won't really matter much because this will really hurt. Imagine a paper cut multiplied by a thousand and lasting several minutes." Then she pulled out a syringe and stuck me in the ass. In short order a numbing wave crested and splashed over me. Then a second and third. I felt good. Bring on the paper.

Two large men in white entered pushing a padded gurney. They raised me, sheet and all, from the bed and onto the four wheeled chariot. Then we were off. I had a vertical view of ceiling tile and fluorescent light fixtures. Soon a door opened and the ride was over. Nurse Jane bent over me. "We are going to remove all of your bandages except for your face. Then we will slide a matt very carefully under your body and lift you into the air. We will then move you over the tub and lower you into the cleansing solution." I was buzzing along and wanted to ask if I needed a ticket for this ride.

Maneuvers took place with practiced precision and soon I was airborne. "Fly me to the moon." was bouncing between my ears. A little turbulence as we changed elevation and moved to the left. "Big old jet airliner." replaced Sinatra. Then we began our approach and descended into the healing waters. "Swing low sweet chariot." played for splashdown.

At that instant I became pain. Packs of dogs with teeth of fire ravaged me from toe to head. Insatiable, relentless, throbbing pain. My voice returned as I wailed "Shiiiiiiiiiiit!" There was no response. I caught my breath and yelled again, "Fuuuuck." And so it went until the matt began to rise and the agony fell away a drop at a time. When I landed on the gurney Jane stuck another needle in my hip. A tug of war ensued between relief and pain. By the time the flag reached the border of numb land I was back in my bed.

Nurse Jane wiped my brow and pitched a few ice chips. I looked at her with contempt, "Get a little closer and I'll bite a finger off. Or maybe that pug nose of yours" A seething anger occupied my mind. Jane, of course, knew the tune. "I know you are upset, pissed and want to lash out and I don't blame you. Let us finish your dressings. That shot should be kicking in by now. Try to relax and we will talk later" She was right about my latest fix. The buzz band was in full swing, I managed to mumble "O.K." before nodding off.

The human voice puts us at the top of the food chain; it is the bullhorn of the soul, our interface with the world. Having just recovered mine I could appreciate the power of speech. I had issues to discuss, information to obtain, requests to make, and songs to sing. It was early morning when I awoke. My room was still in full night shade mode, I was a plant waiting for the grow lights to come on.

In the peaceful dimness I could make out fresh bandages, archipelagos on each arm and lower leg. Some appeared to have decreased in size. I was still restrained, not that I had any desire for mobility after my last journey down the hall. I felt irritations here and there, an itch, twinge, and ache. No pain. My barbiturate balloon was fully inflated.

Living in a narcotized state was becoming normal. I appreciated that the alternative was unacceptable. Modern medicine was working a miracle. No longer a shish-ka-bob, I was on the road to recovery. My thought process remained disjointed, three steps in one direction only to veer off toward a roadside distraction. The click of a computer key, morphed into the click of Iris's heels on the dance floor, which begot the click of the door opening.

"Good morning Mr. Lawton" said a smiling Nurse Blitz. "I hope you're feeling better after that nasty, old bath." Nurse Blitz was young, with brown hair to the shoulders, a dimpled, apple cheek face, flat of chest and long of leg. I watched as she made a few notations on my chart before checking the dressings, replacing bags of solutions, adjusting Velcro straps, and finally lifting the sheet and checking out my catheter. I knew my dick was down there but at this point it was a one trick appendage. All must have been in order because Nurse Blitz carefully lowered the sheet and looked up at me. "I hear your voice has returned, is there anything you need." I looked into her young face, checked my vault of one liners and came up with, "How about some Jim Beam with the ice chips." She gave a quick chuckle, "It is good to keep a sense of humor. I will relay your request to Nurse Meyer she is coming on duty soon." Blitz then turned to the door. After a couple of steps she looked over her shoulder, "Although I do believe she is a Jack Daniels woman."

It felt good to engage in conversation, my give and take was up and running. Comprehension and retention kicked into gear. The memory motor sputtered to life. A lot of me was back in the race. The rest bounced around, tin cans tied to my undercarriage. Background static, bolts of light, vaporous images colliding with the pavement sending sparks into the mix.

The return of my sense of self was a two edged sword. I was back in the game but it was the majorly fucked league. Anger and self-pity fogged any reflection. "Why me?" echoed behind every thought. Why me indeed. Grills shouldn't explode. Did I do something wrong? What happened?

I was staring at a pattern on the ceiling tile and missed Nurse Jane's entrance. "Paul, how are you this fine day?" she said. I almost jumped out of what little skin I had left. She was quick to apologize, "Sorry, I should have noticed that faraway look in your eyes." Jane pulled a pen out of her hair and made chart notes. She gave me a few sideways glances, set the clipboard down, and pulled up a chair. "Let's talk." she stated, more of a command than a request.

"I have been working this ward for almost ten years." Jane began, "and I have seen the process unfold hundreds of times. You are at the end of the beginning. Your body took a great shock and so did your mind. We must heal both. Your wounds are improving every day. I cannot read your thoughts so we need to discuss your feelings."

Jane's words were more than just beaten air; she had a professional yet caring tone. Her eyes reached into mine with genuine concern, beacons of hope. I wanted to head toward the light. A clearing of the throat brought me back. O.K. let's talk.

"Well-- I--- am--- pissed--- off." My new found voice chopping the words like hard wood. "Everything was going good and now---- this" I stammered. Tears started to form at the corners of my eyes. I wanted to look away but my head wouldn't move. Frustration boiled up, "And what the fuck is it with my head nailed down to the fucking bed anyway. Not to mention my fucking arms and legs" I raised my limbs in anger. Jane sat like the Buddha. Her calmness floated toward me lowering my agitation meter. I relaxed for a moment before proceeding, "And another thing, how about a mirror

I want to see my face. I have heard enough about it; guess I have two more ass cheeks." The good nurse suppressed a smile, lips and wine stain quivering.

Jane stood up and crossed her arms over her chest. Distraction alarms sounded in my brain. I looked up into her face. "Good questions let me start with the mirror. We have found that mirrors are not helpful. The doctors are like artists they do not want to show off their work until it is complete. You are past the plasmatic imbibition stage and into inosculation." At this Jane broke out into a grin. "How's that for some medical mumbo jumbo. In layman's terms your graft is taking root; it is like repotting a plant. We need to make the connection between the graft and the surrounding skin. Get the blood and nutrients flowing."

"So how is my garden doing?" I asked. Jane grabbed my chart then bent over and examined both sides of my face. "You're doing well; the skin is turning from white to pink. I believe suture removal should occur in a few days. Of course it will be some time before we can determine if reinnervation has taken place." I gave her a quizzical look. She responded, "If the nerves have made a connection, if you will have feeling in the skin."

O.K. No mirrors until Van Gough has finished. Who am I to question the hands that heal? I was about to move on to my restraints when Jane's pager went off. She excused herself and left me alone with images of sun flowers poking through my pores.

My interlude was interrupted by Dr. Gibbs and the internees. "Hello Paul," Gibbs practically bellowed, "I am Dr. Gibbs and these are doctors in training who are rotating through the burn unit for a few weeks." He motioned to the attentive group with a wave of his hand. "We are going to do everything to speed your recovery and get you back home." The doctor was an inch or so short of six feet, with a full head of short cropped light brown hair, black rimmed glasses, a spreading paunch and a little too much of a tan.

As he picked up the chart I took the opportunity to mutter, "We already met asshole." Gibbs looked up, cocked his head to one side and said, "Excuse me, did you say something."

My eyes roamed over the eager faces surrounding the bed. Mr. Southern Drawl was standing next to Mr. Olive, three lab coats removed from Gibbs. "I said that we already met, you all were here before." After setting down the chart Gibbs moved a little closer toward me and in a soft, concerned tone stated, "Paul, sometimes the mind plays tricks. You have been through a lot and unless you golf at Cypress Hills I do not believe we have met." This evoked a chuckle or two from the posse which only served to increase my irritation. "Golf is for dicks doc plus it messes up your memory."

Dr. Gibbs took a step back and a little crimson encroached on his neck. I tried not to smile. "You said you were going to take skin off my ass and put it on my face and he compared my face to a mardi gras mask. Remember now doc?" He sputtered like an old lawn mower. I fired one more salvo, "Your bedside manner needs work."

Old Gibbs, to his credit, didn't blow up. He grabbed the chart again and flipped through a few pages. "I see, I see." he pronounced to no one in particular. Then, in a little sterner doctor demeanor, he said, "Paul, first of all everyone at this hospital is here to help you. Fine dedicated people. They deserve your respect, please keep a civil tone. Second, I and these interns have been at your bedside a few times in the past week. If I or anyone else said anything to offend you I apologize. It is certainly possible you regained consciousness during one of our visits." Dr. Gibbs gave me one of those up-tilted nods of the head like a puppy that has just shit on your carpet. I knew it was a close to an apology as I would ever get.

"I'd shake your hand doctor but I am a prisoner of Velcro." A look of relief crossed his face as a few nervous smiles broke in the lab coated herd. "No need for that Paul." he said with a quick look at this watch. "I am sure you have a few questions. I will stop by after we finish our rounds." With that he took a quick turn for the door followed by the buzzing swarm of soon to bees.

I never saw Dr. Gibbs again. A few hours later Nurse Jane returned without so much as a good afternoon. She proceeded to examine my bandages and adjusted the restraints. I detected the tension and took the low road, "Is something wrong?" Jane gave me a stern look. "A nurse is responsible for everything about her patients. Your bit of fun with the doctor and interns earlier was not appreciated." Her brown eyes were on fire. "You have a sharp tongue and a lot of people around here have thin skins."

I liked Nurse Jane and did not want to piss her off. "I am sorry." I replied "But you have to admit Gibbs is a bit of an asshole and I only spoke the truth." Some of the tension left her face. "Dr. Gibbs is a fine surgeon and a good teacher. Let's leave it at that."

I admired her diplomatic approach but sensed she may have agreed with my opinion. Jane sat down and crossed her shapely white sheathed legs causing her skirt to rise up. She cleared her throat and looked at my chart. Again. Everybody looked at the damn thing like it contained all the secrets in the universe. "So," I chirped like the first bird of spring, "can we finish our discussion about me and my prospects."

"Sure." she replied still looking at the chart. "What would you like to know?" I started slow, "When will I be released from the

Velcro?" Jane set the chart down and glanced at my ankles and wrists. "I have had a few fantasies about being tied up in bed." I continued, "This is not one of them." Jane stood up and smiled, "You certainly have an interesting take on things Paul. It looks like tomorrow we will do a bath and reassess. I would say you will be unrestrained by the afternoon."

Good news in the middle of a cow pie. Another bath. "How many more baths will there be?" I groaned. "Depends, you are relatively young and appear to be healing well, maybe two or three." Not a pleasant prospect. Then I remembered the shots.

"Tell me about my medications?" I inquired. Jane grabbed the chart. "Nothing you would recognize. We are fighting off infection, keeping your vitals stable, feeding you, and relieving pain." I watched her sit down again. "Looks like you will begin a solid diet soon; we will remove the catheter and get you back in control of your bowels" Hallelujah and pass the toilet paper. Not to be sidetracked I asked, "What is in the shot you gave me before the bath?" "Fentanyl, an analgesic with a potency eighty times greater than the morphine derivative." Jane lectured. "It gives a real boost to your dopamine levels producing a state of euphoria and relaxation."

She stood up and walked around to the foot of my bed before continuing, "Naturally we are concerned with the potential for addiction. Part of my job is to keep you comfortable with the minimal amount of opioids necessary." I almost felt like I should be taking notes for the next quiz. The words comfort, euphoria and relaxation would be highlighted. I began a slow drift back to a college classroom with pen and pad working overtime.

Jane snapped me back to the present, "How are we doing in that regard?" she inquired. "Do you feel like a potted plant or are

your circuits working?" I did a loop around my cranium before answering, "I have occasional shooting pains but otherwise no complaints. For a while I was mucked up, Jell-O in the gears, rust on
the pulleys. I would run the ball down the field but then the game
changed to hockey and I am on my ass."

Jane smiled, "As I said before you do have a way with words. It
is common to have a period of adjustment."

I again felt the caring in her voice.

"Will I be having any more operations or is this as good as
it gets?" Jane shifted from one foot to another as if she had to
pee. The professor came out again, "Difficult to say, your facial
grafts are healing well. You ears are not in good shape. I am
sure there will be consultations with a plastic surgeon." Another
cow pie. My ears were a little large but proportionate to my size
eight dome. Now they were not in good shape. Coming from
Ms. Optimism that probably meant I had burnt pretzels slapped
on each side of my head. "I think my hearing is fine." Jane was
quick to respond, "Oh yes, there is no damage to the internal
components."

Might as well clear the table and see if the good china is broken. "Any other issues I should be aware of?" I said in that no more
bad news tone as I looked down toward my dick back to Jane and
a return gaze at old helmet head. She picked up on my not too
subtle reference, "Nothing to worry about in the plumbing department or any other area. We just need to get your wounds to heal.
In a few weeks you should be able to start physical therapy. A lot of
time in bed tends to weaken the muscles in your arms and legs."
Arms and legs, big deal, I'll be able to get a boner, now that was
good news.

It was late in her shift and Jane needed to move on. She reached into one of her many pockets and pulled out a hard plastic container. With a quick glance at the door Jane removed a syringe, "So you like Mr. Fentanyl, do you?" I was startled. "In your situation there is no harm in some distractive relief, half a dose should lighten your burden." A slight irritation as the needle penetrated a muscle layer followed by a softening of the edges. A warm cocoon enveloped me as I watched Jane return the syringe to its case. She lifted the water glass and put the straw to my lips. "Hydration, drink as much as you can." I heard, "Hi dink, ash can." Nonetheless I worked the straw like a forty dollar hooker. A gurgling roar echoed up from the bottom of the glass. "Very good." Jane practically whispered, "Very good Paul."

My thank you was drowned in the click of a switch. I drifted off with the fading light.

True to her word Jane and the commando brothers started my morning with a trip down the hall. Things went about the same. I screamed, they ignored me, it mercifully ended. Back to my room, another shot, some relief.

I awoke late in the day, another cotton field in my mouth, zero humidity above the gum line, and instinctively reached for the water glass, watching in amazement as my hand rose up like Lazarus. I was free and shaky. It took great effort to make it half way before my arm plopped back down on the bed. No Velcro anywhere, only one tube in my arm and none leading from my dick. I could even move my head.

I was admiring my wiggling toes when Jane walked in with a look of surprise. "Well who is this man, shouldn't he be tied down. I better get the orderlies in here." Then she covered her mouth in mock horror before stifling a laugh. I smiled myself and said, "When you're done accepting the Oscar would you mind giving me some water, my throat is drier than the Sahara"

A full glass later I smacked my lips which drew another laugh from Jane. "When do I get a steak, baked potato, and chocolate cream pie?" Jane was examining my new leg dressings. She glanced back my way; her brown eye floating above the wine stain. "How about some mashed carrots with lime Jell-O. Maybe with a ginger ale chaser" she replied. Sounded like Chef Gerber. "You are going to have to feed me Nurse Jane; my arms have taken a siesta." She had finished her inspection and was making a few notes. "As much as I would like to," Jane stated with a hint of sarcasm, "We have Candy Striper volunteers for that task. Your meal should be here shortly." She was almost at the door when I called out, "Thanks for keeping your word." Jane turned back, "We are in this together, re-member. If you need help just ask." I rose up a little from the bed, "I appreciate that."

Alone again I went back to testing body parts. The toes wig-gled, I could raise my feet slightly but could not bring them back to bend my knees, fingers moved, and so did the hands. Right arm came up slightly higher than the left. Head movement was a little tight. Not much sensation on the back side or with the dick. Felt a little like a bug coming out of a cocoon. Even the old stomach put forth a weak growl.

As if on cue the door swung open and in came a cart being pushed by a young rosy cheeked girl with page boy hair and a bright smile. A few covered plastic plates crowded together on the top shelf. Without a word this walking candy cane stopped the cart at the corner of the bed before reaching over and swinging a tray down in front of my chest. She then walked back and took the cover off a plate and positioned it in the middle of the tray. It dawned on me that she had yet to look at my face.

I watched as she returned to the cart and hoping to ease the strain said, "Hi, my name is Paul and you must be bringing the pizza and beer." A muffled laugh coincided with a shrug across her shoulders. She turned holding a bib in one hand and a spoon in the other. A confused look crossed her face as if something was out of order. The spoon shook a little before she spoke, "My name is Joyce, Joyce Stoops," she stammered, "I'm afraid there is no pizza or beer just a dinner of big boy baby food."

Joyce tied the bib around my neck and picked up a spoonful of something green with the consistency of whipped squash. "Don't worry it tastes better than it looks." she said before gently placing it in my mouth. Joyce was right, not bad and probably nutritious. She kept up a good pace, spoon following spoon, a Ferris wheel of mush. Joyce wiped my lips with the bib before removing it. Next I finished off a strawberry smoothie concoction. "Good." Joyce said, "Is there anything else you need?" The initial shock of my appearance had worn off. She sat down in the chair with a hopeful smile on her young face.

"How long have you been wearing the stripes?" I asked. "This is my second month." she replied, "I volunteer through Menlo Park High School." "Do you get extra credit?" "No, but I hope it looks good on my college applications. It is all so competitive." Joyce stated a little wistfully. "I wish you well and thanks for helping me out. Will you be here often?" Joyce stood up and went to the cart. "Three times during the week and few hours on Saturday." she replied as she wrestled with the door. "Come back soon, I don't get many visitors, and next time bring pizza." I watched as the stripes bounced back and forth before disappearing. Do not adjust your vertical hold.

A few minutes later the door suddenly reopened. Joyce quickly entered and just as quickly closed the door. "I hope I am not interrupting." she said with a furrowed brow. Her dimples bounced like dice on felt. She took a few tentative steps forward. "You got the pizza?" I asked. Joyce laughed. "No, no, sorry about that but I do have something else you might need." She reached into her pocket and pulled out a business card. "I understand you were in an accident, this is someone who can help you."

Joyce swung the card over to within a foot of my face. I imagined she knew a counselor of sorts, someone to ease me through these troubled waters. My eyes were still focusing when Joyce blurted out, "His name is Dan Plum and he is a great attorney." What the hell, I thought, a cute candy striper shaking it for some ambulance chaser. I was too surprised to be annoyed. She set the card down on my side table. "Time for you to get some rest, Nurse Meyer should be in shortly. See you in a few days."

Sharks have a way of smelling blood across miles of water. Their two legged brethren also have a sharp nose. Always on the scent for accidents, explosions, fires, slips, falls, dog bites, sexual abuse, battery, malpractice, mayhem. Hospitals are obvious fertile feeding grounds. However, like a fin in the offshore waves, a three piece suit would only cause panic on the Burn Ward. Better to use someone much higher on the trust index to relay the message. It doesn't take a legal genius to get cash for a guy whose arm flew out the ass end of a wood chipper. It does, however, take creativity to get Lefty into the office to sign on the dotted line. Runners and cappers they are known in the trade, those who get a little piece of the contingency pie. The bigger the pie the sweeter the taste. I just might be the mother of all pies.

A little pie nightcap would go good right now I was thinking just as Jane entered with a nightcap of her own. "I understand you ate all of your big boy baby food. Of course that good deed brings us a step closer to bed pan action." She grabbed a cord attached to a button and hooked it to my bed rail. "When the need arises push the button. Immediately, if not sooner. Changing out bed sheets is not a wanted job around here." I have a hard enough time pissing in a urinal at the ball park. Twenty guys lined up, dick in hand, staring straight ahead, thinking of Niagara Falls. Now I am supposed to let fly while some nurse checks her watch. Not to mention squeezing out a loaf with my harvested ass cheeks resting on a bloated horseshoe.

Jane finished with the chart and patted her pocket. I knew Mr. Fentanyl was back in the house. "Sure." I murmured as she retrieved the syringe. Soon a river of feel good coursed through me. Jane left the room about the same time I did.

A rumbling in the bowels awoke me just past dawn. Cramp Bros. Trucking roared into the neighborhood spewing exhaust out my newly opened tunnel. "Farting is a natural function and should not be condemned" so said my old friend Roger. This morning was a free fire zone until something other than air appeared on the rectal radar. Severe pucker procedures went into effect. I heeded the warning and pushed the call button.

Luckily the room was still in sleepy mode when an African American nurse poked her head through the door. "Time for the bed pan honey." I gave a vigorous nod. "The orderly will be right in." she said before retreating. Not a lot of jobs where you assist with another's excretory function. I wasn't looking forward to blowing ballast but the situation had reached the point of no return. I recognized Tom as one of the commandos who had helped with the bath process. He went about this task in the same businesslike manner.

I lifted butt as he slid the pan into position and gave me a nod. Ground control to Major Sphincter, "Jettison Cargo." A noise resembling a hippo belch preceded a paint peeling smell. Days of simmering brought forth a strange brew. Tom took it in stride, carefully removing the evacuated and wiping me with an industrial wet one. He even sprayed something in the air, a somewhat successful attempt at arresting the odor. I felt like giving him a tip but had to settle for a mumbled, "Thanks." Tom nodded one more time, popped a lid on the relief vessel and gingerly left the room.

I dozed until breakfast, also brought in by Tom. Neither of us mentioned his earlier visit although it occurred to me, as he spooned powdered eggs that he may be thinking about their eventual deposit into the pan. The removal of my bib coincided with the arrival of another gaggle of interns. There had been a turnover, no Gibbs and all new wannabes. Dr. Scott Vu was in charge. A short, skinny man with deep black hair and gold rimmed glasses who spoke with an accent befitting one whose first tongue mimicked chickens on plucking day. "Hello," he said a little too loudly, "My name is Dr. Vu, let me take a look at your grafts." He removed coverings from both sides of my head. I made a quick tour of the eager intern faces. Their expressions ranged from stoic to amazement to slight eye aversion. These mirrors reinforced the fact that I must live down at the end of Grotesque Street.

"Yes, yes I believe we will have an excellent result. We will remove your sutures tomorrow." Dr. Scotty commented. "I will have Nurse Meyer reapply your dressings. Also, in a week or so you can commence physical therapy." He then turned to the attentive trainees, "Why is such treatment necessary?" It seemed like a soft ball question but a few of the group took a sudden interest in the ceiling tiles. A tall woman with auburn hair and black framed glasses spoke up, "The patient has been bed ridden for a long time causing loss of muscle tone. He will need reconditioning and learn work around measures for any deficit caused by the burns."

Once again I felt like someone's science project. Recondition, work around, suture removal. I could be a piece of furniture.

"Correct." praised Vu, "Let's make a note to track his progress. Any questions Paul?" Questions doc, I got a million of them. For you only one, "When will I be able to leave this palace of pain Sultan Vu?" A giggle rippled through the troops while the doctor raised one eyebrow and tilted his head, "You in pain sir, where does it hurt?" The tall glass came to the rescue, "Dr. Vu the patient would like to know when he can go home." Scotty was a little upset at needing a translator but marched forward, "Four to five weeks I would estimate." he stated to no one in particular. A quick turn and he, as well as the un-credentialed conga line, left. Most likely I was headed into another shit storm with Nurse Jane.

Four to five weeks, a month or so, a good chunk of time no matter how you slice it. And it was not like I would be just like new. Those intern eyes didn't lie. Welcome to my world, Halloween 24/7. The twins, self-pity and anger, again started hop scotching across my mind. It was easy to get caught up in the professional optimism entering my room; real food, suture removal, rehabilitation, good results. While a return to good health appeared inevitable I was not on the conveyor belt to happiness. The one day at a time mantra worked well if you did not think about the past wasted days or those yet to come. I clenched my fists and silently screamed.

Jane had a knack for interrupting my descents into despair. Her voice crackled through my misshapen ears, "If you don't learn some manners there won't be any doctors left to treat you. Cut out the joking and show some respect." Jane and anger did not mix well. I gave her my best wide eyed "What do you mean." look. When the sizzle didn't leave I went for a frontal assault, "You are absolutely correct, couldn't agree more, don't know what I was thinking, will never happen again, if I only could I would cross my heart." Slowly the tension left her and a slight smile staked a claim. "I thought you majored in computers not bullshit." A laugh escaped before I could reel it back.

Jane proceeded to check my wounds. "Dr. Vu is a good guy, you're lucky to have him on your case." I watched her long fingers gracefully reapplied the cotton dressings. There appeared to be less ooze. Jane had me turn toward the wall so she could check the graft site on my ass. "Getting better every day." she noted as I rolled back. "I will return after lunch, is there anything you need?" "I would like to call my parents if that is O.K." I replied. "Good idea." she said, "see you later."

Yeah it was a good idea. And I had a few hours to figure out what to say.

Knowing I would be asked I spent some more time attempting to reconstruct the twist that put me in my present crispy state. There was the final pre-blast frame of my finger hitting the ignition switch on that shiny new Cain grill. Events preceding remained hazy and tangled. A ball of Gordian knotted memories in search of release and reconciliation. Pulling one string just tightened others. Alexander the Great used his sword to solve the problem. Lacking a sharp blade I took the zen approach and let the gnarl roll over me.

Every tale needs a sound track and mine had the lubricated voice of Charles Brown lamenting over life in a "Fool's paradise." He brought me and my Cadillac home that day. Where had we been Chuck? "Drinkin and gambling and staying up all night" Mr. Brown replied. No, it was late afternoon and my breath smelled of garlic and crab. I had been at Thahn Long with Grace the realtor. Grace had sold me the house and we had a couple of rolls in the sack.

Into the house I went and took a nap. Chuck passed the microphone to Jimmy Buffet, "I don't know where I'm a gonna go when the volcano blow." Iris woke me up and the music stopped. She had been shopping for dinner, steaks and a salad. I went to the grill, opened the propane valve and boom. That boom wasn't an explosion it was breaking glass. Iris had dropped a vase; I returned to the kitchen to see what had happened. We cleaned up the mess, then I went back out and boom. No, Iris had served dessert before dinner. Then came the boom.

Nurse Jane arrived midafternoon with the phone. "I got one with a speaker; it will be easy for you to talk to your parents." She set Mr. Bell's invention on the tray and swung it close to my chest. With the cord in one hand Jane looked about the room. "Where is that damn jack?" she muttered to herself. "I think I noticed one under the table in the corner." I said.

Jane got down on all fours and reached toward the wall. Her dress rose up like a window shade revealing gartered white nylons as she struggled with the cord. A bugle called the libido cavalry to attention. The good nurse had an inviting ass. I stared as my shriveled appendage stirred. Arteries dilated, blood flowed, after weeks of hibernation, arousal arrived. Segmental stretching, inch by inch, increasing girth. Boner city, hard on haven, woody acres, erection central, stiffy town, tent pole palace, tripod territory.

"There." Jane announced as she backed away from the wall and stood up, slightly flushed from her efforts. Fortunately for me the bed sheet was crumpled and the return of my manhood obscured. Lust knows no shame.

"So what's the number?" Jane asked her hand over the phone. Shifting gears I easily recalled my parent's digits since they had remained the same my entire life. I had punched them in to get rides home from Little League, to see if I could stay at a friend's home for dinner, to complain about my moldy dorm room, to ask for money, to announce I was moving to California, to offer my congratulations, best wishes, sympathy and regret, and to leave yet another new address.

This time someone else dialed and my mother answered with a cheery, "Hello." Jane looked at me to see if I would take the lead. As the dead air expanded she said, "Mrs. Lawton, this is Nurse Meyer from Stanford Hospital, we met when you came to see Paul." "Yes, yes" my mother replied. Then with a tone of concern she asked, "Is Paul alright, has something bad happened?" Jane turned the dial to soothing reassurance, "Paul is doing much better, and in fact he is here with me. Is your husband available, I'll turn the phone over to your son." At this my mom yelled for my dad to get on the other line. Within a few seconds the old man's voice boomed out, "Paul, you there?" I suddenly had a case of jittering fright. "I thought you said Paul was on the phone." my dad challenged my mother. She replied with a hint of irritation, "Of course he's there, the nurse said so." "Well where the hell is he?"

"I am here." I said, hoping to prevent further phone combat. "Good to hear your voices how is everything on the home front." "We are doing fine dear, keeping busy and getting old." my mom replied. "Never mind about us." my dad barked, "How are you? You looked awful when we were out there." Choosing to spare them the gruesome details of my ongoing resurrection I lied, "Doing pretty well, in fact I should be discharged in no time."

I stole a glance at Jane. She shook her head and gave me one of those "Be careful!" looks. "That's great, maybe you should come live with us for a while." my mother suggested. "Don't rush the boy." dad interjected. "So what the hell happened anyway?" he questioned. I took a breath and replied, "The grill blew up, I guess. My memory is a little sketchy." "You should sue the bastards!" he blasted into the phone. "That is not supposed to happen." My mother put her hand on the receiver and yelled across the house, in a muffled tone I heard, "Calm down would you, he needs our support not your screaming."

After a few seconds she said, "Paul do you need anything, would you like us to come back out?" While I loved my parents we had only been together a few days a year since I moved to California. Hell they didn't even know about my Weezy windfall. Better for them if we kept our distance. "Thanks mom, I appreciate the thought but there is not much you could do here. The staff is great and when I am released I promise to come for a visit." "That would be wonderful." she replied. "Sure," I said, "I am getting a little tired why don't I call you later." "O.K. Paul," my dad said calmly, "And think about a lawyer." "Your right dad, I will make some calls." Good byes traveled the miles and then the mournful tone of disconnection sounded.

We sat in silence for a few minutes. I felt a heart tug at the thought that there was a room in that split level brick house with Lawton on the mail box where my baseball cards rested in a dresser drawer. The lode star where I would be loved and cared for. I turned away as a tear traveled down my cheek. Jane stood up, unhooked the phone and said, "Why don't you rest before dinner, I will check in later." I nodded my head without looking her way.

I drifted away, caught up in the medicated maelstrom, pictures, sound, and finally a story. My mom waving as I rode my bike, a baseball mitt looped over the handle bar, wind splashing my face, both hands in back pockets, not a care in the world. Meet the gang for an early evening tour of the neighborhood; a pack of exuberance, spinning spokes and popping wheelies. Past the creek reduced to a trickle in the late summer heat. Stopping at the gravel pit where the stones fly as brakes strain under sneakered feet. Suddenly a car cuts through, taillights disappearing after the big willow tree. "Bet their going to do it." Murmurs all around. "Let's go watch." "Not yet he ain't even got his dick out." Nervous laughter. Toes kicking dirt.

I move away slowly, stopping after thirty yards. Only mumbling followed. Ahead an intermittent moan pulled me forward into the fading light, heart pounding. The car's shape came into view. It was parked and moving, a slight bounce in counterpoint to guttural ecstasy of increasing decibels. I laid the bike on its side and walked toward the trunk. The rear window had yet to fog. She had one leg over the front seat and the other pressing the door frame. Her face was buried in his right shoulder. "Oh, yeah, uggh, hmmm," A bare butt rose and fell. "I'm coming!" Her head snapped up, eyes wide, teeth gnashed, nostrils flaring. It was Nurse Jane.

This shit was getting weird. I had the twisted dream bends. A pull brought me back to reality, a hooked fish resisting the surface.

My appetite was returning. The stomach demanded attention with ping ponging growls. On cue candy striper extraordinaire Joyce Stoops came through the door. Smiling with excessive strength she rolled a cart of nutrition up to the bed. "How are you doing Paul, hungry I hope? And no it is not pizza and beer" I laughed and said, "Nice of you to remember my preferences." Joyce bent over and placed a bib around my neck. She smelled like a spring breeze. "Looks like your moving up the food chain." she announced. "Solid food is on the menu." There was skinned chicken, broccoli, rice, and Jell-O. My arms were still on strike. Joyce politely fed me, stopping occasionally to dab splatter from my cheeks.

When the last of the wiggly Jell-O slid toward my stomach she asked, "So have you called that lawyer I told you about yet?" "No, not yet," I replied with a hint of remorse. "I don't have phone privileges." A pout of disappointment crossed her face as she cleaned up. "You are going to call him as soon as you can aren't you?" Joyce said with a sense of urgency. Her breathing was a little strained. The pin stripes were all a twitter. One shoulder strap had fallen to the side.

After removing my bib Joyce lifted the tray at which point an empty plastic plate rolled down the sheet coming to rest between my legs. As she reached for the wayward dish Joyce accidently grabbed my dick, which, after my dream, immediately went to full mast. She did not let go.

I looked up at her face, Joyce seemed surprised and amused. There was a flush of color rising up her neck, matching that on her cheeks. She was not going to yell and run out the door. Increasing the tension I said, "I would help myself but my arms are not quite ready." She replied in a voice just above a whisper, "I understand, it's only natural, my brother does it all the time." Joyce blushed even more then turned and pushed the food cart up against the door.

Joyce grabbed the dinner napkin as she walked to the side of the bed where she gently lifted the sheet away from my legs and pulled it toward my chest. Taking a tube of skin lotion from the bedside table she loaded up the palm of her left hand. Joyce gave me a little smile before spreading the lotion on my balls and cock.

Pleasure does not describe the wonderful sensation that accompanied each stroke. She was experienced. Picking up the pace and then slowing down. Massaging, tugging, rubbing, teasing. Weeks of release rose and then ebb away once, twice. Joyce kept her attention on the task, never looking up even as I hit the deep breath and grunting plateau. Quickly the line was crossed. Head thrown back, mouth wide open, silently screaming. White ropes challenged gravity.

I slowly regained focus. Joyce was using the napkin to clean up. She looked my way as she pulled the sheet down. With a sheepish grin I said, "Thanks." Joyce nodded then pulled another business card out of her pocket and put it on the table. "Have a good night." she said after wrestling the cart away from the door. "See you next time."

A new number one on my list of erotic moments: candy striper, hospital bed, threat of discovery. All the elements for a letter to Penthouse and just about all the venal and a few mortal sins. No use, however, exchanging my smile for a ticket to guilt town. I wasn't going there, not tonight. On the cosmic ledger of good/bad this french fry was owed a few more positive checks.

Jane came in a short while later for my nightly checkup. "Exciting day." she commented while giving my wounds the once over. I knew she meant the phone call with my parents, at least I hoped that was the case. "Yes, it was good to talk to mom and dad." I replied. "Your legs and arms are doing very well." Jane told me, "Tomorrow you will start physical therapy."

She bent over to remove the dressings on my face. I watched her pupils, no reflection. Jane applied some medication. "The grafts look fine. Dr. Vu will be pleased." She took a seat and pulled out a few sheets of paper from her front pocket. "These are forms from the counseling department. Why don't I read the questions and you tell me what to write" Jane said. "Sure, do you do taxes too?" She chuckled, "No, math is not my strong suit." And so I began to tell Nurse Jane the facts, figures, and fantasies not many had ever heard.

"The computer has already filled some information." Jane said as she flipped through the pages. "Let's see, here's a blank, the extent of your education." She looked at me with pen poised over paper. "Masters in Computer Science." I replied. "Employment status." An interesting question. Unemployed, retired, between jobs. "I guess I am a consultant." I said. "Last employer?" "That would be Weezy." Jane smiled, "Wasn't that one of the seven dwarfs?" We both grinned. "Describe your average work day." I proceeded to inform Jane that nothing was ever average except long hours and pizza. She listened intently as I explained the intricacies of writing code, increasing speed, decreasing temperature, rerouting, and generally changing the computing world. Her eyes did not glaze over. "Sounds exciting, so why did you leave?" "I didn't, Weezy was bought like a prize winning hog at the county fair." A couple of crinkles crossed her brow before her eyes lit up, "You're a dot com millionaire?" With a shrug of the shoulders I said, "Hope you won't hold it against me." Jane set the forms on her lap. "How does it feel?"

"Actually it hasn't been that long. I mean it obviously changed my life, one day your someone, the next your someone else. But you're really not any different. Does that make any sense?"

"Sure," Jane replied, "Money doesn't change your soul, at least not right away. It opens a lot more doors though. Not that I would know."

"You're right. I bought a new car, house, stereo, T.V., furniture. Of course if I hadn't got that grill I wouldn't be here today. How's that for irony. Get rich, get toasted." An odor of bitterness invaded the room. Anger was right around the corner having a cigarette.

Jane sensed the change. She took my hand, "My grandma told me we are all comets traveling through time. What's past is gone. You need to concentrate on the brightness ahead not the cold tail behind. You are going to feel better."

Jane stared down at the paper on her lap longer than necessary before finally asking, "Any religious preference?"

"Great segue, you mean now or before the kaboom?" I thought for a while then asked, "Is that a yes or no question?" The good nurse bounced uncomfortably back and forth on her chair. Religion will do that.

At the end of every hard day people need a reason to believe. And if your reason lives in a church, mosque, synagogue, pagoda or temple then you have a faith with legions of followers marching alongside. You belong and, therefore, do have a religious preference. If what gets you through is something else-- love, liquid, smoke, work, pill, plastic,-- check the no box.

"I can leave it blank if you want." Jane interrupted. "No, no put down Catholic– baptized, slapped, schooled, and scarred." Catholic up until realizing one Sunday morning while in a balcony pew that guilt should not be the engine that drives a religion.

Dictate standards of behavior beyond the reach of most, cut off salvation for failure, provide a confessional, repeat until death. Mold the conscience, control the person. The institutionalization of what the man from Galilee preached mucked up the message.

"How about you, what is your preference?" I asked Jane. "I thought I was asking the questions." she replied. Jane set her pen down and looked into the distance as if watching the sun set. "In my work there are many opportunities to both curse and praise God. I believe there is a power greater than us; however, he or she must have other interests or a poor attention span because nothing is fair. The good do not always benefit, the bad do not always suffer. There is no preacher who can explain this truth, so I stopped going to church years ago."

Jane redirected her gaze toward her lap. Trouble creased her countenance. My question had caused a disturbance. Accepting responsibility I said, "You are right, the meek don't inherit the Earth, mourners are not always comforted, and turning the cheek usually gets another punch." I sensed something more personal was on Jane's mind. "Hell what of me, and probably everyone else on this floor, did we deserve to smell our own flesh bake. Do I deserve a face like this?"

Jane looked at me with moist eyes, her lip quivered, "I have felt the same way since childhood. The other kids called me 'fright-face' they said I didn't need a mask on Halloween. My mom told me to ignore them but with time I came to the realization they were right. I know how you feel."

What the hell was I supposed to say? Jane knew she was no looker, so did everyone else. We were both on the train taking the dirt road. "Hey you will always be my pal." I said in a lame attempt at cheering her up. She smiled, patted my hand and replied, "I'm sorry, I shouldn't be so emotional. Everyone has their issues."

Issues? More like a core concern worthy of a dissertation. Did Jane choose the burn unit as a way of dealing with her own self-image? Would I be working the crazy mirrors at the carnival or maybe the atomic radiation booth at Los Alamos? Did our faces make us outcasts? Maybe I do need a shrink. I looked at Jane and said, "If I could I would give you a big hug." She stood up and leaned toward me. "Let me take the lead." she said as her arms reached over my shoulders. Jane gently pulled me toward her taking care to avoid making contact with my face. When she pulled away we both felt better.

"So what other details are needed to finish the forms?" I asked. Jane folded the papers and tossed them on the table. "Let's finish tomorrow; we both could use a break. How about a night cap?" Syringe time was always a great way to end the day. Jane had the needle in my arm with due speed. The plunger went down halfway. The needle was removed only this time it did not return to its home in Jane's pocket. This time it found a vein in her arm. Jane gave a slight nod, stood up, said good night and left. She took a little piece of my heart with her.

I awoke to my usual morning rituals: bed pan bowel evacuation, dressing change, and breakfast, after which, like a bull in a china shop, Ralph the physical therapist barged through the door. "Good morning Paul, you don't mind if I call you Paul do you? Good. My name is Ralph and I am here to get your arms and legs working again." He pulled out a large rubber band contraption from a bag under his arm. "Let's start with some resistance work." he said in a booming voice with an Irish accent. "I am usually pretty good at resisting." I replied.

Ignoring my smart ass comment Ralph went to work. Pulling at the band with each hand I grunted and strained. The same occurred with each of my feet. "Not bad, not bad at all." Ralph stated with exaggerated cheerfulness. "You banged your neck, there is some cord swelling which affects your arm strength.

With my help you'll be doing handstands in no time." He spent the good part of an hour awaking my dormant muscles. It felt good even when the soreness arrived. Lying on your harvested ass for several weeks puts a dent in any physique let alone my pizza pummeled body.

"Good work," Ralph said as he packed up. "By the way," he continued "I heard about your accident, sounds like you need a good lawyer." He pulled a card out of his pocket and snapped it down onto the side table. "You can't do better than this guy, tell him Ralph sent you. See you tomorrow."

My accident? Jane's ministrations had kept my mind around the bend from that memory. The particulars had not invaded my thoughts in days. The grill blew up. There must have been an investigation by the Fire Department. Iris was there. Surely the cause is known by now. Somebody will tell me what went wrong. Hopefully someone with more credibility than one of the two lawyers already vying for my affliction. There would be plenty of time for that drama.

Dr. Vu came to call, alone, no posse. "Hello Paul, how are you?" "Been better doc, been better." I said. He looked here and there, checked this and that. "Your body burns are healing nicely. I see you have started physical therapy. You will be walking in a few days. I will allow visitors at that time." He moved closer, removed the dressings from my face and gently probed my new skin. After a few minutes he pronounced, "Your grafts have succeeded very well. The bandages are no longer needed." He crossed the room, opened a drawer and pulled out a mirror.

I drew a deep breath as my heart started to race. Dr. Vu sat his small frame on the edge of my bed. He laid the mirror face down on his lap, took off his glasses, and rubbed his eyes. "Paul it is time for you to see your face. You did have severe burns on each side and we have done our best to improve your condition. Your ears are mostly gone and the skin on your cheeks has a different color and texture. There is more work that can be done to better your appearance. Any questions?"

I had wanted to view my reflection for weeks, now the moment had arrived and I was scared. "No doctor, let the show begin." I said with false bravado. He held the mirror in front of my eyes. A stranger stared back at me.

Well not a complete stranger, blue eyes, pudgy nose, flat forehead, and some hair-- all me. The sidewalls definitely were not original issue. From mid cheek northward rolling hills of pink, brown, red, and tan skin mottled the landscape. Stubs of blackened flesh protruded where my ears used to reside. I had no hair on the cliffs leading to the dome, or the eye brows. Damn nice looking Mohawk however.

I examined my reflection with more curiosity than emotion. It was like looking at a fetus in a jar, a man taking off his wooden leg, a nun in a bathing suit, a three legged dog. You could tell where the ass skin patches were by their crusty border. Other areas resembled steam rolled peanut butter laced with red vines. My ear holes flashed pink, lost planets in deep, dark space.

As Vu lowered the mirror I asked, "Can I keep that?" He set it on the bedside table, "Sure." He spent a few moments turning pages on my chart after which he said, "There are further treatment options available. Would you like to discuss them?" Like an old worn couch I had enough covering to keep the guts in and the all else out. Functional but not fancy. Cheap but not sleazy. "What options doctor?" I choked out in a spasm of hope.

With eyes turned to high beams Vu began, "There are various multimodal therapies that can be used to improve the skin's appearance; such as silicone, steroids, lasers, and additional surgery to give a more natural texture." He stopped and placed a rather clammy hand under my chin and turned my head back and forth. "You also appear to be a good candidate for ear reconstruction. Cartilage can be harvested from you ribs and used to sculpt an ear frame over which a skin flap would grow. We have had some realistic results."

I let the term "realistic results" bounce around a couple of times and then asked, "How long would all this take and how much different would the after picture be than the before?" Dr. Vu tilted his head and grinned, "You get to the point don't you." He took off his glasses again, rubbed at them with his tie, and sighed. "There would be several operations over many months with hospital stays ranging from overnight to a week. The ears would be the most challenging task."

At this he put his glasses back on and looked me in the eye, "With regard to results I stopped kidding myself years ago and stopped giving false hope to my patients shortly thereafter. You were a mess when you got here; we saved your life and did our best with your wounds. You will walk out damaged but with everything working. As for your appearance Mother Nature will smooth out some of the rough edges on her own. The lack of ears is difficult for some; others just consider it part of the package. No matter what, stares will always come your way."

I was taken aback by Dr. Vu's direct and honest response. Better, however, to puncture the hope balloon now than let the air slowly escape. "Guess I will have to think things over Doctor, thanks for the information." I said in a subdued tone. "You're welcome, any more questions just ask, I will stop by again in a few days." He patted me on the shoulder and said, "Keep healing."

Over the next week things moved at a quicker pace. True to his word Ralph had me standing up and taking a few tentative steps with his beefy hand for support. I regained strength in my arms and could feed myself. Jane was absent; another nurse commented that she had taken a few days' vacation

One morning after Ralph had left the door opened, in walked efficiency on high heels. Doris Flatbush, Accounts Receivable Clerk II. Five foot five inches of determination covered in a salmon pant suit with permed helmet hair, too much makeup, and a voice that could grate cheese.

"Mr. Lawton how are you this fine morning?" she asked. "I need a moment of your time to discuss certain financial matters." Doris quickly sat down next to my bed and pulled out a thick spread sheet peppered with codes, fine print, and increasingly larger numbers. "When you were admitted," she began without looking up "A Iris Camp told us you worked for Weezy Inc. and certainly had full medical coverage. Not that we would have turned you away."

There was no hint of caring in her voice just the echo of a calculator on overdrive. "I have made several telephone calls and determined that Weezy Inc. is no longer in existence. I spoke to a, a, now where is that name" Doris mumbled as she shuffled through her notes, "yes here it is, a Mr. Josh who explained that you may or may not have coverage depending on which form you signed upon your departure. He did not have access to the information during our discussion and suggested you might have the paperwork or may recall your situation. My question Mr. Lawton is do you know your insurance situation?" At this she finally looked in my direction, although her gaze avoided my face.

As for my insurance status I had no clue. Hell I could not remember the last time I had been to a doctor. Colds, flu and the occasional bout of the grizzly trots did not require the services of the medical establishment. Iris must have been with me at the beginning and that Doris's call may explain why Josh the sugar vulture had paid a visit. I reached over and picked up the ever present glass of water and drained half. Doris took this opportunity to run her eyes over my assorted repair sites; she even stole a glance at my mug. "I'd like to help you Ms. Furbush, but I really do not know what coverage I have."

She stood and gathered her papers, "It's Flatbush Mr. Lawton I would appreciate you're remembering that, also perhaps you could get in contact with Mr. Josh so we can get to the bottom of this." Doris was coming undone. She turned to leave, stopped suddenly, and pulled a card from her binder. "Mr. Josh's number is written on the back. On the front is the name of a very good lawyer, you should call her. I will check back in a few days." Doris whirled and clicked her heels toward the door

By now I had scanned every square centimeter of my face like a bar code at the Walmart check out. I knew what was pre and post explosion. I knew where the propane firestorm raged by the twisted skinscape left behind, extreme sunburn to beef jerky. At best a sparse crop of hair may one day populate that expanse above my charred ear buds. At best my grafts will look less like patches and my rainbow skin will coalesce into one shade. At best I would still be one strange looking sonofabitch. For the most part I would be healthy. Ralph had discovered some nerve damage in my right leg that would put a twang in my gait; otherwise a finely tuned machine would be propelling this float for the rest of the parade.

As I contemplated whether this was a curse or a blessing in walked Nurse Jane.

"Greetings nurse, how was your time off?" I said. "Nice of you to notice, I had a relaxing few days." she replied before studying my chart and checking my healing wounds. Of course I noticed her absence. Jane had become an advisor, friend, and supplier of the feel good potient. "I see Ralph has worked his magic and you are walking. Why don't we go for a stroll down the hall." Jane stated, more a command than a question. "All right by me, I could use a change of scenery." I replied with cheer in my voice.

Although I had been wearing hospital boxers for quite some time Jane indicated hall cruising required less skin and more coverage. Once on my feet she helped me into a light robe, closing it with a bow. With her hand under my arm we left the room.

My walk was disjointed, the tin man with a broken hip. I ambulated like a cartoon character with a few panels missing. Nonetheless it felt good to be out in the land of the living. The hall was a blur of colors, action, odor, noise. I hugged the wall as Jane ran interference on my left. We passed white clad men and women with intense looks, patients in wheel chairs, and visitors in street clothes. It took a few minutes to hit the first intersection, by that time Jane and I had our dance down. "Let's go right." she directed. With one hand on the corner I pulled my left leg around the bend. "Feels great to be out of the room." I said. Jane smiled, "I am glad to hear that, we can make this part of our routine."

Just as the novelty of the outing was wearing off and my muscles were on the verge of rebellion we came to a large atrium which fronted an enclosed garden. The sky was blue, the air fresh, and the sun bright. I wanted to hobble out and fall down on the grass. Jane motioned to a nearby couch, "Let's take a break, I am sure you could use the rest." I plopped down causing my robe to fly open like a geriatric flasher in a nursing home. Jane casually bundle me back to respectability.

As I watched a bird come in for a three point landing on a tree branch, a boy of two or three ran across the room in pursuit of a big bouncing ball. It came to rest a short distance from Jane and me. The boy picked it up, both arms wrapped around in triumph. He looked in our direction with a huge smile on his face. Our eyes met. A quizzical look replaced his grin. He dropped the ball and walked right up to me, his head barely above my knees. The boy put his hands into the pockets of his blue carpenter pants. He gave me the once over before moving to the side of the couch where he propped his elbows on the armrest.

"Does your owie hurt?" he asked in a high voice tinged with wonder. "No, it doesn't hurt anymore." I said. He thought for a few moments and then said, "That's good, I got an owie on my leg, you wanna see?" "Sure." I replied. After taking a step back the boy pulled up his right pant leg to reveal a purple bruise just below the knee. Returning the concern I inquired, "Does it hurt?" He lowered the corduroy, "Only a little, but I cried when I did it." Then he pointed a chubby finger at me and said, "Did you cry when you got your owie?" "Not right away, but later I did." The boy nodded his head and then asked, "How can you hear without ears?" I looked into his inquisitive face and said, "There are good doctors here and they made me better."

Satisfied he retrieved his ball and returned. "You want to go outside and play catch?" Just as I was about to decline a woman in her early thirties came over, grabbed the boy's hand, and said

"Patrick, there you are, come on now we have to go see grandpa."
"Aw mom, we are going to play catch." Patrick moaned. The woman looked up and noticed Jane and me. She put one hand to her mouth, grabbed Patrick with such force he became airborne, and retreated without a word. The boy managed to wave in my direction before disappearing.

"Nice kid." I said to Jane, "Can't say the same about his mother though." We sat in silence as a shadow began to creep across the garden. My mind drifted. Asleep with eyes open. He was a cute kid. How would I have one my own now? Women will react to me like Patrick's mother. Pack up the babies, grab the old ladies, and run. "You are going to have to get used to that." Jane restarted the conversation, "You're an oddity. You don't fit in." Her tone indicated she was speaking from experience, more personal than professional. "I have spent quite a bit of time with the mirror, there is no doubt I am a walking freak show." I replied, "But underneath I am pretty much the same guy when I'm not pissed off, depressed, or wallowing in self-pity." Jane smiled.

It was time to stop ignoring the elephant on the couch. "I don't know about that, but I am grateful to you and your syringe for getting me this far." Her eyes shot around our perimeter before replying, "My methods are unorthodox to be sure. I feel a special bond with facial injury patients. I know what it is like to get upset over the hand we have been dealt. My little helper is a chemical coping mechanism, a way to adjust, a synthetic sunset. It is also illegal as hell and I would appreciate your keeping our mutual indulgence to yourself."

I wanted to assure Jane I would never rat her out and that she was a good woman, with a great heart, an understanding spirit, and a joyful personality. She had many years of disappointment to throw overboard. I was no stranger to the S.S. Dashed Hope myself. We shared more than the needle. I looked out as dusk pulled the light away, "I would never do anything to hurt you Jane and I hope we can remain friends after the warden gives me my release or I make a run for it, whichever comes first." She gave me a wink and said, "Thanks, I hope so too."

I woke rested. Self-sufficiency had now, for the most part, replaced dependency. I hobbled to the bathroom without an orderly in green or nurse in white where it was easier to do my business seated on the porcelain throne. The glare of fluorescence illuminating the scars on my arms and legs, a hop scotch of strawberry blotches of irregular shape. I could touch most without pain.

As I exited a guy in gray was running a cable to my bedside table. He spoke with the back of his brush topped head facing me, "Just installing the phone, only be a minute." "Take your time," I replied, "not much on my dance card today." He was a large, broad shouldered man who already had sweat stains creeping down the middle of his shirt. There was a worn leather work belt hanging at his waist with assorted tools dangling like a stripper's tassels. He stood and placed the phone next to his ear. "We've got a dial tone." he announced as he turned in my direction, promptly dropping the phone. It bounced twice on the tiled floor.

"What the hell happened to you?" he barked. Above his left shirt pocket, sewn in red with a white background, was the name, Frank. His face was ruddy with a nose that had exploded long ago. An ample belly obscured belt and buckle. "Sorry, they served beans last night; I hope the smell isn't too bad." My attempt at humor only served to perplex, Frank bent over and picked up the phone. He checked to see that it was still working and placed it on the table. Frank's furrowed brow and sad eyes complimented his confusion. "No, no." he said in a softer tone, "I've smelled things around here that would turn your stomach. I meant your face and your ears." Frank looked me straight in the eye. I liked that. "I got a big mouth." he continued with a sheepish expression, "Sorry, I'll just get out of your way."

I raised my hand, "Don't leave, I could use a little company and an assist up, the orderly must be on a cigarette break." Frank placed a calloused hand under my arm. His touch was surprisingly tender. After a few steps he lifted me onto the bed. I propped myself and motioned toward the chair, "Thanks have a seat." He complied, his body coming to rest in stages. Frank crossed his arms over his barrel chest and said, "Good idea, I'm in no hurry to fix a broken toilet two rooms over." Frank gave me a look as if he was waiting for a movie to start. I felt compelled to put on a good show.

"Propane Frank. Propane got me in the state I'm in." I started. The story flowed easily from my lips. New house, girl, Cadillac, grill, boom, hospital guest. Frank listened intently, with an occasional shake of his head. "Shit!" he said "What the fuck was the matter with that grill. I'm a charcoal man myself but I hear those gas grills are nice." I chuckled a bit, "Yeah, from now on I'm a charcoal man too."

Frank smiled and looked toward the door. He opened his tool box, pulled out a can of WD40, and unscrewed the bottom. Out slid a small flask. Frank glanced again at the door before taking a hefty swig. He wiped his mouth with the back of his hand and handed me the bottle. "Care for a snort, it's Canadian Club." I grabbed the flask and poured a gulp down my throat. A herd of hot footed devils raced from my tongue to stomach prompting an exhale like a dragon with gas. "Good stuff." I said as Frank returned the whiskey to its hiding place. "Yeah." he said, "Let me give you my pager number, anytime you want to shoot the shit just use your new phone here and give me a call." He scribbled on a piece of cardboard and left it on the table. As he walked to the door I called out, "Thanks Frank, see you soon." He gave a small wave and left.

The taste of whiskey lingered as I moved the phone to my lap and grabbed the business cards left by Joyce the candy striper, Ralph the therapist, and Doris the number cruncher. Lawyer's names engraved in white, the promise of justice in fine fonts, dollar signs for water marks. I felt a twinge of guilt along with a rush of blood as I recalled the circumstances of my promise to Joyce. Her pony was the obvious choice.

As I located the number my phone went off like a hand grenade. A call for me? I hit the speaker button; my black aural appendages were still not up to direct contact. It was the front desk, "Mr. Lawton, this is Gladys in the lobby there is a Josh Fortner here; he would like to come to your room. I see Dr. Vu has cleared you for visitors, would you like to see Mr. Fortner?" "Only if he brought candy." I replied. After a few seconds of dead air I said, "Sure send him up." I wondered where would Josh max out on the shock meter.

There was not much I could do to pretty up before a tentative knock hit the door. "Come on in the waters fine." I said as loudly as I could. The door opened slowly, very slowly. Two hands gripped the edge, pudgy fingers served to frame Josh's frizzy brown hair, followed by wide eyes, flat nose, tight lips, and a square jaw. His astonished face hung there like a lost party balloon. "Welcome Josh, you win the first visitor prize. There's a chair in here, sit your fat ass down." I said as cheerfully as possible.

He walked across the room as if the floor was covered with land mines, all the while staring at my face. Josh filled the seat much like Frank had earlier, making it disappear. I stuck out my hand, "How you been?" He tentatively exchanged a shake and quickly rubbed his palm on the front of his jeans. With an audible sigh Josh said, "I'm doing alright. Shit I don't know what to say. Sorry about your accident. Fucking buzzkill man, fucking buzzkill."

His eyes roamed the room, "Nice digs, shit you have been here a long time, probably hate the place by now. No television? You want me to bring one? How about a computer? Probably don't have the internet. Maybe we could run a line. Shit, I'm babbling. Sorry, guess I'm nervous." I tried to reel him back in, "Relax, it's still me, just different packaging." Josh gave a quick guffaw, a bullet of spit dropping off to the floor. "It's just that those nurses downstairs gave me this pamphlet to read before they would let me come up here. *Guidelines for Visiting the Facially Injured* it was called. I didn't know what to expect."

"How could you." I commiserated, "Guess I will have to get a copy." "No need." Josh said as he pulled a wrinkled brochure out of his pocket and set in on the table. "I didn't read much but the pictures are nasty." He put his head in both hands and moaned, "Shit, I'm sorry, what the fuck maybe I should leave." Josh stood up with a pained expression on his puffy face. "Sit down, Josh." I calmly said, "Let's talk. What brings you here anyway?" After bouncing back and forth a few times Josh sat back down, grabbed my glass of water and took a big gulp.

"Well Paul it ain't the best of news." he began, "I got a call a while ago from some bean counter asking about your insurance status. Guess she got my name from when I came here the day you had your accident." "Heard about that," I interrupted, "How did you find out." Josh rubbed his two hands together and stared at the floor, "Well that has to do with the other bad news I got for you." I laughed and said, "Didn't that pamphlet mention something about cheering up the patient. Shit your Mr. Doom and Gloom."

Josh stood up again, "Fuck your right, I'll come back some other time when you're feeling better." "Stop the jack in the box routine and stay. Time ain't going to change a damn thing, what you see is what I will be. Get used to it." There was a certain amount of irritation in my voice. "I am sorry Josh; this is a little rough on me. Why don't you just start from the beginning?"

He looked over with watery eyes. "Nothing to be sorry about man, I owe you an explanation."

Josh proceeded to relate that on the day of the boom he was told to call me in for some consultant work. Seems Weesler and Zybtowski, the illustrious founders of Weezy, had taken certain liberties with the work of a few engineers in Bangalore, India who were screaming "patent infringement." All of us legacy engineers were being called upon to save the day.

Josh rang my old phone number and got the disconnected jingle. This did not sit well with his new boss. Being an obliging sort Josh got in his car and drove to my old apartment only to discover a for rent sign. The helpful manager told him I had moved up in the hills, "201 Partridge I think." Josh continued his hunt, stumbling upon my new house just as they were shutting the ambulance door.

"It was crazy. There was this good looking blonde talking to a fireman. I heard her yell,'His name is Paul, Paul Lawton.'" Josh watched as Iris jumped in her Mustang and headed down the hill. He followed her right to the hospital. "I sat in the car for quite a while, half expecting you to walk out with a cast on your leg or something."

Eventually Josh went inside and made an inquiry at the desk. "When they found out I wasn't a relative, it was like, don't call us we'll call you." Josh went back to Weezy where it was decided to messenger the consultant documents to the Partridge address. "Sorry I didn't follow up, but things got busy and I kind of forgot about you until that high strung number cruncher called a few weeks ago and started asking about your insurance status." Ms. Flatbush informed Josh that I had been seriously burned and she needed information right away. "Fuck dude I couldn't believe what she was telling me; hundreds of thousands in bills, bad injury, rehabilitation. I didn't know what to say so I gave her some bullshit about your having the paperwork. I figured they would put you on the street otherwise. Hope that was O.K."

Josh became fairly agitated as his tale unfolded. I poured some more water into the glass. As he was draining it I said, "No problem. What is my insurance anyway?" Josh set the glass down, "That's just it Paul, you don't have any coverage." He explained that when I signed all those papers at my old apartment I declined Cobra and stated I would get my own health insurance. "Guess we should have looked that shit over a little closer." he said.

I was stunned, "That's got to be a mistake. Weezy will make it right, won't they?" Josh's face took on a sucked lemon look. "That's the other problem." He went on to explain that since I had failed to show up for the consultant work my big payout was in jeopardy. "I think they already have a lawyer looking into it." Josh lamented the fact that things had taken a nasty turn. The patent claim was solid and many rupees were about to be transferred. Plus a couple of geeks down the road had cranked out a slicker and faster version of Weezy's prize product. "Those pricks are eating into our market share like maggots on a dead dog." Money had now become so short that any excuse to save a few thousand, let alone the millions I was owed, was jumped on. "They're going to fight you to the max." Josh concluded, "Sorry to say, but that's the fucking truth."

You can't argue with the fucking truth.

The door opened just as Josh completed his tale of woe. It was Joyce in full candy striper regalia pushing in my lunch. She was surprised to see Josh, "Excuse me, I could come back later." I waved her forward, "No, we can't let that great food get cold. My friend won't mind if I eat while we talk. Maybe you have an extra dessert to spare." Josh, who hadn't taken his eyes off Joyce since she walked in, blurted out, "No, that's alright, I probably should be leaving." Joyce blocked his path as she propped a tray of nutrition on my lap. Then she pulled a plate of chocolate cake off the cart. Handing it to Josh she said, "Nobody is going to miss this. Why don't you keep Paul company for a while."

Still the sugar vulture Josh eagerly grabbed the plate and dug in. Joyce gave a nod toward my new phone, "I see you're connected. Have you made that call, as promised?" she asked, Part of my face blushed as I replied, "A little later, I just got the phone this morning." Joyce gave me a stern but hopeful look, "You better. See you soon..."

As the door was closing Josh mopped up the remnants of the frosting with his fingers. "Good cake." he said, "And a cute girl. I like that uniform. Way too young for us though." He set the clean plate down on the table and eyed my tray. "Take mine," I gestured "I'll get another piece at dinner anyway. Let's call it the first visitor prize." Josh did not hesitate. We ate without speaking. When I put down my fork Josh picked up the tray and set it to the side. "Why thank you sir," I said, "If you ever need a job I'll put in a good word. You would look good in green." With a laugh he replied, "The way things are going I just might take you up on that."

Without anything to keep us occupied silence hung in the air, its legs thrashing. Finally I broke the frozen taboo and asked, "So how do I look?" Josh recoiled as the echo of my inquiry rattled off the walls. Then he spoke with hesitation and without conviction, "Good, you look good. I mean a little rough in spots but overall good. You know not great but pretty good. Shit man what do you want me to say?" Guilt grabbed my throat. "I am sorry Josh; I didn't mean to make you uncomfortable. It's just that you're the first civilian I can ask." His eyes had watered up once again. "I would appreciate an honest opinion, don't worry about my feelings, they were toasted in the explosion." My attempt at humor perked Josh up, "Well, if you want to know the truth, when I first saw you it looked like someone had taken a steam iron in each hand and squeezed your head like it was in the devil's vice." I had asked for honesty but was surprised it came in such a descriptive package.

Josh took a short breath and continued, "Those little blobs where your ears used to be really stick out and it looks like somebody sewed new upholstery on each cheek I hope your hair grows back otherwise I'd invest in one of those French Foreign Legion hats." A smile crossed my face like longhorns on a cattle drive, slowly and with effort. Although joining the foreign legion, not just getting the headgear, had its appeal. I was drifting away to the sands of the Sahara when Josh loudly cleared his throat. "Sorry." I mumbled, "My attention span is strung with distraction cable."

After shifting my ass a few times across the bed in order to kill the itch growing at my harvest sites I said, "Appreciate your honesty and if you ever run across one of those hats send it my way." "Hey, no problem." Josh responded as he stood once again to leave. "You probably need to rest. I'll stop by another day." "Sure, they have cake Tuesday and Thursday." Josh gave me thumbs up and closed the door, leaving behind cow pies in my meadow, and storm clouds on my horizon. I was glad he came and hoped he would return. A connection to what once was, to the me I used to be.

There was little time to contemplate Josh's unvarnished comments or the fact that it would take more than chocolate cake to attract most guests. The phone rang. I said hello. A voice flavored with uncertainty came from the speaker, "Is that you Paul, it's Iris." Light years ago at the Club Scirroco the same voice had caused choirs of cupids to sing in my head, now it brought a chorus of confusion. We had a relationship of unclear status with undetermined potential. She was there when the master of misery tapped my shoulder. Flatbush knew her name. The thought had bubbled up more than once, "Where the fuck was she!" Granted Vu and his comrades had put a no fly zone over my airspace but Iris could have landed a letter, note, post card. Then again my flame out could have caused her to seek therapy and forget she ever knew me.

Mustering up my scorched confidence I said, "Well hello Iris, I see you got past security, they usually have the force field up 24/7. How have you been?" With a nervous laugh she replied, "My world is upside down. I have been thinking about you every day. They just let me know you have a phone so I called right away. How are you?"

My condition, glad you're not in the room. "I am doing better. By the way thanks for all your help after the accident. I wouldn't be here if it wasn't for you." My words floated to Iris, clouded up, "Oh Paul..." and caused rain. Muffled sobs filled the air. "It was so awful Paul. I found you on the grass, I thought you were dead. It took forever for the ambulance to come. And then they wouldn't let me in to see you at the hospital." I wanted to give her a hug. Instead I armed my tone with cheerfulness, "Hey, I will be out of this place in a little while and we'll be cruising the town in your Mustang with the Ramones wailing from the speakers."

The sun did not come out, the storm front hung tough. Over more tears Iris said, "Oh Paul I wish we could do that, but my mother.....my mother is really sick. I have to stay with her. The doctors are not very optimistic. She is in a lot of pain. I am sorry; I should be there with you." When it rains trouble it sprouts remorse. I recalled that Iris's mother had been ill a few months ago. That explains why her focus was not on char broiled Paul. I felt like a douche bag for doubting her sincerity.

"Take care of your mother Iris, I really am getting better. I should be able to visit lovely Bakersfield in no time." I sensed a clearing, "You're a great guy Paul, I appreciate your understanding." The tenor of her voice changed, becoming more businesslike. "If you don't mind Paul there are a few things I need to tell you about that night." I was about to tell her any further reenactment could wait when she marched on, her words streaming from the speaker like soldiers on parade.

"A fireman told me there must have been something wrong with the grill. He said I should save it and have someone examine it. The only person I could think of was the lawyer who helped my mom and me after my dad's accident. His name is Jerry Traditore. He is a really good guy, Paul. I called him and he had one of his investigators pick up the grill. It sounds like there is a problem with how it was made or put together or something. You really need to speak with Jerry."

Of course Iris was right and Jerry already had an iron in the fire. "I appreciate your help; do you have Jerry's phone number?" Without missing a step Iris continued, "Jerry can meet you tomorrow at ten in the morning. He will call from the front desk. Will that work for you?" It felt like I was being stroked again. "Sure, I look forward to meeting him." "Great." Iris replied, "I will let him know."

I was about to ask if she had met Josh, tell her of my issues with Weezy, and ask if she felt beauty was really only skin deep when she said, "My mom is waking up Paul, I have to go, is it O.K. if I call you later." "Sure, anytime, I am never far from the phone." Iris laughed, "Good to see your sense of humor is still intact, Bye Paul." The speaker let out the low hum of disconnection. "Good bye, Iris."

Nurse Jane appeared after supper, "Get your mostly healed ass out of bed, we have some walking to do." "You must have been a drill sergeant in a past life." I muttered as she wrapped me in my traveling robe. "No past life, no future life, what you have is what you get." Jane stated, her hand gesturing toward the door. "Kind of takes all the hope and mystery out of it don't you think?" I asked while we doosey doed down the hall. "Hope is for the craps table and mysteries are found in aisle nine."

Traffic was light, hospital staff briskly completing their rounds, orderlies pushing carts full of supplies, janitors mopping. We made the atrium fronting the garden just as the outdoor lights flickered on. The chairs were empty except for a couple seated on a sofa against the far wall. A stone faced, overweight physician had pulled up a seat to their immediate left. The woman sobbed into the man's shoulder. He tenderly held her hand. Bad news delivered the doctor rose with some difficulty, snapped his file shut, said some final words, and left. Jane noticed my wandering eye and said, "Most likely difficult news about a parent, Dr. Packer is an elder care specialist." The couple stood, the man placed his arm around the tearful woman's shoulder and supported her as they slowly walked away.

"Must be difficult having to deliver bad news on a regular basis." I said. "Yes, we try to prevent pain not cause it. However it comes with the territory." Silence surrounded us as another day of healing wound down. Jane spoke up, "I hear you had a visitor." "Well yes I did, and how would you know. Is my room bugged?" She raised her hand to her mouth and stifled a laugh, "Only if they ran out of hot water in the laundry again." Jane's joy at her lame joke caused her grade A body to jiggle like Jell-O in an earthquake. I couldn't help but join in and pretty soon we were laughing hard enough to make our eyes water.

Our mirth dissipated slowly, the last few chuckles bubbling forth. "So who was the young overweight man with the frizzy hair?" Jane repeated her inquiry. "That was Josh the sugar vulture. He used to work at Weezy."I said deciding not to pry into her sources. "It was good to see someone from the old days, but he was the bearer of bad news." Jane's eyes dilated into concern mode. "Can you keep a secret?" I asked. She nodded and moved a little closer. "It appears I have no insurance to pay for this wonderful place. If that battle ax Flatbush finds out my scarred ass will be out on the street." Jane shook her head in disagreement, "That would never happen Paul." I raised my voice a notch, "And. And, I probably am an ex millionaire. My stay here in the burn bungalow has prevented me from attending to my consultant duties. That puts future greenbacks in jeopardy."

Jane's comedic synapses were snapping. She grabbed my arm, gave me a soulful look and said, "Well you will always have your looks." I did a triple take and we both laughed again.

When our last cackle echoed of the walls Jane said, "I read somewhere that once you find laughter, no matter how painful your situation might be, you can survive it. We both need to keep our funny bone in shape." Jane and I were shabby store fronts hiding plush interiors. Humor was our welcome mat, the neon sign beckoning, fresh baked cookies on the window sill, a candle in the night. "I have always looked for the grin factor in any situation." I said, "Some people appreciate it, others think I am just a smart ass."

Jane smiled, "You can be witty, sarcastic, offbeat, and charming. It has taken me a while to appreciate that under those layers you are a good person." "We all have defense mechanisms," she continued, "you use that razor sharp tongue of yours to fend off unwanted attention and to engage in verbal jousts for your own amusement. I don't know but you may have missed out on some good relationships." She sat up straight and folded her arms, "Listen to me, babbling on again like some television shrink."

The good nurse was right, of course. Not that I ever gave much thought to why I remained the class clown long after leaving school. "I guess I put up a pretty good front in order to avoid the pain of rejection." I said looking off into the darkened garden. "A connection on the emotional fringe is easy to break and causes little damage."

A janitor passed behind us waxing the floor tile, the gentle hum of the buffing machine tamping down our weighty conversation. Introspection was not usually on my play list. Could good come from listening to the rhythms laid down by our motivations and desires? Hadn't I been happy just going through days like arcade tokens? What was the price of admission to the soul's dance hall? It felt like Jane had already bought me a ticket and shoved me through the swinging doors.

"You should not be worrying about money." Jane announced, "Just take care of your health. We would never send you home unless you are ready. When I see Ms. Flatbush I will tell her you're not yet ready mentally to discuss insurance and bills. O.K.?" "Yes, I would appreciate it. I have a few things to work out."

As we walked back to my room I also told her about Iris's call, going heavy on her sick mother and offer of legal help. Jane helped me into bed and said, "Sounds like you still have feelings for her." Jane had been weaning me off the fentanyl, however picking up on my background music she gave me the needle nightcap. "You're right about that maestro." I mumbled, "feelings....."

It was morning when Dr. Vu strolled in and gave my chart a quick glance. "You have healed well enough to go home in a few days. I would imagine, however, that you would like us to perform some of the procedures to improve your appearance that we recently talked about." Perhaps he wasn't use to impatient patients. Perhaps no one ever rejected the hands that heal before. Whatever the reason Vu was startled when I said, "Thanks, but no thanks Doc. It has been a real slice in more ways than one but the sooner you're in my rear view mirror the better. Let's get the discharge papers typed and signed."

Vu reeled his jaw in, grabbed the chart again and thumbed back a few pages. "I see you have yet to meet with the staff psychologist. Protocol requires an interview before any discharge decision is made. I will see to it that Dr. Plite makes time for you within the next day or two." He scribbled a few lines on the top sheet, gave my arm a quick squeeze and headed out the door where he ran into Frank, the refrigerator with legs. Vu bounced left, right, left before escaping the janitor's gravity. "Uh, sorry doctor," Frank muttered as he crashed forward, throwing his tool bag down at the foot of my bed.

"How are you doing Paul, was in the neighborhood thought I would stop by." Frank said as he settled into my bedside chair. "On my way over to the fat fucks wing, another plugged up toilet. Those bastards are supposed to be losing weight and they pay people to smuggle food in. Last time I found half a fucking chicken jammed down the pipe. Of course the shithead acted like he had no clue how it got there. Like the sonofabitchen chicken flew in the fucking window and drowned in the toilet bowl. Shit."

Frank was agitated but it must have been too early for a little WD 40 action. He slowly calmed. I waited a few beats then said, "Vu and I were just discussing my release. I have decided not to have any more work done; he thinks I need to see a shrink." Frank brought his beefy hands together, intertwining the fingers as if in prayer. "Hell it's your face. These butchers will keep dicking around if you let them. Shit, look what they did to that Jackson kid, he looks like a fucking alien." Frank had a way of connecting dots that weren't even on the same page.

"Watch out for those damn shrinks." he continued, "They don't know shit from shinola. I wouldn't let one of them assholes fix me breakfast." Just as I was about to ask his opinion on lawyers Frank's pager buzzed like a bee in a meth hive. "Sonofafuckingbitch, now they got water on the floor, fat fuck probably took a shit after plugging the toilet with a fucking pizza. Got to go buddy, you know how to reach me." "See you Frank, thanks for the advice and good luck with the pipes."

I had little time to digest Frank's words of wisdom before the phone rang. "Mr. Lawton, this is Jan at the front desk there is a Mr.

Traditore here to see you." Then in a whisper she said, "I think he's a lawyer." I let out a mock gasp, "It's O.K. he's on my side, send him up." In a few moments a firm knock on the door was followed by the entrance of Jerry Traditore, Esquire, briefcase in hand. From his wing tip shoes to the gel in his hair he reeked of confidence and expensive cologne. His tailored suit, tone on tone shirt and tie, gold watch and cufflinks set off a tanned face which surrounded gleaming teeth. Jerry was just the kind of guy I wouldn't cross the street to piss on if he was ablaze. Now I reached to shake his outstretched hand, "Hello Paul, I am Jerry the attorney Iris told you about. Is this a good time for a chat?" He looked at me straight on with no hint of surprise or disgust.

Jerry sat down without being asked. I took a drink of water and said, "Chat away counselor, I am all ears, appearances to the contrary." A confused ripple crossed his tight face before he chuckled, "Iris told me you had a sense of humor, now I see what she meant." I took it as a compliment and asked, "How long have you known Iris?" Jerry crossed his arms over his chest. His cufflinks glittered. "I met her a few years ago. I get a lot of my cases due to referrals from other clients. Iris called me the day after your incident."

He reached into his brief case and pulled out a binder. On the spine, in large red letters was Lawton v. Grills R Us. Several tabs stuck out, each neatly numbered. I was surprised, "You have a file on me?" Jerry laid the binder on the lap of his pleated pants, "Yes, we took the liberty of doing a little background work while you were in the hospital. Of course this doesn't mean I am your attorney, yet. That's why I am here, to see if we can come to an arrangement." There was a little Italian hiding in his vocal chords.

When I didn't reply Jerry appeared slightly confused. He opened the binder, looked at a few pages, lowered his voice a notch and said, "If it is O.K. with you why don't I go over some of the information we have obtained." I felt a touch of remorse. It was clear attorney Traditore was trying to be helpful. Yet I couldn't get over the feeling that he considered me a large dollar sign in a hospital gown. "Sure, I would like to know what you have found out." I said. Jerry went on to explain that after Iris's phone call he had the Cain grill and tank sent to a lab that specializes in accident investigation. "They are the best." he assured me, "Working on everything from plane crashes to tooth paste tube failures."

While I imagined gobs of Crest flying around assorted bathrooms he related that the lab determined that the grill had a defective propane gas connection. The regulator, which controls the amount of gas released to the burner, can leak propane when the propane cylinder is turned on and not in use. "Plus," he said, "The rotten egg smell you should notice when venting of the propane occurs fades within a few weeks of the tank being filled." Jerry went on to explain that Cain knew about the problem and recalled the defective grills. Grills R Us should have received the notice and never sold the grill.

"We have a really good case against the retailer and possibly the manufacturer." He pulled out a sheet of paper and handed it to me, "This is our standard retention agreement. You do not have to pay us a dime unless we get you money. If you settle before trial we get one-third of that amount plus expenses, if you go to trial we get forty per cent. There is a line at the bottom for your signature." Jerry held out one of those fancy pens that are only sold in jewelry stores. I grabbed it and did a quick read of the contract. I needed a lawyer to explain what this lawyer had written.

I looked up at Jerry and said, "If I have such a good case why should you take one third or more of my money?" Like any good trial attorney he didn't flinch at the curve ball, "Good question. Our office takes a lot of cases; some have better potential than others. In the end it all balances out, the good cases allow us to take the tougher matters. It is the way the system works best." Yeah for you and the other cast of characters in the pain and suffering industry, none of whom will ever wake up and see my face in the mirror. I'll just be another binder on the shelf and a few digits added to the bottom line.

When I made no effort to sign Jerry developed a pained look and reached for the contract. "Since you know Iris I could reduce the percentages to twenty five and thirty." He crossed out a few numbers and rewrote the deal. I still felt as if I just gave my money for some snake oil but at least I got an extra bottle.

With my signature safely on the bottom line Jerry snapped the agreement into the binder. He stood up and shook my hand again, "We will file a complaint in Superior Court next week. Don't you worry about anything but getting well. I will keep in touch." Jerry seemed anxious to hit the road, like a guy who just scored a few grams of coke and saw no reason to continue making small talk with his dealer.

Just as his hand hit the door he stopped, turned back, reached into his jacket pocket and pulled out a camera. "I almost forgot," he said, "We need a few pictures for the file. It helps to document your injuries so the defendants can see what they are dealing with." He squatted at the foot of my bed, "Don't smile Paul, in fact a sad look it best." Jerry took several shots of my face and body. I reflected sadness until his lens fogged up with sorrow.

"Why don't you speak with your parents more often?" Jane asked as we began our nightly stroll. I no longer needed her support although she still stayed close.

I had spoken with my mom and dad just before dinner, the news that I had hired an attorney was greeted with applause. All was well on the home front. An offer to come out was met with my insistence that my release was impending and I would be at their door step in no time. Love yous crossed our respective borders, good byes in their wake.

Jane's statement was a question and not a criticism. "I don't know, we didn't talk that much before and now I don't want to upset them with details of my condition." A drift had occurred over time and distance. I had strayed a long way from the roost both physically and vocationally. Talk of the weather, my single state, work status, and health, in no particular order, exhausted our topics of discussion and resulted in silence over the air waves. Unless a relative was sick or died, a classmate married or had a baby, a local business went bankrupt, or someone hit the Lotto we ended our conversations with take cares and call soon. As time passed "soon" lasted longer and longer. The familial bond wasn't broken just stretched. We were there for each other and, at a moment's notice, we could snap back into familiar arms. As the child who left the nest, tree, forest, and state I had come to realize how difficult it was for my parents as I took flight. A bigger piece of their hearts went with me than what I left behind.

"Don't you think it would be better to start letting them know about your recovery and plans. Especially before you visit in person." Jane commented. We had reached our usual couch and sat down. "You're right." I replied, "But I figure there is still time for that and no news is good news." "Your call. So how did the visit with the lawyer go?" she asked. I described attorney Traditore's casting call looks, GQ clothes, and fancy leather brief case. "Yes," Jane said, "The nursing corps was all heated up. He spent several minutes with Nurse Blitz inquiring about your condition and appearance." That would explain his cool demeanor upon first viewing my mangled mug. I told Jane how he thought I had a good case and that he agreed to cut himself a smaller piece of my pie. "Good for you Paul," Jane said, "I hope it works out for the best." I did not know, my hope chest had shrunk to an A cup. It did not provide a mouthful of expectation.

"So was the lawyer the one recommended by your friend Iris?" Jane asked. "Yeah, one and the same." I said. "You're lucky to have an outside contact. There are a lot of vultures circling the Center looking to feed. Some law keeps them off the grounds but they do recruit our employees. The orthopedic and burn wings get the most action. Band Aid bounty hunters. I hear they get a piece of the recovery. One physical therapist bought a BMW."

We got up and started the walk back to my room. "Are you upset Iris hasn't come to see you?" Jane's inquiry zapped through me. Her big brown eyes roamed my face. "No, not really. Well yeah, I guess." I numb tongued a response. Truth be told, I still expected her to show. It would be the orderlies turn to heat up. "You might want to prepare yourself for the possibility she is unable to handle your injuries. I have seen marriages break apart. Was your relationship strong?" A cattle prod question, no less of a zap. I told Jane the saga of Paul and Iris. How we met before Weezy turned into a gold mine. "We dated before I came into the money. She was way out of my league in the looks department but we hit it off. Good conversation, shared interests, fun times." I said, each word coated in deepening shades of wistfulness. I explained how Iris helped with furnishing the house, "Hell she was there when I bought the damn grill."

We had reached the room. I slid out of the robe and onto the bed. Jane scribbled something on my chart and took her usual seat. She kicked off her shoes and massaged white stocking feet. "So you never did answer my question, was your relationship strong?" Zap. "I liked her a lot; we were at the end of the beginning. Sleeping together, making some plans. I hoped we had a future." Jane curled up on the chair bringing both legs under her shapely bottom. "And how did she feel?" Zap, zap. "I'm not sure, at times she was distracted. Maybe her mother's problems were bothering her. It is not like we spent every waking moment falling over each other like teenagers in love. Yet, there was something between us."

Jane reached into her pocket and pulled out her night cap case. "Sounds to me like Cupid might have shot a one way arrow." Maybe that was the street I was on. It had all merged together so fast. Bucks and a babe, house and a car, moon and the stars. "You may be right." I told Jane, "Back then it didn't matter too much. I wanted her to love me, sometimes I felt she might. If not I would move on, but now..." My voice trailed off, I could see the bus for Lonely Street coming around the corner.

"Now." Jane said, "Now-- you still are witty, charming, and interesting. Don't let Iris, your accident, or anything else pull a black curtain over your head." Not the best choice of words for a guy who would be better off with complete face coverage. Give me a sex change, conversion to Islam, and I would be a happy hijab wearing Sunni woman. Jane soldiered on with her encouragement, "Our spirits define us not our flesh. Happiness is not found in a mirror. When we reflect love and joy the world is a better place. You have a lot to give, don't forget that."

She reached over and gave my hand a squeeze. I reciprocated and smiled. "Thanks. You always seem to give off a good vibe. I appreciate it." And then, my mouth engaged before my brain could pull the switch and change tracks, "You must be making some guy really happy." Jane looked toward the floor. I began to wish it would swallow us both up, a wave of linoleum washing away my words.

After a few moments she began to speak in a low, soft voice. "I have had a few relationships. My face makes it difficult to get to the phone number exchange stage. In fact the last guy met me at a masked ball." Jane looked in my direction, "I have never told anyone about this, I hope you don't mind, I need a sympathetic listener." "Be happy to lend a crusty ear." I said. She rolled her eyes and began the tale of Chuck the pharmaceutical salesman.

Every year the hospital has a masked ball to raise money for research. The hundred dollar per person tickets were out of her price range but one of the doctors had a family emergency and gave Jane his. She went into the city, found a dress on sale at Macy's, and a rhinestone, feathered mask in the Castro. "I looked good in the dress." Jane said with a "it ain't bragging if it's fact" tone. She arrived a little late, the band was in full swing, the drinks were flowing, and the lights had been dimmed. "There was a lot of jewelry, hair spray, and fashion on the floor. Everyone was in a mask. I found it exotic and intoxicating."

Taking refuge at the bar Jane grabbed a glass of wine. It wasn't long before a tall, tuxedoed, man with a black mask came over and asked her to dance. The band was just beginning a sad attempt at the Stones tune 'Satisfaction'. Jane bounced to the beat. Catering to the declining lung capacity of its audience the orchestra slowed the pace to a waltz. The partners came together. "It had been a while since I had been in a man's arms. It felt good. I melted into his chest." The night became a whirl of music, drinks, laughter, color, and dancing. "He was Chuck, I was Jane. We kept our masks on and the conversation light."

The evening ended as the last notes of "Good Night Irene" drifted over the remaining revelers. Chuck bent down and kissed Jane, a jolt shot through her, she reciprocated with vigor; soon their tongues were engaged in slippery battle. It took the near blinding glare of turned up lights to end their embrace. "He escorted me out the door. I felt like a princess." At the valet lot Jane wrote down her address on the back of his ticket. "It's a fifteen minute drive, I'll leave the light on." she whispered in his ear.

Jane rushed home. "I ran two red lights." she confessed with a chuckle. After unlocking the door and turning on the porch light she quickly stepped out of her dress. "I like sexy lingerie, garter belts, bustier, and nylons." Jane said with a slight blush. She barely had time to put on a slinky robe and adjust her mask before the doorbell rang. Chuck stood transfixed as Jane loosened the front of her gown. She took his hand, guided him across the threshold and gently shut the door. "We took up where we had left off on the dance floor. His hands were all over me. I was beyond excited. It had been so long." Jane led him to her darkened bedroom, only then did she remove her mask. For the next few hours Chuck found pleasure in Jane's willing body. "The more he gave the more I wanted." Chuck left before dawn. Jane found a note with his name and number scrawled inside a heart. "I walked on air the rest of the day."

She decided to call him that afternoon. "It was Sunday; I had to work the next day so I figured what the heck." Voice mail picked up,

Jane left her number with a breathy "Call me." Then she waited and waited. As the days past it appeared to be a one-time thing. "I didn't mind too much, it was a great night with a very happy ending. Still I was disappointed." Then the phone rang early Thursday evening. Chuck explained he had been out of town selling drugs. "He liked to say he was just a highly paid pusher man." Chuck said he had to catch the red eye to Chicago in a few hours. Would Jane mind if he dropped in on his way to the airport. "I knew he wanted sex, I didn't mind, I was definitely in the mood. What did worry me was there would be no camouflage." She told Chuck to hurry, "And I hope you will recognize me without the feathered mask." He laughed and said he would be over in twenty minutes. Jane took a quick shower before sliding into a sheer white teddy. She put on some jazz and lowered the lights.

"I will never forget the look on his face when I opened the door." He was carrying a dozen roses. Chuck looked Jane over from bottom to top. His eyes slowly climbed up her shapely legs, rose to her breasts and finally fell upon her face. He momentarily froze, confusion in the headlights. Jane reached out, took the roses, turned and walked toward the kitchen. "I waited; afraid he would retreat to his car. When I heard the door shut and his steps on the hardwood floor I sighed with joy."

Chuck helped her put the roses in a vase. He mentioned how happy her message had made him feel. "I wish I could have come over sooner, my job has been a bitch lately." Jane told him she was glad he didn't turn out to be a one night stand. Chuck assured her he was not that kind of guy. "I wanted to believe that." Jane took his hand and led him to the bedroom. Passion quickly ignited. Jane straddled his firm body and rode them both to a vigorous climax. As they rested in each other arms Chuck asked if she would accompany him to New York the following week. He had meetings

Thursday and Friday but his nights were free and they could stay the weekend. "I had to pinch myself, this never happened to me. Of course I said yes." They made love one more time before Chuck had to leave for the airport. Jane kissed him good bye at the door. He said he would pick her up around five on Wednesday. "He left without ever mentioning my face."

The next few days flew by as Jane pulled dusty luggage out of the garage, arranged for time off, and selected her wardrobe. "I felt like I was going on my honeymoon." Promptly at five on Wednesday afternoon the bell rang. Jane had her bag waiting by the door. Chuck came in and gave her an extended kiss "The flight is running late, how about a quick one for the road." Chuck whispered. Jane was taken aback but turned toward the bedroom. Chuck reached out and grabbed her shoulders. "We don't have that much time, why don't you just bend over the couch." She could feel his growing hardness. "A small part of me wanted to slap his face, while the rest was tingling with sudden excitement."

Jane dropped her jeans as she placed both hands firmly on the back of her leather sofa. Chuck pulled her panty to one side and ran a finger over her increasing wetness. Jane heard a zipper release and his pants hit the floor. He entered her slowly. Soon his thrusts quickened, Jane lowered her arms to the cushion, the sound of slapping flesh filled the room. Her hands pulled at the cowhide as she moaned. Chuck grabbed her breasts, grunting loudly. Their mutual spasms slowly subsided. After catching her breath Jane turned into Chuck's arms, they embraced before she looked up at him and said, "This has the makings of a great trip." He laughed as she pulled her pants up and headed to the bathroom. "I'll take your bag out to the car, don't take too long."

After a few drinks on the plane Chuck grew serious, "I have a confession, about your face. At the dance, someone said, I over-heard a guy say." Chuck sputtered, mistimed spark plugs in his truth engine. "You know how guy's talk, awesome body bad face, I didn't think anything of it. I mean we had a great, great time. Then when I was leaving your place I saw a key ring hanging by the door with your hospital security card."

At that moment two slides projected onto Chuck's frontal lobe; a drunk pissing in the bathroom telling his buddy about that nurse Jane, how he'd love to fuck her if she had a bag over her head and Jane closing the door of her darkened bedroom before removing her mask. "Well, I really don't know why, anyway, I looked at your picture on the card. I'm sorry if..." Jane grabbed his hand and in-terrupted, "No, no don't be sorry, I am the one who should apolo-gize. It was rude of me to hide behind the feathers, it's just that I was having so much fun and didn't want it to end."

A tear slowly trickled down her cheek, a rivulet released by memo-ries of rejection. Chuck missed the "please hug me" cue, instead he finished his drink and said, "I think were past all that now. I mean we got a good thing going here. O.K.?" Jane didn't know what to make of his question. Are we past something we never discussed? Is that why we have a good thing? A man who believes my face is a non-issue. She leaned into Chuck's shoulder and told him it was O.K. with her. "I began to think he may be the one." Jane said.

There stay in New York was filled with good eating, sightseeing, and much lovemaking. Chuck was generous with his time and money. One night, on their way to a show he asked if she would mind meeting an old friend of his before the performance. They took a cab over to 42nd Street. Chuck introduced her to Tom, a pal from college. They shared a few laughs over drinks. Chuck excused himself and headed out to make a phone call. "He's a busy guy." Tom said. He then asked a few questions about her family and job before commenting, "I have a friend with a facial discoloration like yours, was it present at birth?" When Jane replied in the affirmative Tom asked about laser surgery, steroid treatments, cryotherapy, and concealing cosmetics. Seemingly satisfied with her responses Tom finished his beer, shook Jane's hand, and left. Jane noticed that he went directly over to Chuck who was standing just outside the lounge entrance. They engaged in conversation for a few minutes before Tom patted Chuck on the back and walked away.

Jane rearranged her legs on the chair and said, "I suspected Tom was not an old college friend of Chuck's, their conversation was a little forced." She went on to tell me that Tom was most likely a dermatologist. "His questions were clinical." Jane did not fault Chuck for the ruse.

"I was touched that he would arrange for someone to check my condition without embarrassing me." "What exactly is your condition?" I asked. I knew that was one helluva birth mark on her face. Shaped like a kidney it flowed down from her right eye to the edge of her mouth, mostly dark red with shades of purple streaking across her cheek. I had ignored it from the start; she was my angel of mercy.

"The medical term is flat hemangioma." Jane began, "More commonly known as a port-wine stain." She went on to explain that they are always present at birth and are thought to be associated with a deficiency in the nerve supply to the blood vessels. It occurs in 3 out of every 1,000 infants. "I have had pulse dye and photoderm laser treatments. The recovery was awful, my skin turned black, swelled up and bled. No real hope for improvement." There was little emotion in her voice; she spoke as if the subject was one of her patients. "That's why Chuck's calling me even after seeing my picture and then having a doctor look me over made me feel special."

After returning from New York Sunday evening Chuck drove Jane home. She wanted him to spend the night but he had a lot to get done by morning. "It was a good trip; I made some nice sales, now comes the paperwork. I'll call you tomorrow." They kissed at the door. She watched him walk to his car and waved as he drove away. "I was happier than I had ever been." She wasn't bothered when he didn't call the next day. "I figured he was hard at work. I didn't want to call him, didn't want to come across as pushy."

By Thursday, however, Jane was feeling pensive. Razor winged butterflies were clouding up her stomach. She was about to right him off as a better class of asshole, but an asshole nonetheless, when he phoned. He apologized before explaining he had to drive to Modesto for a few days of meetings. "I forgot to bring your phone number and I didn't want to call the hospital."

Jane tried to act nonchalant but her heart was racing like a fox in front of a pack of hounds. "That's O.K. I figured you were busy, I was pretty busy too." Chuck suggested they have dinner on Sunday. "I'll bring the steaks and wine, you make a salad, maybe we can watch a movie." She didn't want to wait that long. "Can't you come by sooner or I could come to your place." He said he was really swamped but would make up for lost time on Sunday. "See you soon sweetheart." Jane liked the "sweetheart" reference. "Can't wait." she replied before hanging up.

On Saturday Jane went to the Farmer's Market, she was intent on making the best salad Chuck ever had. It was crowded, canvas covered stalls of fruits and vegetables competed for customers. Jane had just bought organic carrots and green peppers when she saw Chuck near a stand selling honey. She had to look twice to make sure before hurrying to his side. The same instant Jane tapped him on the shoulder, a cute, curly haired girl of five or six grabbed his hand and said, "But daddy you promised I could get some cotton candy, you promised." The girl's words shot through Jane, taking her breath with them.

"It's bad for your teeth Mandy." Chuck said before looking toward Jane. His face turned ashen, a vein in his neck throbbed, and his eyes desperately sought a way out. Mandy followed her father's gaze, pointed a finger in Jane's direction and said, "Daddy why is that woman's face so dirty. She didn't use enough soap?" Before Chuck or Jane could react an attractive blonde, in jeans and a sweater, carrying a bag of apples came to Mandy's side, "Is something wrong sweetie?" she said. The young girl grabbed the woman's leg with one hand and pointed with the other, "Mommy, that lady has a funny looking face." The young mother looked quizzically at Jane then handed the apples to Chuck. She bent down and spoke quietly to her daughter, "Mandy it is not polite to point at other people. That lady just has a big birth mark."

She took the girl in her arms and stood up. After taking a step toward Jane she said, "Sorry about that, kids can be a little insensitive." Jane still had that punched in the stomach look. Her eyes turned to Chuck. He was holding the apples in one hand and kicking at the dirt with his worn loafers. "I knew he was expecting the worse, I thought about slapping his face and going hysterical. But I didn't have the strength." Instead, Jane handed the peppers and carrots to Chuck, nodded at this wife and walked away. After a few steps she heard Chuck say, "No I don't know her, how would I know her? She is just upset because of Mandy."

It was my turn to squeeze Jane's hand. "Men are assholes; we should all be castrated at birth." Jane smiled, "Not all, but certainly some." A difficult silence ensued. I did not know how to respond to her story. Up to this point we had talked mostly about me and my issues. Bringing comfort to others was not my strong suit and, having avoided deaths, divorces, injury, and tragedies, I really had no opportunity to practice.

Jane sensed my unease, "Paul, please forgive me, I shouldn't have brought my problems into your world." "Why not," I quickly retorted, "I've been raining mine on your head for weeks." Jane smiled again, "Yeah, but I get paid for that." She stood and wrapped her arms around my back in a strong embrace. Her hair smelled of lavender, her body was warm and soft. We held tightly, shifting pain, transferring confidence.

"Sorry" Jane said, "Enough about poor, old Nurse Meyer." "You're neither old nor poor, and I have every intention of keeping you as a friend for as long as your will have me." "You know," Jane said, "If I didn't know better I'd think you were trying to get in my pants." Before I could protest she continued, "I do like you a lot, but I don't see romance in our future. Besides, with our faces, we would always get the worst table in restaurants." She was right about that, "Yeah well at least you would be the better half." Jane stood up and stretched her curves, "You are a silver tongued devil with a good sense of humor." "Thanks for that back handed compliment." I replied. "You're welcome, I think it is time for bed, you have a big day tomorrow meeting with the psychiatrist."

"I am going to tell him I want to see you naked." "And I am going to tell him that explosion rattled your brain to mush." she said

Morning came like many before, short of breath and already tired. In those moments before reality shoved an icicle up my ass I often felt a different bed warming my bones. The twin in that small room in the well-kept Midwest subdivision tri-level. Visions of various futures projected on the ceiling. Boyhood dreams replayed nightly. The musty, abused metal framed college dorm bed. The first out- of- home sleep port which often comforted a head in various stages of confusion, intoxication, relief, remorse, doubt. Later futons and mattresses thrown down in an assortment of bee hive apartments during those extended educational years. Less confusion more intoxication and doubt. Then real beds, full size, complete with headboards, as the paychecks came every other Friday. Self-worth on the upswing, the occasional overnight squeeze, dreams of love, discovery, and wealth. Finally the big soft mattress on Partridge Avenue. Laughing myself to sleep, bouncing with Iris, and a new set of options. I would linger in one of these beds, warm blankets shielding another cold day, until hospital sounds jerked me to life.

This day it was the sand paper voice of Frank filtering through the door, "I told you there's an emergency over here in the Burn Unit, I'll get to your fucking problem soon. Hang up the damn phone, you're wasting my time." Using his large behind as a battering ram Frank backed into my room as he jammed a cell phone into his shirt pocket.

"Shit, can't get a moments peace in this godforsaken place. How you been Paul, win any beauty contests lately?" He had a grin on his face as he sat at my side. "Just one Frank," I replied, "Your mother came in second place." We both laughed, Frank's belly shook like a cement mixer. "That's a good one, you smart ass bastard. Seriously, how you doing?" His blood shot eyes gave me the once over. "Doing pretty well, should be getting my walking papers in a day or two."

Frank looked a little surprised, "That soon, why good for you. You know if you need a place to stay the Mrs. and I have a spare room." His generosity was genuine, the offer touched my heart. "Thanks Frank, I appreciate that, but, I do believe I still own a house unless old Fuzzbush sold it to pay my rent here." Frank's phone buzzed, he gave it a look of disdain before sending the caller to voice mail. "Well, you'll have to give me your address before you leave so I can stop by for a few beers." He raised his massive frame up from the chair. "I'll be around again, got to go see about a broken vent in pediatrics, some kid probably hiding porno magazines."

There was time to shower before breakfast. Still had a few outposts of skin that rebelled against an attack of hot water. Overall it felt good, soaping up, taking the opportunity to get a stroke and grimace, rattling the pipes, making sure the plumbing worked.

I toweled off and made it back to bed before the powdered eggs, mystery meat patty, cold cereal, and orange juice arrived. My appetite was firing on all cylinders; sometimes the orderly slid a second salvo my way. I was thinking of taking a walk down to the garden when the door suddenly opened and in walked Dr. Daniel Plite, Chief of Psychiatry. Tall, skinny with a shock of receding black hair bouncing off his skull, he quickly strode to my bed, introduced himself and warmly shook my hand. His eyes perused my scorched skin; a slight grimace crossed his face. "Everyone calls me Dr. Dan. I am here at Dr. Vu's request, seems he has some concern about your decision to forego future cosmetic surgery."

Taking a seat Dr. Dan crossed his long legs, placed a notebook on his lap, pulled a pen from his coat pocket, put on black reading glasses, and waited for my response. Like phone sex operators, shrinks get paid by the minute, except they listen more and moan less. "I would hope that sanity doesn't correlate with good looks, otherwise there are a lot of ugly people running around out there that should be locked up." Dr. Dan tapped his pen a few times on his thigh, "The issue is not your appearance, rather whether you are in the right frame of mind to decide how you should look. I just need to ask a few questions before the hospital will feel comfortable sending you home." I wanted to use the "I am almost all ears" line but this doctor appeared to have left his humor at the door and it was more important to get out than get my jollies. "Ask away Doctor, please."

And ask he did. My backgrounds—family, educational, employment, love, religious--all the time studiously taking notes, turning pages with his manicured fingers, occasionally underlining what he had written. "O.K." he said, "I know your history, now I would like to go a little deeper." Deeper? As in just below the surface or plunge to the dark corners of my soul? Dan looked like he dove without a depth gauge.

"Why have you refused your parents' offers to come out?" Anchors fucking away. "Well," I began a little tentatively "They were here once already, there is not a lot of money in their bank account, there is no need to cause them aggravation. I will see them soon enough." My words fell like drops from a leaky faucet. Dr. Dan persisted. "I understand your concern for their finances," he said, "But why only a few phone calls?" "We have never communicated well by telephone," I replied, "We are not big on making small talk and there isn't much to say right now." "I see, I see." he said while adding to his pages of notes. "Are you protecting your parent's feelings or yours?" Wham, depth charge number one. "Never thought about it that way." I said. When I didn't continue no life line was forthcoming. Dan looked at me, I stared at the door. "I don't like to cause anyone discomfort, especially my parents." I finally said. "I suppose I am protecting myself from having to deal with their reaction to the way I look."

Dan began to tap his pen again, "I get the impression you like to keep things light and fun, your injuries are neither. Have you thought about giving your parents and friends the opportunity to be supportive?" Was Dan laying the guilt on me for not sharing my pain? Am I a selfish sonofabitch for not crying in my mother's arms? "I guess I am not there yet, Doc." Dan didn't appear too satisfied with my response but moved on.

"Who do you blame for the accident?" He put a little emphasis on "blame." A lot of variables at play in that five letter word. All those intersections, choices, bumps, that put me in the back yard with the grill. Blame Weezy's success, Iris's beauty, Cain's grills, Grace's salesmanship, my third grade math teacher. The inventor of propane.

"I guess I don't have an answer for that. The lawyers will have to sort it out." Dan leaned forward and asked, "Do you blame yourself?" "Hell no," I quickly responded, "I was just trying to cook some steaks. Why the fuck would I blame myself?" Dan set his notebook down and rocked back in the chair. "Sometimes those involved in bad accidents come to believe they had it coming, that they deserve to suffer for past wrongs. They have a lot of guilt and see an injury as penance for their sins." Now that would deserve a ticket to loony land. "No, that strange interpretation has never crossed my mind."

Dan retrieved his pad and took more notes. He was still writing as he asked, "What about this Iris woman, how do you feel about her?" Depth charge number two. I was surprised how quickly the truth came to the surface, "I am disappointed she hasn't come to see me or called more. It hurts because I thought we had a relationship. Nurse Meyer says a lot of couples break up over this kind of injury. I wanted to believe Iris was better than that. Guess I was wrong." A cyclone of pain erupted in my gut. I had to fight to keep the tear ducts closed.

Picking up on my emotional turmoil, the good shrink recognized disintegrating fiber and handed me a glass of water. I gratefully gulped, slowly regaining my composure. This time Dan did throw a life saver, "It's not your fault Iris or anyone else is not strong enough to deal with the changes in your life. You two did not have much of a history; her betrayal is difficult but understandable." Words of comfort, at last, from the doctor. Betrayal, however, seemed a bit harsh especially when there was still a Welcome Home Iris sign hanging from my heart.

Dan, preferring not to watch as I wallowed in the pity pond, moved on. "Have you thought about what you will do once you leave here?" My mind's juke box whirled; the smart ass 45 hit the platter first. "Well the propane industry has offered me a job in public relations." No smile, just more notes. No further questioning, just waiting. "I plan on returning to my house, the scene of the crime if you will, and try to get a life back. There are issues with my job buy out, my insurance situation is a mess, and I have an attorney suing over the accident, should be enough to keep me occupied for some time." Write that on your paper Doc, patient has a plan, seems determined, good candidate for release.

Dan put his pen down and said, "How will you handle the public's reaction to your face?" Depth charge number three. A voice down inside the canyon containing what was left of my self-worth screamed out, "Fuck em." Recognizing such a comment would not score points I said, "Don't really know, guess I will take what comes and deal with it." "You must understand," Dan said, "Some people will give you second and third looks. You will be a curiosity. Attention will follow you, whispers will reach your ears, pointed fingers will catch your eye. It can be overwhelming."

My "Keep your mouth shut!" conductor once again was asleep at the switch. I whined, "Guess I could shave my ass and walk backwards but somebody beat me to that." There were many comebacks Doctor Dan could have thrown out, most dealing with some combination of "crack" and "cheek." Instead he sat and waited. I spun my wheel of raucous retorts but only landed on bankrupt. "What the hell," I finally said, "I know people will look at me. I can't hide in my room; I have the rest of my life to lead." Dan seemed pleased with my response; a slight smile creased his thin lips. He underlined a few words with extra emphasis.

"So," he began with a deliberate tone, "If you understand that fact why don't you want to take further steps to improve your appearance?" He sat back with a look of satisfaction, an interrogator who has put the last stroke in front of your corner. I needed to kick his paint can over and stick the brush up his ass. "Because," I began, while looking directly into his dark eyes, "According to Dr. Vu there is not much improvement to be gained. I am resigned to my condition, not happy but not depressed. I need to move on; I have been here long enough." My voice had grown a little louder with each word. I took a deep breath, lowered my hand with a dismissive gesture and practically whispered, "If that makes me crazy than crazy I am." More turbulence raked my gut. I looked away. This time I waited. The rustle of pages being turned continued for a few moments then it was quiet. The echo of my pounding heart slowly faded.

Doctor Dan finally spoke, "That's all I have, I will send Dr. Vu my findings." The chair slid back as Dan stood up. I turned and said, "Well what's the verdict am I staying or going, sane or bonkers?" "Proper procedure requires that I report to your doctor." he replied. Proper fucking procedure. "Look Doc you have put me through the ringer, I think I deserve your feedback. Sit down and give it to me straight. With all I have been through I can take whatever you have to say." He was in the corner now. "Give me a few more minutes of your time." I said, with a tone somewhere between a plea and a demand. Dan had one foot toward the door. He swayed in his loafers before returning to my bedside and sitting down. He shuffled his notebook pages yet again before taking off his glasses and placing them into his pocket. "This is going to be a totally off the record conversation." he said, "It is against protocol and I will deny it ever occurred." We were now partners in some medical-legal conspiracy. "I appreciate that Doctor."

"I will tell Dr. Vu he should not question your reasoning abilities. You are doing fairly well, all things considered. Your sarcastic tendencies protect a sensitive nature and guard against rejection. Like many of your generation you have floated through life without any responsibilities other than to yourself. No worries about food and shelter. No wife or children. No war, no service. College extended your adolescence. No real connection to anything spiritual. You have bobbed along, drifting on the current, with very little rudder control. I am sure there is love between you and your parents yet I sense a disconnect; you treat them like characters in a play rather than flesh and blood. Your reluctance to communicate, accept their affection, or tell them the truth about your condition is troubling. I believe you related to Iris in the same way, grateful for her beauty, conversation, companionship, sex but not willing to be totally honest, to put the real you out front."

Doctor Dan put his analysis on pause and gave me a "how you handling this" look. Although it felt like he had crawled into my head and read my diary, I raised my eyebrows as if to say, "Is that all you got." This elicited a second feeble smile. He continued.

"The money from your job buy out provided a better cushion, less chance of discomfort, but no sense of direction. You were still in the gray zone, restless, questioning your future, hoping for love, a sense of purpose, a good reason to get out of bed every day. Your accident, of course, put you over the falls. Physical and psychological trauma can drown your spark. It is up to you to decide if your flame will burn again. The days ahead will be challenging. They can also be rewarding. Don't use your accident as an excuse to keep floating, grab the tiller, and take command."

It felt as if I should throw my chest out, salute, and yell, "Aye, Aye Captain." Dan, however, soon made it clear that this was no pep talk. "When all is said and done you need to grow up. Find some meaning, leave something behind." He stood quickly, placed the notebook in his lab coat pocket, and walked toward the door. As he grasped the handle I choked out, "Thanks Doctor Dan, have a good day." He stopped, paused, and then gave a low wave with his left hand without looking in my direction.

Doctor Dan's words spun around my head, a merry go round of harsh judgment. Psychological acupuncture, white hot criticism needles piercing to the core. Neither anger nor animosity dulled the pain. Pinned like a dissected frog, total awareness without the capacity to respond. The landscape of my life had been ploughed, the soil deemed shallow and barren.

As the minutes passed seeds of a counter attack began to sprout. I knew psychology was an art and not a science. Smoke blown out a PHD's ass is still smoke. He was educated and experienced, so was I.

Granted; Dan made a good living translating actions/speech/inaction/dreams into mental healthese. On the scale of using your shit as a crayon and transcendentally levitating, I certainly plodded along in the great middle. He was going to turn me loose and I was going to be happy to leave. "Grow up. Find some meaning." said the shrink. "Be honest." also said the shrink. "Why?" Is Dan's version of a well-being better than mine? Had I waited too long to turn the page?

More ping pong balls bouncing over the net. I needed a bigger paddle. The phone interrupted my backhand. "Mr. Lawton this is Sally from Attorney Traditore's office, is this a good time to talk?" "Sure," I replied, "As long as there is no analysis involved." She gave a courtesy chuckle before continuing, "We have filed your lawsuit in the Santa Clara Superior Court. Things are moving along. Can you come to our office for a meeting in the next few weeks?" Sally had the kind of voice you couldn't refuse. Molasses tinged with cigarette smoke. "Yes, I should be leaving the hospital pretty soon, why don't I call you when I get out." "Great." she exhaled, "We are looking forward to meeting you." We will see about that, I thought. "Me too." I mumbled before hanging up. Was that the truth? Was I prepared for parole?

I decided to take a walk to the garden, a little fresh air to clear the mind. I put on the robe, stepped into my slippers and wandered down the hall. Hands in pockets, head screwed down into neck, face pointed toward the floor, just another freak shuffling along. I observed my fellow hall mates from the waist down. No civilians, just hospital green, white nylons, staff khaki. Until one of the uglier shades of lime ever to be made into pants passed to my left only to quickly reappear on my right.

After a few steps the efficient voice of Doris Flatbush rose above the din, "Mr. Lawton, we need to talk." I tried to pick up the pace with little success. My sprinting days were over. Flatbush tugged at my sleeve, "Mr. Lawton, we really do need to talk." I stopped and looked down at her hand grasping my robe. Slowly my eyes rose along the path of her jacketed arm, over the shoulder, coming to rest upon her glassed in eyes. She immediately dropped her hand, avoided my gaze and said, "Why don't we find a seat in the lounge. This shouldn't take too long."

Doris found two chairs along the wall separated by a round table with a drooping plant spilling over one side. She motioned toward the closest one before quickly sitting down. After opening a binder she said, "Hope this is comfortable." As Doris scanned several spread sheets I said, "Well I was hoping we could share a couch, get a little cozy." Doctor Dan would be shaking his head. Doris momentarily tightened her brow before completely ignoring my comment. After a few moments she looked at a point somewhere over my left shoulder and began to speak. "As I am sure you know by now there is no insurance coverage available to pay for any of the costs of your treatment. You could have made the process easier if you would have told me this fact several weeks ago." I attempted to sputter out a protest, Flatbush sternly waved her hand across her chest and continued, "None of that matters now, I'm afraid the hospital and my superiors are more inclined to seek full compensation in such a circumstance. Your total bill is approaching two million dollars."

Doris took a quick glance to see if seven digits of greenback debt had any effect. I winked. She frowned. I said, "Can I pay so much a week?" She frowned harder. "No. Mr. Lawton this is a very serious matter." Doris leaned a little closer before stating, "I am afraid it is with the lawyers now." She spoke as if informing the Pope that the Devil was at the door. Flatbush began to gather her papers when her cell phone rang. Doris stood and turned toward the patio, a lime green presence glowing in the sunlight. Her permed head nodded a few times after which she quickly turned back before snapping her phone shut. "I have good news Mr. Lawton, for both of us, your release from care has been approved. You can leave in two days. Congratulations." Flatbush hurried away, I half expected to see her heels kick up, a leprechaun returning to her forest of sharpened pencils.

I was alone. Soon to be released. Alone. In debt up to what was left of my ears. Alone. There would be no one waiting when the hospital door closed behind me. Alone.

The routine of the day continued, oblivious to my impending departure. In a hospital there are always patients, different faces filling the same beds. An assembly line of blood, guts, sutures, metal, bone, pain, death, relief, life. My being on the last conveyor belt didn't seem to matter. Lunch and dinner came and went. I inquired about Nurse Jane and was told it was her day off. She took so few that it always came as a surprise.

Just as I was casting about for some way to stroll away the hours before lights out in walked Dr. Vu. His gleaming black hair was disheveled, glasses smudged, coat stained brown and orange. "Dr. Vu," I piped, "You look like you've been ridden hard and put away wet." Vu gave a tired chuckle and sat down. "Wish I could offer you a beer, looks like you could use one."

He took off his glasses, massaged both temples, rubbed his right eye and said, "Now that is the best idea I have heard all day." Vu went on to explain that three victims of a house fire had been brought in early in the morning. He had spent the entire day assessing and treating. "They are lucky to have you doctor; I want you to know I appreciate your efforts."

A little more life returned to his face. "Anyway I thought I would stop by and deliver some good news before I left. You can go home in two days. How about that?" Vu gave me his usual squeeze and pat on the arm. "That's fine doc but Flatbush already told me, she's happier than I am." Vu grinned again, "Ah Ms. Flatbush, I will have to remind her not to steal my thunder. I have heard of your insurance difficulties. Doris is not happy unless all of our patients shit coins. Don't worry these things usually work out. The hospital did not heal you only to put you into debtor's prison."

I took a drink of water. "Hope so doctor, probably harder to get blood out of me than a turnip anyway." Vu pulled the chair a little closer to my bed. "Along that same vein," he began and then started to laugh. "You see Paul you're not the only one who can engage in humor. Blood, vein, get it?" He was about to break his arm patting himself on the back. "Yeah, good one." I said.

"Anyway," he continued, "I have a proposition for you." I was about to say I already had a lawyer when he went on, "I know you have rejected the idea of future remedial measures, plus Flatbush would probably have a coronary if we suggested it." Vu took a quick look toward the door and went on with a slightly conspiratorial tone, "So, I believe I could recruit Nurse Jane and we could do a little bedside cosmetic surgery. Strictly off the record and off the books. You would look a little better. How about it?"

I was beginning to get the idea that I was a topic around the old water cooler. Jane must have already signed on. "Under two conditions doc, one it is not going to hurt, two I still get out on time. Otherwise trim, cut, and paste to your heart's content." Vu stood up and gave me arm another pat. "Good, good, around ten in the morning should work well."

He lingered as if caught in a web. "You know," he began while tugging the edge of the bed sheet, "You are going to leave in pretty good shape, physically and mentally. I spoke with Dr. Dan and, like every other psych I know, he thinks you, and everyone else, has issues. Hell I'd hate to be on his couch myself. But, overall he feels you are making a decent adjustment. I think he even appreciates your wit." Was he talking about the same Dr. Dan? Or did Dan tone down his critique of my life and times in his official report? I had already put some pavement between me and his analysis. No reason to back track. "Good to hear," I told Vu, "I'll take all the support I can get."

He reached into his pocket, pulled out a card and placed it on the bedside table. "Here are my work and home numbers, call me anytime." Vu sat back down, cupped his hands under his chin and said, "It's not going to be that easy outside these walls. I have had many patients with less of a disfigurement withdraw from the world. It's sad to watch. You need to remain productive." I knew Vu was giving a pep talk but I didn't get much past "disfigurement," another way of saying abnormal. My figure certainly qualified. I was a cartoon character, not bad, just drawn that way. Dr. Vu finally got up to leave, "See you in the morning." he said. "I'll be here Doc, have a good night, you deserve it."

The click of the door hung in the air. I got up and took a piss. Washing my hands with my face reflected in the mirror I once again took stock. The skin was healed, the passing weeks had evened out the colors somewhat, the sorry excuse for ears had not improved. Maybe Vu's bedside magic would help. Jane had trimmed my mohawk, a few hairy outposts had sprouted on the sidewalls.

At ten the next morning my door crashed open as Frank strode in tool bag in one hand and a large yellow sign in the other. "Hey

Paul, how you doing? Looks like we're in for a little renegade surgery." "I hope to hell you're not in charge Frank, I would hate to see what you could do with your hammer, screwdriver, plunger, and drill. My face may look like a plugged up toilet though, I'll give you that." Frank laughed, "Shit, I have seen what a few of these doctors have done. I could do better with plaster, duct tape, and a soldering iron." Frank sat back in the chair, "No, buddy I am just here to provide a little camouflage for the real operation. I will put this "Keep Out" sign by the door and pretend I am fixing some damn thing or another." Just then the rest of the troops arrived. Jane gave me a wide smile as she pushed a cart, Vu followed quickly on her heels.

The musketeers of mercy quickly went to work. Frank moved to the hall and took a few bolts out of the door closer. Jane cleared space at the side of my bed and arranged various instruments along the top of the cart. She and Vu both put on latex gloves and face masks. Jane pulled out a syringe from a case strikingly similar to her nightcap special. "This will relax you." she said with a wink.

Dr. Vu studied a few pages on my chart before taking my head in his hands. His eyes, shining brightly above his mask, traveled over my face. "You have a few contractures which we can help; also some dermabrasion should improve your appearance." Vu said in a professional manner. "I am going to numb several areas." He pulled out a needle and injected each side of my face in two spots. I was already under the soothing effects of Jane's syringe and did not feel more than a pin prick. "Your ears also can be improved. Presently the left remains slightly larger than the right; I will trim to balance them out. It will give your face a more symmetrical appearance."

Dr. Vu and Nurse Jane went to work. He cut and stitched, she handed instruments and wiped my blood with a cotton pad. After the first couple of times Vu came at me with different sharp tools I chose to avoid the incoming by closing my eyes. Time marched without me. Eventually I caught up. My guests were gone. Feeling had returned to my face. Some tingling interfaced with an ache or two.

I instinctively reached for the mirror. The graft borders were a little puffy, skin color was more uniform, and the ears appeared almost identical, small nubs of flesh buttons. A sheen of lotion layered my face. I could barely make out a few incisions closed with stitches. As I took a second lap around my reflection Jane walked into the room, pulling a wheeled duffel bag.

"Welcome back stranger, you have been out several hours, even missed lunch." She heaved the bag onto the chair with a grunt. "Brought me some food to make up for it Nurse Jane?" I asked with a grin that sent a twinge across my retouched face. "Try not to laugh Paul, you might pull a stitch." she said. "And no there's nothing edible in the bag as far as I know. Your friend Iris dropped it off a few days after you were admitted. There should be clothes and shoes to wear when you leave. Shall we have a look?"

My friend Iris had dropped off some clothes. Thoughtful, I won't have to walk out in seared shorts and shirt with melted sandals. Jane pulled the zipper and lifted out a t-shirt. "Wow, I used to love these guys." Hanging from her hands, like Jesus on the cross, was my old Ramones shirt. The one I gave to Iris after our first night of lovemaking.

I caught my breath and told Jane, "Why don't you keep it, a little gift from me for all your help." Jane was pleased, she hug the shirt to her chest, "Why thank you Paul that's very nice. Let's see what else is in here." As it turned out, enough clothes for a weekend at the lake. I settled on a pair of jeans, sneakers, and a long sleeved polo. After returning the remaining items to the bag Jane wrestled it into the closet and hung up my selections. She carefully folded the Ramones into a neat square and placed them in her large front pocket. With a quick wave she said, "Thanks again and I will see you after dinner."

There are moments when desire gasps a last breath, when the heart flat lines, when love dies. The fact Iris had washed and ironed my old shirt, placed it at the top of the bag, and zipped up our relationship qualified. That part of me which still beat the drum of hope was silenced. She had packed the clothes weeks ago. Her intentions were clear, consistent with her subsequent lack of contact. Whatever we had, whatever might have been, was gone.

My last full day as a patient came and went. Dr. Vu examined, "Not bad, not bad at all." he commented. We left the room together. He dropped me off in a small office so I could watch an exit video. Actors or real doctors, I couldn't tell which, gave instruction on home care for the newly released burn survivor. There were creams to use, proper methods of dressing, clothes for the outdoors, activities to avoid, employment potential, and warning signs of trouble.

After initialing a sheet documenting my faithful viewing I walked down to the lounge. It had been raining and the garden plants were crying. I sat and watched the gray clouds roll. After the third wave passed I heard a female voice above the din, "You go ask him, why do I always have to take the lead." Another woman replied, "Because you are better with strangers. Go ahead, we don't have all day."

Shortly thereafter a light tap dropped onto my left shoulder. "Excuse me, my sister and I were wondering if we could have a moment of your time." I turned to find a fortyish woman in jeans and a Cal sweat shirt. She had glasses too big for her face, streaked shoulder length brown hair, and much make up. Hovering behind her was a near double, ten years younger and ten pounds lighter. They introduced themselves as Marge and Betty. I motioned for them to join me on the couch.

Marge, the older of the two, compressed the cushion next to me. Betty settled to her right. "We couldn't help but notice your face. I don't mean to be rude, but our brother had an accident with a water heater, he's down the hall right now with burns to his arms and face. It's only been two days. We're from San Diego. We both have jobs, were the only family he has." Marge started to cry, slowly at first, then gaining in intensity.

I gathered from Marge's run on that they were interested in their brother's future and their place in his recovery. "I'm sorry." she said she dabbing her tears with a tissue, "It's just that we don't know what to do, what to say, what to expect." She stood up, "We shouldn't have intruded." "Please," I said, a catch in my voice, "Sit down. I am sorry to hear about your brother, I don't know if I can help but feel free to ask me anything."

Marge sat back down, a look of relief on her face. Betty spoke up, "Is there a lot of pain?" "Yes, but the drugs help." "How long should we stay?" "I was out of it for the first week or so, after that I didn't have many visitors. You'll have to ask your brother. He is in for a rough time, see what he prefers." "Were you angry?" "You bet. I hope to move forward without a pissed off attitude. It's going to be a struggle." "How is your family handling this?" "My parents live in the Midwest, they were here early on. I haven't shared the extent of my scars with them yet. It is not something I am looking forward to."

Marge took my hand, "Don't worry your family will always love you." It was a nice gesture. "Yeah, well it is not my family that concerns me. How do I look to you?" The sisters exchanged arched eyebrows. Betty began, "When we saw you we gasped. Then we realized you were burned like our brother and we felt sorry for the both of you. It took a little courage to come over and speak." "Now that we have talked," Marge interjected, "I feel comfortable, the initial shock of your appearance is something people are going to have to get over. You seem like a nice guy. Thanks for taking the time and all the best in the future." They both stood up and walked away.

As I shuffled past the doors on the way back down the hall I wondered which one lead to the poor bastard and his water heater wounds. I wished him well in his upcoming battle with the demons that will haunt his days and torment his nights. Hopefully Nurse Jane and Dr. Vu will be in his corner.

I opened the door to my own room for the last time.

They still serve you breakfast on your final day in the hospital. Having no real understanding of the culinary arts I appreciated the food. It would likely be better than what I would have on the outside. Vu came in for a quick look. "Good to go." he pronounced, "I hope you paid attention to that video. We will give you a care kit before you leave. See you at eleven; I hear there's a party."

Jane stopped by as I was heading to the shower. "Sorry I can't stay long; a couple of new patients need my help. Get cleaned up and put on your clothes. See you in bit." I did as instructed. It felt odd to put on pants, shirt, shoes, and socks. I had lost several pounds the hard way. There was excess cloth at the shoulders and waist. The tongue of my belt rested two holes over from its prior home. I looked little better than someone finishing off a stint at San Quentin, with a worse haircut.

As the appointed hour approached in walked Ms. Flatbush clutching a folder and a small paper bag. Still gun shy, she looked everywhere but at me. "Ready to leave I see." she said with contained glee, "You need to sign some forms after which I will return your belongings." After pulling a chair up next to mine Flatbush slid a stack of papers across the table, several yellow "Sign Here" tabs stuck out like guitar picks. "Am I giving up my first born?" I asked. "Of course not," she indignantly replied, "One is a bill acknowledgment, one a release from care, one a promise to reimburse, and the last is for receipt of your personal effects." I looked her way, she pretended not to notice. "I'll take your word for it, can I borrow a pen." Flatbush rolled a blue Bic across the wood.

After I scribbled on the last line she quickly gathered up the documents. "Now for your property. I believe these items were left by a Miss Camp." My keys and wallet fell out of the bag followed by a half sheet of paper. Flatbush stood and spoke to the wall, "Just for the record Mr. Lawton I could have confiscated the four hundred and sixteen dollars in your wallet as partial payment of money owed. I did not, however, because we in Accounts Receivable have a heart. Good luck sir." She turned and reached for the door just as Frank stumbled in.

"Hey Fuzzbush, how's it going. On your way to pry the gold out of some poor patient's teeth?" Doris rose up as if escaping a bad odor. She left without another word. Frank jerked his thumb in the direction of the closing door, "One uptight bean counter, and no sense of humor. Hope she isn't fucking with you." I stood and jammed the wallet and keys in my pocket.

"Not any more than usual. She left me a few things." I picked up the note and immediately recognized Iris's writing. Her voice floated through my head, "Paul, Your car is in Lot D, Aisle 3, full tank of gas. Iris."

Frank noticed my eyes hugging the page, "If that's her phone number throw it away, the idea of bouncing around with Doris gives me the creeps." I neatly folded the inked words, "No chance Frank." "Yeah." he grunted while moving the table and chair next to the wall. "Gotta make some room for dancing."

Frank broke into a plausible moonwalk, many belly pounds fighting gravity. Just as I was about to embarrass myself with a slide across the linoleum, the door opened with a lurch. Jane pushed a cart loaded with cake, a pitcher of juice, glasses, an old tape player, plates and forks. Behind followed Dr. Vu and Josh. "Let's get this party started!" Jane exclaimed, parking the cart at the foot of the bed.

She came to my side, gave me a big hug, and said, "Bet you thought this day would never come." I lingered in her warmth. Of course she was right but now at t-minus 60 minutes the jitters of impending change crept up my spine. "I hope you don't mind," Jane continued in a low voice, "I called Josh, and I tried to reach your friend Iris but the number we had was disconnected." I grabbed each of her hands and gave them a squeeze. "This is fine; you have been great to me." A veil of moisture clouded her eyes.

"Hey, none of that in here," shouted Frank, "I am sure there's a rule against nurses holding hands with patients." He put a weighty arm over my shoulder. "I'm an ex-patient now; I can hold hands with anyone, even you." I grabbed his calloused paw, "I want to thank you too Frank, I enjoyed your company." He took a turn like a circus bear before crunching me in a hug. Just as the last gasp of air left my lungs he let go. "You're a good guy Paul; I wish you all the best."

Suddenly it was Jagger time, "Ride like the wind at double speed, I'll take you places that you've never been. Start it up." I looked toward the cart; Vu was cranking the volume on the boom box. He noticed my gaze, "Can't go wrong with the Rolling Stones." he said before coming to my side. "Let me give you one last exam." Vu bobbled my head, "Not bad at all," he said with a hint of pride. "I have seen worse." "Yeah but were they alive?" I razzed. Vu just smiled and pointed toward the cake, "Did you notice?" A rectangle of white icing served as background for blue letters proclaiming, "Paul Good Rid Dance"

"Nice, special sentiment for me?" I quizzed. "It's tradition," Vu explained, "When a patient is discharged the caregivers do a little dance. Sort of a bon voyage waltz." Sounded corny but tradition is tradition. We got in a circle with our hands on each other's shoulders and did a combination of the hokey pokey and Hava Nagila. Frank's belly, Jane's boobs, and Josh's hair bounced in rhythm. Vu and I did our best just to hang on. As the last bars to Jumpin Jack Flash faded away we all gave a whoop. Everyone laughed and caught their breath.

After a few moments Jane said, "Presents or cake Paul, your choice." Channeling my inner five year old I said, "Presents now, cake later." I sat on the edge of the bed while my farewell troupe gathered in a semi-circle. Frank pulled a crudely wrapped gift out of one of his many pockets. "Something to keep the wheels greased." he said with a wink. I tore the paper open revealing a can of WD40. It was met with head shakes. "Thanks Frank." Jane handed me a scroll tied with a red ribbon. "A degree from the college of pain?" I asked. She gave me yet another roll of her big, brown eyes. "Just open it wise guy." I unrolled the parchment which heralded the fact that I had been awarded five free home cooked dinners upon three days' notice. "Great, today is Monday, how about Thursday?" I said to smiles all around. "Sorry Paul, I am working all week, how about next Tuesday?" "I'll be there."

Josh had been hanging back until now, he stepped forward and handed me a small box wrapped in newsprint. "You might need this in the meantime." Inside was a French Foreign Legion hat, wool felt with a shiny black bill and white cotton draped down from the bottom edge. I put it on and gave a quick salute. "Most appreciated sir, I like it." Vu chirped up, "Not a bad idea to wear it outside, good sun protection." Frank had a pained look on his face, "Maybe if you're in Africa but around here you are going to look a little weird."

I took the hat off and set it on the bed. Weird would be me with or without headgear. Vu reached into his pocket and pulled out an envelope. "It's a free session with a therapist, good for your morale. You can open it later. I placed his present next to the others, "Thank you for putting up with me Dr. Vu, I know I was an asshole at times."

Jane had cut the cake. Plates of sweetness were washed down with apple juice. Frank told the tale of yet another plugged toilet. Josh ate a second piece. I packed the gifts, except for the hat, in my suitcase. Vu needed to see a patient; he shook my hand and wished me well. Frank's cell phone went off, broken pipe in the boiler room. "Take care," he said, "And don't be a stranger. You know where I live." Jane cleaned up and pushed the cart out the door. "Be back with your chariot." she said with a grin.

Josh and I stood around like a couple of lost Shriners. "You know," he confided, "that nurse has one hot body except for that red spot on her face. She should get one of those Phantom of the Opera masks." Josh had a prop for every deformity. "Jane is a great person; I wouldn't have made it without her." "I didn't mean to put her down," Josh replied with a pained look, "she must be someone special to work here." Josh bounced back and forth on his ratty sneakers. "Hey," he said a little too loudly, "do you need a ride?" I put a hand on his shoulder, "Thanks for the offer, I'm good." He seemed relieved. "Well I better hit the road, see you around and take it easy." Josh left, I waited for Jane.

AFTER THE HOSPITAL

Jane had wheel chaired me to the front door despite my protest, "You don't mess with this tradition either." She gave me a kiss on the cheek and hurried back to work.

True to her word Iris had left my car in Lot D. I opened the dust covered trunk and threw in my bag. A few hits of the window washer cleared weeks of particulate. I turned the key and the V-8 Northstar roared to life. It felt could to be the driver and not the driven.

After a couple of turns and one light I was lost. Without thinking I steered the Cady alongside a bus stop, rolled down the passenger window and asked an old man leaning on a cane, "Which way to the freeway?" He hunched over to the car and squinted in my direction. "Next light, go left, four or five blocks, you'll see the sign for the 101." "Thanks a lot." I replied. "Good luck." he said, "And you might want to buy a new razor, your face looks a little rough." I gave a wave before rolling up the window. If only the rest of the world had his old eyes.

As I gunned up the on ramp my back rammed the seat and a whoop shot out my smiling lips. I was back in charge of my life. Ten minutes later my old neighborhood beckoned, a long lost friend. Gas stations, strip malls, fast food joints, assorted offices, apartments, the sundries of suburbia. The Cady needed a bath, it practically steered itself into Mr. Genes Clean Machines.

I pulled up to the attendant and rolled down the window. A plump Latino woman wearing Genes trademark green shirt and khaki pants chirped, "Welcome, what type of service would you like?"

Then she saw my face. Her smile disappeared; she made the sign of the cross, muttered a few words in Spanish, and ran away. I watched in the side view mirror as she approached a male co-worker and excitedly pointed in my direction. The word "diablo" filtered back to me. The man, also Latino, skinny with black hair in a ponytail, motioned for the woman to go inside before slowly walking toward my car.

He issued no greeting, instead his eyes fixated on me. I recognized him from previous visits; Manny usually wore a Dodger cap. We always engaged in some baseball banter. I was a stranger to him now. "I'll take the usual, number four." I said in an attempt to disrupt his eye maneuvers. He came out of his trance with a start. "Sure, yeah a number four." he mumbled. I handed over fifteen dollars. He took the money with a slight tremble in his hand, and then gave it back. "This one is on the house. I am sorry about Carmen, she gets a little excited at times. Your face, it, it, is different, you know." I stuffed the money back in my wallet. "Yeah, I understand." I replied, "Tell Carmen I am sorry if I upset her, next time I'll wear this hat." I put Josh's gift on my head. Manny grinned, "Good idea. Roll the window up and have a Gene Clean day."

There were no welcome home signs on Partridge Avenue, no yellow ribbons tied to the trees; in fact there was no sign of life at all as the now gleaming Cady settled into 201's driveway. I wrestled the suitcase up the stairs to the front door. As I reached for my keys I noticed a paper taped over the entry window. ATTENTION in bold red letters topped several lines of heretos, therefores, in consideration ofs, and furthermores. It appeared Doris the Frizzbush had put a legal hex on my house in order to obtain payment of money owed. Thoughts of suffocation raced through my brain as I jammed the key in the lock. It would not turn. "Son of a fucking bitch!" I loudly muttered. A tiny voice floated over my shoulder, "They changed the lock last week."

I turned to find five feet of Martha Stewart glamour, over jeweled, large glasses, tightened skin and styled gray hair. Luckily I still had the hat on or my next door neighbor, Mrs. Dell, may have pumped her last beat. As it was she narrowed her red lips, bulged her eyes and grabbed at her neck. "Oh my" she said, "You really were hurt. I am so sorry." Mrs. Dell placed a cold hand on my forearm. "Is there anything I can do to help?" I motioned toward the house, "Who changed the locks?" She stood back and lowered her voice, "Two men in suits, they waited for a blue van, must have been a locksmith. Didn't take more than ten minutes." I rattled the door latch one more time. Mrs. Dell stood like a sentry, watching my every move. "They want money for my medical bills; guess they think my house is fair game. Not much of a welcome back." "Yes, I can imagine. My heart bypass cost a small fortune."

We stood like potted plants on the porch. I had no idea where to go, the thought of a spare room at the Dell household began to germinate. "It was an explosion wasn't it?" she asked. When I didn't quickly reply she stammered, "I don't mean to pry; if you don't want to talk that's O.K. It's just there was quite a stir that day." She was trolling for information, over the fence fodder for the next neighborhood gossip session. "Yeah" I replied, "My grill blew up." Mrs. Dell shook her head in affirmation, "I thought so, I saw that cute friend of yours take it away a few days later." Was there anything this manicured matron missed? "I remember because she drove that powder blue Mustang. My late husband had a green one." There was a time drift before Mrs. Dell snapped back to the present.

"Anyway, that grill looked pretty beat up. There was an older man helping her get it in the trunk. I waved when they left but I don't think they saw me." I started to pick up my suitcase, "Thanks for the information Mrs. Dell, have a good day." She didn't move, my exit was blocked. "If I were you," she practically whispered, "I would look under that tub of flowers before you leave." Her eyes motioned toward a ten gallon terra cotta container holding lavender in need of a good soaking. Once again she gripped my arm, "I will pray for you every day." "Thanks." I said as she walked down the stairs, "I appreciate that."

Mrs. Dell was half way home before I pushed the flower pot aside. Underneath was a key. I turned the lock and entered my past.

A layer of dust had settled onto all that I had left behind, a thin film of time, lost sand from life's hour glass. I left the suitcase by the door, threw my hat in the air, and walked to the stereo. The power button clicked without activation. After three attempts I checked the plug. It was snugly in the wall socket. A few flips of the nearest light switch also proved futile. The bastards had turned off the electricity. There would be no rock and roll today.

The backyard drew me like a magnet, across the concrete to the spot of my fiery baptism. Was it an initiation or a cleansing? A calling to a new life or punishment for the old? Just plain bad fucking luck? The last few weeks of hospital routine had dulled the desire to pick at that pimple on fate's ass. Now, as I stood in the high grass surrounding a patch of singed earth, the Woe is Me Chorus opened their hymnals to the dirge section and lamented my state. Remnants of my rescue still littered the lawn. Rubber tubing, plastic saline bags, torn cotton.

A wave of resignation swept over me. I stepped outside my re-aligned skin and objectively reconstructed those fateful moments. The grill was there. I set the steaks here. The propane tank valve opened with a firm twist. There was a crashing noise from the kitchen. I ran inside. Iris broke a vase. A gift for me. And more gifts. Then I returned to this place, pushed the ignition button and blew myself away. Right here, not that long ago. A plaque should be installed. "On this spot Paul Lawton caused quite a stir."

I slowly walked back inside, retrieved the suitcase and dragged it to the bedroom. Clothes in the closet, dirty laundry in the hamper, messy sheets on the bed. I unlatched the bag, my going away gifts rested on top. A twist on the WD 40 can revealed a pint of Frank's favorite. Vu's envelope, Jane's dinner invitations, and underneath a white cardboard box emblazoned with a red cross. Inside was every burn patient's little helper. Syringes and vials of elixir.

A note in Jane's hand was tucked neatly along the edge. "Dear Paul, For those times when you need to return to the womb. Use with care.—your nurse." Liquid invitations to an alternate reality. I was grateful. It was tempting to push the plunger right now. I needed my wits, however, squatting in my own house. I found Traditore's card at the bottom of my bag. He had an office in a high rise along the bay. Time for a road trip.

I hit the bathroom, washed and again looked at my face. Thanks to Vu's efforts I was now a symmetrical horror show, a flat top of hair floating above twin swatches of earless, twisted lizard skin rimming a valley of chin to forehead normalcy. So it is.

Reaching for my hat I realized that an alteration was in order. Not many folks sported foreign legion attire in this neck of the woods. I used scissors from the kitchen to cut off the black bill. Upstairs I picked up a Coyote baseball cap and stuffed the remaining white cotton protective cover into the underside. It fit nicely. A few staples secured all in place..

After returning the key to its hiding place I slid into the Caddy for the drive to the Traditore Law Offices which were located on the tenth floor of a green glassed building hugging the shore. Keeping my eyes straight ahead I avoided human contact until reaching the receptionist. A dishwater blonde wearing a Star Trek head set gave me a nod while stating, "That's right, no recovery no fee. Just come down, no appointment necessary or we can go to you. Thanks for your call." A click of the keyboard and her attention was mine.

"Can I help you?" she said in an overly cheery voice. "I hope so." I haltingly replied, my social skills, such as they were, had rusted in the hospital. "I need to see Mr. Traditore about my case." "I see." she said, "Who should I say is asking for him." "Paul, Paul Lawton." I said with a little more confidence.

She turned and grabbed a clipboard. I watched as her green eyes scanned what appeared to be a list of names. When she hit mine fireworks went off across her pale face. She quickly set the board down, unhooked her headset and crossed to my side of the desk. "Mr. Lawton, please follow me." We turned a corner where she opened a door to a small conference room with a view of the bay and hills beyond. "Would you like water, coffee, tea, fruit juice?"

she asked. "No thanks." I said. "Fine then, I will let the team know you are here. Make yourself comfortable." The team. Hell I had a team, complete with cheerleader.

Leather chairs fronted a shiny wooden table. Two paintings, swirls of bright colors, hung at each end of the room. All was neat and polished a show place not a work place. On both sides of the door, like hunting trophies, hung framed checks, million dollar payouts from various insurance companies. Next to several of the checks were pictures of a smiling Traditore with various poor souls in wheel chairs, or missing limbs, or holding mementos of an untimely deceased relative. None had smiles of nearly the same wattage as their attorney except for one long haired man whose legs abruptly ended just at the knee. He seemed to be in the midst of unfettered glee. Upon closer inspection a check for $7.5 million from Travelers Insurance made payable to Todd Coos and Traditore might have influenced his demeanor. For good measure he was wearing a Ramones shirt. Todd Coos, what the fuck kind of name is that?

I plopped my harvested ass onto the warm leather and turned to admire the view. The San Mateo Bridge stretched over the small bay waves. A few windsurfers cut through the scene. A great convergence of earth, sky, and water. A mind drifter extraordinaire. I thought of days at the lake as a kid, swimming, tanning, throwing the Frisbee. Contentment settled over me. Then the door opened.

"Mr. Lawton, welcome to the office. I am Marcia, assistant to Mr. Traditore." she said while extending her hand in greeting. Marcia was dressed in a beige skirt with a pale white blouse. Her dark brown hair was cut short, framing an attractive face. Like the receptionist before her Marcia had her helpful meter turned way up. "Mr. Traditore is in court but I am very familiar with your case. How are you? Is there anything you need?"

She had a long yellow legal pad in front of her, pen poised at the ready. I took her questions in order. "I just got out of the hospital. When I went to my house the locks had been changed. There was a notice about a lien or something. I have been told my health insurance was cancelled and my buyout money is gone." I was getting emotional, pity spiced with anger. "So I need money, a place to live, and a job. You keep those in the back room?" Marcia reached across and took my hand. "I am sorry Paul; I know you have been through a horrible ordeal. Don't worry we will get through this together." She picked up the phone and spoke in a low tone, "Please bring Mr. Lawton's file in."

While we waited Marcia asked me to take my hat off. I complied without thinking. "I have seen your hospital pictures," she said while looking my face over like a famous painting, "the doctors did a good job considering the extent of your injuries." A quick knock preceded the appearance of young man carrying two red wells full of paper. He appeared startled at first but quickly regained his composure before setting the documents on the table and leaving. Marcia separated a few folders before moving a clipped manila envelope off to one side.

She then explained that my lawsuit was underway, the parties were exchanging written questions. I signed several verification forms. "We will use these as the case continues." Marcia explained. I learned that Traditore had hired all sorts of experts. "We are waiting for reports from our economist and vocational rehabilitationist." she said, "But I have an extra copy of our liability expert's findings should you wish to read why your accident happened." Marcia slid a plastic covered binder in my direction. It looked like a college term paper. I wanted to grab it like a drowning man fighting for a life line. Instead I casually reached over, rolled it up like an old magazine before cramming it into my jacket pocket.

Marcia placed her hands together as if in prayer. "I know your present financial condition is dire." she began. Her eyes gazed out as if addressing multitudes. "And you may not believe it but this is the best thing that could ever have happened for you." Marcia quickly explained how sympathetic I will appear to a jury. "Here's a fine young man who had just achieved the American dream when he was tragically struck down due to the negligence of a big corporation. Further, as if taking away his face was not enough, they caused him to lose his home and all he had worked so long and hard to obtain. You, ladies and gentlemen, must restore that dream." Marcia finished by pounding her small fist on the table. She seemed pleased with herself.

As I mulled over her argument Marcia opened the manila envelope she had set aside earlier. After running her words a few times around the Bullshit Corral I began to see the method to her perversity. The worse off I was the more it would take to make me whole. Whole as in "A whole lot of greenbacks." The more dead presidents for me the more dollars to spread around Traditore Enterprises. Hell I could get my own spot on the wall of fame.

Marcia reached into the envelope and pulled out keys, a small notebook, and a credit card which she neatly arranged in front of her. I detected a slight throat clearing directing my attention upward. "Mr. Lawton I am sure you are aware, but I need to reiterate nonetheless, that whatever you discuss with anyone from this office is strictly confidential. Also you should not discuss your case with anyone else. Do you understand?" It felt a little like being initiated into a secret society. "Sure," I practically whispered, "We are on the same team." Marcia smiled, "Good, I like that." Then she pushed the envelope's contents toward me. "These are for you, to make things a little easier.'

The notebook contained phone numbers, work and home, of various Traditore associates, and addresses for the Sunset Arms Apartments and Square One Parking. The credit card was in my name. The keys had a green plastic tag with SAA #415 stamped on both sides in red. "The apartment is nothing fancy. We need to be consistent with your income from working as an attendant in the parking garage." They had arranged employment and housing in order to keep me occupied as my case ran its course. "Sometimes we have to wait a year or two to get the best result. You should start the job within a month or so." The credit card was to soften the ride. I was to treat myself to the occasional "fun time" or "new toy."

Marcia suggested I leave town for a few weeks, "Maybe you should see your parents. We could use their help at trial." The phone rang before I could admit she made a good point. "I will be right out. Get her some water." Marcia ordered. She stood up quickly and once again extended her hand. "Sorry, another client needs attention. We will keep in touch at every step of the way and if you need anything at all just call." "Thanks, for everything." I meekly said. "Sure," she replied, "Don't forget the keys. I will send Ryan back in for the file."

I picked up my new life: keys and notebook in a pocket, credit card in the wallet. I stood, put on my cap and took in the view one more time. Ryan entered without a sound causing me to practically jump out of my second hand skin when he pronounced, "Impressive sight isn't it." After jamming my heart back down my throat I turned and said, "Yeah, it is something alright."

He started to pick up the folders. "Sorry about your accident. I have been helping out on your case." Another teammate. "Are you a lawyer?" I asked since he looked as if he should still be delivering newspapers on his bike. "Not yet," he responded, "Second year of law school. I am doing an internship here." "Do you like it?" "Yeah, it is interesting, something different every day." "Maybe you'll get your picture on the wall someday." I said. Ryan seemed puzzled for a moment. "Oh, you mean those." he gestured with a roll of his eyes. "There a little too much for my taste but I guess million dollar checks are good advertising."

My attention was again drawn to Coos and his deranged smile. "What do you know about Mr. Big Grin over there?" I inquired. Ryan, files in hand, laughed. "You mean 'Hot Rod' Coos. His lawsuit was before my time but I have heard stories. He was an up and coming race car driver from Stockton before his accident. Quite the character." he said before heading down the hall, my legal hopes under each arm. Go team.

I approached the reception desk knowing that I was a VIP here at Traditore's. "Excuse me," I said, "I was wondering if you could do me a favor." "Sure." she said. Her eyes beckoning. "Marcia suggested I contact Mr. Coos to discuss the legal process." I began my lie. "Only she was called away before I could get his address." I left the inference float in the air like a soap bubble. It finally popped loud enough for the receptionist to suddenly turn toward her computer. "No problem." A few mouse clicks later she scribbled some lines on a large post-it. "Here you go." "Thanks."

1580 East Weber Street, Stockton, CA. was written in a neat, cursive script. I knew I wanted to meet Hot Rod. I just didn't know why.

The Sunset Arms was a non-descript four unit building on a leafy street in Redwood City with a side drive leading to parking in the rear. I maneuvered the Caddy into a covered space. Unit 415 was on the second floor. I opened the door and yelled out, "Honey I'm home." My voice echoed off the freshly painted walls. Traditore had done well. The place was nicely furnished complete with stereo, large screen television, cable, leather chairs and a queen in the single bedroom. On the kitchen counter I found a note indicating maid service was on Tuesdays and it included laundry. Not a house in the hills but not bad.

I had not told Marcia about my unlawful entrance into the old homestead. There was the need for one more break- in to retrieve my things. But first I sat down to read the report of one John Feinman PHD titled **Factors Causing Lawton Accident,** twelve pages of diagrams, pictures, and words. Many words all leading to one conclusion.

The Lawton accident occurred due to a defective regulator on the involved gas grill. A regulator controls the amount of gas released from the propane tank to the grill burner. The Cain grill regulator was susceptible to leaking propane when the cylinder was turned on and the grill was not in use. After an amount of time (anywhere from 8 to 12 minutes) the rotten egg smell caused by the addition of ethyl mercaptan to the odorless propane gas fades. The user has no idea a problem exists. Any attempt to start the grill will result in an explosion and an ensuing fireball. The Cain Company recognized this problem three years ago and issued a recall. The Lawton grill was negligently allowed to remain in the chain of commerce.

I set the report on the couch. The Lawton accident, the Lawton grill. I had been reduced to a commodity, this time in the legal arena. Mr. Feinman PHD was one of many massaging the facts, spouting concern, giving opinions. Others were feeding off the simmering carcass: conomists, psychiatrists, burn specialists, life planners, rehabilitationists, plastic surgeons. They all would chew on my misfortune, earning money analyzing my plight. Traditore had his; the Cain Company would have theirs. Wonk warriors jousting in the legal arena. Justice for Lawton. Justice for Cain. Justice for all.

It dawned on me, contrary to Dr. Dan's exhortations, that life's rudder was still not in my hands. The hospital had set the course before handing the helm to the law men. Here is your health, retrieve your wealth. A system was in place for dealing with us victims tangled in the chain of commerce.

Feinman's analysis threw fuel on the pissed off fire that had been slowly fading out in the backwoods of my soul. It is bad enough Cain made an exploding grill in the first place, it really sucked that they knew about it and still sold one to me. Well technically Grills R Us sold it to me. Traditore also had his foot on their necks. "You fucking bastards." I muttered. "Fucking bastards all."

I resisted the urge to swim in the "why me" river again. It was moving time. Back to the car, back to the house, back to go forward. I felt like a trespasser in my own driveway. Once inside I quickly retrieved my lone luggage and set it by the door. In the garage were a few cardboard boxes which I filled with books and music. There was no need to take anything else, Traditore had seen to that. Two trips to the Caddy, ready to go. Only I didn't.

In the fading light I walked the rooms. There were splices of my time drifting in the air; snapshots of the good life along with miles of unexposed film. What would the future have been for that newly minted young millionaire mugging for the camera? What shots would have filled the reels had the lens not broken?

For grins I buried the key in the planter as I left. There was no looking back once the Caddy hit the street. My life was not here anymore. I was in flux. Instability marked my steps. No navigator sat beside me. I rolled down the window, cranked up the music and drove to the apartment. It wasn't long before my stuff spread out over the new digs, a rash of cds, paperbacks, t-shirts, jeans. While emptying the suit case I finally opened Dr. Vu's envelope. On a prescription form he had written, "For relief in time of stress, call 408-555-1784, mention my name. Two refills." Probably another counselor, I set the paper next to the phone. At this point a pizza sounded better.

About the time I finished a shower the doorbell rang. A pimple faced kid in a Domino's cap was pulling a box out of a warming blanket when he looked up and saw my freshly scrubbed face. He almost dropped the pizza before handing it to me. "That will be $15." he sputtered. I grabbed the box while looking at his name tag. "Dave." I began "My name is Paul and I can't cook to save what is left of my ass." He stood there, mouth slightly agape. "So I order take out a lot, you will, provided this pie doesn't taste like dog shit, be seeing me often."

Dave nodded his head like it was on a spring. "I know you are wondering what happened to my face." The nodding increased in intensity. "I was burned in a gas grill explosion. Everything works and no it doesn't hurt." I handed Dave a twenty, "Keep the change." I motioned, "Any questions?" He stuffed the twenty in his pocket. "Naw," he said, "See you next time." I had a friend in the pizza business, things were looking up.

Pepperoni, mushrooms, and onions had not excited my taste buds since the explosion. Half the pizza was gone before I came up for air. I finished the rest while watching the news on T.V. The world had spun many times during my recuperation, nothing seemed to have changed; news, weather, sports, each with its own drama. No mention of Paul Lawton's release from the burn unit, it would have made a nice human interest story. Channel surfing proved to be only a momentary distraction. I was still hyped up, freedom made my feet bounce. I grabbed Vu's note. What the hell, it was a time of stress.

A throaty, female voice vibrated the air waves. "Hi, it's Mimi." I was taken aback. "Hello, is someone there?" "Yeah, yeah, sorry." I mustered, "I am Paul, Paul Lawton. Dr. Vu said I should call this number." Mimi's tone went from confused to friendly, very friendly. "Hello Paul, I am glad to hear from you. Dr. Vu did mention your name. Would this be a good time for me to come over?" "Sure, sure." I rattled the phone line. After emptying a case of nerves I gave her my address. "I'll be there in about an hour." Mimi said. I picked up Vu's prescription, "For relief in time of stress." What had Vu wrought?

If she knew Vu, Mimi would know who I was. There was no need to worry about impressions or explanations. I put things in neater piles, turned on some tunes, brushed my teeth, and waited. When the bell chimed I was ready, until I opened the door. There stood five foot three shapely inches squeezed into knee high boots, faded blue jeans, a 49er t-shirt and leather jacket. Mimi had waves of curled raven hair splashing onto her shoulders. Her green eyes danced above a white capped smile. A large canvas bag hung over her right shoulder, brushing up against an awesome chest.

"Hi Paul, I'm Mimi" I stuck out my hand. She ignored my greeting, moved past my hand and in for a tight hug. After a few seconds Mimi pulled back, "Well, aren't you going to invite me in?" "Sure, sure." I stumbled, "Sorry, come on in." She walked by, took off her jacket, and headed to the refrigerator. "How about a beer, Paul, the drive over made me thirsty." Traditore had stocked a dozen Anchor Steam bottles. "Sure, sounds good." I said. She laughed while popping the tops, "You sure like to say sure a lot." Mimi handed me the cold bottle, "Don't be nervous, I don't bite on the first visit."

We sat down next to each on the sofa. "Dr. Vu told me they just let you out." "Yeah," I replied, "Just today. How do you know Dr. Vu?" Mimi set her beer on the side table and reached into her bag. "He helped me with my career, Vu is a great guy." She pulled two dvds out and handed them to me. "Here, you can have these, sort of a housewarming gift. I signed them." House warming, more like set the house on fire. The first movie was titled *Bases Loaded* and featured a suggestive picture of Mimi in a skimpy uniform, the second screamed out *Eaten Alive*, with Mimi tied to a jungle tree. Praise the lord and pass the lube, Mimi was a porn star.

"Wow, thanks a lot." I said with a cracking voice. "Have you seen my work?" she asked. My eyes nervously shifted from her sumptuous body inches from mine to a picture on the dvd. Her work? "No, sorry I have been in the hospital quite a while." I replied. Mimi's face dimmed, "Dr. Vu told me about the explosion. It looks like he did a pretty good job fixing you up." We each took a long gulp of beer. "Yeah, he did the best he could with what was left."

"So what did Dr. Vu do for you?" I asked. "Well, aside from the obvious," she began, looking down at her boobs which she suggestively swayed, "He pouted up my lips, shortened my nose, and bleached out the dark skin around my anus." A porno princess check list. "Here's to the good doctor." We toasted with a clink of our bottles. The beer was giving me courage. "So how did you get into the business?".

Mimi was born in San Jose, her dad was a construction worker, and her mother sold kids clothes at Sears. She had two younger sisters, public schools, summer camp, birthday parties, a solid middle class life. After high school came junior college and a part time job selling smoothies. Late one night, a coworker, Julie, confided after a few drinks, that she picked up some good cash working as an "extra" in adult films. Julie said there was no sex involved she mostly just stood around as background. She told Mimi there was a shoot the next day. Julie was sure she could get her a role, two hundred dollars for three hours. Mimi agreed to have Julie pick her up at two o'clock.

"I really didn't know what to expect. I had seen a few pornos. The thought of watching people have sex was pretty exciting." Julie drove to a large house secluded in the woods near Hillsborough. There were plenty of cars and a few large trucks parked in the circular driveway. At the front door a woman sat behind a folding table. She recognized Julie, took one look at Mimi, and agreed to put her in the cast. "I signed a few papers, she handed me one hundred dollars, and said there would be one hundred more when the day was done.'

Once inside they found cameras in the kitchen, living room, and library. A few women with too much make up stood around in short robes. A group of muscular men were off to one side smoking weed. A short, bald headed man with a head set came over. "You girls go back to the bedroom and put on maid outfits then report to the kitchen."

The costumes were skimpy but did not make Mimi uncomfortable. Soon someone yelled for quiet. Two girls, also in maid uniforms, dropped trays of glasses on the counter, opened a pantry door and proceeded to lick, grab, kiss, and finger each other for the next ten minutes. After they each moaned and groaned, the bald man yelled "Cut!" "Everyone clapped and the two women gave each other a high five."

Mimi spent the next few hours in and out of various costumes. She saw a great variety of sexual activity and, as she was leaving for the day, with two hundred dollars in her purse, Mimi was approached by the man with the head set. He handed her a business card. "You have a good look; I think you could do well in this business. Give me a call Monday, we're shooting another film." He squeezed her hand. "My mind yelled 'No way', but I put his card in my purse.' Mimi told him she would think about it. And think she did.

"I was not a slut or anything, I had a few relationships and some one night stands. My sexual appetite was pretty high; I got off one way or another every day. But this was something totally unexpected. Having sex on camera for money had never crossed my mind." Mimi set the card on her dresser. She spent the weekend studying and selling smoothies. On Monday Mimi decided to give Rex Klak, talent agent, a call. "I figured it couldn't hurt to talk. Plus my future employment prospects didn't look all that great. I was a C student without much of a plan."

Rex was happy to speak to Mimi. He explained they were shooting a movie "Out in Nature." and there was a small role she could have. "You and another girl give blow jobs to a couple of park rangers. One scene, five hundred dollars." Mimi hesitated, Rex waited a few moments. "Come on kid, it will be fun." He made it sound like they were going to an amusement park. Mimi was surprised to hear herself say, "O.K. I will give it a shot.' Rex seemed pleased, he gave her the address. "See you tomorrow."

That afternoon Mimi quit her smoothie job. The next afternoon she was on her knees in the woods of Marin performing oral sex on Tom, a guy she had met twenty minutes before. There was much starting and stopping as camera angles were changed. Everyone was friendly and professional. When it was finished the director said "Good work girls." Mimi watched a few more scenes, picked up her check and left. "I felt fine, it was acting after all. Not the kind of movie to show my parents but nothing I was ashamed of either."

Rex received good feedback on Mimi's work. Over the next month he arranged for her to film ten more scenes. There were porno movies shooting almost every week. Mimi was on her knees a few more times before having straight sex. She learned to exaggerate ecstasy, keep track of the camera locations, and a few new positions. "I made almost five thousand dollars, quit school, found an apartment, and told my family I was selling real estate."

Mimi continued to get calls from Rex. She noticed it was always for small parts, sex on the side, never a starring role. When she commented on this fact Rex explained that she was lacking certain attributes required of the lead actresses. "You need larger tits, lips that can suck the chrome off a trailer hitch, bigger hair, smaller nose, and get that ring around your asshole lightened up." Rex was not a diplomat.

Mimi went on line and made some telephone calls. She would have to work over a year at least to afford the surgeries. "That's where Dr. Vu comes in." Mimi's sister babysat for the Vu family, she had met him a few times. She knew he was a plastic surgeon. "He seemed like a nice guy so I drove to his house. He was outside playing basketball." Mimi explained her situation. "I told him I was getting bit parts in movies and wanted to do better." She didn't say anything about adult films. "But I got the impression he knew I wasn't the next Meryl Streep."

They sat down on the porch. Vu lectured Mimi about self-image and self-worth. Mimi replied that it was an occupational issue. "He chuckled and looked off across his big lawn for a few moments." Dr. Vu told Mimi that he was willing to help. He also said he did not want any money. "I almost fell off the step, I wanted to hug him."

"Not so fast," Vu said, "There is a catch." He explained to Mimi how most of his work involved burn victims, some of whom were horribly disfigured. Vu knew that low self-esteem was a major problem and he felt that sharing space with an attractive woman would be beneficial. "I will do the surgeries but you have to promise to spend time with my patients." We shook hands. Four months later a new me came to the dance."

Rex got her three starring roles within the first few weeks. "I was off the charts on the peter meter." Over the next year she made $300,000. Now Mimi was on an extended break. "You get over exposed in the industry." she explained without picking up on the pun. "Everybody has seen you do just about everything. So I am changing my hair color and style, going to tinted contact lenses, and working on a better tan. When I return it will be as Jasmine." I nodded my approval. "Sounds like a smart career move." Mimi smiled as she reached across and rubbed my arm. "Enough about me, how are you doing?"

I awoke late, rested and tired. Vu had performed another miracle. Mimi was great therapy. She listened, she laughed, she held my hand, and she cared. "I know it's tough now." she said, "But you will move on. Besides I like you and I am a good judge of people." Just past midnight she kissed my forehead and left.

After a quick shower I donned the cap and hit the road. The Burger King Drive-Thru went well. I was just another extended hand reaching for cholesterol. I drove to the park and ate on a bench, me and a few pigeons. An early Wednesday afternoon drew patrons from a limited crowd: the disabled, the retired, the unemployed, the homeless, and students killing time.. My comrades were from the fringe, strained out from the 9 to 5 world. The colander of responsibility separated us. We were looking for ways to fill our day, outcastes roaming the landscape in search of sustenance.

Back on the road I wandered the El Camino Real, burning gas, killing time. Then there it was, pulling me, as if a Grills R Us store was my destination all along. I was sure Traditore would shit a hamster if he saw me walking inside. No one noticed my entrance. It was easy to locate the Cain display; big, expensive, meat melters, a few of which looked identical to the monster that barbequed me. It was weird to be standing there, a spy in enemy territory.

A nasal voice came from above my right shoulder, "Those are some beauties alright, which one strikes your fancy." I turned to find Assistant Manager Ray Filarski, six foot two inches and thin as a flag pole. He had a note pad in one hand and pencil in the other. I watched him scribble for a few minutes before taking a step backwards. Ray raised one furry eye brow, "We are running a sale, plus free assembly." The pad came down as he cocked his head to one side and looked upon me. "Got a skin condition, hey" he said. "Smart idea to wear that hat, my sister never did now she has basil cell cancer." "Sorry to hear that." was all I managed to say. "Yeah, well she's pretty stupid anyway."

Ray took a couple of steps to the right, "This is the 690, great grill." I didn't move. "I read something about them blowing up." Ray got a pained look across his face. "That's a load of b.s. One of the idiots at our Tanforan location sold a display model. It should never have left the store. They fired the douche bag and his manager." He gave the nearest Cain a gentle rub with his hand. When I remained silent Ray furrowed his brow, "Funny thing is we always have a bunch of Cains but some guy had come into the place the night before and bought two of the same color and style. Said they were gifts. Cleaned them out. Go figure." Ray's cell phone went off. I gave a slight wave and escaped.

It proved no consolation that my case was known throughout the Grills R Us world. It was a mistake that would never be made again, one customer too late. I was the victim of a douche bag. What the fuck more could be said. I gunned the V-8 down the street, pulsing through a yellow light, getting away.

I rode to the coast, a turn out south of Devil's Slide. Waves crashed on the rocks below. The fog and sun battled for control of the sky. Salt air filled my lungs. I relaxed to the rhythm of the house band at the Pacific Dance Hall. Sea gulls glided by, riding updrafts. It had been a helluva two days. I drifted with the gulls until the fog took the high ground.

Day three began with an annoying tone punctuating the silence. It took several seconds before I realized it was the phone and several more before I found the receiver. My hello reeked of sleep, phlegm, and heart burn. It was Dr. Vu, "Paul, I hope I didn't wake you." "No, no," I lied, "I am still on hospital hours." He laughed, "Mimi gave me your number, I thought I would make sure you are following our treatment plan." For the most part I had remembered to use the right soap and put on skin cream. "Sure, I am doing O.K." "I hope you didn't find my arrangement with Mimi disturbing." Vu said. "No, no," I told the truth, "Thanks for the introduction, she is a great person." Vu agreed, "Yes she is and real down to earth despite her attributes." It was my turn to laugh.

"Paul, I need to explain something," Vu turned serious, "My understanding with Mimi does not involve sex. I only ask that she provide some companionship. I wouldn't want you to get the wrong idea, especially because of the business she is in." I suddenly found myself defending the virtue of a porno star, "I don't doubt that for a minute, we had a nice time and she went home. I would like to see her again, maybe go to a movie or something." Vu didn't press the point. "Oh before I forget," he said, "I trust you won't mind if I give Nurse Jane your number, I am sure she would like to have it." "No, not at all, I probably should call her anyway." I replied. "Good, good. Well I got to run." "Sure, thanks Dr. Vu and good luck." I rolled back onto the mattress.

I dozed away the next hour, the prerogative of the displaced. After a shower and three strawberry pop tarts the itch for action overtook my initial inertia. Only on day three the appointment book was blank. As I put a meager load into the dish washer the note from Traditore's office caught my attention. The address for Todd Coos was written in purple ink, a little heart dotted the i. I recalled the shit eating grin on the legless body, his stock car replaced by a wheel chair. I remembered wanting to meet Mr. Coos. For some reason I still felt the same way. What the hell, Stockton was only ninety miles down the road.

I drove through the Delta, over two lane bridges, across levees, past farms and down I-5. Weber Street was a mac and cheese neighborhood. Worn stucco homes, cars up on blocks, brown lawns. I pulled into the drive way at 1580. Hat on head I pushed the door bell, once, twice, three times. A blaring television suddenly went mute. The door groaned open revealing a large woman in shorts, stained t-shirt, pink curlers, cigarette dangling between chapped lips. She blew smoke over my shoulder, "Yeah, what do you want?" I looked down at the piece of paper, "I am looking for Todd Coos, his lawyer gave me this address." A choking sound preceded another cloud of nicotine exhaust, "That son of a bitch, if I ever see that bastard again it will be too soon." I wasn't certain whether she meant Traditore or Coos. "He hasn't been around here in over a year. I took care of that legless asshole for longer than I care to remember. Then he gets the big check and it's adios Cheryl."

I rocked from side to side, still avoiding eye contact. "You wouldn't happen to know where I might find him, would you." I mumbled. Cheryl flicked her cigarette onto the ground. "Why anyone would want to meet up with that shithead is beyond me. Does he owe you money or something?" I kept my eyes on the smoldering butt, "No, I have a lawsuit going. He had the same lawyers; they suggested it might be helpful if I talk to someone who has gone through the process." I could feel her eyes probing for my disability. "Yeah, well I hear he hangs out a lot at Zeni's, it's a strip club over on Eight Mile Road. Probably owns the place by now." I expressed my thanks and walked toward the car. After a few steps Cheryl called out, "If you do find the ass tell him I said 'Hi.' And tell him to stop by." I turned to acknowledge the request just as the door squeaked to a close.

Zeni's Playworld was nestled in a stand of oak trees off an asphalt road badly in need of repair. The Caddy bounced more than the oversized neon boobs advertising "Cold Beer, Great Girls, Fun Times." In the fleeting late afternoon sun only a handful of vehicles rested in the dirt parking lot. I pushed through the front door, stopped a few feet inside, and waited for my eyes to adjust to the dimly lit flesh emporium. A round, tiled stage with a silver pole planted in the center came into view; Disco balls bounced colored lights across whitewashed linoleum. Chairs fronted every square inch of the dance surface. Small tables populated the area between the stage and a worn pool table on one side and a short bar on the other. In each corner velvet curtains hung below signs announcing "Private Booths." Lou Reed's *Take a Walk on the Wild Side* crackled over a well-worn sound system.

There were no girls, great or otherwise, near the stage. A few backs clad in denim and leather hunched over the bar, nursing long neck beers. They didn't bother to swivel their stools at my entrance. The bartender was on the phone as he rubbed the wooden counter top with a rag. I scanned the room one more time, no sign of a legless asshole. Maybe Cheryl was misinformed.

As I turned to leave a hand tugged at my sleeve, "Come on in, stay awhile. Amanda will be on the stage soon." I turned to find a pixie of a woman clad in a sheer top with a red bra underneath, satin shorts, and skinny legs propped up by white stilettos with six inch heels.

She gently pulled me toward a nearby table. I sat down, the sex sprite quickly landed on my lap. She smelled of lilac, lots of lilac. With her right hand around my neck for balance, the left lightly rubbed my chest. "I am Raven, what's your name?" she murmured. "Paul." I answered. "Nice name," Raven said, her fingers paying more attention to my nipples, "Wasn't he one of the apostles?" Her tight bottom began to slowly gyrate making it difficult to recall biblical history. "Yeah, I think he was Saul a soldier and then changed his name or something." I said. The satin merry go round was moving quicker. My condition had become most obvious. Suddenly the calliope stopped.

"What are you drinking pal?" It was the bartender, dirty towel draped over his shoulder. I could feel a shakedown coming but was in no position to stand up and leave. "I'll have a beer; whatever you have on tap is fine." "Yeah right." he said before adding, "And the usual for Raven, I'll be right back." Raven promptly left my tent pole and sat down on a chair across the table. "Thanks for the drink Paul. Do you live around here? I haven't seen you before. I would have remembered that funky hat." Now it was small talk, no satin shimmy. I let out a sigh, my ass was in a trap, and only dead presidents could win its release. "No, I live by San Francisco. I came here looking for someone. Maybe you know him."

Before I could continue a headless mug of beer landed on the table, quickly followed by a plastic champagne glass. "That'll be five bucks for the beer and fifty for the champagne." the bartender bellowed. I looked up as he folded meaty arms across his chest, daring me to bitch. I pulled out Traditore's credit card, "You take Visa?" He placed one hand on the table. "Yeah but the minimum charge is $100." "No problem," I replied while handing him the plastic, "Why don't you pour yourself one of those fifty dollar glasses of water; you look like you could use a drink." His eyes bulged, "You trying to be a smartass buddy, I'll run you and your stupid hat out of here so fast it will make your ugly head spin." I was tempted to show him what a real ugly head looked like; instead I took a sip of my beer. When I set the glass down he was gone.

"Don't get upset, Charlie is a really nice guy, they just have rules around here." Raven said. I took another hit of beer, the glass was half empty. "So who is this guy you're looking for, maybe I know him." Her query pulled my thoughts away from going Pulp Fiction all over the bartender's fat ass. I finished the beer with one big gulp. Just as I returned the empty glass to the table a full one appeared. "On the house." Charlie announced with a smirk on his face. I signed the slip, $105 even. "Thanks for the beer." I said. He walked away without another word.

My gaze returned to Raven, she seemed a little bored. "He has no legs." I blurted out. Raven looked toward the bar then quizzically back at me. "The guy I am looking for, he doesn't have any legs. His name is Todd, Todd Coos." I said. Raven's face went from dim to bright in a few seconds. She reached over and slapped my arm. "I know that horny bastard, Hot Rod Coos. Shit they practically named one of the private booths after him. He's popped more wads in here than Charlie has champagne corks." Raven chewed on a finger nail, smiling as she looked toward a velvet curtain. "He was good for business, paid with a credit card just like you."

Since she referred to him in the past tense I assumed Mr. Coos would not be gracing this fine establishment anytime soon. "Do you know where I might find him?" I asked, snapping Raven back to the present. She held up her index finger, turned and yelled, "Anyone know where Hot Rod hangs out these days?" A group chortle arose from the bar, several sonsofbitches echoed off the peeling paint.

As the uproar calmed one of the stools turned slightly. "Try Dick's Pool Hall, saw old tripod there a few days ago playing poker in the back." As I finished the beer Raven bent forward, "If you find him tell him to call me at my mom's. He knows the number. Todd can't come in here anymore; Charlie threw him out a few months ago." She leaned even closer and whispered, "Hot Rod did Charlie's wife." I tapped the table, stood up and thanked Raven for her help. "Dick's is over on B street." she said before walking away.

It figured that anyone married to Charlie would consider sex with a legless man a step up. That was a given, however it made me wonder about Mr. Coos. Two women longed for him and one guy had thrown the legless bastard onto the gravel.

These thoughts roamed my beer buzz as I wandered Stockton in search of alphabet streets. After a few trees, statesmen, birds, and animals I discovered J Street. A quick left, six short blocks, brought Dick's Cue Emporium into view a neon eight-ball glowing in a large window. I parked and began to walk across the road just as the door opened followed by a few gallons of dirty water which barely reach the curb. A voice yelled out, "You're late."

The rattle of the screen door announced my entrance. No one was playing pool at any of the six tables. A long haired teenager was slumped over a pin ball machine, his torso jerking as he approached tilt. A mop sat next to a bucket by the ancient juke box. A butterball of a man leaned over a glass counter beneath which various cue sticks rested in leather cases. His gray hair was cut short. He chewed an unlit cigar. It took effort for him to peel his eyes away from a newspaper.

"Yeah." he grunted. "I'm looking for Todd Coos." Two pudgy fingers pulled the cigar from his mouth. He spit residue onto the floor before walking toward a side door marked Private Absolutely No Admittance. "He's in there and like I said you're fucking late." Before I could ask how a total stranger could be late he turned the handle and yelled, "Coos your ride is here."

On the other side of the door dusty boxes were piled along the walls, blue smoke hung in the air with twin fluorescent lights shining over green felt. I stood in the shadows. A pile of cash was heaped at the table's center. Eight chairs were occupied, four cowboy hats, two bald heads, one baseball cap, and the long hair of Mr. Coos. I felt like Stanley finding Livingston. Suddenly the baseball cap yelled, "Fuck me, you hit the damn flush again didn't you Hot Rod." Coos became a statue. Cap man stared darts. Finally he threw in his cards. Hot Rod broke out an ear touching grin as he turned over a bluff. "Thanks boys," he said, "for your contributions."

"Yeah, yeah fuck you." baseball cap replied while motioning in my direction, "Your fucking ride is here, why don't you crawl out the door and hit the fucking road." Hot Rod laughed while stuffing bills into his shirt pocket, "Now Ric, don't kill my buzz, it ain't like I win all the time." He looked in my direction. "Time to go boys, see you ATMs later."

Coos reached to his right and the whirl of a motor rose above the shuffling cards. As he moved from the table his wheel chair seat lowered a few inches. Hot Rod had a red Fresno Bulldog t-shirt covering muscular arms and a broad chest. The stumps of his legs were buttoned into faded blue jeans. There was Arafat stubble across his face. "Nice hat my good man." he said while passing by and punching through the door. I followed.

His wheelchair barely slowed as he tossed money to the cigar cruncher, "Take it easy Fred, and keep the fish in the back happy." I hustled, just making the door before it closed. "Where's the car?" Coos asked, moving his chair back and forth like a tiger in search of prey. I pointed to the Caddy. "Not a stretch," he critiqued "but it will do." I watched as Hot Rod raced to the street center, popped a wheelie, and spun like a top. Why I looked like a limo driver was hard to fathom. Coos headed for the passenger side as I hit the unlock button. He pulled open the door, dropped a side arm down, and hopped onto the seat. This misadventure had already gone past the point of no return. I walked to the chair. "Just hit the red knob," he gestured, "It'll fold up like a cheap suit. Throw it in the trunk." After doing as instructed I got behind the wheel and turned the key. Hot Rod had pulled the seat belt across his torso. "Go up two blocks, there's a Pints and Quarts on the corner."

I drove as he turned the radio to a country station. Hank Williams complained of a cheating heart. As I parked at the liquor store Coos handed me a twenty for "Jim Beam and coke." A fifth of the former and quart of the latter later we left. "Where the fuck are the glasses?" Hot Rod barked. He had a bottle resting on each stump. "Sorry," I said, "Don't have any." Coos gave me a questioning glare before gulping the bourbon and chugging the cola. He shook his body as if suddenly chilled. "Going to have to make do."

Hot Rod rolled down the window, poured half the Coke onto the road, transferred the Beam into its place, and tossed the glass container toward the shoulder. Placing his hand over the open bottle he shook the contents before handing it to me. "I shouldn't, I am driving." Coos didn't move. I grabbed the mixture and took a swig. Caffeine and alcohol, the tingle twins, danced. "Where to Sir?" I asked. "Cache Creek Casino." he replied, "We are going to see Mr. Merle Haggard, the greatest country singer of all time."

Half way to the casino and halfway down the bottle Hot Rod raised an eyebrow and said, "If you're a limo driver I'm a fucking field goal kicker." I couldn't tell if he was angry, surprised, or disappointed. "When you were in the liquor store," he continued between swigs, "the stretch drove by." I grabbed the drink and replied, "Never said I was a limo driver." The last bars of *Whiskey River* drifted away. "That is very true." he said before extending his hand, "I'm Todd Coos." I took my right hand off the steering wheel, "Paul Lawton, nice to meet you."

We rode in silence as Patsy Cline fell to pieces. Hot Rod repositioned himself on the seat; he had a tendency to slide forward until his stubs hit the dashboard. "So Paul," he tentatively began in a thick voice, "what's with the hat?" I grabbed the rim of my creation and set it on top of the nearly empty Coke bottle. Coos did a double take, his eyes squinting. "Well fuck me and the horse I rode in on. That is one nasty excuse for a head."

He threw my cap into the back seat, finished the booze, and said, "You were burned. I had a buddy torched when some racing fuel caught fire, looked just like that after they put a piece of his ass on his neck. His wasn't that bad, I'm surprised you got any ass left. I can see why you wore the hat." I put on the blinker as the Cache Creek exit came into view. "You should have seen me before the accident," I said, "I use to rent my butt out as a movie screen." Hot Rod laughed. As I pulled the Caddy into the casino driveway Coos said, "Don't use the valet, those bastards will siphon half your tank."

We found a parking spot down a nearby row. I retrieved the wheel chair and Coos bounced from the car to the seat. He promptly hit the gas and tore across the asphalt cackling like a prized rooster. I locked the doors and walked halfway to the entrance before realizing my hat was in the back seat. Hesitation gripped my feet. Hot Rod was doing figure eights, I walked toward him, who was going to notice me next to crazy Coos anyway.

We had not gone fifty feet past the door before an Asian woman in a blue dress, with a name tag announcing Ann Phan, Floor Manager, put an arm around Hot Rod. "Todd, so nice of you to visit us again. I hope you enjoy the show; we have a booth down front reserved for you. Don't forget to visit the blackjack tables, your favorite dealers are working tonight." Coos seemed used to the fawning attention. He threw a thumb back toward me, "This is my friend Paul, how about getting him one of those special Haggard cowboy hats before he scares the old ladies away from the slot machines." Ann, who had not paid any attention to me quickly said, "Sure, no problem." She looked up and took a glance in my direction.

Years of dealing with drunks, blowhards, and assorted riff raff did not quite prepare her. Ann momentarily stiffened and a slight shiver crossed her lips, she recovered and stuck out a multi-ringed hand. "Nice to meet you Paul, a friend of Todd's is always welcomed here. Why don't you both have a drink in the lounge and I will send over a couple of hats." She turned and walked away while bringing a phone to her face.

Hot Rod had already motored over to the showroom. He looked up at a bar stool like a puppy eyeing ham slices on a kitchen counter. As I reached his side Coos asked, "How about a lift my good man?" A guy missing knees, calves, ankles and feet still packs weight. Hot Rod instructed me to kneel in front of his chair so he could propel himself off the seat and wrap his arms around my neck. "Lift from the knees." he directed. Having not strained over anything more than a suitcase in many months I envisioned the both of us falling onto the floor.

Coos's technique proved to be true. I rose up, turned toward the nearest stool and roughly deposited him onto the swiveling leather. He steadied himself by grabbing the bar. "Not bad for a beginner, you'll get the hang of it in no time." The exertion had taken the wind out of my sails; I collapsed next to Hot Rod just as he ordered two double shots of tequila. He gulped. I sipped.

A long legged blonde arrived with two buffed out cowboy hats. "Gentlemen, compliments of the house." Coos grabbed one and crammed it over my alien dome. "There you go Tex." he said to me and "Here you go darling." as he handed a fifty to the blonde. He left the other hat on the bar. "You know Paul," he began in a lowered tone, "They say the hat should rest on the ears, in your case that does not apply." Hot Rod pounded a fist on the rail while failing to stifle a laugh. After catching his breath he shouted, "Barkeep a couple of beers please."

Turning back he said, "So Tex what are we doing here?" I knew Coos had maxed out his curiosity governor. After a swallow of draft I came clean, "I saw your picture on the wall at my lawyer's office. They gave me an address. For some reason I felt like I needed to talk to you about the whole legal process, hope you don't mind." Hot Rod took a moment to digest my explanation. "My picture's on a wall and it's not at the post office, I'll drink to that." And so he did. "Yeah." I said, "You're holding a check and grinning like a rabbit in a carrot patch." Tapping his empty glass hard enough on the counter to get the bartender's attention Coos said, "Sure, sure I remember that shot, me in the chair and Traditore showing off like he had just won a blue ribbon at the county fair."

Two more beers appeared. Hot Rod stared into his glass. "That was around two years ago, I moved twice since then. How did you find me?" I replayed my visits with Cheryl on Weber Street and Raven from Zeni's. "And by the way," I concluded, "they both want you to stop by." A wide grin cracked across his face before Coos took another drink. "Cheryl wants to cut my nuts off and Raven wants to move in with me."

Our trip into the past was interrupted by the arrival of two young denim skirted ladies who sat down next to Hot Rod. He immediately turned and said, "Welcome gals, how about I buy you a drink before the show." They were country girls, large of chest, broad of beam, with brown hair curling down to their shoulders. Tammy was first chair, Brenda second. Each gratefully accepted the offer, both ordering rum and cokes. "Good choice," Coos said with a wink in my direction. "Are you here to see Merle, we just love him." Brenda said. "Yeah," Tammy jumped in, "He's a bad boy, been in prison." "Sure," Brenda replied, "just like a lot of your boyfriends." They clinked their glasses with a knowing toast.

It didn't take long for Hot Rod to spin a web around Tammy; they were lost in a silky haze of small talk and giggles. With the dim lighting and upholstered bar the fact Coos was missing the body parts needed for spurs and chaps was not known. He was just another guy tipping back a glass.

After Todd gave Tammy his cowboy hat Brenda recognized her fate and walked down the bar to sit next to me. "You guys come here often." she asked. "It's my first time, seems like a nice place." I replied. We drank in silence. "You know," Brenda broke the ice, "That hat doesn't really fit you right." She was either observant or making a play for my souvenir. "Well," I began with a slow drawl, "Hot Rod says it is because I don't have any ears." Brenda gave me a quizzical grin, "You're bullshitting, right?" I took a long swig of beer. "Wish I was, but the truth is I was in an accident, burned most of my ears off along with a good chunk of my face." The alcohol had washed my disfigured reluctance clean away.

She looked a little closer. "The sides of your face do look a little strange, like beef jerky." A mere statement, neither an insult nor a compliment. "Yeah, well I've got half a steer wrapped around the rest of my head." Brenda let out a nervous laugh, "So there's no way I get the hat?" "No, you can have it, I have another one in the car, we can make a switch later." I leaned over close enough to catch a cheap glance down her blouse, "Frankly I am not a fan of cowboy hats." Brenda laughed again, "Nothing wrong with that, it takes all kinds." Even a one of a kind guy like me.

Our conversation was interrupted by a shocked squeal from Tammy. We both turned to find that Hot Rod had spun his stool around to display his half legged state. "You were not fucking kidding, Jesus, Mary, and Joseph." Tammy didn't know if she should be sad, shocked or mad. Coos had already turned back toward his drink. Tammy leaned into his neck and whispered. They both laughed. Brenda looked at me in amusement, "You guys here for some kind of disabled convention?" "No were just here to see Merle." I replied with a glance toward the showroom. Two double shots of bourbon landed at the rail. Tammy was making up for her outburst. I knew before I lifted the glass that oblivion resided in that caramel colored concoction. Soon I lived next door.

I woke upon a bed covered in sunlight from a window whose curtain had been pulled from the wall and laid across my naked body. The scent of cheap perfume, cigarettes, and assorted bodily excretions terrorized my nose. A throbbing bass pounded my skull vying for attention with a stomach threatening to hurl. I waited for the room to stop spinning before sitting up. There was a condom covering my limp dick. I pealed it off and tossed it toward the floor. It only made it to the corner of the bed, a carnal wind sock lacking a pole.

Standing took effort. I wobbly surveyed a scene of hotel horror. Several bottles of champagne littered the floor. A large television sputtered murky colors through a cracked screen. What appeared to be a bull whip was wrapped around the sitting room chandelier. Several half empty shrimp cocktail glasses balanced precariously on a tilted marble end table. A line of chocolate syrup snaked across the carpet to the opposite side of the carnage. I grabbed a crusty towel off the back of a chair and wrapped it around my waist before gingerly crossing to the door. I took a breath and pushed.

Coos was passed out, his breathing a gentle snore. He also had been left naked and alone. His fleshy pink stumps framed a large cock, a beast at rest.

I found the bathroom after opening two closet doors. This mausoleum of marble had not escaped the battle. A lace bra hung from a wall sconce. The Jacuzzi sat half full, my jockey shorts stopping up the drain. "Merle is God" was scrawled across the mirror in red lipstick. I stumbled into the shower and let the warm water dance to the drumming in my skull. Several chorus lines later control slowly returned to alcohol ravaged regions. It took longer for any semblance of rational thought to hit my frontal lobe.

Disconnected scenes of the previous night began to flash, blurred neon smearing across a tattered canvas. An actual tear rolling down Hot Rod's cheek as Haggard sang "Mama Tried." A topless Tammy pouring champagne over saucer sized nipples. Two security guards lifting Coos off a blackjack chair after he bitched at the dealer "You squaw faced she devil" for hitting a five card 21. Brenda taking the cowboy hat off my head just before she unzipped my pants. A room service worker slapping Hot Rod's face after he grabbed her ass. Tammy arm wrestling a Keno playing truck driver for his Kenworth belt buckle. The four of us singing "Okie From Muskogee" as we did a conga line around two blue haired grandmas playing the slots. Throwing Hot Rod on the bed as he yelled, "Fuck a gimp, and go to heaven." Just from the outtakes it must have been one helluva night.

As I attempted to dry off with three wash cloths a voice strained out, "Where the fuck am I? Where's my fucking chair?' Hot Rod was awake, maybe he knew where my clothes were.

Maneuvering through the debris I spotted the wheelchair turned on its side under the piano. With effort I pulled it out. A thong was stretched from one arm to the other. I returned to the lair. "Fuck me, where's the fucking phone." bounced off the walls as I pushed Coos's ride through the door. He was leaning over the edge of the bed, one hand grabbing the backboard. My arrival attracted his attention. Hot Rod did a double take before sliding off the mattress. He hit the floor with a thud, crawled with his elbows digging into the carpet, bouncing toward the corner. His eyes raging with fear he yelled, "Fucking alien bastard leave me alone!" It was hard to keep from laughing out loud. The poor guy had pulled a sheet over himself.

"Hot Rod, it's me Paul. We're in a hotel, we saw Merle Haggard last night. Had a few drinks." The sheet slowly retreated down his face stopping just below his chin. I pushed the chair a little closer. "Stay the fuck there." Coos said, "I don't know any Paul Haggard.' I stopped and leaned over the chair back. He stared a hole in my forehead. "You're too fucking ugly to be an alien." I smiled. He leaned his head back against the wall. "Jesus, I feel like shit, you wouldn't happen to have a drink on you would you E.T.?" Hot Rod's face was now the color of the sheet, the rush of pure terror replaced by the tremors of a major hangover. "Not on me, but we may be able to scrape something up out in the party zone, why don't you hop up on the chair." Coos was in no shape to argue. He made a quick spin, grabbed the chair rail and propelled his linen covered self onto the seat.

Into the remnants I pushed a naked, sawed offed, caped wonder. "Jesus on a cracker whose room is this anyway." he groaned. "Hope to fuck it's not mine." The wheels mulched broken glass. I pushed cushions and chairs aside to clear a path to a small bar upon which rested three plants without their pots. Someone had watered them causing rivulets of mud to flow onto the floor. Behind the garden I found a half empty decanter of scotch and a bottle of tonic water. Hot Rod watched my every move. When he saw the booze he clapped his hands. "Alright Mr. Alien, don't bother looking for a clean glass." He grabbed the scotch and took a deep drink then shook his head like a dog in from the rain.

We retraced our path. I righted a leather armchair, placed it in front of the window and sat down. Coos pulled next to me. After several sips of flat tonic water hydration began to beat back my hangover. I looked out over the parking lot to the brown hills beyond. A smattering of oaks broke up the heat stroked fields. Hawks circled, seeking out the dead and dying. Fortunately for us the window was tinted.

"What the fuck time is it?" Hot Rod asked, still eying me with caution. "Looks like late afternoon to me, at least on my planet." I replied. "You know" Coos said, "If I was a pencil dicked, earless, naked skinny fuck with patches on my ass, I probably wouldn't be mouthing off." "Yeah, well if I was a half drunk, half legged, half brain hiding under a stained hotel sheet I would just keep my lips shut." After two beats of God's drum we both laughed until it hurt.

Hot Rod gave me a punch in the arm. "So who are you again?" I retraced the previous day's events up to Tammy's bourbon toast. "After that things get a little fuzzy Mr. Coos." I concluded, my hand gesturing around the suite. He spent a few moments staring outside. "Damn roofies." he muttered, "ecstasy my ass, the bitch put roofies in our drinks." Hot Rod went on to explain that Tammy had pulled out a small envelope of white powder and poured the contents into the bourbon shots. Aside from killing off a few brain cells and a few days of crazed flashbacks there wasn't much to worry about. "I've been down this road before, we'll be alright. Must have been one great time, can't wait until I remember it."

As we sunk deeper into our chairs a phone rang, beeping, buzzing, and chiming long enough for me to dig it out from under an ice bucket. I mumbled "Hello." "Yes, Mr. Coos this is the front desk, we have your clothes, and your guest's." I was surprised and inquired as to how our clothes had left the room. The clerk explained, without laughing, that we had stripped to our underwear and mooned the crowd several times from a glass elevator as it rose and fell above the casino floor.

"You caused a real commotion; we hope it was a one time performance." After assuring her we had no encores planned she agreed to send up our laundry. "Just knock and leave them by the door." I said not wanting the state of the room to be discovered, "We will take it from there." "Thank you Mr. Coos, is there anything else you need?" "Yes, yes." I stammered, "How about some chicken soup, Alka-Seltzer, and more towels." I hung up before Hot Rod could yell for booze.

Ten minutes later a knock heralded the arrival of the hangover welcome wagon. I peered out the security peep hole before cautiously opening the door. Our clothes had been laundered, wrapped and tied with string. Beside the crisp bundle were a stack of towels and a tray with bowls, spoons, a covered pot, along with half a dozen foil wrapped stomach settlers. My head swiveled up and down the hallway. The coast was clear. I threw the towels and clothes into the room before gently picking up the tray and retreating into the demolition zone. To my surprise Hot Rod ladled up a bowl of soup and slurped in. I threw four tummy tablets into the tonic water and gulped it down. "Damn good idea ordering the soup, Paul." Coos was back to knowing my name. We finished the broth, the battle for our minds and bodies turned for the better.

Hot Rod belched. "I need a bath, get me to the tub before the flies find me." With renewed vigor I moved furniture, piled garbage to one side, and wheeled Coos next to the tub. It took a few minutes to replace the cold water with hot. "Put some bubbles in." Coos demanded, "I like lots of bubbles." When all was to his satisfaction I helped Hot Rod slide over the tub wall and into the water. He bounced around a few times before growing accustomed to the heat. I left before he could ask me to wash his back.

After putting on laundered pants, shirt, and socks, I retrieved shoes from under the bed. To my surprise someone had placed my keys and wallet in the right one. When I took Hot Rod's clothes into the bathroom he was repeatedly submerging his shampoo covered hair under the last of the bubbles. He drained the water and used two towels to dry off. After Coos turned to face the wall, I reached under his arms and pulled him up and over the side of the tub. "You're not a bad guy to have around." he said while sliding his stumps into faded blue jeans. "If you weren't such an ugly fuck I would take you home to mother."

We went out to the living room. "Time to get the hell out of here, follow me." Coos said. The hall was still empty, Hot Rod lead the way to the freight elevator, apparently this was not his first time partying and dashing from Cache Creek. It too was empty. We rode to the basement, took a tunnel out to the delivery entrance, moved quickly across the parking lot, threw the chair in the trunk, and pointed the Caddy down the road. The clock said 5:30, my body said never again, Hot Rod said, "Adios motherfuckers."

As we spun rubber over the interstate Coos had me take an early exit. A two lane road wandered away from civilization into the coastal foothills. "Where we going?" I asked, hoping it had nothing to do with bourbon, country music, or roofies. "Home" he replied, "Home." A few curves later I stopped at a turn out, chaired up the Coos, and followed him down a dirt path. One hundred yards led us to an outcropping below which stretched a race track, grandstands hugging the oval, banked corners slamming into the back stretch.

Hot Rod gazed into the fading light, "Can you hear it Paul? Twenty four engines roaring, bumpers banging, metal scraping." There was a longing in his voice. He had won many races at this and other tracks throughout California. Nascar owners were starting to take notice. Life was good for the son of divorced mother of three trying to keep food on the table while working as a waitress at Applebees. Coos had gravitated to a gas station across from the restaurant on those days his mom toiled afternoons.

He went from pumping gas and washing windows to helping the mechanics with repairs. Hot Rod turned out to be an artist with a wrench. The day he got his driver's license he drove off in a 1972 Pontiac Ventura under which he had spent many hours of restoration. The day after he barely graduated from high school he entered his first race at a dirt track outside of Lodi. The trophies kept coming as he moved up in class. Jaimie Cousins, a local sports reporter who was rumored to have spent more than one night sharing his bed, gave him the nickname Hot Rod. While he was equally adept at driving both cars and women to the edge, no one bothered to ask Ms. Cousins her intended meaning.

"I lost my cherry right over there." Coos gestured toward a grassy patch next to several weathered boulders. "We came up here to watch the race but she had a different ride in mind." Her name was Betty, she was in her first year at a local junior college, Hot Rod was sixteen. Coos motored over to the site, as if physical proximity would hype up the recollection. "Betty was amazing, we did it all." Hot Rod turned back toward the ridge line, "I wonder where old Betty is today?" I wondered why there was never a Betty for me.

As the light headed west we returned to the car. "Thanks for taking the detour," Coos said, "I enjoyed the memories." "No problem," I replied. The fresh air had done us both good. The effects of the Haggard binge were fading. "How about some food?" I asked, "Seems like a week since I ate." Hot Rod gave me the raised eyebrow, "You like ribs?" I nodded. The high beams scoured the asphalt; John Prine sang about that angel from Montgomery, it was ten miles to Leon's BBQ Shack.

There was a Leon at Leon's. He made the best barbecued chicken, beef, and ribs, served with corn bread, baked beans, along with a choice of potato salad or cole slaw. Unfortunately Leon was not a people person. It was no surprise ninety per cent of his business was take-out. There were three grimy tables with metal folding chairs along the back wall. Each offered a view of the greasy kitchen were Leon, in white t-shirt, soiled apron, and black jeans, did his magic. The food was packed into square Styrofoam containers with push tab lids. Sauce bubbled over the sides like jam oozing out a porked pastry.

Coos popped over the threshold and careened across the faded green and white tile before neatly spinning to a stop next to the middle table. Leon was in the process of putting six orders into two Raley's grocery bags for a young man dressed in L.L. Bean. "I put fucking cole slaw in each one," he growled, "since you didn't fucking state a fucking prerferfuckingance." The customer waved his right hand and said "That's great." before backing out. Leon looked at the door slowly closing, "Asshole college kids." he muttered before turning in our direction.

"All out of cole slaw." he announced. "Glad to hear it," Coos chortled, "Tastes like shredded cardboard and spoiled mayonnaise anyway." Leon slowly shook his head from side to side, "No that would be your mother you sawed off shit for brains. Land of no return." Leon then walked to the entrance and shut an ugly green, wooden door just as three men in camouflage outfits approached. He flipped a sign on the window from Open to Closed before hitting the switch which extinguished a moth covered light bulb above the doorway. "So Hot Rod you buy the beers I'll throw the ribs in for free." he said. Coos rolled his eyes at me then winked, "How about you buy the beer for a change." he said. Leon was busy doling out large mounds of ribs onto two platters. "No can do half pint, got kids to feed."

Soon our table was covered with Leon's finest, a lot of everything surrounded by Budweiser long necks. Leon grabbed each of our hands, bowed his head before thanking God for His bounty. "And Lord," he concluded, "please give your child Paul here the brains to get far away from Hot Rod Coos. Amen." Coos reached for the closest rib, gnawed it like a dog and with sauce splashed on his cheeks sputtered, "Thank you Reverend Leon for those inspiring words, now pass the beans."

For the next ten minutes the room echoed with lip smacking, the sloshing of beer and the rattling of cleaned bones hitting the table. With only sauce and corn bread left we dipped the later into the former until the plates were clean. I pushed away from the table, "Mr. Leon that was one of the finest meals I have ever had." He nodded his head, "Thanks, but please don't tell anyone I got more business than I can handle now." Coos laughed, "I've offered to invest in a new building, get some help, maybe franchise. But this pig headed bastard will have nothing of it." Leon stood up and pulled three Buds out of the cooler. "And work for you," he said, "I may be dumb but I am not crazy."

Hot Rod laughed again before announcing he needed to piss. "Go ahead; wheel yourself in the back room." Leon instructed, "Pull that dick you stole from a black man out and piss in the mop sink." Once Coos left Leon said, "He's a good guy and man could he drive any car on any track. Too bad about his legs." He drank the rest of his beer. "So what the hell happened to your face if you don't mind me asking?" When I explained he chuckled, "Should leave the barbecue to the professionals." I finished my Bud, "Wish I had, believe me."

Leon pulled out another grocery bag and put the bones inside. "For the dogs," he explained, "they're happier to see me than my wife." I picked up the platters and put them on the counter. "Sounds like you got a good lawsuit just like Hot Rod had." "Yeah, I guess so," I said, "what exactly happened to him." Leon was putting the empty long necks into a cardboard case, "He don't talk about it much, I heard a friend bought him some jacks for his car and they broke or something." Coos motored back into the room, "What broke?" he asked, "Your wife's vibrator, is that why she keeps calling me?" Hot Rod popped his chair on its back wheels and spun like a top in the middle of the floor. Leon put his hands on his hips. We could only admire the whirling dervish as his laughter echoed off the walls.

Before Leon left in his white Ford pick-up he reached into the glove box and gave me a baseball cap. "An original Shack hat," he said with a grin, "Very rare, I added the side flaps to keep the bugs away for hunting, use it to keep the sun off that ugly dome of yours."

I expressed my thanks. He pointed his thumb in Hot Rod's direction, "Take care of that asshole." The gravel flew as he left the lot.

Coos was already in the passenger seat. I put his chair in the trunk. "Where to sir?" I said as I turned the key. Hot Rod grabbed my gift. "Sonofabitch never gave me one of these." He plopped the hat on his head. "You're going to have to blow me to get this back." "Yeah well how about I pull this car over and you try dragging your ass down the road." "You got a good point there." Coos said with a smile. "That's why I need the hat." I replied. He laughed but kept the cap on.

"You ever do any hunting?" he asked. I told the story of being ten or eleven, roaming the woods with my friend Burt. We each had new BB guns. Growing bored aiming at branches and rocks our attention was drawn to several robins nesting thirty feet up a maple tree. Our ammo supply exceeded our lack of ability; eventually one of the birds shrieked and fell to the ground. The robin was alive and bleeding, one eye looked toward us, accusing and sad. There was no thrill in the kill. I placed my muzzle a few inches from the orange chest, looked away and pulled the trigger. Bert had a tear down this cheek. Remorse is a bitter fruit. I never shot at a living creature again. Being responsible for ending life was not in my DNA.

As we neared the interstate Hot Rod invited me to spend the night at his place. The shortest distance to a bed sounded good to me.

Hot Rod's house was down a levee road across from an upscale marina on the delta. I parked in front of the three car garage. Once Coos was in his chair he punched in a code and the door rolled up. The space was empty except for an assortment of wheel chairs. "Pick one out, no admittance otherwise." He waited by the hallway entrance while I got comfortable in a motorized model with flame decals on the arms. Coos explained how the joy stick worked before I did a few laps around the garage. "Not bad," he said before hitting a button which opened the door. "Welcome to my world."

The house had been built for midgets on roller skates. Ramps replaced stairs, all counters, sinks, switches, and appliances had been lowered, eye level was three feet off the ground. Coos was pushing buttons at a wall counsel. Suddenly lights came on and music floated in the air. "Make yourself at home," Hot Rod said, "I need the bathroom." He disappeared down a hallway. I maneuvered the wheel chair through the kitchen and out into a large living room. There were leather couches fronting a fireplace. The flooring was oak with a few scuff marks. A bar ran along one wall with several cut out stalls for wheel chairs.

An archway lead to a dining room where a lone table stood under a crystal chandelier. After exiting down one wall I found a hallway with several doors, all with low handles. I opened one and the lights automatically came on. Various trophies lined shelves on the sidewalls. A workbench stretched between them covered with shiny tools and wrenches. I heard a flushing noise from around the corner. I shut the door and followed the sound.

Coos was rolling in my direction. "Nice place." I said. He smiled. "Was part of my settlement, they had to build a home tailored to me."

I followed as he opened a nearby door. "You can sleep here; it's a suite for those with legs." Inside everything was full size including an adjacent bathroom. Hot Rod continued down the hall. "Let's go outside." he said before turning to the left. I tried to keep up without bouncing off the walls. The backyard was pool, palm trees, chairs, fire pit, green grass, and waterfall. Coos pulled up next to a lounger, lowered his chair arm and hopped onto the cushion. I tried the same and promptly fell to the concrete. I sheepishly stood up and sat down. "Fucking rookies." Hot Rod said before throwing a switch which caused the fire pit to flame. The whoosh of the ignition sent a tremor through my gut.

"Been a helluva couple of days Paul, glad you came along." Coos grabbed two beers from the mini fridge and tossed one in my direction. "We make a good team, with your legs and my face we could go places." "Yeah, it's been fun, even the parts I don't remember." We stared at the dancing flames for a few minutes. "So what would you like to know about my lawsuit? I do recall that is why you tracked me down." I was surprised he remembered. "Aw shit, I don't know. Something about that picture on Traditore's wall made me curious about you. Everyone else looked so fucking serious and you were almost laughing. I have only been out of the hospital a few days, nothing really better to do. Hope you don't mind?" "Hell no." Hot Rod replied, "I know the feeling, since my settlement every day has been Saturday night, a year of Saturday nights."

Coos lowered his back cushion and stared into the night sky before continuing. "You're the first guy I have met who has gone through some of the same shit I have. Being in a fucking accident because someone else fucked up is a bitch. Those shrinks talk about anger, denial, acceptance and all that shit. Fuck that. I am still pissed if you want to know the truth." Resentment ran through both our veins. "I went through that in the hospital. Right now I am just glad to be out, spent a lot of time healing. Guess I am at the beginning of the process."

Coos threw his beer bottle into the pool. "There is no fucking process, my legs ain't going to grow back and you ain't going to get any better looking." He was right, of course. "I know that, what I meant was the legal stuff." Hot Rod chuckled, "Shit I could handle your case instead of that vulture. We are double diamonds, clear liability and great damages. You couldn't draw it up any better. Every lawyer's wet dream."

He went on to vent about how Traditore took a third of his settlement then deducted costs for assorted experts. "I ended up with about two million a leg, not a fair fucking trade." Coos rose up and looked at me. "The day you get your money is the day you stop having a reason to get up in the morning. All that time spent answering questions, going in for examinations, meeting with consultants, preparing for trial; it feels like you're in a war with the bastards. Once the fight is done the troops all move on and you're left shell shocked, wandering the battlefield alone." Unsettling imagery from a guy who had spent more time in a grease pit than a classroom.

"Aw fuck, I don't mean to be a buzz kill, let's get some sleep and you can drive me somewhere in the morning." Hot Rod nimbly bounced into his wheel chair and laughed as I cheated and put one leg on the ground. We roared inside and did one lap around the house like a couple of kids with new tricycles. Once in my room I lifted out of the wheel chair and walked into the bathroom.

Later, alone in another strange bed, I decided that my days would not all be Saturday nights. Whether my face was worth more or less than Hot Rod's legs on the scales of justice did not matter. Money would certainly come my way but it would not be pissed down bar toilets. That would not be my future. Hopefully.

I awoke to a voice coming from the ceiling. "Good morning Paul, this is your wake up call. Please get what is left of your ass out of bed. You will find clothes hanging on the door knob. You have twenty minutes to get to the kitchen. That is all." As my head cleared I saw the recessed speaker and realized the Coos home was wired for sound. The bedside clock glowed 7:30 a.m. "It's too fucking early." I mumbled before returning to the pillow.

A few seconds passed before a bugle blasting reveille busted up all the peace and quiet. "Now that I have your attention, get up, it is not too fucking early and, in ten seconds it will be Barry Manilow time." Fearing increasing decibels of "Copacabana" I made it to the shower. After toweling off I found what appeared to be a uniform in a dry cleaner bag at the door. A large yellow rugby style shirt had the number 23 on the front and the back was emblazoned with The Hot Rods in blue letters above a wheelchair which had a stock car engine strapped to the seat. Blue shorts, long white socks, and Leon's Shack hat completed the outfit.

I opened the door before remembering to get into the chair. In the kitchen Coos was in matching attire with the number one across his chest. "Just in time." he said while sliding a plate of pancakes and blueberries onto the counter. I slid the wheel chair into the cut out and grabbed a fork. Two mouthfuls later I downed half a glass of orange juice. "I am hungry and you're not a bad cook." Hot Rod was busy with the dishwasher. "With a working mother I had to learn a few tricks in the kitchen or starve. I also make a mean mac and cheese."

After cleaning up we motored into the garage. Coos pointed to two wheel chairs that appeared to be outfitted for combat. "Those will fit in the trunk if we tie the lid with rope." I got to my feet and helped push the road warriors out to the Cadillac. After a bit of shoving they were safely secured. Hot Rod hopped into the passenger seat, leaving his tricked out ride behind.

As we rode into the morning Coos explained that today was the finals of the Valley Indoor Wheelchair Hockey League. The Hot Rods were playing a team from Tracy. "If we win it is on to San Francisco for the state championships." It dawned on me that my uniform and the extra chair meant Coos expected something more from me than cheerleading. "We're playing at the University of Pacific gym, take the March Street exit." He was getting more amped up with each passing mile. As we approached the parking lot Coos reached into the backseat and pulled a catcher's mask from a tattered duffel bag. He eyed me with a slight squint, "What's your hat size?" "Well before the explosion it was an eight, now I am probably an earless seven." I replied. He tugged at a few straps on the mask. "This should fit."

Hot Rod directed me to park at the edge of brown, block building. "Get the chairs out and put them on my side of the car, make sure nobody sees you." Trying to be inconspicuous while dressed like a stuffed canary I managed to do as directed. Coos scrambled into his seat while motioning for me to sit down. "Leave your hat in the car and follow me." It was difficult moving the wheelchair with my arms for a motor. After much effort I made it to the door where Hot Rod explained that the team's regular goalie was back in rehab. "A little problem with the nose candy." He assured me that I could handle the job. "Just move around and stick your hands up, the way we play there won't be many shots anyway." Before I could question or protest he opened the door and rolled inside.

Armored wheel chairs roamed the large gym floor like stampeding buffalo. Black rubber softballs were being thrown at two nets twice the size of hockey goals. The riders were missing legs or had withered limbs strapped down to the stirrups. The Tracy Tigers were at the far end of the building wearing orange shirts with black stripes. They weaved across the floor passing the ball back and forth. The Hot Rods were gathered near their goal doing some sort of wheel chair calisthenics.

Coos tossed me the mask, "Do not let on that you can walk, they're a little picky about that." As I tried to figure out which end of the face protector was up two teammates chugged over. They were both paraplegics with muscled arms, bald heads and three day beards. Hot Rod gave them each a high five, "Mitch and Jeff this is Paul our new goalie." Mitch looked me over and exclaimed, "Coos, where the hell you get him? We may be a bunch of gimps but that one is scary." "Guess there are no mirrors at your house." Hot Rod replied.

I managed to get the mask on just as a whistle blew. Two referees, "walkers" each, stood at half court. I rolled to the front of the closest net stopping more or less in the middle. The rest of the Hot Rods, two defensemen, a center and two forwards, spread out before me. Coos and his counterpart met for something resembling a jump ball. The Tiger had a longer arm and swatted the ball to a teammate who quickly heaved it in my direction. I promptly ducked. The ball flew over the net. Hot Rod came over for the throw in. He handed me the ball, it was softer than it looked. "It doesn't hurt much," he said, "don't be afraid to get in front of the damn thing."

The game was two forty minutes halves. Eighty minutes of wheel-chair warfare. Players were often knocked over like tipped cows only to righted by a nearby teammate. It was polo without water, hockey without sticks, soccer without kicks, wheeled mayhem. I let in many goals, only stopping throws that managed to hit me. Yet the Hot Rods stayed in the game. Coos played as if possessed. He stormed both ends of the court trading metal with anyone in his way. With thirty seconds left the score was tied. Jeff intercepted a pass and lobbed it across the court. Hot Rod caught it with his right hand while crank-ing his left wheel. He spun in front of the Tigers net and bounced in a goal. I was in the midst of cheering when the Tigers made two quick passes. Suddenly their left wing skidded to a halt thirty feet to my right, rose up in his chair and fired a black blur.

I woke up on the floor surrounded by the front wheels of five wheelchairs. My mask was lying nearby, a ball jammed between the metal bars. As I made an attempt to sit up Coos yelled, "Don't move Paul, remember what I said, the refs will help you back into the chair." The cobwebs had cleared enough that I remembered that "picky" rule about having the use of one's legs. After being assisted back into my seat and given the "how many fingers" test I was cleared to leave.

I followed the team out to the parking lot where we gathered around Mitch's van which had a pony keg on ice in the back. "Figured we would need this no matter how the game turned out." he said while passing out plastic glasses of cold Bud. The first toast was to the team captain, benefactor, and leading scorer Hot Rod Coos. A glass was also raised to Paul the new goalie for stopping the tying score with his face. The decision was made to bronze the mask and ball as a memorial to the great victory.

Once the beer was gone the team began to roll away. Coo hand-ed out directions to Diablo Valley College where the state cham-pionships would begin in three days. "Don't forget to wash your uniform." He said. As we waited for all witnesses to leave the scene I chided Hot Rod for doing a good deed by sponsoring the team. "Aw shit," he said in reply "between the uniforms, gym rental, and league fees I am only out a few thousand. All those guys only get a disability check once a month, they look forward to these games more than you know." "Yeah, well it still is good of you to put up the cash." The coast was clear; I loaded the chairs in the trunk. Hot Rod asked me to drop him off at Dick's Pool Hall. "The afternoon session should be starting." Having just been knocked senseless playing a game I never heard of I had no desire to lose money in another one.

After parking in front of Dick's I retrieved Coos's warrior chariot. He slid into the seat as I took out the other chair and closed the trunk. I pushed the spare through the door. Fred was still behind the counter chewing on the same cigar while reading a different paper. He didn't look up. "A few fish in the pond Hot Rod, the rest will be here within the hour." Before Coos could head for the back room I explained that I would not be going for a swim. He tried to tempt me with a thousand dollar loan, no interest. When I balked he borrowed pen and paper from Fred and had me right down my address and phone number. "We are going to need you in goal. I'll call you in a couple of days." He grabbed my hand and pulled me down into a hug. "It's been fun, take care of yourself." "You too." I replied. As he rolled toward the back door he yelled out, "Don't forget to wash your uniform."

As I turned to leave Fred piped up, "Good to see you brought him back, I thought you fucking kidnapped Hot Rod or something when the real limo driver showed up." "Yeah we had a little mix up there, been an interesting couple of days." Fred bounced the stogie back and forth like a log roller. "You spend time with Todd you better keep your seat belt on." "You know him long?" I asked, "As long as anybody I guess, gave him a job at a gas station years ago. He turned into a real wizard with the wrench then a heckofa race car driver."

Fred grabbed a coffee cup and took a long drink. "Damn shame what happened to that boy, he hasn't been the same since the accident. I am hoping he comes out of the tail spin soon. He has no direction, just parties." I pointed to the wheel chair. "He's doing some good with the team." Fred waved his hand dismissively, "Blowing off steam a few times a week, another excuse to drink beer."

A man with a chalky complexion, dirty t-shirt, golf shorts, and a Bay 101 Poker Room hat came through the door. He threw a twenty on the counter and went into the back room. Fred put the money in his pocket. "He should be doing something in the racing business, instead he can't even drive. Shit they gave him two cars with hand controls, wrecked them both. Drunk driving. I think it was a death wish. Hell even if he grows legs they won't let him behind the wheel again." Fred picked up his paper. The conversation was over. I left.

I had returned from Stockton in need of rest, the calamity of Coos had taken its toll. After devouring a Domino's Hawaiian that was promptly delivered by Dave I noticed the message button blinking on the phone. Three calls from my parents, each with increasing intensity. "Paul why haven't you called us?" "Paul you should call us." "Paul call." They had contacted the hospital, were told of my release, and got my number from Jane. I decided to sleep before reaching out to their area code.

The next morning, after a bowl of cereal, I called. They both seemed glad, with an undercurrent of irritation. "So you finally decided to give us a ring." my dad said. "It's O.K.. Paul," my mom soothed, "We understand you have probably been busy." As the conversation progressed it became obvious I had no choice but to agree to a visit home. "I'll be there next week; will call you with the day when I get a ticket." They smiled across the line. The deal was done.

A few minutes later Jane phoned, she wanted to let me know that my parents had called. A little late but it was good to hear her voice. Jane had moved on to different patients. "Don't worry you will always be my favorite." she said with a laugh. I told her about a few of my adventures with Coos. "Sounds like you have found a friend." When I mentioned the wheelchair hockey tournament Jane wanted to be there. "Don't worry I won't blow your cover, just let me know the time." I promised to call.

There was mail; all junk except for a letter from Traditore informing me that the battle was in full swing. The enemy wanted me to appear for an independent medical examination with a doctor of their choice. It was in a month, I had more pressing concerns. On the computer, after several clicks and with assistance from my lawyer issued credit card, I had an airplane ticket to Minneapolis. First class, I figured there would be fewer bulging eyeballs in the front cabin. Leave next Wednesday, return on Sunday, plenty of time to overstay my welcome.

A few hours later, between Jeopardy and Wheel of Fortune, the doorbell rang. It was Mimi stopping by to see how I was doing. She was on her way to a shoot down at Coyote Point. "We're doing a scene on a sailboat, there will be plenty of bouncing on the waves, hope I don't throw up." We shared a soda as I gave her a rundown of my last few days. Mimi also expressed an interest in attending the tournament. "Maybe I can bring some of the girls to cheer you on." With that she kissed me good bye.

On Saturday morning Coos arrived in a black Escalade. Our battle chairs were in the back, along with one of his many regular rides. He was happy that I had washed my uniform. "We are going to kick some ass today." Hot Rod shouted as we pulled onto the freeway. He explained that Mitch was bringing the rest of the team in his van. "Those bastards better not tap the keg until after the game."

He was in good spirits, bouncing on the seat while Willie Nelson blared from the speakers. As we pulled into the college parking lot Coos reminded me to let the driver set up the wheelchairs. "This is the real deal here, don't fuck it up." I saluted, "Yes my captain." Coos was not amused. "Where is your damn hat, the crowd might head for the exits once you roll in." I had forgotten my facial fence. "Here, but I want it back." It was his own Leon Shack hat. Hot Rod grinned at my surprise. "Had to buy the ribs and the beer before he came across."

With the help of the driver we saddled up and wheeled into the gym. A large banner announced, "Welcome to the California Wheelchair Hockey Championships" The rest of the team was already there and appeared sober. We watched as the final seconds ticked down to a win for the Hollister Hayseeds. The announcer thanked their opponents, the Fighting Spokes from San Diego, and informed the crowd that the next match between the Hot Rods of Stockton and the Blades of Hollywood would start in fifteen minutes. Jeff led us out onto the court for warm-ups. I exchanged my hat for the face mask.

In between attempting to dodge balls thrown my way I scanned the bleachers. Jane was in the third row reading a program. She was wearing jeans and the Ramones shirt; her hair fell over her shoulders. It was strange to see the nurse out of uniform. Large sunglasses partially covered her wine stain. When Jane looked up I waved. She gave a quizzical look, I raised my mask. She stood up and yelled, "Good luck Paul." Two seconds later a ball hit me on the side of the head. Jane put her face in her hands. She was laughing. I put the mask back on. Just as Coos went over to meet the Blade captain and the referee a buzz went through the crowd. Mimi and three friends were in the house.

They each wore white cheerleader outfits with "Hot Rod" in red letters busting forth over their ample chests. I later learned the costumes were left over from the best-selling movie, "Hot Rod High" starring Mimi as the head cheerleader and Franz Pearl as the star quarterback. The foursome marched around the court waving pom poms. As they turned the corner by our net I rolled over and said, "Mimi, thanks for coming." She promptly sat on my lap. The rest of the team moved closer, eyes wide with amazement. Introductions were interrupted by the buzzer. Mimi bent over, "Good luck Paul." she said. The fantastic four retreated to the sideline where they promptly broke into a cheer, "We like our Rods hot, Go Hot Rods Go." It wasn't poetic but you could not beat the presentation. The crowd gravitated toward our side of the gym, except for the Blade supporters who held their place.

The game was another edition of wheelchair mayhem. Coos was tipped over three times in the first five minutes. He played hard, slamming his chair fighting for position. Unfortunately the rest of the team did not match his intensity. Goals went by me sight unseen, I only heard the rattle of the net. Hot Rod and Jeff worked their magic a few times. The girls, sensing something good had happened, shouted, "Go Hot Rods, put it in some more." Then did a dance that usually requires a pole.

At halftime the score was 6-3 in favor of the Blades. Coos bitched us out, "We should be beating these sorry bastards." At the same time Mimi's troupe ran onto the court, one girl did a cartwheel while the rest cheered, "You can't beat our Rods." The fans applauded.

The second half played out like the first. The buzzer concluded with a 11-5 Blades win. As the Hot Rods rolled toward the door I motioned for Jane and our cheer team to follow. We congregated at Mitch's Dodge. The keg was tapped. I put on the Shack hat. Beer soothed our wounds, except for Coos who still wore a scowl. He did not like to lose at anything. I introduced Jane to the team and Mimi introduced Tish, Jen, and Mandy. It was an odd tailgate party; five guys on wheels with five women looming above.

Hot Rod took me aside, "Your cheerleader friends cost us the game, they distracted the team, fucked up our chemistry." I argued that the Blades had to be similarly affected. Coos rolled his eyes and shook his sweaty hair, "You stupid sonofabitch, they are all gay." He rolled back toward the keg. Jane poured him another glass. "Thanks," he said while pointing in my direction, "Did you guys take out his brain when you took off his ears?" Jane laughed, "No, he left with what he had upon arrival" Hot Rod drained the cup, "Couldn't have been much then."

I pulled up between them, "Jane you will have to excuse my friend here, he's upset over losing to disabled homosexuals. Trying to blame it on our lovely cheerleaders." Jane looked down upon us, a slight grin on her face, "They certainly attracted attention, although Mr. Hotrod you still played really well." "Yeah Mr. Hotrod, maybe you were on the wrong team." I hooted. Ignoring my jab he extended his hand to Jane, "My name is Todd Coos, alien boy has mentioned your good work, nurses have a tough job taking care of assholes like Paul and me."

Realizing her mistake Jane blushed, "Thanks for the encouragement, and sorry about messing up your name." "Don't worry about that, Hot Rod is a nickname from a long time ago." "Putting mister in front of it was a nice touch." I interjected. They ignored me, having moved on to discussing Jane's revelation that her Uncle

Ray used to race at dirt tracks and Hot Rod's admiration of her Ramones shirt. Taking the hint I spun and wheeled toward Mimi, she was throwing the ball around with Mitch.

With my arrival we made it a three corner toss and catch. Mitch told Mimi the story about how I saved the last game by taking one in the mask. "No hero today," he said, "we played like shit and those Blades were pretty good. It was still fun and we had the best cheerleaders." Mimi smiled. Jeff yelled over that the beer was gone. "We are going to find the nearest bar." Mitch tossed me the ball, "Keep it as a souvenir, I better go." Mimi gave him a hug and we high fived as he and the cheerleaders went by.

"They are all good guys." Mimi commented. "And so are you for helping them out." She stood in front of my chair, raised her hands toward the sky, and commanded, "Now get up and walk!" I looked toward Coos and Jane, they were watching with smiles. The limo driver, leaning against the back of the Escalade, peered up from his magazine. When I stood and took two steps Mimi did a pirouette before taking a deep bow. "Bravo!" Hot Rod yelled out, "Can you do anything for me?" Mimi frowned, "Sorry only one miracle a day." We all laughed. The driver shook his head and went back to his reading. I shared the last of my beer with Mimi. "Shit, I forgot about the driver, hope he isn't offended." "I am sure he has seen stranger things. By the way you were pretty convincing." "Well I have been known to raise more than one guy from the dead." she said with a mischievous grin.

I put my arm around her shoulder, "Thanks for showing up." "Glad to Paul, I hope we weren't too much of a distraction." Her eyes, today, were a deep emerald. I was transfixed. "No, you guys were just the right amount of a distraction." Mimi grabbed my hat and put it on her head. I felt a chill. Inside and out. "You don't need to hide." she said, reading my mind. "You are who you are."

I took the cap back. "Yeah, except it is easier on everyone else if I conceal some of the blast damage." Mimi shook her head. "That's bullshit, you mean it is easier on you." I was getting irritated with the porn star. "You're not the one who looks like E.T.'s cousin. Cut me some slack." She punched me in the arm, "O.K., but just today, this fight ain't over."

Hot Rod wheeled up, "You two going to fight? I'll put my money on the star of *Bases Loaded,* she is one helluva athlete." Coos, as I should have expected, had a large porno collection. Mimi was surprised he recognized her considering the new look. "I didn't place you at first," he continued, "your hair is different, and your eyes, but you still have a great ass. Mimi gave him a wink. "You were in *Bases Loaded*?" Jane interrupted, "One of my friends left it behind must admit I enjoyed it a few times myself." Hot Rod gave her a pat on the butt, "Now that's my kind of nurse."

The driver walked over, "Mr. Coos, if we are going to be at the restaurant on time we should leave now." He took my chair and wheeled it to the back of the Escalade. "Shit, I almost forgot we have reservations at Spanglers, hope you all like fish." "Damn thoughtful of you Mr. Coos." I said. Mimi mentioned she had a shoot in four hours. "No problem we can drop you off."

The next morning I awoke early on the couch at the Sunset Arms. A bed frame rattle echoed from my bedroom with an occasional moan interrupting the beat. Hot Rod and Nurse Jane were fucking. Again. This time I joined in, aurally enhanced, grunting as the groaning faded. We fell back to sleep, us three.

As dawn turned the dimmer switch up a notch I was paying for abusing alcohol. There was a pounding in my brain as Jane kissed me on the forehead. Out of focus and disheveled, she said, "I need to get to work, call me when you wake up." "Sure." I muttered before pressing my face into the pillow, "As soon as the world stops spinning."

A few hours later the effects of ethanol, a tide of nausea, chills, dizziness, mind ache, ebbed. I stood on shaky legs, stuck my head in the freezer, drank water, felt better. A look into the bedroom revealed Coos's chair tipped over in the corner, two pillows, one without a cover, lying next to the bed, the headboard was bent away from the wall, the sheets were piled in the center of the mattress, and out of a turban of percale protruded three rolls of flesh. From the other side of cotton mountain came a hoarse voice, "Turn off the damn light." I slowly shut the door and headed out to the deck, pausing to pick up the phone.

Nurse Jane answered on the third ring, "Good timing Paul, I just finished my rounds." She put me on hold while walking to the lobby fronting the garden. "You sound a little better than when I left." Jane said upon returning to the line. "I thought about running an I.V." "Yeah," I replied, "Well I just looked in on Coos, he is still out of it but possibly for different reasons." "It was quite the day and night." Jane said, "I hope you're not upset." While I would admit to a few nurse-patient fantasies with Jane in a starring role, there was never any impetus to act. Now, however, a jar of jealousy spilled over my heart.

Looking back Hot Rod's courtship of Jane was a thing of beauty. He sat next to her in the limo except for a few miles when he grabbed the interior straps and pulled an iron man gymnastics move. His head was two feet off the floor while his legs stuck out the sun roof. Two pale poles cutting through the afternoon air, permanently at half-mast. He spoke only to her except for the few minutes when he talked to Mimi about a movie. "I just remembered you were in that picture about that guy with huge dick, it had a weird title." Mimi had no trouble remembering Martillo del Monstruo.

She laughed before telling us that the title was Spanish for Monster Cock. Coos laughed too. "That really described that guy; I don't see how you handled that thing." Mimi laughed some more, "I didn't, we had a stunt pussy." She explained that the porno world, like many businesses, had its specialists. "There are guys that can pop a wad across the room, girls with tongues like snakes, guys with all kinds of dicks, and girls who can handle a bat." Coos shook his head, "Well I'll be damned." It was a shock to his system. He turned back to Jane. I gave Mimi a pat on the back, "You should write a book." She looked around the car, "I think we all could."

Our arrival at the restaurant was noted by the owner. He came to the table with a bottle of champagne. "This is on the house Mr. Coos if you promise not to urinate on the floor." Hot Rod mocked offense. "No problem if you've put in an accessible bathroom since my last visit." He then lectured us and the uncomfortable restaurateur on the Americans with Disabilities Act and how everyone deserved equal rights no matter how they moved around. "I could have turned you over to the access army and their nasty lawyers." A bead of sweat began to move across Mr. Spangler's forehead. "No need for that Mr. Coos, you just let the waiter know your needs and I will personally see to it that they are met." He left with a slight bow.

We talked, ate, laughed and drank. Jane spent a few moments instructing me to call Frank. "I am sure he would like to hear from you." I put it on my to- do list. "By the way I am going to see my parents next week, any advice?" Jane was pleased at the news. "Paul your parents are good people, I am glad you are getting together." When I didn't respond a frown jumped her face, "You haven't told them how you look?" I shook my head. "That's going to make for some scene." Jane said, "Maybe I should call them." A little leaflet drop before the invasion. "What would you say?" I asked.

Her face turned stern, "What you should have told them weeks ago. You're the same lovable guy with a different face." Coos had been eavesdropping. "Tell them it doesn't hurt except to look at." Jane gave him and elbow in the ribs. "I'll call tomorrow." She then returned to the Coos cocoon.

I had watched a Hot Rod charm channel episode with the cow girl at Cache Creek. He was back at it. Jane enjoyed the attention. Mimi felt they made a good couple. "She has a good bullshit detector." Mimi had stopped drinking. "No one appreciates a drunk on the set." She became, therefore, our designated decider: assisting with the food order, sending a plate out to the driver, telling us to tone it down, calling the waiter when Hot Rod needed to piss.

On one of Coos's later safaris to the bathroom Mimi asked how he lost his legs. To my surprise Jane took the lead and explained that he had been repairing his prized Mustang when jacks he got as a gift from his latest girlfriend failed. "Half the car fell on his knees." Mimi shook her head, "That's so sad. I can't imagine how bad his girlfriend must have felt." I finished another glass of champagne just as the check arrived. "What the hell." I said pulling out the credit card "Can't let Stumpy pay for everything." I was the only one to laugh.

We drove Mimi to a seedy motel just off Bayshore. "We've rented the whole place. It is a takeoff on the whole Bates Motel thing; they are calling it "Dates Don'tell. I'd invite you in but it is a closed set." "Can't be too closed." Coos chirped while waggling his thumb at what sure looked like Mitch's van. Mimi laughed as she headed out the door. "Coming soon to a theatre near you Hot Rod's buddies. Those girls must have signed them up as extras. I'll let you know how they do. Thanks for a fun day."

As the Escalade motored up the on ramp Coos commented that Mitch and the boys may have found new careers. "There's a market for gimp porn, hope they're not too drunk to get it up." Having no experience with the genre Jane and I just nodded. A few minutes later we arrived at the Sunset Arms. Hot Rod gave the driver several Benjamins and told him he could leave. "My scary friend here can give me a ride back tomorrow." I pulled his regular chair out of the back. He hopped on while whispering, "I am going to need your bedroom tonight." I wasn't surprised.

"Paul you're not upset are you?" Jane said with a sense of urgency the phone line barely contained. "No, no." I said, "I could tell you two made a connection." "He is an interesting guy underneath layers of anger, regret, and fear. Reminds me a little of you." I half expected her to continue with, "Except for the big dick of course." But Jane was thoughtfully silent. "I haven't known him that long." I replied, "Coos is more than the hell raiser he shows the world." she stated. "It's been a couple years since his accident and he still hasn't moved on. It's like he is looking for answers without knowing the questions." Sounded like Jane was channeling Dr. Dan. Her analysis included comments on how money hasn't brought happiness, he has no goals, drinks too much, needs better friends, and is great in the sack. "I think in the bedroom Todd still has his legs."

I heard Jane's pager go off. "I have to hang up Paul; I almost forgot I did call your parents. They know what to expect. You should have done that yourself." "Yeah, I know I'm gutless. Thanks for taking the time." I knew she was smiling. "You're welcome, now go wake up your guest and get some breakfast." I hung up.

I decided to let the sleeping Coos lie and go out for the paper just as the phone rang, it was Mimi, she had just gotten home. "What a night, they shot two movies, Dates Don'tell and Dates Moantel. Let Hot Rod know his buddies only held the mikes and lights, they weren't in on the action." I told her I would pass on the news. Mimi, fortunately, didn't ask about my night, but did bring up my upcoming trip home. "I think you should lose the hat. We all are what we are." "I don't know if it's time yet." Eyes walking over you, some barefoot others with army boots, leave tracks.

Mimi sighed, "It's like jumping in a lake, once you do it, the water feels fine. People stare at me every day, I have gotten past that." Comparing a big breasted, hot bodied porno star to a guy out of a late night fright show didn't make a lot of sense, unless a stare feels the same no matter the reason. "I had this same talk with Jane." Mimi said, "She needs to put herself out there. Big sunglasses and scarves are silly." I didn't respond. "Jane has no problems at the hospital; it shouldn't change when she walks out the door."

A few seconds of dead air brought another sigh. "I'm sorry Paul; I need to get some rest instead of bitching. You know we have some great make-up people at work, I could bring one over before you go to the airport." "Thanks, but I'll just wear the hat." I said. "And thanks for the advice; it gives me something to think about." She wished me good luck with Coos and my parents. We made plans for dinner in a week. "I'll buy this time." Mimi said with a yawn before hanging up.

I grabbed my Shack hat and walked to the corner market. Herb was busy tenderizing a slab of meat with a worn, wooden mallet. His chubby wife Rose sat at the cash register reading a Chinese newspaper. Neither was big on small talk. The place served those without transportation, those with transportation but too lazy to drive to Safeway, those in dire need of cereal, diapers, cigarettes, munchies, beer, and those needing tough meat for dinner. I bought orange juice, donuts, and a Chronicle. Rose barely looked up as she handed me my change.

I ate a donut on the walk back home. The sugar rush and the fresh air both felt good. The sun was high in the sky, it wasn't morning anymore. Two young mothers pushed strollers in my direction. They were discussing pre-schools. I stepped to the curb to let them pass. Neither acknowledged my gesture although one of the kids spit out his pacifier and started to cry. The wail subsided only to be replaced by the hacking yell of Mr. Coos as the Sunset Arms came into view.

Before I could open the door it was clear he was not happy. "Where are my fucking clothes? What the fuck is going on? Fuck me!" I poured us each a glass of juice, slapped a donut on a dish, and entered the bedroom. Hot Rod was on the floor. Naked. As he struggled to upright his chair I turned on the light. He blinked several times. "Good morning sir," I cheerfully said, "Hope you slept well, a little breakfast if you please."

As I set the glass and plate on the night stand his eyes burned a hole in my chest. "Paul you are one sick, ugly bastard. In case you haven't noticed half my legs are missing which makes it a little difficult to get around. You're lucky I didn't piss on the wall." I walked to his side, righted the wheelchair and asked, "You want me to lift you up?" In response Coos placed one hand on the side of the bed, lifted himself off the floor, bounced off the mattress and landed on the chair. The Russian judge would have given him an 8.5. He grabbed the donut, finishing it in two bites, before gulping down the O.J. I found his clothes half under the bed. As he buttoned his shirt I grabbed the plate.

"You might want to empty that jug while you're at it." he said before leaving.

The artificial flowers that came with the vase were lying in the corner. In their place I found several ounces of warm urine. The gag reflex kicked in just as I reached the bathroom sink. I poured the contents down the drain and took the dishes and vase to the kitchen. Coos was on his third donut. The empty orange juice container lay on the table. He belched long and loud. "We are going to need some more food my friend." When I didn't reply Coos gave me sheepish look, "I am sorry about yelling earlier." When I didn't reply he said, "And I'm sorry if you're upset because I made it with Jane." When I didn't reply he threw his hands up in the air, "And I'm sorry grills were ever invented, there is no Santa Claus, and I am an asshole." I turned from the dishwasher, "Guess we are both a couple of sorry fucks, I shouldn't have left for so long. Where you want to eat?"

I drove to a Mel's Diner. It was three in the afternoon. We had a big breakfast. Hot Rod flirted with the waitress. Having forgotten my hat I kept my head down low. Back in the car Coos announced, "You need to get laid." and told me to drive north to San Francisco. Thirty minutes later I was helping push the wheel chair up Jones Street. We were in a fringe neighborhood, a block one way you could buy a smoking jacket, a block the other, crack. Hot Rod was not the only guy in a chair but the others; sporting signs proclaiming "Disabled Vietnam Vet, Have AIDS, Need Money for Food" would fold theirs up at dark and walk away.

At a metal gate two thirds of the way up the hill Coos ordered, "Push the doorbell." We were under a sign announcing, "Orchid Massage Parlor-Therapeutic and Sensual" There were cameras pointed at us from both directions. Hot Rod looked up at one, smiled and stroked his hand up and down over an exaggerated length, even for him. A loud buzz announced our acceptance. I opened the gate, Coos hopped the threshold.

A dimly lit hall led to another door which was opened by a petite, Asian girl with long black hair, a short white lab coat and red high heels. She pranced the few steps between us before jumping onto Hot Rod's lap. "Jeff, it is so good to see you. It has been too long." After giving me a wink he replied, "You're right Amy but I had to wait for my friend Marty here to get out of the hospital. He had a little accident." Apparently no one used their real name at the Orchid. Amy looked up at me with dark brown eyes, she had the perfect angle to see my messed up mug. "Oh, you were burned. I have an uncle who got napalmed during the war. He is missing one ear." Coos then wheeled his comely cargo through the door. "Come on in Marty," he yelled out, "You are home."

As Amy skirted off for tea Hot Rod explained that the Orchid was a Vietnamese establishment. He had reconnoitered the neighborhood. There were Korean, Chinese, and Filipino competitors within two blocks. He also commented on parlor etiquette, "You pay the guy at the table forty bucks, this gets you in a private room from there it's two hundred more to travel down the ecstasy highway." Considering the twenty three dollars in my pocket it appeared I would need to hitchhike.

Hot Rod recognized my poor boy look and shook his head. He handed me a fistful of twenties. "The First Bank of Coos to the rescue." "Thanks, if I had known..." My voice trailed off as Amy returned. She was accompanied by a taller version of herself. "This is Shari, she would be a good choice for you." Her voice lowered, "I explained about your accident." I sipped the weak tea as Shari sat very close. Her hand rubbed my back, the sweet smell of jasmine floated in the air. Amy and Hot Rod left, a few moments later Shari took my hand.

I paid the forty and we walked into a small, dimly lit room. The back wall was mostly mirrored under which a single bed, with a crisp white sheet and large cotton towel to match, beckoned. There was a small sink in the corner. After asking me to remove my clothes and wrap the towel around my waist Shari exited. Doing as instructed I sat on the edge of the bed, anticipation revved up my heart and nerve endings.

Shari returned with two more towels under her arm. Again she grabbed my hand, "You need a nice shower." Considering it had been over a day I understood completely. We walked down another hall to a room which held a two foot high, tiled, table covered with a blue rubber mattress. Overhead a hose dangled, a large, adjustable nozzle attached. Removing my towel Shari told me to sit down. "Cross your legs, like the Buddha." She motioned to a small table which held a smiling statue and an incense burner. After testing the water Shari slowly covered me with a gentle, warm rain.

A few moments later she brought out a blind fold, washcloth and a bar of sandal wood soap. Shari covered my eyes. "Stand up please." I managed to get to my feet. She stood behind me and spread the warm lather over my shoulders and down my back. Being washed by another is a return to childhood. It felt more comforting than erotic. She did not mention my numerous scars. After another rinse cycle Shari gently toweled me dry and took off the blind fold. "That's better." she said with a smile while wrapping the towel around my waist. I nodded in agreement and floated behind her back to our room.

As I lay face down on the bed Shari turned on a small boom box, drippy, soothing new age music filled the space. She removed my towel. I felt her weight straddle me. "Some oil to relax you." The first drop hit just below my neck, several more bounced down the line to the base of my back. Her palms gently spread the warmth. Firm fingers needed my doughy flesh. Shari hesitated at my harvested ass before applying more lotion, slowly squeezing my patchy cheeks, occasionally flicking a finger down the canyon. Spreading my legs farther apart she massaged each to the foot. Relaxation turned into excitation as her fingers, barely touching the skin, made the return trip. The massage had taken a turn down the road to arousal.

Shari lowered herself onto my back, bent down and whispered in my ear, "Time to turn over." before sliding off the bed. I rolled over. Her oiled hands went to work on my shoulders and chest. I closed my eyes as she lowered her attentions. Sergeant Semi-erect was preparing for battle. Shari bypassed the commotion completing the tour back to my feet before crawling back on the bed, a stalking cat.

"Would you like something more?" she purred. I opened my eyes. A layer of make-up aged her young face; blue eye shadow deepened her sockets, with pink lipstick completing the look. "What else is there?" Her right hand grabbed my boner. "For two hundred dollars there is everything." she said with a squeeze. The sales pitch was irresistible. "Sure." I said. Shari stood up, "Please, the money now." I thanked Coos again as I pulled the Jacksons from my jeans. After taking the cash Shari said, "Lie down, I'll be back."

With sex just around the corner I drifted with the music. The Orchid was proving to be a fine rest stop; time out of mind, a little something for myself. Hot Rod had sensed a dip in my happiness index. Truth be told I wasn't looking forward to going home and I was a little upset over Jane's dance session on my bed.

Shari returned and quickly removed the lab coat revealing a short, pastel printed camisole. She faced the wall and let it drop to the floor. In the dim light Shari glowed, shapely and exotic. I smiled as she returned to the bed and put her knees on either side of my chest, took my hands and placed one on each breast. I went into massage mode. There was no response. This was clearly about my pleasure and not hers. The sooner I came, the better. She wasn't getting paid by the hour. As I squeezed Shari reached down to retrieve a condom. The sight of a wiener wrapper was comforting. After ripping the packet she threw it on the floor, reached up and gently placed her hand over my eyes. "Close. "She whispered "I am going to make you feel good."

And that she did, forcefully and efficiently. Her mouth wrapped around me, deftly rolling out the rubber. Lips met latex, saliva saturated, suction brought moans. Close, very close, then back. Twice. Suddenly Shari rose up, a catcher squatting. Her hand guided my cock into wetness, warmth. The oral foreplay had primed the pump. Up good, down better, up, down. I exploded, eyes closed, grunting. The cock sock was removed. "Lay back, relax." As my breathing slowed she dressed, retrieved a wash cloth soaked in warm water from the sink, and carefully cleaned the remnants. "You had a good time? Nothing hurt?" I laughed, "Very nice, thank you, I look bad but feel good." Shari placed her hand on the top of my head. "You're not so bad; come back next week and I make you feel good again."

At the hall corner I ran straight into the old sugar vulture himself, Josh Fortner from Finance, baggy shorts, hooded sweatshirt, pudgy face, frazzled hair. We were both surprised. "Well Paul you sore site, how's it hanging?" "Just fine, just fine how about you?" He gave a thumbs up. "Around here it's always happy days." At the lobby there was no sign of Hot Rod. Josh went over to the candy dish and popped mints into his mouth, "Glad to see you found out about this place, I should have told you myself. It is perfect for fat guys, old men, and ugly dudes. Shit I saw a guy in a wheel chair go by earlier."

Right on cue Coos rolled up, Amy on his lap. "Marty," he practically bellowed, "knees stop shaking yet? Ready to hit the road?" As Josh looked quizzically in my direction I said, "Guess that's a problem you don't have Jeff." Amy stood up and ran interference, "You two be nice, and come back soon." She gave me a big smile before walking away.

We filed out into the fading sunshine. Parachuting back into the real world, heads swiveling to see who noticed our reentry. I pushed the chair up the hill to the corner. Josh followed, gasping the last few feet. I introduced him to Coos. "Todd?" he questioned, "I thought your name was Jeff." "That's my undercover handle; no one uses their real name in the massage trade." Josh's face scrunched up. Hot Rod pulled a wheelie, "Let's go to the Saloon boys, first beers are on me."

We escaped the underworld; in fact the denizens allowed passage without hassle. Moses had nothing on us, the Red Sea is a snap compared to meth freaks a half hour from a tweak, mentally impaired homeless, hyped crack heads, and assorted ex-cons. An alien with shocks of hair busting out of his head like sad feathers pushing a legless smile on wheels parted the puddle of fright with no problem. Josh sucked through in our wake although one cross-dresser with hairy legs did pinch his ass.

Union Square, the promised land of high end retail, also cleared a route. Mothers grabbed the pointing arms of their gaping children, large matrons clucked, office workers gave a glance, old men laughed. We kept moving. Through Chinatown, where

Hot Rod bought me a green Mao hat with a bright red star and insisted I put it on. "Cover up; you're scaring the quack out of the Peking ducks. Into North Beach, the corner of Grant and Fresno, The Saloon, Established 1861.

The light had been sucked out of the sky as we found the open door. The place was narrow and not very long, a bar brought around the Horn over a century earlier stood guard to the left. The far corner was reserved for whatever blues band was playing that day. A small dance floor fronted the stage. Stools were at a premium, ten around the bar, even less along the wall. Our arrival was greeted with the last few notes of Johnny Nitro lamenting, "I'm workin'nights, your're working days. If we get together, someone's got to change their ways." As the saxophone grew silent three suits left three stools. Josh and I grabbed the left two, Coos slammed into the other. "Give me a lift you dick and tie the chair up to the meter outside." he said in my general direction. Josh looked down, "Dick? Marty? I thought his name was Paul?" As I struggled lifting under his arms Hot Rod gave Josh the finger before grabbing the edge of the bar and propelling his ass squarely on the worn seat.

The bartender, Gladys, a women not hired for her looks, greeted us warmly. There were no freaks at The Saloon. Coos ordered three Anchor Steams and three shots of Yukon Jack. He paid with a fifty and told Gladys to keep the change. Hot Rod grabbed the shot glass, "Here's to us, happy bastards that we are." Disappointment would not drive us home tonight. We downed the hundred proof and called for more, nursing our beer between salvos from Gladys. Josh asked how I had been spending my time. I gave him the condensed version of my lawsuit, new apartment, escapades with Coos. "Shit," he complained, "You've been having more fun than me."

Hot Rod, sitting to my right, was engaged in conversation with a skinny black man who promised, "Buy me a drink and I'll tell you who really shot MLK." Coos motioned toward Gladys but the band started up before the answer could be revealed. A jolt of blue lightning zapped the room. Crying guitars, wheezing harmonica, wailing sax, and graveled voices took us to the crossroads and back. Our spines swayed, feet tapped, heads bobbed. The congregation was uplifted.

The sermon was delivered by the saxophonist who used a beer case as a step up onto the bar. She deftly maneuvered her black stilettos over the bottle strewn pulpit while raining the rich notes of Stormy Monday upon the grateful flock. As the service concluded an empty pitcher passed through the crowd, collecting green for the band. Everyone was happy to give. Coos finished his beer, "If there ain't no blues in heaven I don't want to go." We said goodbye to Gladys. I retrieved Hot Rod's chair. Josh patted his paunch, "Time to eat, and I know the place."

As we rolled along Green Street Hot Rod stopped to admire an old Detroit jewel with shiny chrome rims and sweeping curves, spilling out of its parking space. Josh and Coos began arguing whether it was a 1971 or 1972 Pontiac Firebird. Back and forth they went, pointing at the grill, spoiler, and trim. I did not share their enthusiasm or knowledge. Josh informed us, "I made models of just about every muscle car ever made, I know it's a 71." Hot Rod spun around, "Yeah, bullshit, you must have sniffed way too much glue. It is a 72." "Gentlemen," I said, placing a hand on each shoulder, "We could wait here all night until the owner returns and ask him, or we could go to dinner." Josh was the first to blink, "He makes a good point. Let's go."

And go they did, side by side talking about Cobras, Chargers, Z-28s, Vettes, Gran Ams. It became white noise to me. I was glad when we reached Caffé Sport. A funky Sicilian place serving family style portions. The staff helped as the chariot barely fit down the only aisle. We all slid into a booth. The waiter took the chair to the back. "Aren't you afraid of losing that thing?" Josh asked. "Not tonight, I have you two to carry me around." "That's not his usual ride." I said, "You should see the power he normally controls."

I explained to Josh about yesterday's unfortunate loss to the Gay Blades. A look of severe indigestion spread across the captain's face. The waiter returned with three Peronis, "On the house, sorry for the inconvenience." Coos picked up the beer. "Looks like Josh knows more about restaurants than cars, good choice my friend."

Josh ordered platters of food: pastas, chicken, fish. We used big spoons to load our plates. Flavors exploded. We toasted to a good day. After Josh used a hunk of bread to soak up the last of the thick scampi sauce he looked at Coos, "So what's up with your legs anyway?" It was an intrusive question, lacking in both taste and tact. Josh, who was licking his fingers, had no clue. Hot Rod took a swig of beer and told his story.

Four years ago Todd Coos was living a dream. His stock car career was going well. Racing, partying, and wrenching. "Every day was a good day." He had rented a house up on a hill with a three car garage and a pool. "I could work on my cars, swim, entertain, nice place." Hot Rod had several girls of interest, but one, Jackie, had pulled away from the pack. She had moved a few things into the house and spent more nights there than anywhere else. Coos bought her a sparkling tennis bracelet. "Just because I liked her." A few days later Jackie brought home four hydraulic car jacks. "The guy at the store said there the latest thing, just hook them up to an air compressor." "I was impressed she had found something I could really use."

He tried them out that evening, they worked as advertised. The next afternoon Hot Rod reattached the jacks and went to work with his back on a dolly. "I was under the middle of the chassis, legs sticking out." It happened quickly, first the front passenger jack, then the rear, lost pressure. Coos had no time to react. The frame hit him at the knees. "I stopped cold. There was no pain. At first I thought everything was O.K. Then I looked down, my femoral arteries were pumping blood on to the driveway. I laid my head back and waited to die." Each beat of his heart pounded a nail in his coffin.

The noise brought Jackie out of the house. She grabbed two bungee cords and used them as tourniquets. "Saved my life." The paramedics arrived, put Hot Rod on a gurney and pushed him to the ambulance. He was still conscious. "As they wheeled me around the front of the car I saw my legs sticking out from the door frame. For some reason I tried to move my feet." Coos set his beer on the table. "I still have nightmares, and sometimes my fucking feet move."

We sat in silence. The waiter came and cleared the plates. Josh ordered more beers. I tried to lighten the mood by pointing at one of the many carvings on the wall. "Looks like my fifth grade teacher, old prune face." No change in emotional pressure. Josh took a turn, "So what kind of car was it?" The cold front moved out. Hot Rod got that Detroit look in his eyes again, "A sweet Mustang, 1966 Hertz Shelby GT350H." "Shit," Josh yelled, "They only made 1001 of those." Then he said what he shouldn't have, "You sure that's what it was?" Coos put his hands on the stained cloth and pushed himself upward with muscled arms until his head was halfway across the table. Josh's eyes doubled in size as he tilted his chair back. "Look Humpty-Dumpty, I know cars, if I tell you it's a GT350H it's a fucking GT350H. Candy apple red with side stripes, Cobra 289 V8, 306 horse power."

Coos lowered himself back down on to the chair. Some color returned to Josh's face. He crossed his arms over his man boobs. "Zero to sixty in 6.6 seconds, standing quarter mile in 15.2 seconds, top speed 117 miles per hour. Only fifty were made in candy apple red. I know cars too." Hot Rod seemed impressed; he lifted his glass in toast. "You do know your shit, next time you're at my place I'll show you a few pictures." "Pictures," Josh sputtered, "why don't we go for a ride?"

Coos looked up toward the corner, "Jackie got so pissed after the accident that she drove the car out to the slough, covered it with gasoline, and torched it. Not that I blamed the car but she couldn't stand to look at it. And it wasn't long before she couldn't stand me either, of course I was a bitter asshole. She probably should have torched me and saved the Mustang." We were still contemplating when the check arrived. Josh had forgotten it was a cash only restaurant. "I left all my money at the Orchid, there's an ATM around the corner." Hot Rod put up his hand," Your lack of money is understandable, in fact you look like you should be spending more on pussy than food anyway," I didn't even reach into my pocket. Coos paid and tipped the guy who brought his chair from the kitchen.

We found the street thick with fog. The neon lights smudged in the mist. Hot Rod damn near got us all killed cutting across Columbus to City Lights Books. He went inside without looking back. Josh peered through the window, "Think they got any porno in there?" "No, at least not in English." Josh turned and faced the street; the fog was kissing the pavement. We would hear the cars before they passed, shadows on wheels. "I like your buddy Coos, you know where you're at with him." I smiled, "Yeah he is out front, alright."

Josh tightened the hood of his sweatshirt against the chill. "Damn shame about his legs, helluva story." A MUNI bus went by, sparks flashing blue above the wires. "It's too bad his girl burned that Shelby, one sweet ride that Mustang." I nodded sociably, my ignorance of cars allowed for nothing more. "That girl you knew had a blue Mustang; I followed her to the hospital after your accident."

Josh was right, I had forgotten, Iris did drive a Mustang Hot Rod muscled between us, a book wrapped in brown paper on his lap. "Paul, this guy still talking shit?" "Not that I would know." Coos shook his head then whistled at a taxi. "Too damn cold to walk back to the car. Throw my chair in the trunk, I'll buy." Josh didn't need a ride. "Guess I'll see you guys later." Hot Rod tossed the book, "Here, thought you might need this." By the time Josh tore up the paper Coos was in the cab. It was a hardback titled, "The History of the Pontiac Firebird." Josh was still staring at the cover as the taxi pulled away. Coos stuck his head out the window and yelled, "Check out page 42, it's a 1972."

It took the taxi twenty minutes to find my car. Couldn't blame the driver since neither Coos nor I could remember where we left it. The cabby, a turbaned Sikh with a manicured white mustache, finally pulled to the curb.

"Gentlemen," he began in a lilting tone, "the meter is running, you don't want me to drive all over town looking for your Cadillac, perhaps you have a receipt from the parking lot." Hot Rod and I looked at each other, a couple of dumb fucks sharing a brain fart. I pulled a green piece of cardboard out of my pocket and handed it to the front. He held it up to the light before putting the big

Dodge in gear. Two blocks later we sat in front of Douglas Parking. "Thirty two and fifty cents please." he said, his piercing black eyes in the rear view mirror. Coos gave him a fifty and waved off the change. "Just pop the trunk."

On the way down the 101 I told Hot Rod he could have the bed again. The carnal cloud still hung over the room. He jabbed me in the arm, "You're not still pissed about me and Jane are you? I figured the Orchid would have cured that." "Hell I don't have a disease, and I am not still pissed. It's just that I know a lot about Jane and I don't want to see her hurt." "I wouldn't call what we did painful. The good nurse and I hit it off. She knows a little about cars. I know a little about hospitals. We had fun."

With Coos it always came down to fun. "You think Jane feels the same way?" He gave me the raised eye brow, perplexed look. "I never thought about it, getting laid is getting laid." "You want to see her again?" "Sure, she's interesting and has a great body, but what's up with the red blotch on her face?" I explained about the wine stain. "Never knew there was such a thing." "She's been toyed with in the past; I don't want to see that happen." Hot Rod fiddled with the radio, "I'll keep that in mind." He found a country station. Ray Price took us along For the Good Times.

My expertise with the wheelchair was improving. Ten minutes after our arrival Coos was resting on the couch, beer in hand. I ignored the message light on the phone and joined him. "That was quite the story you told tonight." "I'm surprised you never asked." "I just figured you would bring it up when ready, I don't go talking up my tale of woe either." Hot Rod spun so his back pressed up against the sofa arm, his stumps resting across the cushion. "Jane filled me in on what happened, you had the world by the ass then a shit storm blew in. We have that in common, but your stay in the hospital makes mine look like a vacation. Don't know how you did it." "One day at a fucking time, plus there were some good people who cared." I grabbed the stereo remote.

An old Eagles album cued up. "About as close to country as I got." Coos tapped his beer bottle to the Hollywood Waltz. "I had a lot of folks show up the first few days. I was shitty company. Nobody knew what to say. It didn't take long until it was just my mom and Jackie. And old Traditore showed his face a few times. Then Jackie stopped coming. She sent a card. Said she was sorry for burning the Mustang, sorry she bought me the gift, and sorry she couldn't see me anymore. It wasn't me it was her. Funny, I had used that same line a few times myself." I thought of Iris. "At least you got a card, I got a phone call."

Hot Rod perked up, "You had a main squeeze?" he said with more astonishment than inquiry. "What was her name? Give me the details after your get me another beer." I complied on both fronts. He downed half the brew as I related the romance that was Iris and Paul. Coos gave a snort, "You were banging a hot girl for a few months She probably was looking for easy street. Then you turned into more that it was worth. So she left, good riddance if your ask me." A bubble of anger popped in my throat. I took the low road, "Yeah, well your Jackie wasn't any better." Hot Rod smiled, "You're right, but the difference is I never hoped she was."

He was a perceptive bastard. I stared at the big screen; our reflections flickered off the blank glass. "I'm sorry; I can be a dick at times." "No, you're right. I wanted happily ever after with Iris. Just another thing the accident fucked up." Coos belched before informing me he needed to piss like a race horse. He quickly lowered himself off the couch, placed his knuckles on the carpet, and propelled his ass toward the bathroom. "Don't worry," he said "I can shoot a stream into the bowl from three feet away."

I imagined him on the floor, leaning against the door, dick in hand, with a yellow rainbow stretching over the linoleum. He returned and announced, "Didn't spill a drop." "Glad to hear it." I listened to Glen Frey ask, "What can you do when your dreams come true and it's not quite like you planned?" Coos interrupted, "So why did you come looking for me and not this Iris chick?" I explained how I found the Ramones shirt in my bag. "Shit that's worse than giving a ring back. Jackie kept everything I gave her and burned my car."

"You know Iris drove a Mustang, baby blue with a stretched out rear window." Auto scholar Professor Hot Rod lectured, "It must have been a fastback, the roof slants down toward the trunk. Mine was the same way, slick looking." "She said it was a 1965." "Highly unlikely, that was the first year for the fastback. They didn't make that many. Did you happen to notice the grill if it had chrome edged horizontal inserts it was a 1966, the 65 had a honeycomb grill." "Can't say I paid that much attention." "Where was she from?" "Bakersfield I think."

Coos finished his beer, "I smell a road trip." I gave a grunt of disbelief, "Two minutes ago you were telling her good riddance now you want to go find Iris." He threw his beer can toward the kitchen sink and gave a fist pump when it clanged in. "I don't give a shit about Iris but the Mustang interests me. I have been looking to replace mine and hers sounds like a possibility." "Iris won't part with it, too much sentimental value. Her dad had one like it." Hot Rod slowly shook his head from side to side. "She doesn't strike me as the sentimental type, left your skinned ass in a hurry, besides money overcomes resistance most of the time." The Eagles warned, "Somebody is going to hurt someone before the night is through. Somebody is gonna come undone, there's nothin we can do."

"It's a fucking crazy idea, I don't need the aggravation. We could never find her anyway; there must be a lot of Camps in Bakersfield." Coos dismissively waved his hand, "Shit you found me, and we should be able to find her. You don't have to see her, I'll do the talking. "Yeah, well I had an address for you; we can't just ride around looking for a hot blonde in a Mustang." "You got a point, let me worry about that. In fact it's time to sleep on it." Hot Rod's spring had finally wound out. It had been another roller coaster of a day. At least, I thought while throwing a blanket on the couch, the idea of seeking out Iris should die on the pillow. That would be one hangover without a cure.

It was way past noon when the phone rang long enough to wake me up. "You too busy to return messages." It took a few moments for the gauze to lift, "It's Frank, from the hospital." "Sure," I mumbled, "how you doing? Sorry about the messages I got in late last night." "And you just woke you up, what the hell." "You're right." I confessed. "I've been trying to invite you over for dinner, tonight, my wife suggested we grill, I nixed that idea so she's making turkey with the trimmings." He didn't mind if I brought Coos, "Gladys makes enough for an army anyway." I gave him the heads up about the wheelchair, he gave me directions. "See you at five, you better leave soon."

In the bathroom I found piss on the floor, Hot Rod wasn't the sure shot he claimed to be. I threw a towel down and wiped up the mess before taking a shower and walking into my room in search of clean clothes. Coos was hugging a pillow and softly snoring. After dressing in the corner I kicked the mattress a few times. "Rise and shine sleeping beauty we've been invited to dinner." Both he and the pillow rolled over. "I know you can hear me. I am going to set up the bath." Hot Rod raised his right hand and gave me the middle finger salute.

The tub was half full when he swung his ass over the doorway. "Don't forget the bubbles." Coos was naked except for a pair of white boxers covered in red hearts. He put his hand in the water. "Just right, help me in and I'll take it from there." As I closed the door he yelled, "I need a new shirt." I found an old Hawaiian one someone at Weezy had left in my car. Coos was resting his head on the edge of the tub, a washcloth over his eyes. I draped the shirt over the sink. "This should fit."

We left a half hour later. It was a little past four. Frank lived in Pacifica, a coastal community often shrouded in fog. I explained to Hot Rod Frank's role in my recovery. "We're hungry, his wife is cooking, can't beat that." "Couldn't agree more," he replied, "and may I suggest a stop for a gift." Canadian Club, being Frank's drink of choice was a good idea. U Save Liquors sold fifths. They did not take plastic. Coos bought again.

Frank's house was in a subdivision a few miles east of the ocean. A gray Dodge Ram pickup was parked in the driveway. The garage door was open. Since there were steps up to the front door I figured Frank wanted us to use the back way in. Hot Rod rolled into the garage stopping to admire a large, multi-drawered, black tool chest. He whistled, "A fifty six inch Montezuma. What a beauty, costs more than my first car."

Suddenly a booming voice broke out, "Probably drives better too." Frank had come in from the side door. He wrapped me in a big bear hug, knocking my Leon's hat to the concrete. "Paul, good to see you. Glad you made it across the city line; they don't like weirdoes here in Pacifica." He turned toward Coos, "You must be Todd, nice you came along." Hot Rod extended his hand, "Somebody has to keep an eye on Paul, they might grab him for the circus." Frank laughed, "You boys come around the back, easier to get through the sliding door.'

We followed and found ourselves in a large den on the ground floor of the tri-level home. Two couches, a Barcalounger, end tables, an oak cabinet, a desk with computer, and a large television decorated the space. Coos hopped from the chair to the couch. Frank was impressed. I handed him the paper bag from U Save. He pulled out the fifth and smiled. "Nice. Thanks."

Frank took three glasses from the cabinet, placed them on the table and filled each half way to the brim with the whiskey. "Here's to your health gentlemen." Both he and Hot Rod downed the liquid dynamite in one gulp. I took a small sip. Frank grabbed the bottle, "One more before dinner." I placed my hand over the glass, "Maybe later." Coos took seconds. A high pitched voice rang down from above, "Frank could you come up her please, I need a little help." "Be right there Gladys," he said while stashing the bottle behind the computer monitor. "The wife doesn't appreciate liquor in the house."

Frank and Gladys had thoughtfully decided to serve dinner in the den. There would be no need to get Coos up the stairs. They brought out wooden television trays. Gladys, a shapely woman with short gray hair, tortoise shell glasses, and a hint of makeup, placed steaming plates of mashed potatoes, turkey, gravy and green beans in front of us. Her eyes nervously moved from my face to Hot Rods stumps. "What would you like to drink; we have ice tea and Pepsi?" After delivering the sodas Gladys appeared relieved her waitress duties were complete. "You boys enjoy yourselves. I'll leave you alone; you must have a lot to talk about." She quickly retreated up the stairs.

Coos and I ate like starved dogs at a meatball factory. Frank served us seconds, "Better than that hospital food hey Paul?" I stopped chewing on a leg long enough to agree, "You got that right. How are things back on the ward?" Even though it had only been a couple of weeks it seemed as if months had passed. New place, different pace, and the hurricane called Hot Rod had spun my world. Frank filled his own plate, "Just as you remember I imagine, pain, suffering, clogged pipes." I told Coos the story of the fat farm internees flushing pizzas down the toilets. He practically snorted a piece of turkey out his nose.

The plates were empty. Frank grabbed the Canadian Club and freshened our drinks. After returning the bottle to its hiding place he gathered the dishes and went up the stairs. Coos took the opportunity to slide back into his chair, roll out the door and piss on the grass. He made it back before Frank returned carrying a tray with three large pieces of raspberry pie topped with vanilla ice cream. Once again silence ensued as we dove into the tangy sweetness.

As the last bite was put to rest Frank suggested another piece. We both declined, "Frank, I am full up to what's left of my ears." I said. "That's why you're here, you are always welcome. You too Todd." He put our plates back on the tray and placed it on the desk top. A gray wall of fog pressed up against the glass obscuring the backyard. Frank turned on a lamp. "So what have guys been up to, sounds like a lot of partying?" I told of our adventures going light on the sex, drugs, and alcohol. Frank was amused, "Call me up next time, as long as I unscrew my dick and put it on the mantle, Gladys lets me go out."

"We are on a mission right now." Hot Rod announced. "Trying to find a Mustang Paul's old girlfriend drove." Contrary to my expectations, sleep had not wiped away Coos's desire to find Iris and her car. He was busy explaining to Frank how she was from Bakersfield and his belief that there could not be many Camps with 1966 Mustangs. "Paul and I are going down there to scout around." "Speak for yourself kimosabe," I piped up, "Wild goose chases are not in my plans." Frank raised a beefy hand, "I might be able to help." He turned toward the stairs and yelled, "Gladys honey could you come here please."

As she took a few tentative steps down the stairs Frank explained that his wife worked for the Department of Motor Vehicles. She had access to a lot of records. "Sweetheart the boys need to find a car, thought maybe you could help them out." Gladys did not appear too thrilled with the request. "Frank you know I am only supposed to log on for official business." He smirked, "Yeah like the time you tracked down your sister's deadbeat boyfriend."

Gladys glared at her husband before sitting at the desk and turning on the computer. As the screen glowed to life she said, "Paul and Todd you must never tell anyone about this, I could lose my job." Coos turned on his charm voice, "We appreciate your help mame." Frank walked over and attempted to slide the booze away from the monitor. Gladys waved her hand, "Too late Frank." He grabbed the bottle and sheepishly put it inside the cabinet.

After a few keystrokes Gladys asked, "So what do you know about the owner?" She still was not making eye contact. "Her name is Iris Camp and the car is a 1965 or 66 Mustang." Hot Rod took exception, "Actually it is a 1966 Mustang." As her fingers tapped away Gladys said, "I will do a state wide search for Iris Camp and Mustang." The screen blinked a few times. "Sorry no match. Any other names?" Coos gave me a what the fuck look. "Why don't you just try Camp and Mustang." This resulted in over a hundred matches, none earlier than a 1995 model. The power of the DMV was of no assistance in our quest. Gladys was bouncing nervously on her chair.

Frank spoke out, "Anybody else you want to check on, it's kind of fun to look up old friends or coworkers." Hot Rod replied, "How about looking me up, bet there will be twenty cars on there." After giving Frank a stare Gladys entered Todd Coos and all cars. "You're right," she said with a chuckle, "twenty-two cars starting with a 1972 Pontiac Ventura." "Shit, I am forty five years old and have owned six vehicles, what did you do with all those wheels?" Frank asked. "Sold a few, wrecked a lot." Hot Rod said.

Gladys was shaking her head, "Twenty went to salvage and one, a 1998 Corvette, was sold to a Fred Barnes." Hot Rod got a pained look, "Now that was a sweet car, lost it to Fred in a poker game. He rivered a straight flush, lucky bastard." "And you wrecked the rest?" Frank said. I explained how Coos was in the racing business before his accident. "A lot of them died on the track." he said wistfully.

"What about the other one?" I asked. "There aren't any more, my last ride went up in flames." Hot Rod said. "Not according to these records," Gladys stated, "You transferred title on a 1966 Mustang to a James Paizer." Coos sat in disbelief. "Must be a mistake, that car was destroyed a couple of years ago." I said. Gladys looked in my direction, "Our system is reliable Paul, let me double check just to be sure." As she went back to the key board I could see Hot Rod squeezing the arm of the couch, his face was flushed. "Just as I thought," Gladys said with a hint of vindication, "The car is now registered to James Paizer, 129 Summerset, Half Moon Bay, California." She hit a button, the printer came to life, and a sheet dropped the information on the desk.

Gladys shut off the computer, stood up and handed the paper to me. "Please destroy this when you are done." As she walked by Gladys put a hand on Coos's shoulder before disappearing up the stairs. "That fucking bitch." Hot Rod mumbled under his breath. Frank was busy retrieving the Canadian Club. I filled him in on the accident and Jackie's role. "So she told you the car was burnt." Frank began while handing a glass to Coos. "Yeah, only I'm the one who got burned, I can't believe she fucked me over like that." "Maybe she figured you would be better off without the reminder and didn't have the guts to trash the Mustang." I said. Frank nodded, "Yeah that makes sense." "Bullshit!" Hot Rod said, "She lied to me, pure and simple." He grabbed the printout from my hand, "I want to see the car and then I want to find Jackie."

The party was over. We finished our drinks. "Tell Gladys thanks for everything." I told Frank. Coos was already out the door. "Sorry for the quick exit." Frank handed me my hat, "That's alright; Half Moon Bay is just down the coast. Call me when you can and be careful."

Hot Rod was in the Caddy. I put the wheelchair in the trunk. We drove south in silence. The fog danced with the low beams.

As we slowed for the curves at Devil's Slide Hot Rod spoke, "I don't know her last name." I was busy keeping the right wheels away from the guard rails. "Who?" He sighed while bouncing his left stump. "Jackie. I lived with her but I can't remember her last name, if I ever knew it." It was a testament to his days of slam bam one night stands. Things hadn't changed much, I was sure he didn't know Jane's either.

"Going to make it a little tough to find her." I said as we passed the Moonside Bakery. At the stop light I grabbed the printout off the dash. Summerset was on the right. Near the end of the block a large, two story house with a three car garage had 129 painted on the mail box. Coos got in his chair. I put on my flap hat, we would be surprising enough.

After navigating a sidewalk lined with yellow and white seaside daisies, I hit the bell. Twice. Suddenly the light went on. The oversized, white maple door slowly opened. A sandy haired older man with wire rim glasses stood staring. Since it wasn't Halloween his hesitancy was understandable. "Good evening sir." Hot Rod said. "I heard you have a Mustang for sale. Could we take a look at it?" James Paizer, left hand firmly on the door knob, changed expression, crossing from surprise to puzzlement. Coos, sensing the possibility of rejection, pleaded, "I understand it is a rare model, if you don't have the time tonight we could come back tomorrow."

The thought of a daylight visit was too much for Paizer. He let out a strangled laugh. "Did the guys at the club put you up to this? Those hackers, how much did they pay you?" Hot Rod played along. It was pretty obvious from his Dockers and polo shirt that James would be a country club member. "You got us, we were down at the bar when your buddy started talking about this Mustang. Said it was a Hertz Shelby, I told him he was full of shit." James took his hand off the door handle. "It was that pecker Fred, never should have shown him the car."

Coos looked up with eager eyes. Paizer took off his glasses, cleaning them with his shirt. "So you know the Hertz Shelby?" Hot Rod rattled off the horsepower, cubic inches, and quarter mile times. "Only 1001 ever made." This appeared to satisfy the keeper of the classic, he deemed us worthy of a viewing. "As long as you're here you might as well have a look." Paizer reached back to hit a wall button. The garage door on the far left quietly rose as a light illuminated a vehicle covered in tan canvas. "Appreciate the opportunity." Coos said as he quickly wheeled down the walk and across the driveway. I walked along with James, "Surprised you found me tonight with all this fog." "Glad we did, he really wants to see the car."

The car had been backed in. Hot Rod was in the garage pawing at the cover. Paizer unhooked a few Velcro straps before coming to the front and pulling the canvas off with a flourish. A candy apple red work of art shone like the last rays of sunset. Even standing still it took your breath away.

Coos placed his hand on the fastback before slowly caressing the curves of the Mustang, stopping at the driver's door where he stared through the open window, lost in thought. Paizer returned after putting the cover along the side wall. "There it is, as advertised, a 1966 Hertz Shelby, one of only fifty in this color."

Hot Rod slowly rolled around to the front of the car. Mustering up some enthusiasm I said, "Really impressive." "It is fun to drive, handles really well." Paizer proudly declared. Coos retreated a few feet and peered under the bumper. "Pulls a little to the right if you take a corner over fifty." he said. James was slack jawed, "How would you know that?" Hot Rod didn't reply before disappearing along the passenger side. Paizer took a peek under the car before walking to my side. "Is your buddy a mechanic or something, I never told Fred about the cornering issue." Not knowing what to say I stared at my dirty sneakers.

Coos reappeared from the back of the Mustang. "I know," Coos said as he rolled up to us, "because this is my car and I was going to fix that problem when this beautiful machine sliced off my legs." James put his hands on his hips, his mouth was a tight line, "Look guys I don't know what Fred put you up to. This joke has gone too far, I am going to have to ask you to leave." Hot Rod's voice rose a notch, "This is no joke sir, that is my car. Show me the pink slip and I will prove it." Paizer wasn't use to taking orders from anyone, let alone a shaggy haired, half pint in a wheelchair. His face began to approach the hue of the Mustang. He abruptly turned and walked back into the house.

Coos took another spin around the car. "Hope he is getting the title and not a gun." I said. "I don't give a shit if he brings an Uzi, we aren't leaving without my baby." His ammunition did not match his determination, we would be leaving the way we came, probably with a police escort. "Take your hat off." he ordered. I was mildly offended, "What, you expect old Jim to see me and run off into the fog screaming for his life." "Just take the fucking hat off." Hot Rod spit the words. I put the cap in my back pocket.

Paizer marched back into the garage, face down, staring at a plastic covered pink sheet of paper. "Here is the title. As you can clearly see the prior registered owner, Todd Jasper Coos, signed it over to me more than two years ago." James, looking up while handing the pink slip to Hot Rod, saw me and dropped the document to the floor. I smiled, picked it up and gave it to Coos. He squinted at the signatures. "Right you are sir except for one thing, I am Todd Coos." Between seeing my face and hearing the challenge to his ownership James was flustered. "That can't be." he stuttered, "I bought the car fair and square." Coos replied, "Go take that tricked out red, white, and blue cobra gas cap off and look at the side. You will see my initials." Paizer complied. He found TJC stamped into the metal.

As Jim replaced the cap, Hot Rod reached down into his pocket pulling out his beat up wallet, my sugar tit. Paizer started moving toward the car cover, "Guess we will have to let the lawyers sort it out." Coos grabbed his arm, "Here's my driver's license and an article about my accident." Jim reluctantly took the evidence, placed each on the car hood, sighed and read. I whispered to Hot Rod, "You have a write up in your wallet; I would like to see that." He grinned, "I need it sometimes to get laid, it helps close the deal. You'll have to give me a blow job to read it."

I flipped him the bird just as Paizer turned around to hand the items back. "Sorry about your accident." Coos waved off the pity. "I don't understand how the Mustang left you, was it stolen?" Hot Rod explained Jackie's role in the affair. James shook his head, "I saw the car in a parking lot and left a note. A guy called me the next day said he was interested in selling. We met at the beach lot. I took it for a ride. It was great. He told me to make an offer. I started at sixty thousand, to my surprise he said fine."

Coos almost came out of his chair, "Shit, it's worth twice that." Paizer turned apologetic, "I know, looking back it probably should have raised a red flag." Hot Rod sensed a turn in the battle, "How did you pay for it?" "In cash, he dropped it off at my office the next day." Coos whistled, "Another red flag James. Did you ever ask for i.d.?" "Never felt the need, he was nicely dressed, seemed like a stand up guy." "A low down crook." Hot Rod replied.

Paizer went back on offense. "Hell, I had no idea, you can't blame me. Besides I spent a good deal of money on the new paint job and some upholstery work." "Legally," I interrupted, "the true owner gets possession of an item that was stolen even if someone has paid for it fair and square." I then went on to tell the story of my uncle who bought a snowmobile at a swap meet, turned out to be hot, lost his money and his winter ride. James didn't think much of my tale. "That can't be the law, how am I supposed to get my money back."

Hot Rod gave me a wink, "I don't want to see you lose out James. The car is no good to you now, every time you go for a drive my stumps will be sticking out the passenger door. That's one image you don't need." He rolled alongside Paizer and reached up to his shoulder, "How about you trade the Mustang for that Cadillac out there, straight up, title for title." Before "What the fuck!" could make it out of my stunned mouth Paizer and Coos were shaking hands. "I'll get the keys." he said, practically skipping back to the house.

I stared bullets into Hot Rod's face. He raised both palms up, "Hope you don't mind Paul, trust me it's a good deal." "You hope I don't mind. Why would I fucking mind the Caddy is the only thing I own that's worth a shit. Sonofabitch." Coos smiled with his hands now clasped together in mock prayer. "Don't worry, I'll make it right. It's the only way to get my car back. Do it for me. Go get the title before he has a change of heart. Please." I pulled the hat out of my pocket, crammed it on my dome, and stormed out of the garage.

As I rummaged in the glove box James peered through the door. "Looks clean, how many miles?" "A little over a thousand." I said while handing him the pink slip. He reciprocated with a binder of papers and a set of keys. "Part of me really wants to keep that Mustang, but Todd's story is just too much. He's right I would think about him whenever I drove it."

I tossed the keys to Coos before asking for a pen. Paizer and I put it all right, the Hertz Shelby back to Hot Rod, GM's finest to James. Coos had unlocked his beauty. He was sitting in the driver's seat, turning the wheel with his eyes closed. I took the keys, opened the trunk and maneuvered the wheel chair. James graciously tossed the car cover in, "Had it specially made, fits like a glove." Hot Rod had managed to slide onto to the passenger seat. Paizer walked over and shook his hand. I turned the ignition, the engine roared to life, a caged beast smelling asphalt. As we slowly left the garage I waved goodbye to the Caddy.

I drove the Mustang like a man on his first horse, alternately feeling in control and holding on for dear life. I recalled being a passenger with Iris at the wheel of another Mustang; it was not as easy on the driver's side. Hot Rod made me pull over five blocks down the road. "This is a sensitive but powerful machine. It can quickly get you in and out of trouble. Go easy on the gas. Hold the steering wheel like it was your dick." A few lines floated by, Coos, however, was in no mood for a verbal joust. He had his right hand on the dash, tension rose up his arm.

As I slowly gained proficiency driving his baby, Hot Rod began to relax. On the freeway he swiveled his head, "Punch it once." As the gas pedal reached the floor my spine headed for the backseat. The speedometer needle buried itself. We passed a Volkswagen like a house on the side of the road. I let off the gas; the roar subsided just north of eighty. "Fuck, that was amazing!" I shouted. Coos smiled, "Good to see Paizer treated her well." "That's what you meant about getting into trouble. Holy shit I'd be jumping everything on the street." Hot Rod turned toward the window. "Nothing like it my friend, nothing like it."

Memories fell down upon him; he drove the Mustang, he had legs, he had thrills. "You know Paul a couple of months ago I met this guy who tried to convince me that our whole life is laid out before we are born. He said our scripts are written, we just act them out. Well what crazy bastard would have me riding shotgun in the car that made me the half man I am today." I had no response.

"And what about that bitch Jackie. She gives me the jacks, lies about burning the car before selling it. I am going to find her." He punched me in the shoulder. "We are going to find her. I want to see the look on her face when the Mustang pulls up." "Maybe she didn't sell it, maybe she asked someone else to burn it, maybe that's the guy who sold it to Pazier." Hot Rod was having none of that, "Yeah, and maybe pigs fucking fly. She was in on this, I guarantee it." "When was the last time you saw her?" Coos stared into the night, reeling in time. "She came to the hospital a few times. Didn't say much. Gave me Traditore's card on one visit. Told me he helped out her cousin or something. I wasn't in the mood. Said she gave him the jacks. I really didn't care."

We hit the 380/101 interchange. "Never saw her after that. She sent the Dear John card, told me the Mustang was destroyed and good bye." "Jane told me a lot of relationships go sour over a catastrophic injury." I slowed to seventy as a CHP cruiser slid across the Ralston on-ramp. "Besides, you didn't even know her last name." Coos laughed, "Some fucking kind of script." I decided to turn the page.

"So what did Traditore do for you?" "He showed up at the hospital, all spiffed out. He already knew there had been a major fuck up. I signed some papers and didn't see him again for months." The good lawyer had learned of a manufacturing defect with the jacks. Varying degrees of failure occurred within a few months. Most of the mechanics were able to push away but a few had lost limbs with one death. The company came up with a quick fix, a thicker set pin, only instead of recalling all the packages they sent out red plastic bags with the new hardware and instructions. Each supplier was to heat seal the bag to the cardboard container. Somehow the ones Jackie bought never got the treatment.

It was an easy, lucrative case. Traditore had Nascar experts lined up testify Hot Rod would have made the big time. He had a young man whose dreams were taken away along with his legs. The case settled eighteen months after the accident. "Seven and one half million dollars"

At the exit we pulled up to a stop light where three teen-age girls yelled at the car. Coos rolled down the window, "Sorry, no rides tonight, maybe tomorrow." I accelerated a little too vigorously as the light turned green. "Get that all the time, the car is a babe magnet. Even you, citizen of another planet, would get action with the mighty Mustang."

After parking the prize in the car port, Hot Rod supervised while I attached the canvas cover. Several "dumb shits" we uttered as I demonstrated my ineptitude with all things remotely mechanical. A few minutes later the shroud was in place. "If your neighbors only knew, they wouldn't sleep." he said.

The apartment had been refreshed by the cleaning lady, erasing the last two days. Things were as they should be. "I need a drink." Coos announced after plopping onto the couch. "You got any real booze?" I was about to disappoint when the memory of Frank's WD40 gift went off. It was on the closet floor. Hot Rod was impressed when the secret was revealed, "Better than a paper bag."

I filled two juice glasses before sitting down. "Here's to finding your Mustang, against all odds." Downing the entire drink he replied, "If we hadn't met, it wouldn't have happened." "You have Traditore to thank for that." I said, refilling Hot Rod's glass, refreshing mine, and placing the empty bottle on the table. "That's where I am going to start." "Start what?" "My search for Jackie, she said Traditore represented a relative, they must have some useful information." "You still need a last name; even then the client could be from the other side of her family. Plus releasing information is probably against all sorts of laws." "No problem, I got an in. As in the old in and out, if you know what I mean."

Hot Rod had charmed the pants off many women, not surprising someone in the office had succumbed. "You ever meet Marcia,

one of the assistants?" First Jane, now Marcia. "Yeah, she helped
me when I got out of the hospital. Tall, short hair, a little older?"
"That's the one; we did it a couple of times in her office." That
could explain his smile on the wall of fame. "I'll call a tow truck in
the morning. Once I am home there has to be something laying
around with Jackie's name on it."

With the Canadian Club gone it was time for sleep. I wanted
my freshly made bed but the thought of Coos rolling off the couch
was disturbing. "You can have the bed if you promise not to piss on
the bathroom floor." He feigned shock before conceding, "Don't
worry, I am not nearly as wasted." That was true. "You take the
bed," he insisted, "I won't be able to sleep, too much bubbling in
the brain." Coos took my flight information. "See you when you
get back, I'll be gone before you get up. Take care of yourself." I
turned out the light "You too Jasper."

It was late morning when my eyes opened. Hot Rod had managed to leave without help. There was a note on the table. "See you
in a few days. I took the car keys. Thanks for your help. Hot Rod.
P.S. Don't ever call me Jasper again." Two bowls of cereal later I
dragged out the suitcase. Thanks to the maid service all my clothes
were clean. Pants, shirts, underwear, toothbrush thrown in leaving plenty of room for the gifts I had yet to buy, sourdough bread,
Ghirardelli chocolate, a snow globe of the bridge, thankfully all
available at the airport.

I cleaned up fairly well. My hair was long enough to comb over.
A hat was still required. I found a weathered Giants cap.

Two hours preflight Yellow Cab delivered me to the Northwest
door. The driver paid little attention, he looked half asleep. I gave
him my last twenty. "Keep the change." He mumbled something.

After finding an ATM from which Traditore's Visa card produced my $300 limit I located one shop with all three presents. I also bought a 49ers sweatshirt and pulled the hood over my hat and head. I looked like an orange beaked redbird, odd but not worth a second glance.

The check in procession was in full swing. Bags up, move ten feet, bags down. Repeat. A dance without partners. It took several minutes before I realized First Class had its own line. I did a double u-turn in an attempt to avoid looking the rube. When I finally walked between the red ropes an attendant quickly motioned me to the counter. All smiles and warmth, she took my bag and handed me a boarding pass before wishing me a wonderful journey.

The line for security wound back and forth, switchbacks of impatience. I took off my shoes, put belt, change, MP3 into the tray before turning toward the metal detector. "Sir, please remove your jacket and hat." The TSA officer was a large black man in no mood for argument. A bead of sweat crossed his brow. I shrugged and complied. As my plumage hit the gray box the officer raised an eyebrow, a few passengers nearby took a sideways glance as I crossed over the threshold. No alarm. A few fingers pointed while I wrestled into my sweatshirt. Several steps later I was one of the crowd, again.

Airlines pulse their passengers aboard, first Class, frequent fliers, those with young children. Seat 2A was to be mine for the next five hours, four inches wider with thirty-eight inches more legroom than Coach. A fact not lost on the faces of the next spurt passing by toward the back.

When the door closed, the treatment began. Hot towels, drinks, a pouch of treats all offered before the wheels left the ground. I settled in. As we rose Candlestick Park winked, the bay shimmered, and the bridges waved good bye. Headset on, U2's Vertigo blaring, I watched as the Sierras rose and fell. Five miles high the tube of tin leveled off. It was safe to walk about the cabin.

And safe to time travel, heading home I always drifted, years peeling away along with the nautical miles. Soon I was that laughing kid with the baseball glove hanging from the handle bars bouncing down the path to the diamond. The world was small, your bed always warm, and you were loved. I stared at the popped corn clouds, retrieving other moments recorded in days long past. Hanging between the heavens and earth, my fate in Northwest's hands, it was easy.

"More wine Sir?" Gail the stewardess asked, interrupting my reverie, a bottle in each hand. I refilled with the red. 1A had the white. He was a middle age Brooks Brothers type with a lap top on the tray table. Sensing my stare he looked toward the brick of fading light over my shoulder. "Great way to fly, you pay or using miles?" "Put it on the credit card. Going to see my parents." "Jack Wunch." I shook his hand, "Paul Lawton." Jack sipped his wine, "So you a rapper? You got the outfit for it." Hell of an assumption, plus I had no bling. "No, I work in the computer industry." "Yeah, I should have guessed it, the geek look."

I was beginning to suspect Mr. Wunch was a major asshole when he explained he was in the advertising business. It was his job to filter, categorize, entice, and sell. "The hooded sweatshirt was a nowhere item until the bad boys started wearing them. Sales took off. I predict that kind of action." Amazing how many ways there are to make a buck. Jack flipped the computer screen in my direction, "For instance what do you think of this girl. We need a new look for a motor oil ad." A short haired blonde with snow white teeth, large boobs, and long tanned legs filled the screen. Seen one, seen them all. He flashed a few similar models before a familiar green eyed beauty emerged. It was Mimi, dressed in a grease monkey outfit, holding a can of oil. Jack was ready to click forward, "No wait," I said, "that's the one."

Jack took a long look. "She has a different appeal, a little exotic. Let's check her bio." He pulled up a new screen. "Hell she does porno. That's great." Jack explained that motor oil buyers also rent a lot of adult movies. "They might not remember where they saw her, but they will have a vague recollection of pleasure." Couldn't argue with that. "I'll make her a finalist." He transferred Mimi's picture to another folder. I looked back out the window into the creeping darkness as globs of light spread across miles of Utah. Maybe a few street mechanics were stroking to Mimi unaware that while it would not cause blindness it may later result in an urge for Penzoil.

Dinner arrived on real plates. Chicken, pasta, salad, cake, washed down with a beer. Better yet everything was gone with my last sip of Budweiser. I returned to the concert between my ears and wondered how Paizer was doing with my Cadillac. I was without a ride and Traditore's credit card wasn't up to the challenge. Hot Rod was good for it although he wouldn't come across unless I helped him find Jackie, another mission for stumpy and the freak.

I hadn't yet given much thought to my homecoming. Hopefully Jane's talk with my parents prepared them for the new me. If not I would be spending a lot of time in my old room.

The 737 fell from the sky at six p.m. local time. First Class exits while Coach rumbles. I didn't want to leave. At the gate Wunch thanked me for my motor oil momma advice. "Maybe I will see you up front soon." he said, leather bag draped over his sport coat. "Sure, take it easy." I replied. He headed for the exit while I sought out the correct carousel. People who had just spent five hours hanging together in the sky now ignored each other while watching a revolving parade of luggage. My ratty bag led the band. I lugged it over the side and made my way to the rental car bus.

Twenty minutes later my driver's license was on the Budget counter. The clerk looked between the plastic face and my mug a few times. "O.K. Mr. Lawton what would you like to rent?" Make a show or go incognito? I decided on a Ford Taurus, neutral and plentiful. With suitcase in trunk I navigated out of the airport. It was getting late; traffic on the freeway was light. I had made the drive many times before, both directions, coming and going. I could see versions of myself in the mirror. The Pontiac had burned a lot of gas hauling my ass through those years.

Eighty miles passed before the right blinker was needed. Exit 48 leads onto two lanes of state highway. Home was an hour away. Farms dotted the landscape, plowed fields running into stands of hardwoods. It used to be that only an occasional cluster of buildings hugged the road: bar, post office, general store, church, and school, passing in the blink of an eye.

Over time the drive of my youth was interrupted more frequently by condos, golf courses, development. Pimples on good memories. Hell raising country bars became Seven/Elevens, mom and pop burger joints boarded up, dirt roads to a hidden lake gated, hunting camps morphed into retirement homes, hills of pines leveled. More people encroaching, shrapnel from the population explosion cutting into nature's flesh.

I drove through the night, a sliver of a moon smiling in the sky, listening to an FM station playing album sides. Soon familiar billboards shown in the headlights, beacons guiding travelers toward town. Not uptown or downtown, just town. Side roads became more frequent, houses appeared, then a stop for the first red light in sixty miles. The

Shell station on the corner was closed, a man sat in the window of the Northside Restaurant drinking coffee while reading a paper, a teenager was wrestling shopping carts in the Wal-Mart parking lot, two pickup trucks sat by the door to the Bluebird Tavern. On the green I wheeled the Taurus down Second Avenue past Krogers, the second entry on my resume. It was now a thrift store. The streets were empty, lights out in most of the homes.

I stopped at a turnout on the river, a mile from the house. A picnic table and grill stood above a small dock used for boarding canoes. With the window down, the sound of water splashing over rocks blended with the wind rustling the leaves. It was a long way from rodding the Mustang through the fog to sitting in a Taurus at this river's edge. The miracle of flying shortened a journey, crossing great spaces much too quickly. The suddenness of change in time and place is disconcerting; the mind needs to catch up with the body.

I had spent many hours up around the bend. A short hike led to a small overlook, ten feet above the water with just enough room between the birch trees for a straw mat. Reading a book, daydreaming, listening to baseball, and thinking. It was a lodestone location. A spirit checkup, how close was that needle to full. It never failed to nurture, a chapel without walls. The moon wasn't bright enough to make the walk this night.

A left off the four lane, quick turn past the IGA, slow for the curve, sixth driveway on the right. It was almost eleven, a light was on in the living room, and the kid was home. I put the Giants cap on, pulled the hood tight, popped the trunk and got my bag. It wasn't cold, I shivered. The screen made the same tired squeak as I entered the garage. I banged the wall feeling my way to the steps. Suddenly the light came on; my mom's face appeared in the window. She smiled, I smiled back. The door opened we hugged on the porch. "Welcome Paul, it's good to have you home." "You're going to crush his ribs Betty, let the boy in." My dad was holding the door open. I gave him a quick hug before bouncing my suitcase into the kitchen. "Cliff, you could help with the bag." my mom said. "Hell, he's younger than me."

It was as if nothing had changed; I had pushed through the membrane into the protoplasm of my was. I was a baby, I was a kid, and I was a teenager here.

"You must be hungry Paul, I can make you a sandwich." my mother said gesturing toward a plate of cold cuts on the table next to a loaf of homemade bread. "Sure, that would be great." I replied. As she pulled out some mustard and mayo from the fridge my dad leaned against the stove top peering at me through his bifocals. When I pulled out my old chair to sit down he rocked forward, "Take that jacket off, and let us see how you look." Betty turned, a small vein on the side of her head pulsing, "Cliff, don't you remember what the nurse told us. I can't believe you sometimes. I swear you are going senile."

The tone in my mother's voice was just below her pissed off octave. I intervened before my dad could push her up the scale. "Sorry I've been wearing this all day, forgot I had it on" "You don't have to apologize Paul, and you don't have to do anything you're not comfortable with." my mom said, finishing the ham sandwich while giving my dad another stink eye. Cliff was used to it; he often engaged his mouth before his brain. Betty had done damage control many, many times over the years.

I savored the soft bread. They sat down. We were in the places where thousands of meals had been shared, information exchanged, orders given, futures planned. It was a lot easier to finish the sandwich than to look at their faces. The kid had been bad. Confessing at the table was always preferable to being convicted. With the plate empty I said, "Thanks mom, that was good." "You're welcome honey." She reached across and grabbed my right hand. "Why don't you go to bed now, we can talk in the morning." It was a motherly gesture designed to lesson my discomfort, however delaying the inevitable was not an option. "No, I'm fine. I need to bring you up to date, it's long overdue."

In a few minutes I took them from my Wheezy windfall to living in an apartment on a lawyer's tab. Dad was glad to hear of the lawsuit, "Pick those bastards' bones clean." Mom nodded. The story concluded without reference to my burns. Nurse Jane had done the prep work; it was up to me to close the deal. I looked back and forth between concern and anger. After a deep breath I said, "I was burned pretty bad, the doctors did the best they could. My skin is discolored, but it doesn't hurt. My ears are mostly gone and my hair is a little weird. But what the hell my brain still works and it's good to be among the living. They told me there were surgeries that would give me a better appearance but I needed to get away from the hospital. Maybe I'll let them work their wonders later."

The unveiling was at hand, my audience sat attentively. I lowered the hood and took off my hat. My mother gasped before putting a palm to her mouth. My dad stared before slowly moving his head from side to side. The only child of their love was damaged goods. It was a shock, no doubt. "Hey," I practically shouted, "It is not that bad, don't get upset. You always said it's what inside that counts, well I've been through a rough time but I am still the kid that used to drive you crazy." They both were fighting tears, a rare sight for the old man.

He quickly stood up, pulled a bottle of Seagram's Seven from the cupboard and thoughtfully brought three small glasses to the table. Dad poured one, looked at Betty poured another, glanced toward me, I smiled, he poured a third. He was on his second as I finished, while my mom took a third sip. The alcohol ran head long into my jet lag lowering my awareness level. I stared into the eyes of Jesus looking down from a painting of the Last Supper which had hung on the wall since before I was born, his expression as pious as ever. I winked. "I can see why you wear that outfit." my dad spoke a little loudly, his third Seagrams gone. "You are one helluva sight." "Cliff!" my mother yelled, "didn't you hear Paul, the doctors are not done yet." She finished her drink.

An uneasy silence hung over the table. Jesus didn't mind. I stood up, grabbed my bag and said, "It's just going to take some time. You'll see." My mom managed a smile, "Your room is ready, sleep well." The light from the kitchen cast shadows down the hallway. My bedroom was the second door on the right. A flick of the switch took me back one decade, then another. Artifacts of my youth greeted me. The dented metal Tonka cement mixer in the corner, the framed state math award propped on the dresser, two old mitts hugging a cracked bat, a football helmet piggy bank jammed with coins, Bobo the stuffed monkey resting on the bed. I hit the mattress like a fallen tree. Head on the same pillow, staring up at the same etched glass light fixture, feeling the same sense of safety. My room.

My eye lids opened slowly, busted blinds blinking in the bright light. It was still morning in California but not in God's country. In a place where people woke roosters, my bedded state was reserved only for the dead and dying. I slowly rose to join the living and headed to the shower. The hot water felt good. A fresh towel rested by the sink. I dried off before wiping the condensation from the mirror. My reflection became clearer with each pass of the cotton. Over the years the looking glass had revealed raging acne, sprouting facial hair, hang overs, and grins. Now the new me came into view. What the hell, the mirror didn't crack.

Lunch was on the table. The Price is Right was on the television. "Lazarus is up." my dad barked, "We were going to call for a priest." "Cliff you know he is from a different time zone." "More like a different planet." dad muttered before finishing his coffee. I gave him a pat on the back, "I've heard them all by now." "Heard what?' Betty asked as she brought me a plate of mac and cheese. "Nothing mom, just talking sports." Cliff gave me a nod of thanks as he stood up and headed toward the door. "Fred is picking me up, got a meeting down at the Lodge, be home in a couple of hours."

I was hungry, the noodles disappeared. "You always were a good eater." "You always were a good cook." Mom laughed. "I told your father he could miss one meeting." "It's O.K., we've got time to catch up." I could feel her watching me as I forked my way through the last of the gooey pasta. After declining thirds the table was cleared. Mom filled the sink with soapy water. I grabbed the dish towel. We took our stations. This duet had played many, many times before.

"Tell me about the girl." Betty said as she rinsed a glass. "What girl?" I asked. "The one who put you in the fix you're in."

Mom had a way of tracing events back to the most unlikely sources. She blamed her father Bert's heart attack on Frank Seiberling the founder of Goodyear which made the tire on the old Ford pickup her dad was driving across the state to a 4H convention. The tire went flat. No spare necessitated a long tow to a lonely garage which resulted in a good fix but bad directions. Bert became lost as the road turned from black top to gravel. He pulled into a country store for help where the proprietor's mother coincidently needed a lift to the nearest town, a place of sufficient size to be on the coffee stained map spread over the truck's seat.

An hour of dust later Bert dropped Mabel off at the Baptist church where she insisted he remain, "For just a little while." Five minutes later Mabel handed him a paper bag bulging with peanut butter clusters. A confectionary delight Bert had never tasted. He quickly fell in love. According to Betty her dad started eating them after leaving the curb and didn't stop until he gained fifty pounds, clogged his veins, and blew up the blood pump. If it wasn't for Frank Seiberling Bert would be alive today.

"Which girl is that?" Jet lag and Seagram's had hazed out what details of my ordeal I had revealed upon my arrival.

"The one you bought the house to impress." Mom had cast way out there to reel in the cause of my misfortune. I was tempted to tell her it was Frank Seiberling's granddaughter. "You mean Iris, did I mention her last night." Betty scrubbed the old frying pan, bits of Brillo Pad spraying into the murky water. She spoke into the sink, her voice bouncing off the worn metal. "If you hadn't bought the home you wouldn't have had the accident. You wouldn't have bought it but for this Iris girl."

My sigh fogged the water glass. "I bought the house because I was tired of living in a noisy apartment next to a strip mall." That argument could be made. "There was all this money, a home was a logical investment." That made sense. "Iris had nothing to do with it." That, of course, was a necessary lie. Mom shook her head, the dishwater kept time. "I know you don't appreciate my logic but that girl was a turning point. Your compass was off, if it had been working…."

The unspoken inference, if Iris had been right she should still be with me. "No need to analyze. Some guy screwed up and made a bad grill. That's all." I put the last of the silverware away as the drain gurgled. Mom grabbed my hands, "You will always be my son and I will always love you." She reached up; her reddened hands gently touched my face. A tear sliced her cheek. I cradled her in my arms as she had comforted the boy in me. The blare of the phone tore the moment.

Mom stepped back, brushing her face with the back of a wet sleeve. "Oh, that's probably John, I told him to call back after lunch." Only my mother, and possibly his parents called John Mentor by his first name, everyone else knew him as Zinger. We had been friends since third grade. His younger sister gave him the name when she saw him give the middle digit salute. She spit out "zinger" through several missing teeth. And so he was ever since. "Should I tell him you're available?" "No, say I'll meet him at Shorty's in an hour." I needed some reentry time.

Mom started doing laundry. "You go see your friend; I have plenty here to keep me busy." Guilt had never creased my brow all those times I had left her in an empty house; it was no different this day. The Taurus was waiting, as were more memories and artifacts.

The Route, as it was known in my youth, highlighted all the action in the county. Time and the economy had chiseled away a few stops. Tops Burgers was a drive-thru cleaner. The bowling alley a house of worship. The rest stop off the highway became a storage yard. John's Tavern, where under aged drinking had accounted for half the revenue, had burned down. Driving by rattled moments out of the past, nuggets of time sifted through the brain pan: first date, first beer, first smoke. I eventually turned down Maple where in a few blocks another heart string would bend as the Skye home appeared on the left. I didn't know if any Skyes still inhabited that green split level with the detached two car garage. The first Iris, according to the last report, had moved away with husband and three kids. The stomach twinge, with Old Faithful predictability, knotted up as the Taurus slowed. No sense could be made of this emotional scab picking.

Shorty's was an armpit disguised as a saloon. It had been planted on the east side for over a hundred years. The wooden bar, however, was a work of art having arrived by train in the 1800's, a gift from a brewery hoping to make it big in the north woods. It was a flower in a weed patch. Hand crafted mahogany dressed out with intricate carvings of assorted wildlife. A large, yellowed mirror eyeballed the patrons. The rest of the establishment was held together with spent chewing tobacco, spilled beer, and dust. The décor was a mish mash of wooden tables and chairs with two beat up sofas fronting a stone fire place. A juke box held scratchy 45s; Neil Diamond's Sweet Caroline was worn through.

Shorty's opened at six and closed at two, both on the a.m. dial. Night shift workers shuffled in first, shirts stained with sweat. Boilermakers all around. Lunch brought the retail crowd clutching bags of burgers and fries bought from Bob's Take Out across the street. A beer or two washed the grease away. Traffic slowed mid-afternoon to early evening: a few retirees avoiding their wives, a few wives whispering to their boyfriends, a few hard cores looking for answers. Most evenings chairs were scarce. Card playing, pool shooting, shuffle boarding, bullshitting kept the tap pulled. "If you don't have a good time at Shorty's," as Zinger was fond of saying, "You are in need of a serious retooling." I tightened the hood on my sweatshirt and shoved the door.

Before the state banned indoor smoking it was impossible to see the moose head on the wall opposite the entrance, now the antlers stood out through the slight haze that was always attributed to the fireplace. I scanned the room, Zinger was at the far end of the bar playing liar's poker with a woman old enough to be his mother. He took note of my arrival while slamming the cup down. "Shit, you win again." he whined before throwing a Lincoln down.

Zinger tipped away from the bar and slowly walked toward me, squinting as his head moved side to side. "That you Paul?" "In the flesh." "It's been way too long." We hugged. Mumbling agreement into his old cardigan I got in the last squeeze. Zinger stepped back; he was two to three inches taller than me which forced him to lean away in an attempt to find my face. I took a step toward a table. "You got a car close by?" he asked. "Sure." "Let's go, I got a cd you should hear."

There was no music of course, Zinger either needed a toke or felt the moment did. As the Taurus unlocked he whistled, "Slick ride dude, you selling insurance now?" "It's a rental." "Isn't everything." I cranked the key. Zinger pulled out a beat up Sucrets box, no lozenges just machined joints as fine as Camels. He never got the hang of hand rolling, a small plastic roller and Zig Zags made up for this deficit. "If God had meant for you to smoke he would have given you the talent to hand roll." Stan Milk used to say every time the Sucrets lid popped. Zinger always ignored the jab, he was proud of his handiwork.

I drove while Zinger opened everything with a hinge. "Where's the lighter?" He hadn't driven anything made after 1985. "They

don't install them anymore, part of the cancer stick war I guess."
"Fucking cigarette smokers ruining it for everybody. Pull over at
Jimmeys, I'll scam some matches."

The party store of choice, Jimmeys was a local fixture welcom-
ing its third generation of alcohol and munchy fans. The radio
blasted the entire farm report before Zinger returned. "She wanted me to buy something, had to remind her I had bought enough
beer to float a boat. She gave me the, only this time, line. What
the fuck." Traffic was light, I backed onto the street. "Why don't
you buy a lighter?" "What do I look like, Rockefeller." "Maybe I'll
get you one for Christmas." "Yeah, maybe you'll kiss my ass." End
of conversation. "Head down to the river, we can walk to that spot
you always liked."

Ten minutes later we were dangling our feet above the muddy
current. Zinger pulled two Buds out of his jacket pockets. "Didn't
tell her how much beer I have stolen." His head snapped back with
a cackle, dirty brown hair bounced off his shoulders. "No free
matches, fuck me." Zinger lit a joint, pulling the glowing tip toward his dry lips. Eyes closed he unleashed a blue cloud over the
water. "Good weed got it from guy downstate." Good or bad, it had
been a long time. I coughed part of a lung. "Yeah, tastes sweet."
Zinger smiled then threw a short stick upstream.

The curtain rose on a new show. Colors rushed down like rain,
the wind danced with the river, a bird sang. I blended in, tossed
from the palette to the canvas.

"So you going to take that hat off and show me what all the
fuss is about." I stared in the direction of the aural invasion. For a
moment the words stood at attention before marching one by one
into my right ear, never to be heard again. "Fuss", however, slipped,

tripped and became "fuzz". "What the hell, whose been talking about my fuzz?" Zinger, assuming he had sent out the wrong soldier, got a pained look. "I heard your mother talking about your accident, sounded like you were pretty messed up." These troops never breached the outer armaments. My eyes were fixed upon a blue heron on the opposite bank, its wings stretched. A pebble hit my arm. "Dude you stoned or what?" The thread snapped as the bird took flight. "Both, I think."

My attention retrieved, Zinger repeated his inquiry. I spoke more to the place, this space that nurtured me over the years, than to my friend. All of my incarnations sat in a semicircle as the story of their future unfolded: wealth, explosion, pain, recovery, quest. At the finale I removed hood and hat, no bow was necessary. "Shit, that's a helluva look, does it hurt?" The upturned faces slowly dissolved, expectations lost in the breeze. "No, it doesn't hurt anymore." "That's good, it ain't that bad. The hat is a good idea."

We finished the beer. Zinger caught me up on the lives and loves of a few mutual friends. Charlie Martin had won a short story contest with a tale about a young boy who rode through the park late at night with his father when their truck hit a bump which his dad said was an old log. Later the boy learns a man had been killed the same evening and rats his dad out. "Yeah my mom sent me a write up in the paper." "Well," Zinger paused for effect, "turns out there was a guy run over years ago in Charlie's old home town, guess who is in jail now?"

Ben Stentz, who had been voted most likely to succeed, was doing time at a federal prison after getting caught blackmailing businessmen. He would lurk around airport hotels, have a few drinks with the boys before handing out a number. At least once a night the phone would ring in a young blonde's room nearby. Ben would hide in the closet taking pictures which later were sold to the usually married, respected schmuck who let the little head lead him astray. "He'll be out in eighteen months, rumor has it there's a shitload of money waiting in the Bahamas."

The wind changed causing commotion in the birch leaves. Tom Nell had died trying to reach his ride parked across the highway after a night of drinking at a bar outside town. He outran the approaching semi-truck but didn't count for the motorcycle passing it. "Bad fucking luck." Zinger commented. "Sort of like you and that grill, no way to anticipate a hidden Harley."

The weed rebounded. Maybe I should buy a motorcycle, good excuse to wear a helmet. Probably could get into a gang with my looks. They'd call me Lightning because I caught a bolt on Route 66. Yeah, the biker women would worship my nob. I could have sparks tattooed on the shaft. Might have to shoot a few cops. What the fuck, live fast.

"Paul, have you heard a word I said. Sonofabtich you fucking amateurs." Apparently I had taken the elevator to a different floor. "Sorry, kind of drifted off there." Zinger's face hit the serious channel. "It's O.K. dude, you got a lot going on. Take your time I was just talking about Iris." The Michigan Marching Band came around the corner, barely splashing the water. The Blue Angels pulled seven Gs in the sky. James Bond whispered in my ear, "Play it cool kid." Mr. Casual strummed my vocal chords, "So what were you saying?"

Zinger had gone to a wedding a few months back, sort of Deer Hunter meets Saturday Night Fever, three hours to the north. Iris was with the DeNiro crowd. "I didn't recognize her at first, shorter hair, more weight. She noticed me, we met at the bar." Iris had a coke. She pointed out her husband and daughters. They lived in an old farm house on forty acres. "Seemed like there was lots of work and," Zinger paused, "I picked up a hint of the Jesus Freak. Was invited to some service the next morning. Imagine that."

He had long ago decided that following the teachings of guys who lived two thousand years ago didn't make any sense. "It's like taking advice from Fred Flintstone."

"Sounds like you had a nice chat anyway." "Yeah, I always thought she was alright, too bad you guys didn't last."

"She did ask if you were still in California." A memory tug. "I didn't mention your accident since it was only a rumor, nice of you not to let me know." Maybe there should have been a full page announcement in the local paper, *Former Resident Burned Beyond Belief.* "Guess I didn't want to be a bother." Zinger stood up, dusting the dirt from his jeans. "Got to get back to Shorty's, Euchre tournament starts in a half hour." My buzz had stabilized, would be no problem keeping the Taurus between the lines. "You should know," Zinger said as we walked through the trees, "you can call me anytime no matter what." He was sincere and disappointed, getting shit again for not sharing the pain. "I know Zinger, appreciate that."

Zinger had another toke before Shorty's came into view. I pulled a u-turn stopping at the door. "Come by later I'll be here all night." "Sure, take it easy."

The radio spoke of love lost at the bottom of a bottle as the familiar streets looped me across the river toward the north side. The American Legion Lodge, flag proudly flying above its pink blocked home, stood alone on Kingman Avenue surrounded by a large gravel parking lot twice expanded to handle the relentless bingo crowds. In the lonely time before the ping pong balls rolled it was a local practice to turn in one driveway and out the opposite in order to avoid a traffic light.

Just as I started this maneuver my dad exited the double glass doors. The Taurus kicked up a few stones before stopping. Cliff looked more annoyed than startled. I rolled down the window, "Your limo, sir." He squinted in the late afternoon light. "Geezus put on your hood before the guys come out." After double timing it around the rear of the car dad slid into the passenger seat and slammed the door. He motioned toward the exit. "Not until you put on your seat belt. Clickit or ticket the sign says." Cliff gave me a look of total exasperation. I smiled. He sat. "I'll put on the hood." He buckled. I pulled the cotton shroud. As we turned down Eighth dad wrinkled his nose, "What's that smell, you hit a skunk?"

My father was a good man. He had built a life out of much less kindling than most. Sweat, muscle, long hours, and a second job had taken him up the ladder. A family, nice home, cars, travel, benefits, and respect well earned. Still robust in his sixties, even with thinning gray hair and a slight paunch, he neither gave nor took shit. Several minutes were needed for him to get over my ill-advised attempt at humor. He settled down as we passed the Dairy Queen. "You think you can find the hunting camp?"

Calling Green Hollow a hunting camp was a complete misnomer since no one had fired a shot in anger for the last twenty years and it had no beds. Seven hundred and fifty square feet of ramshackle dedicated to alcohol consumption, card playing, and bullshit. Farting was not only condoned but often applauded. A five gallon bucket held chew juice, it was emptied with the first snow. A generator provided the lighting while a propane tank fed the heat, stove, and refrigerator. A few years back a couple of the guys nearly died from carbon monoxide, more attention was now paid to filter maintenance. The "No Women Allowed" sign had been removed from the front door but could still be found on the outhouse wall.

"Green Hollow?" I said while turning onto the state highway heading west, "Do believe I had my first beer there, should be able to get us close." Cliff still wasn't going to look in my direction. His head pivoted toward the last few houses before a wall of trees lined the road. "Good, need to check on the gate, Chet said some punks busted the lock."

A few miles of silence later the old man cleared his throat, "It ain't easy being a parent you know. Hell I probably wasn't around enough, too busy working. Then you left for California....." His voice faded. I now knew how tough it is to build a life, raise a family. "Dad, you and mom are great parents, I always felt loved even if I didn't always show it." Cliff smiled. The pavement hummed a tune. "You know none of this would have happened if you had stayed around here, could have worked at the plant, got married, had kids....."

Was it too late to retrieve those recently uttered words of parental praise? We had a tug of war over the issue many times; the white victory rag had never made it to either side. I still left. At this point, however, it was difficult to argue that the right choice had been made. The rope needed a big tug. "Oh I don't know, a few million in the bank wouldn't have happened downing shots at the Hollow."

More pavement music. "How come you never told us about the money?" Good pull. "Things were moving pretty fast. I was planning on having you come out and being surprised. The accident happened, wasn't much point then." "You really had millions?" Cliff sputtered. "Eight of them." I nonchalantly replied. He shook his head. "That's Lotto money, never met anyone with that kind of cash." I tapped a hand on his shoulder, "Paul Lawton, nice to meet you." Dad laughed, more than necessary. "Keep your eyes on the road." It was getting warm, I pulled the hood down. "I could work," Cliff said, looking in my direction, "a hundred lifetimes and not get half of that."

The wealthy, those five per cent of Americans who have most of the money, are usually isolated from the ninety five per cent. The system works best when the have nots stay on their side of the red rope. Cliff and his friends never missed what they did not possess. Their wants were met. Their dreams, however, dimmed with time, fading from Technicolor to gray as the reel played out. My cash encounter upset the norm. Dad knew where eight million lived, he just couldn't go down that street.

"Yeah, I know it is crazy, before the accident I was just starting to figure it out. I was searching for some meaning besides the dollar bills." Cliff had a bemused look. He was no psychologist. We had never discussed life. It was a surprise to hear him reply, "There is no reason for anything, shit happens and we all take turns getting splattered." After rolling down the window and spitting with the wind he continued, "You hit the jackpot and then got robbed on the way to the bank." I slowed the Taurus and turned right onto a gravel road. Dust followed, covering our tracks. "Well if my attorney is to be believed I should own part of the bank soon enough." Dad grinned, "Yeah and you're going to have to wear a mask to get your money out." We both laughed. He wagged a finger in my direction, "Don't tell your mother I said that."

Our progress was slowed as deferred maintenance had left the road blanketed with pot holes. Cliff bitched as the Ford bottomed out. "What the hell are they using our tax money for, the road to the country club is smooth as ice and we get this." Cliff had no use for golf. In his mind it was not a sport but a game, like horse shoes. Plus a major expense and a time suck. I tended to agree but failed to see the connection between Green Hollow and the Rolling Hills CC.

"Pull over I need to drain the snake." As I stopped the dust swooped down. Dad waited for the grit storm to pass before making his way behind a ragged cedar. There was no need for privacy he could have pissed out the car window. As he shook, zipped and returned I noticed how much we used to look alike. I would age but no longer into his image. "What's up?" he asked before shutting the door, "You look like you saw a ghost." Could there be a ghost of someone who will no longer be? "Nothing wrong, just a touch of indigestion." "Just wait," dad said as I put the car in drive, "the plumbing really acts up as you get older."

A weathered wooden sign peppered with bullet holes greeted all who survived the trip to Green Hollow. The gate, a hundred yards from the road, was open. I killed the engine. Cliff didn't move. "I need to get a few things off my chest." A squirrel scampered up a pine tree to the left, stopping every few feet to sniff the breeze. I expected a pep talk, you'll always have a home here homily. What I got was something much different. "As I said before being a parent ain't easy, it sure ain't natural. Hell they don't give you an instruction manual." Truth be told it is harder to get a dog license than have a kid. "We got married back then just to get laid, babies were a certain consequence. Your generation is lucky to have the pill and all that, shit they sell rubbers next to candy at the drug store."

Cliff looked me in the eye, "Don't get me wrong I love your mother and was proud when you were born. It just that at my age, when there are more miles behind than ahead, things are clearer." Dad twirled the wedding ring on his calloused finger. "It's like we were pin balls bouncing along, here and there, but always down. Shit no one knew any better, if we did maybe the game would have changed." The hamster does not jump off the wheel. "Too late to bitch now, but when it comes to you there is still lots of road left."

He waved his hand toward the windshield. "Make the days good, don't just get through. And if you have kids enjoy them because one day you wake up and that life is over. They have moved on. It is like being on a roller coaster, great ride and then it suddenly stops. Parents get off, the children keep going." He slapped me on the knee, opened the door and said, "Let's see what the little vandals have done this time."

Resignation tinged with regret hung in the air. I appreciated his gift. Dad had let me see through his eyes and feel through his heart. I wanted to give him a hug

"Look what the stupid bastards did." Cliff was pointing to the U-bolt on the concrete post, it was bent and a good foot higher that than the gate. Someone had slammed down on the top hard enough to break the lock and lower the red metal bars. After trying unsuccessfully to level the two dad had me get the tire jack from the Taurus. He placed it under the bottom bar and slowly cranked the handle. Several minutes later the gate rested on the bolt. Cliff took a new lock out of his pocket. "We're going to have to leave the jack here, hope you don't mind." Budget might, I didn't. "No problem, my little contribution to Green Hollow."

We met darkness on the trip home. It was dinner time, "Betty is going to be mad if we are late, she's making your favorite, lasagna."

My stomach had been doing the munchies march since I dropped off Zinger. Dad commented on the changing demographic as we passed the half empty industrial park. The area was turning into a retirement community. "No jobs, kids leave town when they graduate." Several schools had closed; the high school housed less than half the students as during my time. The biggest employer was the medical center. "Of course the undertakers have no complaints, you know what it costs to get potted?"

Discussing death with someone you should outlive is disconcerting. "Don't worry your mom and I have everything planned out and paid for." Both the planning and paying were evidence of the practical nature my parents shared. They were also a rather sad commentary on the ability of their son to navigate through the passing on process. Could not, however, argue.

I pulled into the driveway. Before Cliff could get out I said, "Dad wait a minute." He turned toward me, his face in the glare of the dome light. "I need to say a few things too. I did some thinking during those weeks in the hospital. I know I have been pretty selfish the last few years. Shit, probably my whole life. I just want to say that I am sorry for not calling or visiting more. That's going to change, I promise." It felt good to unload. "Paul, it's been a two way street. I couldn't understand your world, didn't really try. You're a man now, I respect that. And we will talk more, especially when you move back to town." The light clicked off. It was tempting-- settle my case, get some cash, buy a place on the lake, spend afternoons at Shorty's. Hell if I bought enough drinks it didn't matter how I looked. "Don't know dad maybe I will, still got a few things to finish up out there."

Dinner was great. The novelty of my appearance had worn off. It was the three of us, plus Jesus, talking about the old days. Dad and I had a few beers. Mom had baked a cake. We laughed a lot. The phone rang as the dishes were being cleared. It was Zinger, "Hey dude I got some Puerto Rican girls just dying to meet you." He knew about five song lyrics, that was his favorite. "Thanks, but I'm staying in tonight, still a little jet lagged." A whine blared through the line, "No really, I got a couple of babes here. They want to party."

The last time he had made a similar proposal I spent the night listening to a large girl extol the virtues of the Oprah Show while her sister put her oral talents to better use between Zinger's legs. "That's alright, maybe another time" Major whine. "How about if I drive by and you stick your head in the car and say hello." He had either made a bet or taken a bribe with regard to my disfiguration. "Geez Zinger maybe you could set up a tent in the parking lot and sell tickets. Five bucks for thirty seconds with the freak." He didn't pick up on the fact I was teasing. "Fuck no man, you're cool with me. Shit I'm sorry." A long pause later, in a hushed tone, "It's just that this girl has a rack a moose would be proud of." I was tempted to channel Nicholson and make a "Here's Pauley" appearance. "No need to apologize, just not tonight." "O.K., take it easy." Zinger would have to find another route to the treasure chest.

The next few days were relaxing. We spent the hours together, except for church. My parents appeared relieved when I declined that invitation. One afternoon I drove us out to my uncle's farm. He had died the previous year. A big for sale sign hung on the side of the barn. "You know a guy with some cash could pick this place up for a song." Cliff said. "And maybe it would be a good place for some quality retirement time." I replied. Dad was eligible for the pasture, I could open the gate. "Anything to keep him away from that dreadful Green Hollow" mom chirped. I wrote down the realtor's number.

Half way home the Taurus was thirsty. Self-serve Union 76. Hopping out of the car without my hoody hide out I soon had gas gurgling. Across the island two young boys were pointing out a van window and laughing so hard their car seats were bouncing. I gave them a smile and a thumbs up which brought a howl. To their left a young woman in jeans, sweatshirt, and bandana stretched across brown curls, stood like a statue, nozzle straining her right hand. I waved. She dropped the hose, got in the Caravan and drove away. The kids craned their necks in my direction. My pump clicked off with a burp.

Back on the road Betty said, "That women looked like she saw a ghost." "Yeah but her kids were laughing." Cliff chuckled. "It ain't easy being me," I replied, "but it can be entertaining." "You are going back to the doctor." mom stated a command not a question. "Not until after Halloween." Betty tapped my arm, barely suppressing a smile.

Leaving wasn't easy. I promised to be careful, to milk the Cain Corporation dry, to call often and to go back to Dr. Vu for more work. They stood in the drive waving as I pulled away with a honk of the horn. Miles were needed to shove down the lump in my throat.

Outside of town, at the stop sign fronting the state highway, a lone hitchhiker stood. He was tall, barrel-chested, holding a cardboard sign displaying a hand drawn airplane. Hitchhikers always got the accelerator pedal from me but this guy appeared different. He was wearing an army surplus jacket, blue beanie, jeans, boots and had a red duffel bag. It was a few hours from the airport; I was certainly the only non-stop transport available. I pulled over twenty yards short of the intersection, he grabbed his bag and semi-hustled toward the Taurus.

I put the hood over my head and popped the trunk, in went the sign and bag, down came the lid. He opened the door and squeezed his oversized frame onto the seat. "Thanks, how far you heading?" "From the looks of your artwork, right where you want to go." He banged the dash. "Alright, been sucking exhaust out there for an hour."

Reaching into his pocket he pulled out two bottles of water, "Would you like one Paul?" Grabbing the Arrowhead with thanks I was on the second gulp before it dawned on me that he knew my name. A closer look at this hitcher revealed an L branded into his forearm. L for Lee, Lee Bay, two grades behind at Grover Cleveland High and years advanced on the political front. Lee had led protests every month against anything from ROTC on campus to banning salt in the cafeteria. His blonde hair was shorter, a wispy goatee adorned a ruddy face, and his eyes were still a piercing gray.

"You know my name?" Lee's shoulders slumped. "I am such a dumb shit." He went on to explain how Zinger was scamming beers in exchange for telling the tale of Paul Lawton, barbecued victim. "Zinger said you were flying out today, I figured you would come this way."

I lowered the hood, gave him a quick glance and pulled out onto the highway. "So do I live up to Zinger's billing?" Lee didn't flinch, "Yeah, skinned rabbit, about right." Having never butchered a bunny I had no frame of reference. "You can move to the back seat, I would understand." Incredulity crossed his face, "You're dicking with me right? Hell I have woken up with women scarier than you. Lee finished his water, crushed the bottle, and returned it to his pocket. Two guys on Harleys blew by, leaving a muffled roar in their wake. The Taurus quivered. "Yeah." I announced a little too loudly, "yeah, I was dicking with you." He rolled his eyes, "They didn't burn the smartass out of you."

As we ate the miles Lee caught me up on his life and times. A degree in sociology was followed by two years teaching at an inner city school in Philadelphia. Took a year to write a book about the flaws in the educational system, titled it "Recessed Minds.' "No one would publish it, chicken shits." Now he worked for a think tank called, Keep It Simple. "We are attempting to stop the voracious appetite for consumption that drives our economy and will soon ruin the planet."

Lee was heading back to D.C. where he shared an apartment with three other low paid employees. "The pricks that are ruining things live like kings while those of us doing good barely keep our noses above the poverty line." Lee was on the ultimate crusade. My accomplishments paled. Nonetheless the story of my code crunching pot of gold, mini-mansion purchase, exploding grill was told as the forest gave way to fields. Instead of condolences Lee barked, "See that's just what the fuck I was talking about, that grill never would have had the chance to do harm in my world." A bold statement. He justified his confidence with a twenty minute lecture.

The problem, according to Lee, was the fact quantity was valued over quality, new was better than old, replace more important than recycle. "It is stupid to have so many choices for everyday items such as a grill. After Zinger told your story I looked it up, do you know there are over a hundred grill manufactures with over a thousand model types." His voice rose, "We waste time and resources with the unnecessary duplication of products. Meat can be cooked just as well on one standard grill, efficiently designed and safely constructed. No explosions, ever." Lee went on to argue that product variety in general was a capitalistic tool. "A society should first satisfy all citizens' basic needs: food, shelter, health care, and education, before building twenty different kinds of lawn mowers or fifty different models of phones."

Keep It Simple advocated coring production of quality goods everyone needed, from toilet paper to cars. "Our possessions should not define us," Lee said, his voice rising, "We are better than that, keeping up with the Jones's is killing us." He also sounded off on population growth contending that Earth has more than enough people now; we should only be replacing not expanding. "Seven billion of our species is enough, put out the no vacancy sign, close the door."

Of course big money would never agree, more consumers mean more profit. People can only eat so much sausage, if you want to sell more you need more mouths. "I know we are advocating a complete revamping of the economic system, but it doesn't take much to see the train we are on is quickly running out of track." Lee looked out the window, a few miles of silence passed before we reached the freeway. "Mind stopping at Forwards, I need to take a leak?" Combination of gas station, general store, and restaurant Forwards was a shrine on the pilgrimage to civilization. "No problem," I replied, stringing up the hood.

I pumped the tank full before going inside. Lee was standing off to the right, his head visible above the shelves. "See this is what I mean, five brands of toothpaste, six different deodorants, three kinds of shoe polish. Unnecessary products competing for our attention, all fed to us by advertising. Half the brands are made by the same company anyway. The energy, time and money could be put too much better use." He made sense. One or two choices for most things we buy would be enough. Stop the ads, but then who would pay for the television shows, magazines, newspapers, and live sports. A million bucks for thirty seconds of Super Bowl time greases the gears. Lee wanted to get rid of the gears

Lee didn't offer to split the gas but did buy me a diet Pepsi and a bag of cheese corn. He continued to complain while my fingers turned varying shades of yellow. "Would we choose to live like this if we had to do it all over again? No fucking way! One percent of the population owns just about everything. The land is being raped, global warming, wildlife extinction, billions in poverty, genocide, corruption, and other assorted cluster fucks."

I wanted to shout out a big "Amen." "Of course we at Keep It Simple are pissing into the wind right now, but our time will come. It is inevitable." He crushed another water bottle before doing the same with my can. I envied Lee his passion and the certainty of his belief. "You got a card or something; I would like to keep in touch." I said as the airport off ramp came into sight. He grinned while putting a green card on the console. "Recycled paper, has my address and e-mail."

Lee's flight was an hour from take-off. I pulled to the departure curb and hit the trunk switch. He stretched across the seat and gave me a hug. "Thanks for the lift and for listening. Take is easy. And," he grinned, "Zinger was right, after a while your face ain't a distraction. Good luck with the future." "Yeah, you too." I replied. Lee barged into the terminal, a man on a mission

.

I returned the rental, hooded up, checked in, and flew west. Also on a mission.

I was surprised to see Coos as I left the Northwest jet way. He was spinning a wheelie while four toddlers ran around him laughing hysterically. After several revolutions, hair a brown blur, he stopped. More dizzy than tired, Todd didn't object as two of the young boys tried to climb on to his chair. They were quickly corralled by their mother who apologized profusely.

Unable to speak Coos gestured with his right hand that all was fine.

I walked up from behind, "Hey buddy you should take that act on the road, the gimp circus is looking for talent." His back muscles tightened, the chair slowly rotated as he barked, "Who you calling a gimp." When his eyes met mine I laughed, "You shorty." Coos punched me in the stomach which caught the attention of a nearby security guard.

He walked over just as I regained my breath. "Is everything alright here gentlemen?" Todd was laughing now. "No problem officer, just a little misunderstanding. Everything is fine." The guard was in his mid-twenties, blue pants neatly pressed, white shirt spotless, assorted offensive items hanging from a shiny black belt. "I will give you two minutes to vacate this area." Coos appeared ready to hop down and wrestle his badge away. I grabbed the chair handles and began to push toward the exit.

Forty yards down the walkway I asked, "What the hell you doing here?" Coos gestured toward the Bay Bridge Bar. It was almost noon. I maneuvered us into a corner table, opposite the harried traveler pathway. Coos ordered two beers before answering my question, "It's time for another road trip Paul, I got a lead on that bitch Jackie." It had been a while since I had given any thought to that candy apple red Mustang and the dirty deed. Of course it was all that my friend thought about. "Before you go detective on me, where is the car? You know the car that I traded my ride for, which I guess makes it my car?"

Coos set his glass down, a little foam settled on his upper lip. "Didn't I leave you a note, I couldn't sleep so around four I called my buddy Ryan, he owns a towing service. We had the Mustang on the truck by daylight. Back in Stockton two hours later." He went on to explain it was in the shop being outfitted so he could return to driving. "I paid a lawyer plenty, whatever it takes to get me back on the road." When that happened I wanted to be indoors.

"How was your trip?" Coos asked, gesturing for another round. I filled him in on my return to the womb. "So what has Sherlock discovered about Jackie?" "I have discovered," he loudly announced, "she is slipperier than a greased pig."

After taking care of his Mustang Coos had returned to his large house in search of Jackie's last name. Jackie had never lived there but Todd had transferred boxes from his old place. He called in his maid, Ramona and the two spent a full day going through every drawer, closet, and shelf. Ramona had come with the house as part of the settlement package. Her English did not match her cleaning skills; however, after being shown the name, she worked like a blood hound and sniffed out the only trace, a dry cleaner receipt with the letters J. S-N-I-P on the customer line. The rest of the faded paper had been torn away.

Disappointed at his lack of success and not sure if he even had a clue Coos awoke early for a limo ride to Traditore's office. "I figured Marcia the office manager might be able to help, plus we had a history."

It had been a few years but Marcia came out quickly after the receptionist announced a Mr. Todd Coos was waiting. "She still looked good." "Yeah and she was still old enough to be your mother." He could tell she hadn't forgotten their earlier bump and grinds. They went to an interior conference room and closed the door. After some small talk Coos explained his quest. He gave her the "Snip" clue and suggested she check clients six or seven years back for a match. Marcia got that sucked lemon look, "Any information would be confidential, I don't know." Todd placed a hand along the inside of her thigh while sliding hers onto his crotch. She feigned shock before smiling, "It is good to see some things haven't changed." Marcia pulled out a set of keys and quietly locked the door.

By the time she turned around Coos had lowered the chair arms and unzipped. Marcia quickly pulled her skirt up, stretched flowered panties to one side revealing more gray than Todd remembered, and mounted. Coos held her ass as she balanced over the chair, hands pressed into the wall, feet barely on the floor. She worked the rhythm, he braced with each bounce. They had done this dance before. Marcia's soft moans turned into sporadic grunts. Todd buried his face in her silk blouse. The locked wheels strained in protest. They came within seconds of each other. Marcia caught her breath, a red hue slowly faded from her face and neck. "You are incorrigible Mr. Coos." "I hope that's a compliment." he replied. She laughed, wrote down the clue and went to her office.

A few minutes later Marcia returned, pulling a torn envelope from her pocket. "We had a Snipnell and a Snipperton as clients years back. Snipperton was an older women, Snipnell was twenty or twenty one. It sounds crazy to me but Snipnell appears to be your only hope. Here's his address. You did not get it from this office." Coos grabbed the paper. He rolled down the hall and back to the entrance. Marcia pushed the button for the elevator, leaned over and whispered, "You owe me one more, I am going to call you in a few weeks." A cloud of confusion muddled his mind, who was using whom "Sure, anytime, least I can do, should have this cleared up by then, thanks, take care." he sputtered as the doors opened.. By the time he spun the chair she was gone, by the time the lobby bell sounded he felt like the trade had been fair. Information for satisfaction, the fact he got both didn't bother him.

274

Regency Court in Danville was a forty minute drive from Traditore's office. The community was gated, a fortress for the affluent. Luckily Coos's driver recognized the guard from their kid's soccer team. He confirmed that Mr. Snipnell lived on the first cul de sac to the right. The red bricked home was set back from the road; large arched windows looked out on the manicured lawn.

Coos was surprised to see a ramp leading to an imposing wooden door. He hopped on the chair, easily navigating the tiled switchback before pushing the bell. A metallic gong tolled inside followed by a whirling noise as a camera above zoomed its eye. Moments later a disembodied voice coming from a speaker built into the brick asked, "Can I help you?" Coos felt a little like Dorothy; he had no idea who was behind the curtain. "Yeah, I hope so, I got your name from Traditore, he was my lawyer too." Guilt momentarily tightened his chest as he broke his promise to Marcia. "I am trying to find Jackie, she helped me out and I wanted to thank her now that I have my settlement." He was heartened that the wizard didn't demand, "Jackie who?" Suddenly the door silently opened, he crossed the flat threshold.

The interior design was a mixture of Star Wars and Wild Kingdom. Polished glass and metal gleamed, animal heads were mounted on several walls, various audio-video-computer equipment hummed, everything was wheel chair accessible, a ramp lead toward a back room. As the door shut behind him Todd whistled, "Looks like this gimp has died and gone to heaven." "Or hell" a hoarse voice stated from the right.

There sat Edward Snipnell, a shriveled husk strapped to the fanciest wheel chair Coos had ever seen; motorized, electrified, digitized chrome. Sniper, as he was known in his youth, after extensive, costly physical therapy had movement in two fingers on his right hand as well as everything above the neck. With the aid of technology he could operate all the entertainment wonders gracing his home. The chair was his coach, the house his kingdom.

It had been years since a settlement brokered by Traditore had funded the gutting and remodeling of the spacious tri-level. Caregivers provided twenty four hour assistance. A button push would quickly summon help from a guest apartment on the ground floor. He was washed, dried, fed and turned out to play. Pampered like an over indulgent matron's prized Yorkie, Sniper's days were as pleasant and worry free as partial quad could ever hope to have.

His presence limited to an active mind and two miracle digits, Edward Snipnell did his best to be relevant. He was on the internet with an alias in forums spanning the social spectrum. The stuffed trophies were shot remotely using his monitor and keyboard space bar, thousands changed hands weekly on sports betting sites, four scrabble tournaments ran at once, and he gave no bullshit advice on a paralysis web page. Sniper had slowly become a recluse finding less and less of a reason to leave home. He lived in a cloud, floating in a world where feeling did not require touching.

Coos had seen many chair riders, but this was different, it took a moment to get his bearings. He wheeled toward his host intending to shake his hand, realized that could not happen, stopped and gave a weak wave. "Thanks for letting me in, I'm Todd Coos." Snipnell left a bank of security monitors and rolled directly in front of Hot Rod, his perch was higher by a foot; he looked down with a bemused look. "Another victim of the industrial complex I see." "Yeah, had a bad set of car jacks." "That sucks; Traditore must have picked their bones clean." He let out a groan of a laugh, "Of course the lawyer still has his legs, and his dick still works, not to mention all the other appendages I no longer have any use for." Coos moved his chair in a 180 degree arc, "Not a fair trade that's for sure." Edward was preaching to the choir, it was the last service, that song had been sung.

"You got anything to drink in this fun house?" Sniper grinned, he didn't know this guy but he liked his style. "One push of a button and I can get a cute Filipino girl with big knockers to bring you a cold beer, how does that sound. Follow me." His chair practically jumped across the foyer as he sped into a large living room, sparsely furnished with one leather couch and a few tables. Todd's overdrive was no match, by the time he arrived Snipnell had placed the order.

True to his word a short, young lady dressed in white with shiny black hair down to the middle of her back appeared with a tray containing two cold glasses of Anchor Steam. She placed one into a cup holder on Sniper's chair and attached a long, plastic straw to a piece of Velcro near his mouth, before bending down and handing Coos his beer. As the caretaker left Sniper drained several ounces. "This will play hell with my plumbing but I don't get many guests. Cheers." He took another long pull. Todd drained half his glass before coming up for air. "So what put you in the chair?" having shared his story Coos felt entitled.

Sniper hit one of several buttons near his functioning fingers. A saxophone lead off an assortment of instruments filling the air with a techno vibe. "I had the unfortunate timing to hit a step suffering from years of neglect just as it gave up the ghost. Concrete separated from the rebar causing me to fall head first. Woke up broken."

The apartment complex owners, management company, and janitorial service all paid policy limits. More lager worked its way up the straw. "You must know the routine, all that rah rah from relatives, nurses, therapists, doctors. You still have your life in front of you. There will be a cure soon. Take it a day at a time. And my personal favorite, It is all part of God's plan. After a while I just nodded and smiled."

Coos agreed, although on the fucked-up scale Snipnell was on a much higher rung. Just the fact that his dick no longer worked made Todd wince. "Yeah, I hear you. A lot of bullshit." The beer was a memory. Sniper motioned for Coos to follow him up a ramp and into the kitchen. "I am not supposed to have another so soon." he said pointing at a double door stainless steel fridge. "And the fact is I can't help myself, but you Todd can do the deed." Coos found the beer on a bottom shelf, popped the tops and refilled their glasses. Snipnell had him hide the evidence behind a large ficus tree in the corner. They laughed like little kids. "Fuck em!" Sniper yelled spinning down another ramp.

Two right turns brought the duo to a large door which slid open by voice command. Inside was five hundred square feet of sensory overload. A dozen monitors of varying sizes ringed the walls and ceiling. The queen sized bed was motorized allowing Snipnell to adjust his position in all directions. Racks of amps, tuners, pcus, and gaming equipment travelled along grooves in the floor. "I have spent full days without leaving this space." Sniper stated. "Getting out of bed isn't always necessary."

Coos was attracted to a large collection of dvds near the heavily draped window. As he browsed his eye was drawn to a dusty picture frame. A much different Snipnell, tanned, in a red muscle shirt, smiled: his arm draped around the shoulders of an attractive auburn haired girl with twinkling blue eyes. It was Jackie. Just as Todd grabbed the evidence half the screens flickered on revealing a double amputee with metal leg prosthesis running down a tartan track. "Why haven't you gotten these?" Sniper asked, "They look awesome." Truth be told Coos had tried a few different versions. He always felt uncomfortable. "Too slow, plus I get more pussy with the chair."

Snipnell had maneuvered himself into a u-shaped counsel; he was plugged into a virtual command center. "You mean like this." All the monitors were set to vaginal vision. Assorted female nether regions came and went, a slide show of lips and clits. "Took me half a day to set up this program, close to a thousand different women" Coos was impressed. "Of course," Snipnell sighed, "it's like a castrated dog outside a poodle convention, all I can do is look."

A few moments passed before the parade of beaver was replaced with geometric figures dancing to a salsa beat. He had a lot of time on his fingers and created elaborate presentations which he placed on various web pages with the intention of disturbing as much shit as possible. Sniper enjoyed the internet interaction. He would spend hours replying to e-mails.

"You want to see my latest project; it is titled 'Enough Already.'" A somber melody played in the background as pictures of Jesus, Mohammed, Buddha, and other assorted religious deities preceded a quick timeline of human history, the good and the awful: Mona Lisa and Dachau, Hiroshima and penicillin, Pol Pot and Gandhi. A disembodied voice laced the slides with prayers and chanting. The pixels then made the case for the end of all religions. The first salvo centered on the contention that in the age of space shuttles, medical miracles, and technological advancement should we place any credence in prophets who had no understanding of atoms, energy, or the universe. Images of men on camels contrasted with leathered up motorcycle riders.

The argument continued with the claim that if a religion is to have any credence at all it should be universally accepted. Why would there be more than one afterlife or more than one route to get there. The piece went forward with years rolling off a cliff. Two thousand years for Christians, thousands more for Jews, all spent waiting. "Maybe," the announcer boomed, "the promise of a savior is a way of stringing us along, the out of reach carrot. We don't live long enough, if just one human was a few hundred years old he would have wised up by now. We should too."

There was also a riff on reincarnation, calling the Hindu and Buddhist belief a mathematically impossible conveyor belt of poor souls stuck in an endless loop. Dollar signs concluded the presentation, tallying billions of dollars in wealth controlled by those pretending to have the keys to heaven. A crier yelled for the coffers to be emptied, for houses of worship to be turned into homes for the poor, for the gold to be melted and the icons sold. "I'll be putting this on the net soon, should create a bigger storm than my last project proving that the US government shot down that plane in Pennsylvania on 9/11."

Coos didn't know what to say. He gripped the picture frame on his lap, tapping it with his fingers like Dorothy and her shoes, hoping to regain his bearings. Just as Snipnell's whirlwind was settling down another attendant entered the room. She too was young and attractive. "Mr. Edward, the alarm went off for your urine output." It was a polite way of saying his piss bag was full. Her uniformed body hid the exchange from view. The discharge was in a small white bag as she left the room. Sniper didn't acknowledge the event. He was checking an arriving e-mail. Todd drank more beer.

"What do you have in your hand, Mr. Coos?" Snipnell backed his wheel chair until he was at Todd's side. "Where did you find that, I told them to throw away all my old pictures. It hurts to see what I was." "Sorry," Todd replied, "I thought I recognized the girl." Sniper stared down into the print. "That's my cousin Phyllis, must have been taken ten years ago. She is hot, poor choice for a name. A Phyllis should work in a library, go in a convent or take tolls, she sure as shit shouldn't look like a centerfold." Coos was beginning to doubt his identification. "Did she change her name?" Sniper finished his beer, and then belched. "Oh she didn't like the name, was always calling herself something else, drove her parents crazy." "Ever use Jackie?" "Hell, I don't know, probably easier to pick one she didn't use."

He rolled back over to mission control. Shortly several pictures of Phyllis graced the screens. Coos recognized the "fuck you world" look in a few shots. He was certain it was Jackie. "Where is she now?" Sniper lined the monitors with maps. "Mr. Coos I recall you mentioning a Jackie before I let you in the door. Is my cousin Phyllis your Jackie, and if so, what do you want with her?" Todd was at another conscience crossroad, telling the truth might be the wrong way to go. "I think she is, and it's a long story." Beethoven's Fifth blasted from all directions. "A story you would rather not get into, I believe." Coos rode his chair toward the far wall, still cradling the picture. He did not reply. "Well I doubt you could cause her much harm, and from one chair jockey to another, I don't feel a bad vibe. I will tell you what I know, but you must promise to return and spill the whole story."

Coos smiled and readily agreed. It had been months since Snipnell had spoken with Phyllis, years since he had seen her. "We were pretty close before my accident, cried on each other shoulders. After I got hurt she just broke down every time we got together, wasn't good for either of us." "She put you in touch with Traditore." Sniper shook his head, "No, that was some guy at the hospital, an orderly or something. But she did take an interest in my case. Was happy I cashed in, came to the house once and told me I deserved anything I wanted." He tapped a finger and a dial tone filled the air followed by the notice that the number was no longer in service. "Well this is not going to be easy." More tapping. "No e-mail, no net presence at all."

The speakers blared, "What you going to do when the well runs dry." Sniper lowered his seat back and stared at the ceiling. Todd became uncomfortable as the moments past. He had invaded Snipnell's space and taken up too much of his time. "That's alright, I appreciate your help." He said before setting the picture back on the shelf. Sniper ignored him. Coos began to roll toward the door. "Cards, that's it, why didn't I think of that before."

Snipnell was back at his bank of computers. "Double fucking down, what was her handle?" In the past few years Phyllis had discovered internet poker. She played Texas Holdem on line and had occasionally accumulated enough wins to get a free entry into live table tournaments. "She liked that car tune." A song filled the room, "I bought you a brand new Mustang, nineteen sixty five… you don't wanna let me ride..one of these early mornings I am going to be wipin your weepin eyes." Two monitors suddenly displayed a list of names, all champions of the month from the Poker Stars web site, highlighted in yellow was WilsonP. "That's Phyllis," Sniper announced, "Get it, Wilson Pickett sang it, so WilsonP makes sense."

Hot Rod felt a blast of irony at the Mustang reference. "Looks like she has qualified for the Micronesian Millions Tournament, starts tomorrow on Saipan. Bet you will find her there." Coos had no clue where there was, he also wasn't going to admit it. "I owe you one, can't thank you enough." Todd came up to Sniper's chair, grabbed his two working fingers and gave them a squeeze. He felt a slight pressure in response. "No problem, I enjoyed our time, and you owe me a return visit." Snipnell followed Coos to the door which swung open at their approach. Todd turned and waved before wheeling to the limo. As he moved onto the back seat he asked the driver how far it was to Saipan. "I don't think you can get there from here." came the reply.

As the limousine made its way over the coastal hills Coos called Fred at Dick's Pool Emporium, "Where the fuck is Saipan?" Fred muttered a few words about the tragic state of public education. "It's one of the islands in Micronesia, not too far from Guam." "So down off the coast of Mexico?" Fred almost swallowed his cigar. "Shit, no geography or World War Two history at your school."

Todd had spent a minimal amount of time studying or concentrating. "World War Two, fuck, it's over in Germany?" The phone line went dead, Coos blamed the hills. He called back. "It's in the Western Pacific you idiot, about a four hour flight from Japan. You know where that is don't you!" Upset that he was being dicked with but grateful for the information Coos refrained from going off on Fred. "Thanks man, I'll bring you some Cubans when I…" the phone went to tone again. There wasn't a hill in sight.

Once home Todd did an internet search. Fred was right Saipan was a long way out in the ocean, a speck of green surrounded by turquoise. 1458 miles south east of Tokyo, 1475 miles east of the Philippines, and 5000 miles from San Francisco. Sixty five square miles of limestone, jungle, cliffs, and beaches. Home to sixty thousand trying to earn a living off tourists, the garment industry, and the Commonwealth government. On June 15, 1944 American forces commenced a battle which resulted in the deaths of thirty thousand Japanese soldiers some of whom jumped off the aptly named Banzai Cliff. Coos was once again reminded of his lack of knowledge. Once again he vowed to spend an hour a day filling in the gaps in his education. Remediation was on hold, however, as he called up the Micronesian Millions web site. Sniper was right about the tournament, off on the date. Coos pulled out his credit card.

"All my work." Todd stated tossing a packet of paper on the table. Inside were first class seats to Saipan via Tokyo, two entries into the tournament, two rooms at a resort hotel, and a laminated sheet of Texas Hold-em terms, hand rankings, and drawing odds. "Had your luggage transferred, we should head over to the gate." He gave me the familiar-- what the hell else you got that's better to do-- grin. "Do I have time to take a piss?" "Only if you don't sit down."

I left while Todd paid the tab. He was parked just outside the men's room as I exited. "I don't know shit about poker." "Yeah, well I do but these guys are going to be tougher than those bums back at Dick's. I got some books in my carry on, we can both pick up a few pointers." "Plus," he cackled while putting his chair in another gear, "I figure you must have the greatest poker face of all time." Coos was weaving around startled travelers, I hustled to keep up.

Up in the air, first class again, ate the food and drank two beers. Todd's competitive nature had him hitting the books. I pulled out the tournament information. "The entry fee is ten thousand dollars?" Coos looked up from Doyle Brunson's *Super System*, "Yeah it was the only way to get a room." The logic escaped me. "We probably could have bought a house for twenty thousand." "I figured in order to find Jackie we need to get close to the tables anyway. Don't get upset, it ain't your money." True, but I did not want to look like a total asshole. Grabbing *Harrington on Hold Em* I began my education.

Texas Holdem takes twenty minutes to learn and a life time to master. Players are dealt two hole cards, bet, and then the flop-- three communal cards face up on the felt, bet, then the turn card, bet, and finally the river card, last bet. In "no limit" a player can bet all his chips, go all in, at any time. Simple enough until you start reading about pot odds, calling station, anticipated value, position, and a dozen other concepts and theories. I would be a fish swimming with hungry sharks. Setting Harrington aside I resigned myself to an early exit from the tournament, hammered a shot of bourbon and went to sleep.

Switching planes in Tokyo went smoothly. Back in the air Coos and I played a few practice hands. He became irritated when I made a flush. "That's what makes this game such a pain, I should have won that hand nine times out of ten." He went on to tell me the odds of flopping a flush are 0.8 percent. It was heartening to realize luck could make up for stupidity. An hour later I attempted to bring his attention back to the reason we were flying halfway around the world. "So, what is the plan for finding Jackie?" "Two ways," he began, "There must be a roster somewhere, try to find her name. If that doesn't work we need to keep our eyes open." It was unfortunate Coos had not kept a picture of his prey.

Saipan International Airport welcomes tens of thousands visitors a year. As the DC-10 touched down I realized my hooded look would not be practical on a tropical island. To my surprise Coos pulled out a foreign legion hat, similar to the one Josh had given me. "It almost makes sense here." he said. It was five a.m. local time. I had no idea what time it was back at the old homestead. "The cards start flying at noon." Todd mentioned as we watched the luggage carousel. My bag hit the belt with a thud. I helped wrestle a Samsonite belonging to Coos and schlepped them both to Customs. Todd had called my mother and had her find and deposit my passport in my backpack. "You talked to Betty?" "Yeah, told her it was a surprise trip to Mexico." Mom had kept the secret.

As the doors closed behind us a hammer of heat pounded down, seventy eight degrees with seventy per cent humidity before the break of dawn. On the sidewalk a bead of sweat swam down my spine. There were shuttles set aside for tourney players. Coos made a production out of hopping into the front seat of the van. Our driver, a sleepy eyed young man with brown skin and black hair, was wearing the tourism standard white shorts, sandals, and a flowered shirt. Todd wasted no time peppering him with questions about blondes with nice boobs. He handed us a card for *Sally's Roundevouz,* "Great girls there, tell them Rocky sent you."

The ride to Garapan, the main hotel area and tournament site, took us past tin roofed buildings, creeping jungle, white sand beaches with rusted WWII tanks half submerged on the reef, strip malls, golf courses, poured concrete office buildings, and low slung garment factories. "Check your shirt," Rocky said, "odds are it was made here." The sun rose as we arrived at the Nimitz Carlton Hotel. I got the chair while Rocky wrestled the luggage. Coos gave him a twenty, a good start to his day.

The lobby desk was not disability compliant. Todd had to stop ten feet away just to see the clerk's face. Our names were on the list, keys were provided, along with a complimentary breakfast buffet. Coos inquired if a Jackie Snipnell was registered only to be told that guest information was private. He was too far back to attempt a bribe and I was too slow to understand his gesture. The phone rang and the opportunity was lost.

The activity level was low this early; a few Japanese with bags of scuba gear were finishing breakfast. Otherwise more cleaning staff than guests walked the spacious ground floor. I continued carrying our luggage as we found our eighth floor room. Coos immediately ran a hot tub while I hit the shower. We left an eleven

a.m. wake up call. Four hours of sleep would have to do. All too
soon it would be shuffle up and deal.

The Marianas Trench passes by Saipan, 35,810 feet of water. I
was below that, sleeping soundly, when a ringing phone brought me
up from the depths. The wakeup call alternated between English
and Japanese. With Coos snoring, the air conditioner gasping,
and palm trees swaying outside the window it took a few moments
before I remembered ten thousand dollars' worth of chips were
waiting.

I pulled a clean pair of pants out of the suitcase along with a
faded Giants t-shirt. Todd required two pokes in the shoulder before he sat up. "Fuck, whose idea was this anyway." He put on his
usual half pants before buttoning up a shirt decorated with suited
cards. Next came a Nascar hat and large sunglasses. "The books
say you should keep your eyes hidden, won't give away your hand."
The fact he looked like a refuge from a Florida trailer park was
irrelevant. He tossed me an even larger pair of shades. "With your
hat you should be good to go."

We hit the soda machine for cans of caffeine before elevating
down to the lobby. Hordes of soon to be felt combatants were making their way toward the convention center, a large Quonset hut
shaped structure one hundred yards down a crushed stone path.
"Keep an eye out, you never know." Coos admonished. I was lucky
to keep an eye open. The crowd was ninety per cent male, and
one hundred per cent abnormal. Professional poker players live indoors. Sedentary hours spent passing chips, listening to music on
headphones, calculating odds, rushing to the bathroom, and eating junk food produce pale, pudgy bodies and razor sharp minds.
Bets, bluffs, raises, folds, re-raises are the weapons employed by

these table warriors. Tournaments were three or four day affairs, a test of acumen, luck, will, and bladder control.

As we approached the row of entry tables Todd's head was on a swivel. After being handed our seat assignments Coos again inquired about Jackie only to be told all entrants' names were confidential. The word "taxes" was bandied about. "I really need to find her." he practically begged only to be ignored. Not a lot of sentiment at tournament time. Our tables were on opposite sides of the large room. Todd decided to roll up and down the rows, a wheeled hound dog hoping for a scent.

I found table 56 with a little guidance from strategically placed young women wearing coconut bras and flowered skirts. Once there I was clueless as to where seat five was located. "Over here baby." gestured a middle aged Filipino man with an excessive amount of gold jewelry hanging down his chest. Not knowing seat location was blood in the water, just dole my chips out right now. Suddenly the lights dimmed, a drum roll preceded strobes of light blanketing the crowd before resting upon an older woman in a crisp navy blue outfit. Gratitude was expressed to island hosts, various sponsors and the 1897 players. The Governor of the Commonwealth was introduced and given the honor of announcing, "Shuffle up and deal."

I spent the next hour trying not to look like a total douche bag. It took three hands before Mr. Gold Chains was kind enough to inform me that picking up my two hole cards like it was blackjack exposed them to more eyes than my own. "Make a cave with your hands baby, don't let no one in your cave, baby." He smiled. It was an honorable gesture. Posting of the blinds, big and small, was each player's responsibility every circuit. I managed to comply with a little prodding from the dealer. My chip control needed work, twice one rolled away, zig-zagging across the green.

There were ten of us around the table; elbow room was at a premium. Other than pegging me as a fish no one paid any attention. The hat and sunglasses worked well, in fact everyone but the dealer was shaded and six wore hats. No women so no Jackie unless she was a helluva cross dresser and had gained weight. The group was a mix of Asian and American with one guy from Sweden. A few were acquainted and made small talk about the last tournament in Macau. I played one hand forty minutes in when two sixes showed up in my cave. Pocket sixes in poker lingo. The flop came with a face card, a gentleman chewing a cigar sporting a large panama hat threw out two one hundred dollar chips I tossed my cards in front of the dealer an area known as the muck. At this point losing was O.K. as long as I followed protocol.

After a while a rhythm developed. Not many hands were contested and those that were didn't involve a lot of chips. Occasionally, usually when I was paying more attention to one of the island girls pushing a drink cart, the words "All in!" would ring out, The first time it was a pudgy faced Chinese guy wearing a coffee stained polo shirt three seats to my left. He had just put his tournament life at risk, challenging the Swede, a dapper looking young man with blonde hair falling out of a Panama hat. All necks at the table stretched toward the cards, three small hearts and the two black tens. The Swede stared at Mr. All In, looking for a tell. Finally he threw his cards in the muck. The victor smiled and revealed a six and eight of clubs. His move was a stone, cold bluff. Everybody laughed but the Panama hat.

Four hours and two bathroom breaks later we paused for lunch, the fact it was three in the afternoon didn't seem to matter. I had won a hand with three sevens and another with two pair, still my chip count was one thousand less than at the start. Coos had positioned himself in a hallway outside the room, his head bobbling as I came up on the right. "All I'm seeing is cocks and balls." "Well you're the perfect height for that." He was not amused. When an official with a World Poker Tour name tag locked the doors without a Jackie sighting Todd spun around in disgust. "She is here." he slowly stated, it sounded more like hope than a fact.

By the time we reached the buffet it looked like hyenas had ravaged the long row of gleaming, metal trays. Rice and pancit noodles with a few skinny pork ribs were the most edible remains. Coos filled two plates and muscled his way to a table that was quickly vacated by two middle aged Germans who seemed shocked at his arrival. "Maybe gimps are bad luck." I said. "Yeah, or maybe they saw your fried face."

We were both running on fumes. It had been a long time since I had sat at my parent's table having breakfast. Between bites I asked, "How you doing?" He waggled a fork in my face, "These fucks are good, half the time they know my hand better than I do." Even though under the average chip level we still had plenty of ammo because the blinds were not that high. Coos liked playing; it fueled his competitive nature, just a different finish line.

With enough time to take a piss I made it back to the table. No one had busted out yet, the same group took their seats. It was the hottest time of the day and the island was experiencing a power outage. Before the hotel could switch to emergency generators the room heated up. Beads of sweat were rolling down the back of my neck. The hat had to go. I put it under the table. No one noticed until the next hand was dealt. As I looked in the cave Mr. Gold Chains said, "Baby anybody ever tell you to use sunscreen." I mucked a king deuce unsuited. The Swede chirped up, "He was burned; I spent a few months driving an ambulance in Stockholm." "Yeah but he don't look half as bad as that guy at the Aussie Millions." "Your right about that, half his face was twisted over, he had teeth coming out a cheek."

Another flop hit the felt, the conversation faded away. I was just guy with a dwindling chip stack. Poker players did not judge by looks but by position and bankroll. I could have had two noses and blended in after a few hands. The air conditioning restarted, the hat stayed on the floor.

After the next break I sat down in the big blind to a five – seven of clubs. The bet was raised to four hundred fifty chips with four callers. My cards reminded me of Heinz ketchup, which made me think of French fries, which reminded me of the time I found ten bucks on the bathroom floor at McDonalds, which lead me to believe I should play this hand. I called. The flop came three-four-six of clubs, a straight flush. My heart was banging so hard I was sure my rib cage was bouncing. It took all I had just to tap the table signaling check.

The original raiser followed with a continuation bet, three folds and a call from Mr. Gold Chains. Jack of diamonds. Three checks. Ten of diamonds. I wasn't sure what to do, so I checked again. Another check. "All in baby." Gold Chains had me out-chipped two to one. I couldn't speak so I pushed all my chips to the middle. The original raiser showed the two black jacks and folded. Gold Chains flipped over the Ace-ten of clubs for a flush. "Sorry baby guess you'll have to put your hat back on and walk home."

My hands shook as I turned the winning cards over. A few seconds of recognition brought forth a storm of "holy shits," "sonofabitches," and laughter. As the dealer carved away chips from Gold Chain's stack he tilted back in his chair, "Good hand baby, fucking stupid, calling a pre-flop raise with garbage." He continued muttering to himself. I flagged down the drink cart for a soda, Gold Chains made me buy him a beer.

My win brought more attention. The Swede said, "Lucky at cards not so lucky with your face?" I explained the grilling accident. Murmurs all around. "A real bad beat." Poker often mimicked life. A bad beat was an underserved loss, a kick in the balls delivered against all odds, an illogical occurrence. It was, however, an accepted part of the game. "You got to move on and get back in the action." I nodded. The chips continued to fly.

Four hands later I boldly raised with ace-queen of hearts. Two callers and a flop of ace-ten-queen rainbow followed. I bet the pot, one fold, and an all-in. "I call." came out of my mouth without a moments consideration. In poker, as in many other endeavors, a little reflection can often prevent trouble. Blame it on jet lag, inexperience, or ignorance. It never occurred to me anyone could have king-jack, the coffee stained polo shirt did and my tournament ended with no help on the turn or river. I picked up my hat, gave my sunglasses to gold chains, shook a few hands and took the long walk out of the money. It ends suddenly, this card competition.

The sun was pulling out as I walked the path toward the hotel. The sweet smell of plumeria hung in the air, the adrenaline of shuffling cards slowly faded. I pulled the hat on, continued down the driveway and across the road to the white sand beach. In the dimming light waves broke softly at the edge of the reef two hundred yards off shore. Billowing clouds passed slowly to the right propelled by a gentle breeze. I took off shoes and socks, sand surrounded my feet, micro massaging pebbles. A string of colored lights turned on at a point jutting out into the water. An invitation if I ever did see one. By the time I reached Tiger's Oasis moonlight was exploding on the beach side palm trees, fresh from the set of a WWII movie where nervous GIs await the bell for the final round.

A few plastic chairs dotted the sand leading up to the open air bar being tended by a large, black woman in a flowered muumuu. Her smile rivaled the moon, "Looks like you're a man in search of a cold one." She threw two ice cubes in a glass and filled it with a San Miguel. I drained half before expressing my thanks.

"You must be with that bunch of card players." I looked to my right. A leather faced old man with a shock of gray hair sat at the bar's corner. "Can't be doing too good if you're here." I tilted my glass in his direction before finishing the contents. "Oh I don't know, looks like a nice joint." He let out a high pitched cackle. "Doris bring my new friend another beer, he needs a change of luck." Two ice cubes later I moved to the seat next to his, "Thanks, my name is Paul, Paul Lawton." He stuck out his hand, "Les Fields, pleased to meet you." Les grabbed his drink and spun the chair so it faced the water. "A buck a beer, with a view like this, can't beat it."

He was right; we had a clear shot down the coast. A few spots of light punctuated the shore. Night had arrived; it was seventy eight degrees. "This is the best time of the day," Les said, "the sun is off but the heat is still on." He was wearing khaki shorts, flip flops, and a faded short sleeve shirt, sun glasses tucked in the pocket. I had failed to notice that the left side of his body was withered, a forty per cent mark down of muscle and tissue. He felt my gaze and pointed toward the sea where the moon's light now illuminated the crashing surf, a rolling marquee. "It happened right out there, sixty some years ago, here at Chalan Kanoa."

Doris plopped two more beers on the wood behind us. "Now Les, nobody wants to hear those old war stories." I grabbed both bottles and handed one to Les. We buried the ice cubes in foam. "Shit Doris," Les said over his shoulder, "I'll listen to his tales of the French Foreign Legion." My hat had been noticed. I took it off. Les gave my face the once over. "Looks like we both got fucked in the fight." "Not exactly," I said, "unless you consider battling barbecue warfare." After quickly describing my misfortune I inquired, "So what happened out in the water?" Les looked toward the reef and started the projector.

"I was with the Higgins Boats; you know the landing assault craft. We dropped guys off at every fucking island in the South Pacific. I saw turquoise water turn red many times." Les explained that each of the barge- like boats had a crew of four. "I was all of twenty-one by the time we made it here in 1944." He had a buddy, Ted Goslin, who had been with him for three years. "Goose and I should have been gay, we were that close."

The men often dodged bullets and artillery shells "We had our rituals; it was a crap shoot out there, a lot of close calls." The two said a quick prayer, exchanged lucky pennies, and moved stations on each run. "Except that last transport, our second of the day. Goose said he would man the ramp again." Les objected, "I told him we shouldn't mess with our routine. He just waved me off, said he knew one of the jarheads up front, and that everything would be fine."

Thirty six Marines were deposited on the beach. As the landing craft returned to the troop transport gravity's rainbow delivered a "pistol pete", 105mm of Japanese artillery shell. "I was thinking about grabbing some chow before the next run when the explosion hit, the ramp end of the boat disappeared. Threw me in the water, a hunk of shrapnel in my guts." Goose was gone, "They never found a piece of him, he's still all around this place." Les waved his arm over the beach.

"I woke up on a hospital ship, halfway back to Hawaii. There wasn't much they could do; a good chunk of me came out with the metal. Took months before I could stand up and try to walk." The fighting had been over a few weeks when Les was finally released from rehab. He flew back to Dayton, Ohio. "Not much of a welcome, everyone was putting the war in the closet, getting on with their lives. No time for a messed up sailor, the parades were over, the only heroes left were sandwiches."

Doris brought another round. "I got a job with the post office. My mom knew the boss. She told him the government owed me one." Les spent forty years in the backroom. Never married. "Hell I had a hard time getting hookers to give me some." Lived with his parents until they passed then got the house. "I took to reading, going to the movies, getting food delivered." He visited with relatives during the holidays. "Took a fcw vacation tours around the states and Europe." Time passed. "Retired with plenty of money and plenty of time." Les decided to revisit Saipan, came in a month ago. Spent one night at the hotel before finding Tiger's Oasis. "Doris told me about a house up the road with a room for rent. Nice old couple, they make me breakfast. Might never leave."

The beers were sedating. I closed my eyes and listened to the waves' powerful rhythm. My head slowly found my chest. The smell of salt air was interrupted by aged body odor and barley breath. Les was a foot away when I opened my lids, "Of course we are not here to discuss the mundane." he whispered. "You and me, you and me," his voice rising, "you and me want to know why the hell us. Why were we present at the explosion?" His face was boiling. Jolted out of my decent I crossed my arms, extracting a few additional inches of distance between us. Les stated,"Truth be told that's why I came back here. Getting closer to ground zero was supposed to provide some closure." It hadn't.

A lot of whys are never answered. It should have occurred to Les that my mere presence was a big question. What was the likelihood of our ever meeting, let alone on this beach? He didn't see it that way. "We are here, you and me and Doris, for a reason. Let us figure this out my friend." He put his good hand on my shoulder; a tear went down his face. I needed a rescue, someone throw a lifeline. "It's been over six decades and I think about it every day."

Les returned to his chair, slowly regained his composure and in an almost professorial tone stated, "Some explanations come easy." He listed: fate, God's plan, bad luck, timing, karma, a long forgotten misstep, chance, genetics, kismet, and destiny. "I am sure you have run this list thinking about your accident, what put us in that place at that time." I had, of course, but not in a while. The "get over it and move on" mantra must have been lost on Les. His fixation was troubling.

Les locked his eyes on mine. "I would like to think we had a choice, but that requires acceptance of a certain amount of responsibility for our own misfortune." He looked back toward the surf. "Of course better minds disagree." Les than quoted Einstein, "Everything is determined, the beginning as well as the end, by forces over which we have no control. It is determined for the insect, as well as for the star. Human beings, vegetables, or cosmic dust, we all dance to a mysterious tune, intoned in the distance by an invisible piper."

"That's fucked up." I said, "What's the point of life if we are just connecting dots drawn by someone else." "There are those," Les replied "who believe choice is an illusion, that when God throws—the dice are loaded." "Bullshit," I eloquently responded, "like that guy said in the movies, 'We are the masters of our fate, captain of our ships." There had to be some control, otherwise everyone is a puppet. "O.K.," Les said, "run with that, why did you end up in front of that grill, why didn't Goose and I switch places, why did that shell hit our landing craft." "Shit, you were in a war and some asshole made a bad product which I bought." "Yeah well a lot guys were in the war and a lot of folks bought grills that didn't explode."

My head was starting to hurt. Doris brought over a plate of sashimi with a tangy dipping sauce. "You guys might as well have a snack while you're solving the world's problems." She smiled and returned to the other end of the bar where a small television glared.

The tuna was cold and tasty. I downed three pieces in quick succession. We were on a philosophical merry-go-round, I needed to jump off. "Les, maybe you just got to move on." He finished another San Miguel and said, "A priest told me how a person responds to his fate is more important than what his fate is. I told him he should spend some time in my shoes and left the church." It was time to stop the music. "What should I know?"

Les was taken aback; he drew up in his seat, a vein pulsing out his neck. "Aw fuck, I am just an old drunk with an excuse to be pissed. Some days I wish that Goose had changed places like he should have, he probably would have handled this better."

Maybe chance is a word void of sense but it does bring to shore some boats that are not steered. It had brought me to this sand bar so I could drink beer with an alternative future. Les turned in my direction, "I guess you should know that I don't know. Some guy wrote that the grave is the best shelter against the storms of destiny. I believe it also may be where my answer lies."

I picked up my hat. Les motioned to Doris, "I'll pay for us both, Paul here put up with my ranting, it's the least I can do." I shook Les's hand, "Thanks, I appreciate both your words and the beers."

He placed his free hand over mine. "Good luck to you, it ain't easy being us but it's all we got."

Doris gave me a wave as I stumbled up to the road, "The hotel is to the right." she said with a chuckle. I was glad for the direction.

It was the next afternoon when I woke up. My mouth needed sweeping. A long shower helped. I found clean clothes and a note from Coos. He hoped I was just sleeping and not dead. His fortunes had turned at the tables, he was confident of finishing in the money Dinner was in an hour, he wanted me to meet him at the buffet. I found a half-eaten fruit plate next to the television. A few slices of papaya, pineapple and banana would tide me over.

Just as I finished the man himself burst into the room. "Motherfucking douche bag, how can you call an all-in with four/ five suited, cracked my pocket Aces with a runner, runner straight. Shit me a river." Coos hopped from his chair to the bed, bouncing back to the headboard. He had made it within five spots of cashing. Exasperation covered his face. "Hell you did better than me.' I said. "Fuck, a one eyed monkey could have done better than you.' "Last time I'll try to cheer you up." He flipped me off. "Give me the phone, let's order some food. I ain't eating with all those assholes smiling over making the money."

The steaks came from Australia, the rice Japan, the vegetables were local, and the beer was once again San Miguel. Halfway through the meal Todd said, "I might have a lead on Jackie. The bartender last night said he saw a woman with the finest ass this side of the Philippines. I gave him a twenty and told him to call. He thinks he can get her room number off some receipt." "That's one heck of a lead, Sherlock." His twenty was long gone.

Coos pointed a steak knife, "And, ass wipe, I posted a bounty, two hundred bucks for information leading to the whereabouts. Don't know why I didn't think of this sooner." He reasoned that of the small percentage of female entrants most would be like their male card flinging counter parts, out of shape and overweight. "A hot bod has to be rarer than this steak. I am a fucking genius."

"So all we need to do is wait, I can handle that. You want to check out some of the sights, saw a brochure for the Blue Grotto and a cave that was the Japanese headquarters during the war. They even have a jail that may have held Earhart." I got the cockeyed look, "Why the hell would that western sheriff be in prison way out here." "Earhart not Earp, Wyatt Earp was a gunslinger, Amelia Earhart was an aviatrix." He finished his beer, "Yeah I knew that." Coos belched. "Let's go to that grotto place, sounds like more fun than a cave or jail."

We hired a cab, a fair fare to the attraction and back; fifty dollars according to Danny the driver which seemed steep until he pulled out a large joint. "No extra charge, the grotto is best seen with hazy eyes." The taste was clean and strong, the effect immediate, a shine was on the world, a shimmer in the air. Danny laughed as he pulled into the parking lot, a worn piece of island asphalt with a solar powered phone under a sign shouting, "For Emergencies Only." "Here we are, the great Blue Grotto. I'll be back in an hour."

I retrieved the chair from the trunk. As we moved across the lot Danny turned out onto the road. Coos, who made it to the trail's edge first, yelled out, "It's piggy back time, Paul, sooyee, sooyee." The path lead to stairs, 109 steps according to the sign, which also warned of tidal surges, hungry marine life, and assorted scuba diving dangers. "Guess Danny never thought to bring this obstacle to our attention.

Let's find a bar or something and wait for him to come back."
Todd spun his chair like a top. "What's a matter pussy; you can't
get me down a few steps." "Shit I can get you down half pint, it's
getting back up that will suck." Coos rolled over to a nearby bench,
transferred from chair to wood, then to the ground. He started
doing the two armed rabbit hop toward the first step.

"What the hell!" I yelled into the wind. We met at the third step,
his knuckles were already bruised. I bent down; he hit my back
like a dropped bowling ball, his arms over my shoulders, hands
clasped below my neck. "I love you too." he whispered in my ear
before reaching back and slapping my ass, "Let's go pilgrim, we're
burning daylight." Once the decent took hold it was all I could do
to remain upright, fortunately the last several steps flattened out.
We came to rest near a large outcropping of rock. "Nice job Porky."
Todd commented as he slid down to the ground.

A collapsed cave filled with sea water the grotto gets its name
from sun shining into the space filling the area with a strange,
blue light. Seventy feet below are three openings to the sea, door-
ways for white tip reef sharks, barracuda, turtles, and rays. "Wow,
this is something!" his voice echoed off the walls as Coos bounced
over to the rock's edge. The place was empty. I sat down and enjoyed the marvel. Soon we were both drifting away.

There was a frequent tidal surge, bringing a muffled roar.
Several minutes into our reverie large bubbles popped the surface followed by three scuba divers. The surprise was mutual.
Todd, pot headed, mistook them for strange sea creatures. He
shuffled back ten feet, "What the hell Paul." he choked. The
divers, bug eyed, timed the surge and plopped up onto the outcropping. Two men and a woman exchanged high fives. Pulling
off their masks and fins they stood up, air tanks straightening
their spines.

"Great dive." exclaimed one guy with a soggy, red beard. The others nodded with a sideways glance in our direction. Todd reclaimed his position next to me as the three walked toward the stairs. "You ain't getting me down there, I prefer muff diving." He gave me a poke in the ribs. "Besides I don't think they make fins for stumps." He was probably right about that. "You," he continued with a laugh, "would look a lot better in one of those masks." The thought of cutting through the water like Superman was appealing.

The combination of weed and nature's art work caused a slippage in time. Danny found us still amazed at the changing light. "You guys going to have pay for overtime." he announced in a voice that invaded our tranquility. Todd spoke first, "Danny, glad to see you, ever hear of an arm chair?" Before either of us knew what was happening Coos had Danny and me grab each other at the wrists with our arms crossed. He then sat down and placed one hand on each of our shoulders. "To the top, gentlemen, glory awaits." Some arm chair. Danny was too flustered to object and I was just happy to have help. We stopped three times over the next ten minutes. Todd's ride was where we left it. A small cowrie shell rested on the seat, a gift from the divers.

Danny wanted another twenty before starting the car. Coos agreed provided he gave us the rest of the joint. He complied. Fifteen minutes later we were back in the room, the red message light blinking on the phone. Todd grabbed the receiver, listened intently before breaking into a large grin, "Bingo baby, the bitch is mine."

He bounced off the bed and toward the bathroom. "We got a good lead, time for a quick rinse, meeting the guy in the lobby. Turn on the water would you." I left Coos singing four feet below the shower head. "Don't open your mouth too wide you'll drown like a goose in the rain." Once again he flipped me the bird. I laid

two towels by the door. "Don't get your dick caught in the drain."
Another bird.

I shut the door and sat out on the balcony. The shade had just
fallen; a few stars twinkled over the water. It didn't seem plausible
that Todd's bounty would result in a meeting with Jackie, but as
Les down at the bar said we are all dancing to the same piper.
Maybe the notes would line up.

It felt good to throw my feet up on the railing. Sleep and blue
smoke had charged my battery. I was in tune with this latitude
after my recent jump through time and space. Palm trees swayed,
waving at the passing clouds. A warm cocoon wrapped around
me.

I thought of what had brought me here, all the ifs and but fors.
Weezy to Cain to Coos. Some double play combo, here at Saipan
Field. Half way across the world because of a vintage Ford Mustang,
a car Todd had already recovered. Some would have been happy
just getting the car back, some would have mailed a nasty letter or
bitched over the phone, and one half pint with plenty of cash and
time would track her down. I came along for the ride; however the
finish line was giving me second thoughts. Leaving Coos alone to
face the woman who done him wrong was racking up points in my
poll. I was becoming one with the soft lounge chair. It was dark,
the choice was clear. I wondered where the rest of that joint was
hiding out.

"What the fuck you doing out here. Let's go, we're on a mission."
Todd had cleaned up well. "I borrowed a shirt, hope you don't
mind." He had found one of dad's white dress shirts my mother
had saw fit to throw in my bag. "In case you need to go to Court"
she had reasoned. Already on his chair, Todd was as anxious as a

police blood hound. "Come on Paul, my contact is waiting." I left my concerns, grabbed my hat, and followed him to the door.

In the lobby we met Joe, a local in his thirties carrying too many pounds and sporting too much jewelry. His thick black hair was combed back. A double X blue rayon shirt falling over brown khakis above leather sandals completed the look. We walked to a corner where Joe and I sat in large rattan chairs with Coos positioned between us, his back to the concierge desk where he had grabbed a couple of diving brochures.

"Let's go see some fish." he demanded a little too loudly. Joe laughed, "Between your wheel chair and his desert rat look, everybody is going to remember we talked." Todd grimaced at this intrusion into his detective fantasy. "So what do you got?" he asked in a barely audible tone. Joe rubbed his thumb across his fingers. Coos handed him two C notes. After taking the money and shoving it into his shirt pocket Joe leaned over, "Found her, one fine ass, she played in that poker tournament, had short black hair, and looked kind of strange."

Joe gave us a suite number in a building behind our tower. "It's where they put the big money from Japan and Korea." Coos turned to leave. "You might be interested in this." Joe placed a key card on the table. "It's a master, will get you in her room." Todd reached down, the key flew back into Joe's pocket. "That will be two hundred more." For the first time he looked around the lobby. "A worthwhile investment, sir, and difficult to come by."

Todd put two bills where the card used to be. Joe reached across and shook his hand, exchanging the master in the process. We broke camp with Coos and I heading toward the rear entrance. "Glad that's done," I said, "much longer and we would have needed another shower." "As long as he is right I don't give a shit." Coos replied as we exited and found a small sign pointing in the direction of "Paradise Suites".

A winding path bordered by banana trees and manicured white sand ended in a complex of four two story tan buildings. Three suites were in each structure, the bottom took the entire floor while uppers shared a stairwell. There was no adherence to any disability protocol, luckily for Todd Suite 415 was ground level on our immediate right. He wheeled up to the oversized teak door with tarnished brass fittings and pulled out the master key. "You sure you want to do this?" I nervously asked. He gave me his favorite finger before sliding the card. The lock popped.

Coos nudged the door with the edge of his chair; it opened revealing a short hallway leading to a large sitting area with brightly colored leather sofas, dark wood tables, canned lights, television, a dining table with chairs, and a sliding door fronting a covered patio. I could hear music coming from the left; a mellow jazz tune competed with running water. Whoever the occupant was, he/she was in the shower.

Todd motioned for me to sit in one of the chairs; he slowly maneuvered around a rattan table and stopped next to the patio door. My heart was racing, sweat beaded up on my neck even though the air conditioner was running high. A bar and small kitchen separated us from the door to the bedroom. A half-filled glass of red wine rested next to a cheese plate. Coos was able to reach up and nonchalantly threw a couple of slices in my direction. My mouth was too dry to eat. The shower stopped along with my heart. Todd retreated to my side; we were on odd pair of book ends.

A rustling was audible, footsteps approaching then retreating, a blow dryer wailing, coat hangers clacking, and time passing. Ten minutes by the clock on the microwave lead Todd to finish all the cheese and eye the wine. I started to wonder what Saipan jails were like. Then, without warning the music stopped and a woman walked out. She reached for the wine glass, brought it halfway to her lips before dropping it on the bar causing shards to spray into the air.

"Todd, is that you?" she stammered. "Half of me." he loudly replied moving a few feet in her direction. Anger flowed over his face. "What are you doing here?" she said stumbling back toward the bedroom door. "I misplaced the keys to my Mustang thought you might know where they were." Confusion clouded her eyes. She looked from Todd to me and back. Shoulder length blonde hair whipsawing. "Are you drunk or what." Indignation had replaced fear in her voice. "Todd, I don't know what you are talking about or why you tracked me down. Your making me uncomfortable, please leave before I call the front desk."

Coos rocked his chair back and forth, a pissed off metronome. "Jackie, you lied to me about the Mustang. I want an explanation." She grabbed the telephone, "You are freaking me out, take your friend and leave now."

I stood up, gained her full attention, and took off my hat. The phone followed the same trajectory as the wine glass. Tremors ruffled her robe, eyes fluttered before tilting back; she collapsed in a heap to the floor.

Iris had fainted.

Upon hearing her body hit the tile with a thud Coos started to slowly laugh, a chuckle blooming into a full blown guffaw, as he struggled to get his breath while pointing a finger in my direction. "One look and she fainted; your face should have a warning label." "A real fucking comedian," I countered while walking around the bar. My brain rejected the idea that Iris was on the floor, an impossibility, until I found her laying, left leg turned up under the right, arms over head, sporadically moaning. It was definitely Iris Camp, we had met at the Club Scirroco in another lifetime.

I held onto the counter, my legs were shaking. Coos pushed his way through to my right. "Let's grab the bitch and tie her up. As Ricky used to say, 'She's got some splaining to do.'" I bent down and carried a semi-conscious memory a few feet across the floor. It was difficult to rotate her limp body onto one of the wooden kitchen chairs. Todd rolled along side and grabbed her waist while I positioned her legs. He then untied the belt on the robe, crossed the ends and retied them behind the chair. We used rolled up plastic dry cleaning bags to secure legs and arms. Head tilted onto her shoulder she looked like a victim of the electric chair.

"I know this woman." Coos was trying to fill a cup with water but was having difficulty reaching the faucet. He finally propped himself up on the lip of the sink, almost kicking his ride backwards. Succeeding, Todd bounced down, spilling a few drops. He pulled in front of the whimpering blonde, prepared to splash her to reality, when she loudly moaned, "Paul, no, Paul." Coos stopped mid throw, he slowly turned his head, looking up into my face. "What the fucking fuck!" I smiled at his consternation, "You really have a way with words. I told you, I know her." He set the glass down on an end table cluttered with poker magazines. "When the fuck did you say that." "Just now, when you were over there sink diving."

We both looked at the woman in the chair. Her face vacillated from calm to troubled, a nightmare on Saipan.

"When did you ever meet Jackie?" "I knew her as Iris, she grew up in Bakersfield, her mom was sick, we met in a bar." I had told

Todd the tale after that night in North Beach a few weeks ago. His recognition platter started to turn, "Yeah I remember, she was there when you blew up, didn't come to the hospital, I told you she was probably a gold digger." He looked at the fainted one, "You sure this is her?" "It's her, it is definitely her." Todd was overloaded, the combination of finding Jackie/Iris along with the knowledge that I had scored with her was too much. "You banged her." I needed to get his big head re-engaged. "Get over it; let's concentrate on figuring out what the hell is going on here."

Coos wheeled over to the fridge, popped the caps on two Sapporos and handed me one. Night had fallen; I closed the curtains on the sliding door.

Improbabilities, detours, shooting stars, double rainbows, curve balls, road blocks, do occur with some frequency. The present situation had no viable peer. Coos and I had a relationship with the same woman at different times and in different places. We had no explanation. Todd picked up the water and threw it on her face. "Get up sleeping beauty; the dwarfs have a few questions."

The shower snapped her back to reality. "What the hell." she said while pulling at our make shift restraints. They held. I was leaning against the bar to her right, Coos was a similar distance to the left. Her eyes once again ping ponged between us. "Todd, Paul what are you doing? Untie me. Please." Years of pouting had resulted in the perfect facial contortion. Her lips were turned downward, eyes slightly teary, forehead creased. "Since you know our names, what's yours?" I asked. She strained again, tilting the chair slightly forward. Todd banged his armrest, "It's Phyllis Snipnell. Your cousin told me, you remember Edward, all brain no body." Biting her lip nervously, she looked down at the floor. "I never liked that name."

"That's not why I'm here." Coos said. Her eyes still eyeballing the tile Phyllis replied, "I know, it's the Mustang. Can't believe you tracked me down over a car." "It wasn't just a car," his voice rising, "you knew what it meant to me. You told me you burned it, and then you turned around and sold it to some guy. That's fucking bullshit." She started to cry, real tears down the cheeks, plopping on the floor. Phyllis looked up shaking her head, snuffling nose, red eyes. "I'm sorry Todd, really sorry. You were in the hospital; I didn't see how you could ever drive again….." "So you told me you burnt it." "I really thought about doing that but then it seemed like such a waste. Plus I needed the money for my mom." "Yeah, sure, so what did you get for it?" A pained look returned to her face, "Oh you know I am not good with numbers it was quite a bit, ten thousand I think."

Coos turned and rolled toward the flat screen television, he knocked it to the floor with one arm. More broken glass. "You are so full of shit, the guy I found it with paid sixty thousand." Phyllis stared right through me, the look of someone seeking the right puzzle piece. "So what do you want from me, the cash?" Todd spun his chair, "I wipe my ass with twenty dollar bills, I don't need any fucking money." Tension filled the room, frustration stirred the air.

"He bought it from a guy." I interjected. They both looked at me as if I had three heads. "Paizer bought your car from a guy, at a parking lot by the beach." "That's right Watson, he did say that." It felt good to be involved in the conversation, I mushed forward, "And what about that Mustang you drove with me?" Phyllis resumed a downward stare. "You told me your dad had one like and you were making payments." The sobbing began anew. "My dad did have one, I was making payments. I even thought about giving it to you Todd."

"So how come you were using a different name when we met?" I was in fine Perry Mason mode. "I told you I don't like Phyllis." she said her voice rising with her head. "Guess you didn't like Jackie anymore either." Todd commented. Phyllis looked toward Coos, "Whenever someone called me that I thought of you, it got to be too much." I went to the fridge and pulled out two more beers. "Why didn't you visit me in the hospital?" I asked while passing a bottle to Todd. She didn't miss a beat, "My mom was really sick, then the weeks went by, it secmed you would be better off without me, everyone would be better off without me." Tears flowed. "I knew two great guys and both got hurt." Phyllis leaned forward, chest heaving. "Come on, untie me. I'll do what you want."

Coos went back across the room, rocking his wheels over the broken TV glass. He suddenly looked tired and dejected. This adventure had not ended well. "Fuck, Jackie the whole thing was pretty stupid on my part. Since the accident I have been riding a wild hair up my ass, looking for action. When I found out about the Mustang something went off. Now here we are on an island in the middle of nowhere. And the buzz is gone." He stared out the door into the dark night. "Shit Paul untie her and let's get out of here. There has to be a plane leaving for some-where soon."

And that is what I would have done if the telephone had not rung.

Coos picked up the receiver, grunted something and hung up. He quickly rolled to the sliding door, ripped the drapery cord out, and yelled, "Paul, get your ass at the end of the hall." His sense of urgency overcame my need to know what the hell was going on. As I walked to the left side of the hallway leading to the door, Hot Rod maneuvered into the kitchen, grabbed a small dish towel and stuck it in Phyllis's mouth. She shook her head, protest muted.

Coos quickly took a spot opposite mine and tossed an end of the cord. "Get down, when the guy walks in pull your side, he'll trip and you jump and tie him up." Before I could ask the who and why, the lock clicked, the door opened, footsteps echoed. I remember thinking it was odd to see a tasseled sandal just before yanking the cord. A yelp of surprise preceded a loud thunk as a head hit the side of the sofa.

There would be no need for a further attack, the guest was out cold. I stood up taking in the body south to north. Sandals, white khakis, blue dress shirt, black hair on a head turned in my direction, broken sunglasses resting nearby. It had been some time since we last spoke, Jerry Traditore, Esquire, and I, now he was in no shape for conversation.

What kind of rabbit hole was Suite 415?

Todd's gracious removal of the gag was met with a rising crescendo, "You fucking killed him, you stupid bastards, ignorant assholes. Let me ..." Before she could continue Coos returned the towel to her mouth causing several seconds of chair dancing. Todd wagged a finger, "Settle down or I'll put you on the floor with your boyfriend."

Coos went over to Traditore, slamming a wheel into his ribs. The lawyer moaned. "Better tie him before he wakes up."

Our experience with Phyllis made the job fairly easy even though he was twice her weight. We cut the drapery rope with a kitchen knife using the pieces to bind him to a chair next to the broken television. Traditore's body remained mostly limp with an occasional spasm accompanied by a groan. Phyllis had ceased rebelling although there was clearly fire in her eyes.

Todd and I took up positions between the two. "Nice work." he complimented me. "You could have told me what the fuck was going on." "No time, besides I didn't want you to chicken out." "And why would I do that, we are already on the hook for burglary, what's another crime."

The phone rang again, this time I answered. There had been a report of yelling by one of the neighbors, I explained we were having a little reunion and promised to keep the noise down. "How about when he wakes up, maybe we should gag him now." I said to Coos. "No, no these two don't want to draw any more attention, isn't that right Phyllis?" She shook her head affirmatively. Todd reached over and took out the towel. "Thanks, that thing tastes like shit."

Coos did not reply, he wheeled over to the fridge for more beers. I walked to the bar, grabbed a bottle, and took a lean. "How about sharing some of that?" Phyllis asked. Tipping the bottle to her lips; she managed two large gulps before a slight gag. "So what do you have to say for yourself now?" Todd practically sneered.

It was clear that Jackie/Iris/Phyllis was involved with the married, father of two, Traditore. It was not coincidence that he had found his way to Suite 415. There was an overnight bag and brief case lying by the door. You don't bring a change of clothes half way around the world just to say hello.

"How long has this been going on?" Coos asked pointing toward the semi-comatose barrister. Phyllis gave a look of resignation, raising her eyebrows, turning a slight smile. "We have been good friends for a few years. After Paul's accident I was upset and he had issues at home. Guess we gave each other a shoulder to cry on." Todd laughed, "What the fuck is he doing here?" "He knew I was here for the tournament, decided to come out for a few days of sun." "Coos laughed even harder, "Sure, like you were going to spend anytime outside." A guy doesn't fly for thirteen hours just for the scent of Coppertone. "Go to hell Todd, we had some good times, why can't you leave it at that."

Hot Rod rolled to the door and picked up the brief case. He tried to open it without success. The fine grain tanned leather bag had a brass combination lock. "Yeah we had some good times, imagine Paul would say the same and many others. You haven't kept those legs closed very much." "You're still a crude bastard," Phyllis replied, "my feelings for you were genuine. Things change, people move on." Coos erupted, his face a trembling, red mass, "Move on my ass. You left when things were the worst. My fucking legs were gone." He jerked his thumb in my direction. "You pulled the same shit with Paul. Now you're fucking our lawyer. What a heartless bitch." Phyllis didn't blink, "You've been screwing anything that moved for years, why am I any different." The logic bounced off Todd.

I finished the beer. Traditore was still out; there was a large lump over his right eye. Todd was poking a knife at the brief case lock, scarring the rawhide with each attempt. "So what's it going to be boys? You might be able to walk away now but once Jerry comes to I see handcuffs in your future." Phyllis was smiling.

It was time to rejoin the fray. "He was the guy who sold the Mustang to Paizer." The smile disappeared. "No, he wasn't involved, why would he be." This relationship with Traditore seemed odd. "Isn't he a little old for you?" Phyllis smirked, "Age is less important as you get older; he is a generous and caring man." Her voice was mechanical. She was looking down at the floor again. Maybe Phyllis was tired, maybe she was playing us like a drum.

"Fuck." Coos yelped he had cut his thumb; drops of blood splattered the leather. "Paul," he started between thumb sucks, "she needs a sugar daddy. Bet he paid for the trip here." Phyllis twisted in his direction, "I won the seat for the tournament. Damn near made the money too."

Not wanting more bad beat stories I changed the subject, "Didn't you ever wonder how Hot Rod and I were doing?" She shut her eyes and let out a deep breath, "Sure I did, I should have kept in touch." Phyllis made eye contact, "I am sorry about your face, you were a good looking guy." A compliment that hurt.

The weed, beer, and late hour were taking a toll. I was tired. "Yeah, well, don't worry about it. Everybody has to move on. I'm sorry about this mess, Todd got the better of me." I made a move to grab the knife from Hot Rod, it was time to cut the captives loose. Coos lifted the blade up into the air. "She isn't making it with him, that's all bullshit. She's been lying since we got here. I smell a rat."

He was going off on another ride. "Give me the knife Todd; let's end this thing before anything else happens." Coos rolled in front of Phyllis. He ran the steel down her neck toward the tied belt, partially opening the white robe. She strained against the chair, her chest heaving. "Get the fuck away from me Todd; I swear I'll scream so loud they will hear me in Guam." Coos pulled the knife back, "I am right ain't I, you aren't spreading it for the lawyer." I took the opportunity to grab the knife. "Give me that before you cut yourself again." He rocked back in his chair, grinning, "Jackie I know you too well, you're a lot like me or at least like I was, no way have you climbed in bed with gelled hair over there. Admit it and the game is over."

Phyllis looked longingly toward the passed out counselor, "You are amazingly conceited, there are plenty of men who would make better partners than one Todd "Hot Rod" Coos. Why you think I didn't find that with Jerry is so egotistical. We have been lovers for months." Todd laughed, a chuckle tinged with sarcasm. "Got to hand it to you, one hell of an act. Cut the crap, speak the truth for once." "Coos what difference does it make," I intervened, "let's get out of here." He gave me a stern look. "It makes all the difference in the world, can't you see that." All I could see was a wardrobe of orange. "I got to piss, don't do anything stupid." He wheeled around the bar and disappeared into the back room.

The fridge was barren of beer so I took a bottle of water. As the glass hit my lips I looked across at a scene out of a B movie. The good looking blonde tied to one chair, her lover at another, broken glass, and blood. It was time for a knock on the door. Instead the babe whined, "Paul please untie me before Todd comes back. He's gone off the deep end. You saw him with that knife." She could be right. "Don't worry, nothing is going to happen. I have been on a few road trips with Hot Rod, once the fun is done we move on." And the fun here was definitely done.

"You can't be serious Paul, let me go." "Can't do that," I said sipping the water, "we need to finish the story." Phyllis turned surly, "Bullshit, Jerry could really be hurt. You have only known Todd a short time, we had feelings, and you know I am a good person. Wise up." It was a machine gun of words, everything but invoking God and country.

"You shouldn't have messed with his Mustang. Bad karma." "That's no reason to kidnap me. And Jerry, why bring him into all of this." "Is Coos correct about you two?" "Of course not. Why would I lie about that." Good point, it is not something most women would admit. "Did you really have feelings for me?" Her face brightened. "Well you weren't much of a dancer." I didn't laugh. "Sure, there was something between us. We were at the beginning. Who knows if the accident hadn't happened, if I hadn't freaked out......"

I didn't know what to think, sincerity was in short supply this evening. "Yeah, if I hadn't blown myself up, everything would be different. That might be me tied up over there." A lot of ifs brought the four of us together. "I'll go talk to Todd, give me a minute."

The large bedroom was at the end of short hall. The few lights were set on dim. Coos had his chair in front of a small vanity, admiring a black wig he had somehow managed to cram over his head. Hot Rod didn't look half bad, a cleaner cut than his usual shag. He saw me in the mirror, "Why do you suppose she was wearing this thing?" "Better her than you." Coos pulled it off and threw it at me, missing the target. "Probably one of those poker things, like hats and sunglasses." I said. "It really doesn't matter, we got to let them loose and get the hell out of here." Coos rocked the chair up and down. "I will let them go if Jackie answers one question right, a simple yes or no. If not we got more work to do."

"Is he circumcised?" Coos spit the question at Phyllis. "Answer correctly and you never see us again."

I had expected something more profound. Todd pointed at Traditore, who was a little more active since our return to the scene

315

of the crime. His body twisted every few minutes; weak sounds escaped his mouth. "Should be an easy question, if you are lovers." Phyllis rolled her eyes in my direction, "Told you he was losing it. What kind of crude bullshit. How about I talk about your dicks." Hot Rod laughed. "That's the point; you know our cocks on a first name basis. How about Jerry?"

Phyllis became indignant, "You are a low life." Hot Rod continued, "I am sure you have given him a blow job or two, Paul she ever give you some head?" I did have a film clip in the archive, the day of the boom. I looked at Phyllis, "Didn't you, just before the explosion? My memory of that time is badly bent." She slowly shook her head, "Son of a bitch Paul, are you joining in this nonsense." I was drifting back to lingerie in the kitchen, her head bobbing.

"Paul," it was Coos, "snap to, go stand over by the lawyer." I walked across the room. Traditore had some drool dripping down his chin. "Phyllis, yes or no. Cut or not. It's getting late." Todd's chair was bumping up against hers. "Alright, he is circumcised just like you two assholes." Phyllis appeared to be preparing to spit in Coos's face. "Now cut me loose." Hot Rod pulled back and turned toward me, "Check his dick Paul."

The request that I examine another's penis set off a lot of bells. "What the fuck did you just say?" "Take a look at his cock; see if he has been snipped." Coos was sitting straight up, his hands tightly gripping the armrests. Phyllis was staring at me, smiling, "No touching Paul." "It's your bullshit idea Coos, come over here and look for yourself." "I would but Jackie wouldn't believe me and neither would you. Just do it." His logic was correct, the bells, however, were just as loud.

I reached over and grabbed the top of Jerry's pants in an attempt at a pull and peek. Not enough of an opening. Feeling eyes upon me I walked to the opposite side of the chair, fumbled with the tan Gucci belt, cursing my short, stubby fingers. The leather restraint was for show since the pants pressed tightly against his gut. One button and two snaps later it was time to unzip. I tugged downward, grinding over a bulge, revealing red boxers.

The audience heard the normally erotic tone of metal being released. "How exciting." Phyllis mocked. The member was angled off to the right necessitating a tug on the elastic. A mass of curly black hair sprouted above a fleshy tube of wrinkled skin. His dick looked like mine wearing a turtleneck. I let go of the waistband. It snapped against his belly, Jerry moaned. Having no desire to rewrap the package I turned around and announced, "Definitely not circumcised." before sitting down on the couch.

Coos slowly turned toward Phyllis, her face was blank. A cloud of confusion passed through my skull. Why didn't she know? Why was Todd so upset? Why did it matter? Why did I unzip a guy's pants? Phyllis spoke first, "Jerry can't get it up, he's got a medical condition. We've never had sex, but we are very much in love." Todd smiled before wheeling to my side. He ignored Phyllis completely, speaking only to me in a slow, measured voice. "Now that we know these two assholes aren't getting it on there remains the issue of their meeting. What the fuck are they doing together here, across the fucking Pacific Ocean?" I was surprised at the turn of events but what did it matter. "Who gives a shit, let's get out of here." "Listen to Paul." Phyllis chirped.

Coos was not deterred, "Don't you see, it is all too weird. Jackie is your Iris, we both had relationships with her, and she's got something going with our lawyer. You think that is a coincidence, you don't want to know why?" "What do you suggest Sherlock, we got them both tied up and Jerry looks like he's been abused." Too bad we didn't have a camera; the next meeting of the State Bar would have had a new star. "I suggest we reconvene in the bedroom." Hot Rod moved across the floor, stopping to reinsert the rag in Phyllis's mouth, before disappearing around the corner. She yelled again, a muffled "fucker." I walked by without making eye contact.

Coos had hopped onto the king sized bed; his face was buried in a violet camisole. "The same perfume." he announced upon coming up for air. "I'm getting a little wood here." "Yeah, maybe you should visit Jerry, he's almost ready." Out came the middle finger, "Maybe I should go out there and reintroduce my dick to her mouth." "Why not, what's another felony between friends." I sat on a rattan rocker next to the vanity. "Seriously, it is time to leave." He threw the scented satin in my direction. "Take a few whiffs, it will calm you down." I rubbed the shimmer, it was therapeutic. Todd did the knuckle bounce across the mattress. "We'll be leaving soon I promise, but let's think this thing through first. That women, Jackie, Phyllis, whatever, is a first rate liar. I sighed and set the camisole on my lap.

The minutes passed, I relaxed. The mayhem in the next room left my thoughts. I was numb to it all. Occasional mumbles filtered through, Coos lamenting that Jackie had bought the car jacks and that we were perfect cases. I rubbed the satin harder. Hot Rod got the drift,"I am going to check on our guests."

The thought that Iris was somehow involved in our accidents was painful. Looking back with a cynical eye she was clearly out of my league. I had fallen for her, the times were good, was it all an act? The idea was bullshit, Todd's legs, my burns were cosmic coincidences. It was insane to think otherwise. I threw the camisole back on the bed and walked out to the storm.

Coos was back in front of Phyllis, running numbers through Traditore's briefcase lock. He hadn't bothered to remove the gag. "Nothing but bad vibes here Hot Rod, let's hit the road and find a couple of cold ones." He was lost in his fiddling, clicking and pulling at the clasp. "You have a better chance of picking the Lotto digits." Traditore appeared to be coming to, the moaning had stopped, his body would tense, and then relax. If he awoke tied, with underwear exposed, a major vocal outburst could be expected. Todd was not concerned; his attention remained with the lock. "Why the fuck would anyone bring a briefcase to paradise?" he wondered.

Phyllis looked pale. I held an index finger in front of my lips. She nodded in agreement. The rag was moist with saliva; I set it on the bar. "Thanks Paul, please don't hurt me anymore." She started to sob. "Hurt you," Coos snarled, "how do you think his face felt burned to shit or my legs, hurt you my ass." I filled a glass with water and gave Phyllis a drink.

"So," I began, making eye contact, "did you know Todd's jacks and my grill were bad?" She took a dismissive tone, "No, of course not, how would I?" "I seem to remember you insisted on a silver one, it was a display model." "I just wanted it to match your patio furniture." "That's understandable, but I went back to the store a few weeks ago and the clerk said a guy had bought two silver ones earlier that day. That guy wouldn't be Jerry would it?" Phyllis rolled her eyes, "No, no, when did you get so paranoid?" "Probably when he lost eight layers of skin." Todd interjected.

Phyllis glared. I crossed my arms, leaned against the bar and cleared my throat. "Jerry hired an expert; he said the grill only explodes if the gas is turned on for a few minutes before ignition." "Paul, I swear on my father's grave, I didn't know anything about

319

the grill." Silence. "You should know I would never hurt you Paul."
I did not know what to know anymore.

"Time out." I said too loudly, walking out of the confusion and
toward the bathroom.

Our hosts slide the International Herald Tribune under the door
in the early morning hours while Coos and I attempt to sleep off another drunk. It is our third or fourth day at the Nikko Kanaya near
the shores of Lake Chuzenji, Tochigi Prefecture, Japan. They say there
are trout in the lake, a tram up a mountain, and a large waterfall
nearby. We have yet to leave the building, a series of bartenders keep
our blood alcohol levels high.

A long shower had cleared my head sufficiently so the letters
pounded into the newsprint do not hop over each other creating
an unintelligible tangle. Pages of governmental bickering, financial intrigue, assorted disputes, fashion updates, sports, and international weather barely held my attention.

The the lower right corner of page five, however, announced,
AMERICAN COUPLE FOUND DEAD IN SAIPAN LOVE NEST.
A short paragraph antiseptically explained that a female entrant
in a large poker tournament and her male companion had been
discovered by a hotel maid. Local police suspected narcotics were
involved. An investigation was underway. Names were not released
pending notification of next of kin. I creased the page, placing it
on the toilet so Hot Rod would not miss it when he crawled into
consciousness. Time for a walk.

It was the offseason at the lake. I had the trail to myself. Low
clouds and fog played hide and seek with the mountains. The
air was crisp and clean. My mind turned off as the path weaved
through trees and boulders with occasional snap shots of the

water. A few deer stood still at my approach, returning to nibbling the short green grass after I passed. A sharp corner surprised with a shrine, the year 1487 chiseled in the rock base. I stopped and sat on a worn stone bench. A large gold Buddha reigned high up the side of a granite outcropping. Prayer flags hung from parallel ropes. An altar rested below the deity, smudged black from burnt incense sticks. The Buddha smiled. I thought of the Jesus on my parent's kitchen wall. It was time to confess.

It was as if I was just coming out of that bathroom in Suite 415 once again.

Phyllis was slumped over in her chair, gaping mouth and big, blank eyes. Traditore's head pressed into his chest, vomit covered his shirt. Coos was removing the last of the cord from the lawyer's arms. He noticed my arrival while wheeling toward Phyllis. "Take a look at those papers on the bar." he said, motioning toward the counter. The brief case was open; a few manila folders lay next to several typed pages. "The bastards set us up, and God knows how many others." The first sheet I grabbed had contact information for several men in California; all were professionals, under thirty, and single.

There were names of old girlfriends, schools attended, career highlights. Each entry contained a section titled Potential Accident Scenarios. One was involved with off road vehicles, another wanted to skydive, and a third was a noted scuba enthusiast. Pertinent products that had been recalled were listed along with possible store locations, such as The Underwater Emporium, Santa Cruz, California, still selling regulator prone to jamming at depth. At the bottom of the page was a bullet point highlighting the fact that a few recalled Cain grills may still be at some rural stores. I also found a bank draft for $500,000 payable to Phyllis Snipnell with a note line reading, "Expenses for PD matter."

The impossible was reality; Phyllis went on a personal injury safari and bagged Coos and me. She and Traditore cashed in on our suffering. I crumpled the check in my hand. A fury rose within me, drying my mouth and boiling my brain. "You fucking bitch, you rotten fucking bitch." I spit at Phyllis. "Save your breath, she can't hear you."

Hot Rod had removed the make shift restraints and steadied her limp body with his right hand. "Carry her to the bedroom." As I lifted Phyllis her robe partially opened revealing firm white breasts tinged with blue. There was no life in this load

.

I tossed her roughly on the bed, arms and legs slowly bounced, as if infused with lead, Phyllis's eyes remained open. My finger on each cold lid pulled the shades down. "Prop her up against some pillows before she gets too stiff to move." I complied with the order; the weight of the moment had not yet fallen. "Now let's get that shithead lawyer." "You going to zip up his pants?" I asked. "No, we are going to take them off, and his shirt." Coos maneuvered behind and managed to lift Jerry's ass above the seat. I pulled his sandals off and jerked the khakis down. Unbuttoning the puke stained shirt, I ripped the last four buttons apart, they flew across the floor, tingling off the broken glass.

Traditore was a pale, heavy, bastard. The weight proved a struggle and after twice almost losing him to the floor, I said, "He needs to ride on your chair." Todd saw the logic. He hopped onto the couch, thoughtfully lowering an arm rest. I positioned the open side of the seat next to the slumping barrister. His chair was high enough that a slight push and gravity transferred the body. "Put him next to the bitch." Hot Rod ordered.

I managed to stabilize and propel around the bar and back to the bedroom. The landing zone was a good half foot above the wheelchair. I squatted in front of the wheels, facing the bed and pulled Jerry over my back, his head rested between my shoulder blades. I could feel beard stubble through my shirt. Lifting with my legs I gained enough leverage to put him on the mattress. "Lean him up next to her." Todd said. This required climbing onto the bed, pushing the body up into a semi-seated position, placing one foot on either side of the torso, then lifting by the arm pits and dragging. Almost apologizing when Jerry hit the wall, I put a few pillows behind his back.

In the dim light the two could be mistaken for a couple discussing the day's events. Phyllis's head was buried in a pillow, her long hair falling on each shoulder. Traditore was two feet higher, chin resting on chest, appearing deep in thought. They were both taking on a grayish pallor, as if turning to stone. I shut off the light and left them alone, conspirators to the end.

Hot Rod was on the couch, staring at the busted television. "We need to do a little cleaning up." he announced. I rolled the chair in his direction; he made no attempt to get on. "I still can't fucking believe it, I would kill them again if I could." The reference to the dark deed shot an arrow through my mind. I was no longer on auto pilot, void of understanding or emotion. Phyllis and Jerry were dead. In the next room. Dead.

Leaning against the bar my legs trembled. "How did you do it?" I dry mouthed. Coos continued to stare at the broken screen as if waiting for a replay. "I used your drugs,' he monotoned, "you really shouldn't be doing that shit, it could kill you." The words "your drugs" penetrated. "What the fuck do you mean,

I don't have any drugs." "Then someone planted a shit load of fentanyl in your bag."

Earlier Hot Rod had borrowed a shirt, taking it from my luggage. The same suitcase I left the hospital with, the one with the gift from Nurse Jane, which hadn't moved during my movements. Coos had put the stash in a pouch on the side of his chair. "I was going to throw it away, crazy to travel with that stuff." Instead. "I first thought about giving those two a dose so we could make an easy getaway. By the time they woke up we'd have been on a plane." Todd moved over and slid back onto his wheels. "Then I busted the lock and found those papers. Our names were on a sheet like that, we were fucking targets. I did what needed to be done."

What needed to be done was pumping all the fentanyl into their veins. "Jerry was starting to come to, so I gave him a quick needle. Jackie bounced the chair, shit she almost fell over." Coos loaded another vial. "I told her it was a medicinal sedative." Phyllis wasn't buying it; she threw her body into the restraints. This, however, made a vein in her left forearm stand out. "I hit it first try." Her eyes rolled back, the fight left. "I was so fucking angry, my legs are gone because of these assholes." Hot Rod then administered a lethal dose to each. "Saved everybody's time and money." There was no doubt in his voice. "It would have been better to cut their legs off and burn their faces. Pieces of shit."

The Buddha had visitors; an elderly duo in large grey shawls stopped and lit incense. The women bowed for several seconds, oblivious. I envied their peace. Walking slowly away the taller of the two stopped and grabbed my hand. Her skin was leathered yet soft. She pointed toward the smiling deity, and clasped her hands together. It couldn't hurt.

I stood up and walked to the makeshift altar. The incense still burned, filling me with the scent of cedar. I bent low with clasped hands. My heart beat an echo that slowly faded. For a time the marching memories stopped. When I turned around the women were gone.

As the moments passed darker clouds moved in, it was time to leave. A bend in the path gave me a clear view of green hills supporting acres of mist. My time with the Buddha had not resulted in a cleansing although it was settling.

I managed another hundred yards before the parade in my head resumed. The fezed ones drove their tiny carts in zig zag patterns across my brain. Everyone was laughing, the kids ran for candy thrown toward the curb. No need to move, it all would pass by in due time and at the end the police cars, lights flashing, sirens wailing. We are going to jail.

That's what I had told Coos, with knees knocking, as I almost sat in Phyllis's chair. A shudder or two later I made it to the couch near the sliding door. Hot Rod was rocking back and forth over the picture tube glass. The intermittent crackle charged my conscience, jolts of guilt lit up the shadows.

Two dead. My fault. Pre-vomit stomach clenches. Wait. They deserved it. They deserved worse. I didn't kill them, was taking a piss at the time. You would have. Can you believe she set me up like that, leading me along, sex and sincerity. You wanted to be lead, you loved it. Put her on the bed, propped up like a kid's doll. She was cold, waxy. I was a payday, weeks of work. What kind of person could do that? For five hundred grand they would be lining up around the block. She waited until I turned the grill on before breaking that vase. What if I had turned it off before running back in, what was plan B. How long would the effort have gone?

Jerry was a prick, probably had a stable like Phyllis, stalking big verdicts. He wasn't the one sucking your dick while the grill percolated. So he didn't buy the gun just the bullets. The bitch took Hot Rod's legs. Wonder what that was worth. Fuck them both. He was a load getting on the bed, not human, just flesh, guts, and bone. She wasn't making it with him. It came down to money. Did she set up her cousin, what about her dad, if she had one? I was burned like bacon, she didn't care. They did look like lovers, nested on the sheet, blood pooling down their torsos.

Death is final. Time fucking up. Nobody could forgive what they did, not even some sanctimonious bible thumper. Give me some wood from the cross to jam into their hearts. Who are you to judge, you who are still alive? Fuck that, look in my mirror. Judge, jury, executioner. Would I have done it? Game, set, match. Probably not, I would have called the cops. Bullshit, things were too far gone.

It was painless, Jerry never woke up. Iris must have seen it coming. Good, she still got off easy. Fuck she's dead. I am going to pay for this. You already have. Stomach spasm, vomit now at mezzanine level. Sweating and cold. I wished it was yesterday. It is done; move on, that's what they said in the hospital. Make the best of it

.

Pounding, pounding, a drumbeat of fear. You saved future victims. You widowed a wife, messed up some kids, and took a daughter from her mother. Excuse me, who started the ball rolling. Fuck everyone. Look in my mirror.

"What the fuck are we going to do now?" My voice was surprisingly calm. Hot Rod rolled in front of me, and grabbed my hands,

"I should have talked to you before…." His voice faded, while his grip tightened. "I am sorry, really." Coos pulled back, unclenching. "I was in a rage, now we are both in the shit."

It was we; no way would I turn on Coos, not with what the demons had done. "Don't worry about it, let's fix this mess and vanish." He managed a quick grin. "We can always drown in guilt somewhere else."

Find a deliverance box in the church, go inside, kneel, wait for the carved lattice to slide open, "Bless me father for I have sinned." There ain't a confessional tough enough for this tale. I could be on both sides of that sanctifying screen. Forgive and be forgiven. Too late for that padre, the sinners are starting to decay, rigor mortis their last act. You could still forgive. You first padre. A hand slides the panel closed. No absolution. Maybe later, maybe not.

I proceeded to pick up the television glass and place it closer to the busted flat screen trying to make it look like it accidently tipped over. Coos was busy wiping everything we touched with a wet rag in the hope our fingerprints would disappear. "What did you do with the drugs?" I asked throwing the last of the jagged fragments under the stand. "I put a couple of syringes and some vials in Jackie's robe pocket, the rest I'll toss in the jungle." During the corpse transport the sound of tinkling glass wasn't heard over the crackling bones and pounding heart. Hot Rod was certain the local authorities would take the easy way out. "They won't give two shits about a couple of statesiders overdosing. Plus it plays better for future poker tournaments if no foul play was involved." His logic was almost comforting.

We debated moving Traditore's luggage from the entrance hall. Neither one of us was too keen on returning to the bedroom, the bag stayed where it was. I cleaned up the kitchen, putting the empty bottles in the sink. The cords from the drapes got tossed behind the fridge. Coos pulled the briefcase and papers down to his lap. "I still can't believe this shit; it's like the devil's roadmap." I noticed the lock had been violently twisted off.

"You know" Hot Rod began, "I remember Jerry telling me about a few cases where trees had fallen on people." To be in the zone of danger when an oak decides to kiss the ground is an unfortunate combination of both bad timing and bad luck. A million steps ending with one at that instant, if that is not the ultimate "what the fuck", it is in the top three. "Those two waited with chain saws for us to come down the path."

Our attempt at cleansing the suite complete I stood at the door, hat on head, eye balling the peep hole. We had decided to split up. I would take the longer loop back to the front of the hotel while Coos would retrace our earlier route. He gave me the brief case, "Throw it out past the landscaping." The papers had been soaked before serving as a meal for the garbage disposal. The room key went in for dessert.

I stuck my head out the door, no sounds except for geckos chirping in the darkness. Hot Rod followed down to the path, stopping to wipe the door handle with the stolen dish rag. "See you back in the room." he whispered before spinning his wheels. I walked the other way trying to appear like a guy out for cigarettes. Yeah, enough cigarettes to fill this brief case. A breeze was blowing, the palm fronds rumbled. A sharp turn presented the perfect spot for a cowhide discus throw. The satchel landed with a thump, somewhere in the night. My blood pressure plummeted upon reaching the driveway sidewalk. I gave a nod to the doorman before sauntering into the lobby.

"Bodies, what bodies."

It was pushing midnight, a few Hawaiian shirts murmured at the bar. The guy at the counter didn't look up as I passed toward the elevator bank.

"Man and woman dead in a fancy suite, shocking, very shocking."

The door opened, an empty box, up forty feet. My hand shook as I swiped the room key. Green light.

"No visible signs of a struggle, probably addicts. Get them to the morgue, they were checking out in two days anyway. Keep the woman away from Joaquin, you know how he gets."

Coos was in the shower, soaping off the night. He had called the airline, the flight to Tokyo left in two hours. Other than pointing out the ticket purchase no words were exchanged. Hot Rod emptied every little bottle of booze in the mini-bar into the ice bucket and poured the contents equally into two glasses. We drank without a toast. I grabbed our suitcases; the desk clerk ravaged the credit card on file, a taxi ride later Customs waived us through. Saipan receded as the DC10 beat gravity. More little bottles. Fitful sleep, faces with no eyes, screams with no sound.

Our actions would go unchallenged except for the battle in our heads.

After my visit with the Buddha I gave up the sauce. Todd didn't notice. We still shared a corner table in the hotel lounge, taking food and drink from a rotating shift of hostesses. Sleep, as it was, took place between two and ten a.m. As my mind cleared I tried to engage Hot Rod in conversation. He grunted, shook his head, and occasionally spit out nonsense. A pickled brain reverts to primordial functioning, keep the plumbing going with the hope the storm will pass. I took it upon myself to wean him off the liquor, paying the bartender to water down the libations. Two days later the lights came back on. After an extended visit to the bathroom Coos returned, downed the last of a mostly coke and rum, and announced, "Let's go home."

When we left Lake Chuzeni our drink tab was higher than our room and meals. Miyoko, the desk clerk, was certain there had been an error with the placement of a decimal. She excused herself to check with the bartender. He reassured her that we had consumed enough alcohol to float two battleships. Kanpai and Banzai. Many brain cells had died, not the ones, however, replaying the drama that was Ritz Carlton Suite 415, they were tough bastards. On the plane Coos took one more shot, drinking whatever wasn't locked up, searching for his own cold nothingness. The stewardess was too polite to cut him off; he eventually passed out, his head resting against the closed window shade

I kept pushing the memory down, hoping to drown it under the weight of time and distance. I knew it was time to move forward. We had gotten away with justifiable homicide at least that was how it splashed around in my reason bucket.

The tin can bounced down at San Francisco International thirty minutes early. I told the Customs man the truth: poker on Saipan, holiday in Japan. Baggage? Not much. Did you win? Broke even. He winced when I took off my hat. The passport photo still held a few truths, a piece here and there. No need for a supervisor, the tired jig saw puzzle was me, Paul Lawton. It had been many days since anyone had stared or I had noticed. "Tan marks, shit, look at that Marge." I pulled the head gear down low and waited for Coos. His addled state had delayed the process; he was the last citizen to exit the doors, a half opened suit case spilling off his lap. "Fucking bureaucrats," he muttered, "do I look like a fucking terrorist."

It was limo time again. The 101 was jammed with rush hour traffic, a gray marine layer pushed down to the road, we drove into cotton. Todd half-heartedly drank a beer. It took the two of us five minutes to remember my address. The driver, a large Hispanic woman with bleached hair, didn't mind, she was on the clock. "You boys look like something even the cat wouldn't touch." "Yeah it's been a rough few days." I replied. "Don't worry," she said, "I will have you home in no time."

Forty minutes later we arrived at the Sunset Arms. Hot Rod grabbed my wrist as I went for the door. "We played some poker, drank some sake. Nothing else." I stated. His grip tightened. "Those bastards took my legs; it was bad enough believing it was an accident. Now..." his voice drifted off. The driver was pulling on the handle, I fought back. She got the message. Giving advice to Coos was mostly futile and sometimes dangerous. "We're back home, let's get some rest and get on with it." I gave him a hug. He clenched back, a ball of tension. "I'll call you in a couple of days." The air was cold as I stepped into the light. Hot Rod was reaching for another beer; it was a long ride to Stockton.

The apartment had been cleaned. I tossed my bag on the floor. The shower felt very good, the bed better. The next day, whatever it was, was when I woke up. It was the afternoon, late enough for pizza delivery. I met the driver hooded up against the fog, he didn't give me a glance. Balancing the pie on my knee I managed to pull out a few items from the mail box. Three credit card applications and one letter from the Traditore Law Offices. I ate four slices, washed it all down with a soda, and opened the envelope. It was from a trustee sadly reporting on the untimely passing of the firm's founder, announcing a memorial service for the upcoming Saturday and stating future communication would be forthcoming regarding the status of my lawsuit.

I would not attend the funeral. Coos would, having been summoned by office manager Marcia to pay off the second round he had promised days before when she supplied Snipnell's address. They would consummate in a small office at the crowded, non-denominational church. Pre and post-coital talk centered on Jerry's demise. "Such a shame for his family, he even had that girl on the payroll. I don't remember ever meeting her." If Marcia knew the girl's name she didn't mention it. The connection between Snipnell and Coos was not made.

There was no mention of Phyllis/Iris/Jackie in any of the central or northern California newspapers; I checked dozens on line my first days back. A little digging did turn up an announcement in the Bakersfield Californian congratulating Reginald and Phyllis Snipnell on their marriage. A check of the county records revealed a divorce three years later.

No word from Saipan either. The headline there concerned one Joe Totto, described as a local hustler, who was found dead in the sand, a heart attack victim. An old mug shot accompanied the article; it was the same guy we had met at the Nimitz. He had provided the room key to 415. A large loose end Coos and I had overlooked was no more. I forwarded the article to Todd with the subject line, "Lucky us!"

Time crept by. I spoke with my parents, silently taking a scolding for not calling sooner. Mimi answered her cell phone in LA, "I am up for a role in a commercial, can't say what." There was a message from Frank inviting me back for dinner, "You can even bring that Hot Rod character if you want." I called Jane once, she was on her way to work, we promised to meet for lunch.

And so it went, the Saipan memory bubbled up to the surface less often. Another letter arrived from the trustee, the defendants had offered ten million dollars, and the law firm would cut its fee to two million if I accepted. One flick of the pen brought another upgrade to my bank account. More cash than the Weezy windfall, at a much greater cost. I reconciled my debt with the hospital and sent a couple hundred grand back home with instructions to buy my uncle's farm. My mom cried, my dad laughed. They both again suggested additional plastic surgery.

I thought about getting in touch with my old realtor Grace, it seemed like years since she sold me the house on Partridge. There was a new residence to be found, the trustee had given thirty days notice and the Sunset Arms landlord had brought a couple of college kids by to look at the apartment. The largesse provided by my legal team was at an end. Don't let the door hit you in the ass and if you run into any unfortunate victim of tortuous conduct remember who got you your millions.

Buying another home seemed too permanent. A pensive restlessness had set in; it didn't take long before I realized I wasn't in the mood to settle down. Three life changing events in less than a year had amped up my expectation meter. I was waking up looking for the next jolt.

The salesman at Sam's RV Haven was surprised that the guy in the 49er hoody, who arrived by cab with a beat up suitcase, wrote a $350,000 check for a Mountain Air diesel motor home. After watching a 45 minute video, accepting a complimentary fill up along with a map of RV resorts, I pulled onto El Camino. By the time I reached the Bay Bridge, the horn honking had slowed down as the mother of all buses learned to stay in one lane. I was Captain Kirk, boldly going to Stockton. The rig had two bedrooms, Coos would be able to hop and slide with no problem. There was a hitch for towing the Mustang. According to the latest figures there are 2,615,870 miles of paved road in the United States. Driving forward, instead of looking back, would be good for both of us.

I scrapped the mail box and damn near side swiped Leon's truck before coming to a stop in Hot Rod's driveway. The barbeque king himself stood shaking his head as I exited the Mountain Air. "My grandma could drive better than that and she's been dead for twenty years. Hope you have a loud horn and plenty of insurance." "Hey, no harm no foul. Plus it was my cherry ride, only into the second hundred miles."

Leon placed a large cooler in the bed of the pick-up. "You come to visit Mr. Personality?" he gestured toward the house. "Yeah, thought we would take a trip." "Well good luck with that, he has been moping around for weeks. I bring him some food on Wednesdays, Fred from the pool hall checks in on the weekends."

Leon explained that Coos had not been himself since he came home from that overseas trip. "I don't know what went on over there, but something twisted him up." Hot Rod spent some days lifting weights and eating right only to be followed by bouts of drinking that would make any sailor proud. "In between he is too hung over to communicate." Leon's eyes shot darts; he knew I knew the cause. I pawed at the concrete, avoiding contact. "Yeah well maybe a cruise along the coast will help." I lamely replied. "O.K., O.K., if you ever need to talk here is my card, call anytime." he shrugged and opened the cab door. "Sure, sure, I will keep you posted." Relief waved my hand more than necessary as he backed out to the street.

My old chair was waiting in the garage; I hopped on and pushed through the open door into the house. Hot Rod was at the kitchen counter, elbows deep in ribs and sauce, two empty beer bottles stood next to a pile of bones. Just when I was about to announce my arrival he barked, "Get more beer out of the fridge Scarface."

The Sub Zero contained equal parts Anchor Steam and Muscle Milk shakes. I banged into a lower cabinet on my return before taking a slot across from the Styrofoam food containers. Coos grabbed a bottle, "Help yourself, Leon's always tastes best the first day." Four ribs later I said, "I got my settlement and bought a little something, it is parked outside." Hot Rod pushed away from the counter and washed his hands and face in the sink, wiping off with a dish towel. "Marcia mentioned your jackpot was coming in, glad to hear it." There was no emotion in his voice. He grabbed another beer, "See you out back."

I finished a few more ribs, stood up from the chair and cleaned the mess. Returning to the ride I took the hall to the yard. Coos had the flames going, it was getting dark, he was on a lounge chair staring into the fire pit. Remembering my last transfer attempt I broke house rules, stood up and sat on the cushion next to the refrigerator. Hot Rod didn't notice. We sat in silence until the security lights popped on around the pool infringing upon whatever was keeping Todd's attention. "You going to stay the night?" he asked. "Guess so." I replied. "You can have the room or crawl into that tin can parked in the driveway." Hot Rod had noted my arrival on the security cameras.

"What the fuck is that for anyway, you starting a tour company?" He obviously didn't see the possibilities. "Thought we could go on a scenic, give Mother Nature a kiss and a feel." Hot Rod snorted and demanded another beer. The fridge was well stocked. "You have to check it out, self-contained party on wheels" "Yeah, bet it is nice, don't know if I am up to leaving." "From what I hear you don't seem up to staying either." Out came the bird. We sat some more.

"No one claimed the body." Todd announced over the chorus of crickets by the hedge. My mind was fixed on the moon peaking above the darkened hills. "What's that?" "Jackie or Phyllis, whatever her name is, was." Hot Rod had one of his pals make a few inquiries. "They were going to plant her in the jungle, I paid for a cremation and had the ashes tossed into the ocean." I was surprised and concerned. "When did this happen?" "The first week back here, and don't worry no one could ever trace it to me." I hoped he was right, it was a strange gesture. "A little odd," I stated, "don't you think, considering...." He went back to staring at the fire, I tracked the moon with Venus now riding shotgun.

"I guess I felt guilty." Coos practically whispered. "I can't recall the last time that happened; now it is an everyday thing." "Yeah, well I hope your interest doesn't backfire. It appears no one is concerned about us, would be good to leave it that way."

"Fuck!" he yelled, throwing the bottle out onto the lawn, "No one cares, we got away with it, my plan worked. We are not going to get caught and that should make me feel great. But it doesn't!"

Maybe because I hadn't pushed the needle, maybe because it happened half way around the world, maybe because I had my time with the Buddha, or maybe because I had gone through enough shit, but I didn't share Hot Rod's harness, pulling a plow through a field of blame. "It's done, time to move on, let's hit the road for a few weeks." "I know, shit, but my legs are gone, I shouldn't have become involved with her in the first fucking place, there is guilt or stupidity over that, then putting an end to her feels the same way." His lens was fogged.

"Get past the guilt, it's a self-inflicted wound." Not that Freud, most faiths, or the law would agree. Maybe guilt is hard wired into our being, a survival mechanism that keeps upright animals in line, a psychic chain jerking us back onto the preferred path. Maybe it is just the currency of religion and controlling parents. "I read that only psychopaths don't feel guilt." Coos said. "Yeah, well I read that guilt is absent when the act is justified." I replied. "Yeah well I read that guilt is an avenging fiend, blowing sorrow in your face." "Where the hell you getting this stuff." "I've been on the internet." He was straying from the sports and porno sites. "You got to get past this, you are rusting, and pretty soon it will eat your heart."

More silence, I grabbed another beer, Hot Rod didn't notice. "How are you doing it?" he finally asked. "I guess I have moved on, no reason to keep picking at the scab. They did and we did back, another bad memory to avoid." Coos gave me that cock-eyed look, "Fuck, I have been trying, my usual remedies are not working, worse than when I used steal my mother's tip money for beer."

"You have been stuck here, not enough action, let's hit the road." "You may be right, it's worth a shot, let's go to Yosemite I want to watch those guys climbing El Capitan. Maybe I should try that, a third less weight to pull." Todd smiled.

The decision was made. I rolled to the able-bodied room after getting Coos to agree that there would be no early morning speaker attack.

In the morning Coos broke his promise as Willie Nelson proclaimed the joys of being on the road again. It was a hopeful sign. I snuck out to the bus for a change of clothes before hitting the shower. Hot Rod was once again at the kitchen counter eating, this time cereal and donuts. I helped myself. "Good choice of morning music." "Thanks but its past noon, as promised." And so it was. He had two duffel bags packed and waiting by the door. "Looks like you are ready to roll." He lapped up the last of the milk. "Yeah, all my clean clothes, figured we might as well keep going east, I have never seen the Atlantic." "Good by me."

When Hot Rod went to his room for his wallet I once again broke protocol and quickly placed the dishes in the sink, pushed the chair out the door to the garage and grabbed the bags. I had just unlocked the Mountain Air as Coos rolled up, guiding a spare chair with his free hand. "Where's the storage and how the hell am I going to get in this monster." "No problem," I countered while pushing a button on the remote which immediately caused an awning to pop out from the side of the roof. "Still learning." I mumbled. Two buttons later a large door opened between the axels. The inside space was meant for motorcycles or a small off road vehicle, it provided just enough room for the chairs. I wrestled both in after informing Coos that he could gain entrance by elevating the lower step. "Hit the button on the side panel."

He did a quick lap around the rig before pronouncing it a rolling palace. "Two beds, a shower, three televisions, internet and kitchen, you did good Paul." I was in the captain's chair cranking up the engine, a display befitting an airliner lit up along the dash. "Thank you sir, you may sit in the copilot seat or lounge in the back." He bounced up next to me and strapped in.

After a few back and forths I managed to get the rig out of the driveway and onto the road. The GPS popped up on an overhead screen while a voice asked for a destination. After announcing

Yosemite a route appeared along with an estimated arrival time and sites along the way. We crossed the Delta, hit I-5 before exiting onto State Highway 120. Hot Rod familiarized himself with every gadget and gizmo, he had country music blaring from ten speakers.

The approach of Don Pedro Lake challenged my new driving skills as the road slithered through the scenic hills. I pulled over to let several irritated drivers pass. At this point the GPS monitor started blinking before a disembodied voice announced, "Do not touch the controls." The other screens around the cabin turned on, revealing alternating pictures from our passports. Coos swiveled in his seat, "What the fuck, you got software issues." "He's got issues alright, and so do you Todd." the voice flatly stated. "Very funny," Hot Rod said, "you got a hidden mike or something." Things were getting spooky. "It's not me, I haven't done anything." At this the speaker blared, "Oh yes you have Paul Lawton, yes you have." The Mountain Air was possessed, probably not covered by the warranty.

The screens went blank for a few seconds before a grainy picture appeared of a tanned young man in a red shirt with his arm on the shoulder of an auburn haired girl who looked very familiar. "Shit," Coos yelled, "I know that picture, it's Jackie and Sniper." Upon further review the woman did look like a young Iris, it took my memory wheel a little longer to spit out the fact Sniper was the guy who provided the Saipan poker connection. The old print was replaced by white noise before Mr. Edward Snipnell himself came into focus. "Hello again Todd and glad to make your acquaintance Paul."

Our smug assumption that the past was cremated had not taken into account the loose string that was Sniper. He told Hot Rod where Phyllis could be located and, with nothing but time on his hands, used his electronic resources to keep an eye on Coos. "I noticed your travel plans included Paul, a quick check and I learned of his lawsuit and the Traditore connection." He knew we had registered for the tournament, our failure to make the money as well as the late night flight to Japan. "Didn't think much of your adventure until this popped up." Sniper stated as the Herald Tribune love nest overdose article appeared on the screen. "It didn't take long before I hacked the local police command center and learned the identities of the unfortunate couple. Their departure so close to yours tweaked my interest."

Hot Rod and I sat in the idling motor home, captives to the machinations of a quadriplegic 200 miles away. Sniper's face was back on the screen. "Todd, in our time together I did not pick up any bad vibes, there was no reason to doubt the overdose explanation. Phyllis had occasionally dabbled in recreational drugs, she could have hooked up with the lawyer, it all appeared to be a coincidence until I decided to see about funeral arrangements."

At this the monitors displayed a receipt from the Lujan Funeral Home, San Antonio, Saipan, a total of $1200 for cremation and sea burial services paid by the credit card of one Jeff Brug. "I wondered why Mr. Brug was picking up the tab for Phyllis's last rites. After some digging I learned that he played wheel chair hockey for The Hot Rods, a team you are both familiar with no doubt." Coos shook his head as I whispered, "Not traceable my ass."

"Now," Sniper said, "I don't know what to think, two are dead and just maybe you know something. So I have alerted the authorities, they should be pulling up at any moment. There is a holding cell in Santa Rita set aside for questioning. Sorry, but it seems like the right thing to do. Good bye."

The monitors went blank a few seconds before a black Crown Victoria with red lights flashing out the rear windows blocked any hope of escape. I opened the door for two burly men in suits who flashed Alameda County Sheriff badges. We were instructed to sit in the rear of the bus at the small kitchen table. One guy drew all the blinds while the other slid into the driver's seat. Our journey east was now u-turned.

Coos looked at me and I at him while the cop watched us both. He gave my face a walk over before resting on the small couch. After thirty minutes Hot Rod asked for a drink. The deputy found the fridge and two diet Pepsis among many bottles of beer. We each said thanks, he did not respond. That tired cop show line about how anything you say can and will be used against you bounced off the walls.

I alternated between fear and hope. They knew everything and were going to send us away or they knew shit and were only fishing. Coos finished his drink and crushed the can. I leaned back, closed my eyes and wondered what the folks would think. The officer was bored, he turned on the television. We watched The Price is Right as the miles passed by. Eventually the Mountain Air slowed for what must have been an off ramp. Ten minutes later we came to a stop.

Our guard motioned toward the exit. Hot Rod mentioned the need for his chair. I pointed out the correct remote button before walking into a tunnel made of canvas. One officer positioned himself by the door while the other opened a flap and retrieved the wheels. Coos did a quick bounce onto the seat. I walked, he rolled, a guard in front and behind. A door was opened, we entered alone, and the lock clicked shut.

The room was dim, white walls and a concrete floor. Just as I was considering what it would be liked to be stripped searched music began blaring. It was Elvis singing "The warden threw a party in the county jail. The prison band was there and they began to wail. Everybody in the whole cell block was dancin to the jailhouse rock."

Prison bars flashed on the walls, alternating colors while a different voice lamented, "I hear the train a comin' it's rollin 'round the bend And I a'int seen the sunshine since I don't know when I'm stuck in Folsom Prison, and time keeps draggin' on"

Hot Rod spun in his chair, "What is this, a fucking disco? Knock it off and let's get on with it." The lights went out, it was pitch black, the sound of metal rattling slowly increased before Sam Cooke joined the party, "(Oh don't you know) that's the sound of the men working on the chain gang."

Suddenly brightness assaulted our eyes, a bewigged judge circled the room before we heard, "There was a friend of mine on murder And the judge's gavel fell Jury found him guilty. Gave him sixteen years in hell"

And then it was quiet as the bulbs dimmed allowing a neon sign to take center stage. Red tubes announcing "Open" shown above a door. "What the fuck." I said before turning the knob and entering a chromed out kitchen. A young, pretty Asian girl stood holding a tray with two beers in frosty glasses. Coos was close behind. "I am going to kill that two fingered excuse for a life form." he stated while reaching up for a mug.

I grabbed a beer, drank deeply hoping for clarity. "You have been here?" Before Hot Rod could respond the voice from the bus stated, "Why yes, Todd Jasper Coos has had a few beers in my lovely home. Welcome gentlemen I trust you enjoyed the ride?" Sniper was positioned at the bottom of a ramp in the middle of large living room. Coos went halfway down the incline and stopped. "Enjoyed the fucking ride, you asshole, ever hear of kidnapping." Sniper held his ground, "Slow down big boy, I admit my method was unorthodox but how else was I going to get you here. You were heading east, and after you promised to keep in touch, I felt neglected." Hot Rod ventured across from Sniper's tricked out ride, "Neglected, shit, how do you think we felt. Where did you get those cops anyway?"

Sniper explained they were actors. "Once I noticed Paul had bought the damn motor home, it didn't take much to figure a trip was in the offing. Luckily one of the guys had been a bus driver." Sniper already had a parking pad for the Mountain Air next to the house. "Had one, was part of the settlement, supposed to help me see the world. Gave it to the guy who cuts the grass." He had rented the tunnel tent from a local party supply house; the music and light show were his own doing.

I walked into the living room and sat down on a sofa below a large Elk head. Sniper gave me the once over, "Nasty patch of skin you got there, can see why they paid the ten million." The settlement was supposed to be confidential; Sniper was plugged into more than just a piss bag.

"Men," he announced turning his chair to the right, "shall we retire to my command center. It is time to talk.'
The command center was the marvel Hot Rod had described, screens, computers, and racks of other electronics buzzed and hummed. Sniper took his spot at the control counsel, Coos roamed the room like a cat smelling a rat, and I found the only chair, which the assistants used to manicure and trim.

"How did you pull that stunt on the motor home?" Sniper looked across a board of blinking lights, his two fingers tapping furiously. "I had a guy visit the rig while you slept at Todd's place, made a few modifications." He had noticed I used a credit card to buy gas at a truck stop off I-5 outside of Stockton and surmised my destination.

"What the fuck you doing all this for?" Hot Rod snapped. Sniper wheeled around to our side of the room, he and Coos came to a stop across from my seat. "Your visit, Todd, was very emotional, it opened a vein of memories I thought were long ago buried."

Sniper had mined the internet for information on both Coos and Phyllis. He dug a lot deeper than his earlier attempt and told us she had a condo in San Francisco, traveled often, especially to Vegas, and had several different bank accounts. "She had one at the Bank of Guam which seemed odd; all of her deposits were under ten thousand, she knew the tax laws."

Sniper delved into Hot Rod's background. "You were some kind of driver." He quickly figured out his connection to me. "Paul, never met anyone would made these machines, very cool." Continuing his initial detective work Sniper deployed a few internet sniffers, keeping a nose out for our names, tournament action, and unusual reports from Saipan. "I saw that Phyllis got bounced out after the third hand, coming up on the wrong end of a seven card straight flush." That bad luck explained our futile attempts at locating her.

After a few days the Herald Tribune article popped up, followed a short time later by our flight home. "I like how you travel first class." He assumed Hot Rod would get in touch, if only to give

A Hard Earned Reason

him the news. When that did not happen Sniper's suspicions were aroused, he decided to reel us in.

"And now that you are here let's talk." He flashed pictures of Coos and I taken just as the fake police pulled up behind the bus. "These are not the faces of total innocence." he commented, "Plus not a word of resistance on the trip." Sniper eyed us both, "I would like to know what you know about that Saipan love nest."

Our mugs on the screens certainly confirmed Sniper's point; we both looked like kids caught with stolen candy in our pockets. It was easy to understand how we could arouse suspicion; of course Hot Rod went into full denial mode.

"Sniper, look I am sorry for not stopping by, but you are way off base here. Sure we did find Phyllis, she was wearing a black wig for some reason but there was no mistaking that body. I yelled at her for selling my Mustang, she yelled at me for being an asshole. That's it, we left, never saw Traditore and didn't know anything about them dying until I got a note from his law office."

Sniper smiled and hit a button with one of his two working fingers. The monitors went blank but the speakers blared a raspy female voice, "A Mr. Traditore is on his way to your room." A slight pause before a reply, "Yeah, kay." It was the one syllable grunt of Todd Coos. "Perhaps," Sniper intoned with rising indignation, "you would like to revise your earlier explanation."

Traditore had also been on Sniper's bloodhound list after his office had breached confidentiality and gave Hot Rod his address. "I thought it was odd you knew how to find me so the lawyer became a person of interest. It was a real surprise to see him clear customs on Saipan. I knew he was acquainted with Phyllis from my lawsuit." He paused, "And Paul might be interested to learn he was in Bangalore, India negotiating some deal for your pals from Weezy." Sniper had calculated driving time from the airport and used a voice mask to call Phyllis's room. "I wanted to hear her reaction to the news; instead I get Mr.Nascar for five seconds before dial tone."

Coos took another shot, "Yeah sure, I remember now, I gave her some shit about the lawyer having an old, soft dick. We left before he ever showed up." Sniper was not impressed. "Two problems with that, first you just lied and second no way Phyllis goes for Jerry, no way. Love nest my ass."

A cornered animal either charges out with teeth bared or tucks tail and moans. I chose the former. "They worked together to fuck us up. The lawyer and his misery mistress. Our accidents were no accident."

If Hot Rod had a leg he would have kicked me, instead I got the gran mal roll of the eyes and sorrowful head shake. Sniper dropped jaw, "What the fuck do you mean?"

It took a few minutes to explain the Jackie/Iris act along with the tire jacks/grill purchases. "She set us up and made sure Traditore got the action. We found papers with other guys' addresses, their hobbies, the names of old girlfriends." Sniper turned and even deeper shade of white. "You are a bigger bull shitter than your shaggy haired friend. I got a detective's number on speed dial. I want the truth."

Coos had enough, "Look, you're the asshole. Paul let's get the hell out of here." He started rolling toward the door. "Wait," I said, "this may convince him." I pulled out my wallet and carefully unfolded the crumpled $500,000 bank draft payable to Phyllis Snipnell. "Here's her blood money." I held the check up to Sniper's eyes. He asked me to set it on a scanner which shortly forwarded a digitized larger image to the screens.

Hot Rod was beside himself, "And you bitched at me for paying the cremation costs, you take her panties too. Fucking idiot."

Sniper was riling the circuits, a wizard pulling information. "The check is legit, and it looks like she received three others like it over the years, all from a Traditore account. She would launder them through banks way out in the Pacific."

"Yeah, she was smart and a nasty bitch." Hot Rod said.

The Preservation Hall Jazz Band leaked from the speakers, a Dixieland funeral march increased in volume. "And now she is dead." Sniper stated. "How did that happen?"

"How should we know, they were alive when we left." Coos stated.

"Well, the toxicologist report, which just came out a few days ago by the way, lists fentanyl as the involved drug."

The screens began dancing again, machines punching out pills, conveyors filling bottles. Then with a flourish red lettered words appeared:

Fentanyl is a potent, synthetic narcotic analgesic with a rapid onset and short duration of action. Fentanyl is approximately 100 times more potent than morphine and is often used for intense pain including......treatment of burn victims.

"I would imagine Paul," Sniper spoke as the words faded, "you are familiar with fentanyl."

"So what," Coos interjected, "he's familiar with bed pans too, doesn't mean he took some home."

"True, however I ran some names at the burn unit through the medical/legal data base, and a nurse, Jane Meyer, popped up. Seems five years ago she was suspected of making off with leftovers, vials of fentanyl were mentioned. Case was dropped for lack of evidence. I do believe she would have had something to do with Paul's care and maybe gave him a few hits for the road."

The sonofabitch was good. It was time for a curve ball. "Yeah, well you haven't been telling the whole truth either." I began, "If Phyllis was your cousin I'm your uncle. You knew a lot more about her than you told Hot Rod, plus it's just plain weird to be cyber stalking a relative." Sniper didn't look up from his keyboard. Coos joined the attack. "He's right you acted like you hadn't thought of her in years, and that picture I found, you two were giving off some heat."

The screens flashed a large bull taking a dump in a barn. Hot Rod countered by pulling out his cell phone. "Perhaps you may recall Traditore's office manager, Marcia; she's on my speed dial. We can easily find out your past." He started to hit some buttons. "No need," Sniper conceded, "No need."

Again the screens flickered, a rollicking version of "Here Comes the Bride" preceded a photo of Sniper, all parts working, in a tuxedo, smiling, next to Phyllis in a wedding dress. Underneath was the caption "Good luck Reginald and Phyllis Snipnell." "Looks like somebody else didn't like there name." I said. Sniper left his counsel and wheeled in our direction. "Yeah," he stated, "I am no Reggie, Edward is my middle name." Sniper pushed a button and ordered more beers, after which he sat across from Coos and me.

"She was an orphan." Sniper began his explanation, "I met her senior year of high school, Phyllis had transferred in first semester, it was her third school in four years." Phyllis Mossstone had been abandoned at a Chico, California Greyhound station when she was six months old. A janitor found her in a cardboard fruit container on a wooden bench. Phyllis was written on the tag sticking out of her jump suit. Mossstone came from the name of the cannery on the box.

In the next twelve years she was handed off more times than a game worn football. Finally an Air Force sergeant and his nurse wife adopted her; they lived at a few bases around the country before her dad retired to Bakersfield. "We were lab partners in Chemistry class, she laughed at my jokes, I loved her sparkling eyes and blonde hair." Sniper introduced Phyllis to his crowd. They were good for each other. "The first time she came over she thought we were millionaires." Sniper's dad was in the dry cleaning business, he owned a large house with a pool and three cars.

They had a great year; proms, parties, and sex. Phyllis got birth control from the nurse at school; she did not want any more unwanted babies in the world. "I wasn't much of a student, spent most of my time messing with computers and playing video games, but after graduation my dad called in a few favors and I got a job at a trucking company." Phyllis worked as a teller at Bank of America. That fall, with nothing better to do, they got married. "We eloped to Reno; it made my folks happy since she was always showing up at the breakfast table anyway."

The couple rented a two bedroom apartment in a large complex west of town. "It wasn't my parent's but I told Phyllis in a year, two max, we could buy a house because the district manager would be retiring and his position would be mine." That carrot got them through months of T.V. dinners with an occasional night out at Applebee's. "I was happy but Phyllis grew impatient, she pointed out every new subdivision on our way to work." Finally, Ed Gerz announced his retirement, thirty five years without missing a day. Sniper and Phyllis attended the gold watch party where it was announced that Ed's replacement was Sam Yarch, nephew of the company vice president, fresh out of UC Santa Cruz with no experience whatsoever. "We drove home in silence; I told Phyllis the guy wouldn't last a month."

Six months later nothing had changed, however it appeared Phyllis had gotten over her disappointment. They talked about moving to the Bay Area, Sniper took some computer courses at night, Phyllis went to paralegal school. "We use to take a short cut out the back of the apartment complex to get to class. There was an overflow parking garage on the way."

The structure was built into the side of a hill, poured concrete with rounded corners giving it a castle look. The back side entrance had two stairwells leading to the street out front. One late October evening Phyllis skipped past their usual stair. "I remember she was pretending be a medieval lady or something, at a door on the opposite side of the floor she bowed and said, 'After you my Lord.'" Sniper played along, insisting she go first. Phyllis would have none of it. "I finally gave in, ten seconds later my neck was broken."

The stairwell had been scheduled for repair; the janitor swore warning tape and signs had been installed although he admitted the lock did not work. It was a clear case of liability. "And Phyllis set you up with Traditore." I stated. "One of the orderlies at the hospital brought up his name, I tracked him down the other day, and," Sniper paused, "it turns out Phyllis paid him fifty bucks to give me Traditore's card."

The attendant arrived with two more beers. "What about me?" Sniper bellowed. She smiled, wagged her finger and left the room.

"Fuck, Paul give me a little waterfall." Not wanting to break house rules I looked at Coos. He nodded. I made my way up to Sniper's chair. The glass held steady as I rivered some lager down his throat. "Don't drown him." Hot Rod cautioned. The amber liquid bubbled away without incident. "Thanks," Sniper said after catching his breath.

"So she set you up too." I stated, a fact, not a question. Sniper nodded affirmatively, "I often wondered why we took those stairs and why Phyllis insisted I go first but until now the idea it was not an accident never seemed right. You two are proof positive." Coos motioned with his glass. I poured the rest of my beer into Sniper's mouth. He tapped his fingers, Jack Nicholson appeared on the monitors yelling, "You can't handle the truth." Followed by a grizzled farmer announcing that "People are no damn good."

Sniper hit a switch and the screens faded to dark, most of the electrical noise went silent. "You have my word, no taping, no eavesdropping. What we say remains here." He motored back to our side of the room. "I never got over her." Phyllis was his last squeeze, her's the final flesh. "I called her all the time once I mastered the voice masking software. Sometimes I pretended to be a pollster or salesman. We had a few conversations. Bullshit I know but her voice made me feel something."

Three young men in Russian roulette relationships. Spin the chamber, pull the trigger. Phyllis had added a few bullets. There was silence in the antiseptic command center. We each wrestled with the she devil who had pinned us to the mat. Coos left in search of more beer.

Sniper rolled up next to my chair. I knew what he wanted.

"We killed them." I stated. "You were right about the fentanyl." I did not go into the details. He seemed satisfied. Hot Rod came back with two mugs, "Sorry Snipe the skirted Gestapo wouldn't let me bring you one." "No problem, my system's been fucked up enough for one day." He turned his world back on; Jagger began to sing about time being on his side. Coos took a gulp before loudly whispering, "You told him, you fuck." I nodded.

"I am happy they are gone." Sniper announced a few minutes later. "And don't worry no one thinks it was a crime. We can all move on." He included himself, an accessory after the fact.

Sniper demanded we keep his improvements in the motor home. "I want to keep an eye on you two." "Hell," I replied, "you will be better company than half pint over here."

Hot Rod managed a smile and a finger. "We better appreciate each other." he said.

"Yes."

"Yes."

⇥ ⇤

Coos and I returned to the road, taking the northern route east and the southern west. Sniper maintained a presence. Every mile broke new ground, we cleared the Sierras about the same time we overcame the gravity of our collective pasts, escaping the tentacles of regret that had clouded our thoughts and slowed our progress. That part of our story was written, there were, hopefully, many blank pages yet to fill.

Six thousand miles later the Mountain Air returned to Regency Court and rolled to a stop at the Snipnell residence, its new home port. Hot Rod had convinced Sniper to leave his cocoon and head up to Alaska. The agreement was reached only after Coos promised to invest in prosthetic legs. The self-improvement push also included my appointment with Dr. Vu for an appearance upgrade.

I will proceed with the knowledge that sometimes a reason can be found buried below the debris of an unfortunate event. Looking back this stretch of river has taught me a few things; most importantly there are those who cast the line, those who bite the hook and those who hold the net.

71131010R00215

Made in the USA
Columbia, SC
21 May 2017